		DATE DUE	

PRAYING

TO A

LAUGHING
GOD

A Novel

—◦—

Kevin McColley

Simon & Schuster

SIMON & SCHUSTER
Rockefeller Center
1230 Avenue of the Americas
New York, NY 10020

Designed by Sam Potts
Manufactured in the United States of America

1 3 5 7 9 10 8 6 4 2

Library of Congress Cataloging-in-Publication Data
McColley, Kevin.
Praying to a laughing god : a novel / Kevin McColley.
p.   cm.
I. Title.
PS3563.O34316P73   1998
813'.54—dc21   97-48720
CIP
ISBN 0-684-83761-7

"Do Not Go Gentle Into That Good Night" by Dylan Thomas, from
The Poems of Dylan Thomas. Copyright © 1952 by Dylan Thomas.
Reprinted by permission of New Directions Publishing Corp.

To Reen,
with love

PRAYING
TO A
LAUGHING GOD

Do not go gentle into that good night,
Old age should burn and rave at close of day;
Rage, rage against the dying of the light.

—Dylan Thomas

Chapter

1

*C*lark Holstrom sees the opera house from the top of the slide. In his
eyes it is a castle, and he is a wizard riding a dragon.

"Come on, raise 'em!" Freddy shouts.

"Give me a second."

"Raise 'em now. You got a yellow streak running down your back a
mile wide!"

Clark raises his hands, the ultimate sign of a ten-year-old's bravery.
His heels grope for the sides and scoot him carefully toward the drop.
Each second is a lifetime.

When he finds the slope he drops in a rush that hooks the pit of his stomach and threatens to fling him into the sky. Courage abandons him, and he grabs for safety. He is going too fast to find it.

The thrill leaps like an animal into his throat. He knows the secret all children know—only on a well-waxed slide are you truly alive. He prays as he jets off the end for this last second of dazzling exhilaration to last forever. He dreams of soaring with eagles.

Growing old, Clark now realized, was like that slide. When he was ten, he'd had to dig his heels into life to get moving. When he was fifty, courage had abandoned him and he had grabbed for a safety he'd been dropping too fast to find. Now he had reached the end. Now the adrenaline was pumping and the eagles were soaring and he was praying blindly with every ounce of life still in him for this last second of dazzling exhilaration to last forever.

At seventy, Clark had traveled to Indiana to visit his brother at the old family farm. The opera house had burned down and the slide rusted to dust. None of the faces had been the same; none of the names he remembered. Freddy had died two years before. Of old age, they had told Clark at the hardware store. It had been his time.

Clark was seventy-two. Two years had slipped by in the space of a heartbeat. He was riding the back of the dragon.

The September sun shone on the grain elevator thrusting into the sky. It shimmered on the two silver lines of the railroad tracks and the Wal-Mart parking lot beyond them. The wind shuttled the greasy smell of bacon from the Bumblebee Café and the reek of dead fish and rotting algae from the lake. Clark sniffed the air and rubbed his eyes.

Maynard Tewle peered through thick lenses at his copy of the *Credibull Weekly Herald*, his eyes nestled in fatty pouches. He squinted at the morning, then tugged on the green bill of his Northrup-King seed cap until it perched just above his eyebrows. "Hog prices are up." He was even older than Clark.

Clark stretched his arms and groaned. He had put up storm windows the day before and was feeling it. "How much?"

"Only an eighth." The paper rustled as Maynard turned a page. Clark watched the traffic creep along the highway. "Well, damn," Maynard said. "Christ in a hand bucket."

"What?"

"The sheriff's report says a house out by the farm got broken into. Some guy's VCR got stolen."

"There's been a lot of that lately." The farm had been Maynard's farm. When he sold it to the Birdseye plant in Waseca, the plant had bulldozed the buildings and plowed up the yard with a profit margin's cruel efficiency. "VCRs and radios."

Maynard grunted. "Never saw crime like this in the old days. Used to be you could invite John Dillinger into your house and the only thing he would steal would be a cookie. People don't give a damn about nothing no more."

Clark watched the sweat gather on the brown wattle hanging over Maynard's shirt collar. "I don't know. Commit a crime, and the earth is made of glass."

Maynard stared at him. Big, watery eyes. "What's that supposed to mean?"

Clark couldn't hold his gaze. "It's a quote. Emerson, I think."

"You and your damned quotes. You read too much."

"So you keep saying." The sun's touch on Clark's lips was so warm he could taste it. You damned fool, he thought, you have to watch what you say. "That was settled a long time ago, Maynard."

"I didn't bring it up."

They were sitting on a bench in front of Henry's feed store, a dusty cattle-feed sweetness tickling Clark's nostrils. To their left clustered what Credibull euphemistically called its business district—two lines of turn-of-the-century brick buildings sagging behind their storefronts like ancient women struggling to keep up with their face-lifts. Across Highway 14 on the railroad's east side stood the new high school, new, to Clark, meaning less than thirty years old; to its west the grain elevator groaned like a mysterious and very constipated giant. The Wal-Mart parking lot teemed with the desperate bustle of dirty cars and dirtier pickups and customers who had to get their shopping done before Oprah Winfrey's ten o'clock broadcast. Someone's sad dream of a housing development loitered behind the store, built in hopes of drawing middle-income families from Waseca, five miles to the east, and Mankato, twenty-two miles to the west. Brown sod now, deserted lots, real estate signs rattling in the breeze. It is amazing, Clark thought, how many things never pan out.

An unlit cigarette hung from Maynard's thick wet lips. "You got a light? Helen keeps taking my lighter away. Damned woman has no sympathy."

"I thought Dr. Donaldson told you to quit smoking."

"Dr. Donaldson, my ass. Dr. Donald Duck is more like it. What a quack."

"You have an irregular heartbeat."

"What do you expect at seventy-eight? I wish I could skip as often as it does."

"It's nothing to joke about, Maynard."

Maynard heaved a wheezy sigh. "Hell, if you can't joke at our age, what can you do? Sit and die, that's what you can do." The cigarette bobbed as he spoke. "So, you got a light?"

"I don't smoke."

"I thought you didn't drink."

"I don't smoke, either."

"I forgot." Maynard took the cigarette from his lips and gazed at it like an old but still-desirable lover. He put it in his pocket and opened the *Herald*. He read silently. "Christ in a hand bucket."

"What now?"

Maynard handed the paper to Clark. He jabbed at the page. "Some Chicago writer is coming to town. He wants to write a book about Albert Wilson."

14

Clark tapped his breast pocket for his bifocals and found it empty. A black-and-white blur of a young man with either a mustache or a harelip stared up at him. "I heard about him."

"You ever read this bird's stuff before?"

His name was too blurry for Clark to know. "That isn't the kind of stuff I read."

"Says he's coming here to do research."

"I suppose he'd have to if he wants to write a book."

"Says he's looking for people to help him."

"I suppose he'd have to do that, too." Clark stretched his legs toward the elevator. Arthritic spurs screwed into his knees and made him flinch. He did not want to talk about this.

"You going to help him?" Maynard asked.

Some answers are as delicate as spiderwebs and others as weighty as lead. Some are both. "It's his book. Let him make his own living."

"Yeah." Maynard closed his eyes against the sun. "Sure." His belly pulled his suspenders away from his chest.

"That was settled a long time ago, Maynard."

"You said that before."

On the high school football field, a line of teenaged girls in blue shorts and white T-shirts were doing jumping jacks, their chants wafting on the breeze. Clark looked down at the paper; the typeset swarmed like ants around a dropped popsicle. On a January evening in 1958, on a farm across from Maynard's, south of Credibull, someone had beaten Albert Wilson to death with a ball-peen hammer. A few months before the murder, Albert Wilson had bought from a failing farmer eighty acres of prime farmland that Maynard had thought to be his rightful due. A bloodstained hammer and a few drunken threats were not enough to convict Maynard of murder, but like a black dot on a white wall, you center your attention on what you have.

Maynard's anger stunk of salt and body odor. His silence said all that he wanted it to.

"I know you didn't do it, Maynard."

"It was that goddamned priest."

"I know." Kenneth Callahan had been priest out at St. Anne's Catholic Church, a country parish a quarter mile down the road from the Wilson farm. On his deathbed he'd confessed to the murder, but suspicion is a stain that does not wear away. "This writer . . . what was his name?"

"It's right in front of you."

"I don't have my glasses."

"Lewell. Ted or Terry or Todd. Ted, I think."

"This Ted Lewell isn't going to find anything that everybody doesn't already know."

"Then why is he writing a book?"

"You'd have to ask him."

Maynard snatched the paper from Clark's lap. "Hell. Maybe I will." Clark let him boil off his indignation. The man could hang on to anger like a dog worrying a bone.

A station wagon crawled into the Wal-Mart parking lot. Ten years ago a dairy farmer named Haas had owned the Wal-Mart land. He'd been a nice guy until he sold out and became a rich braggart—thank God he moved to Minneapolis. Arnold Andresen's sheep had grazed in what was now the high school's mathematics wing. Arnold was dead now.

The elevator glowed in the morning sun. Everything came back. Nineteen fifty-four.

An explosion awakens Clark. He thinks of Hiroshima.

"What was that?" Nora, his wife, asks. Her face is heavy with sleep.

"Must be the elevator."

He runs out of their house and down St. Anne's Road with the pounding of Nora's feet growing softer behind him. Two suns lighten the sky, one in the east, just beginning to rise, and a far brighter one in the north, at the elevator. The air is a hot lick; the elevator spits burning wreckage upon the Andresen flock. The grain dust must have ignited.

16

Clark stops at the highway and shields his face. The sheep scream, God, what a sound, like women being raped. Lambs lie broken backed beneath the glowing timbers, their forelegs pawing the orange-lit ground as they bleat their agony. Skin blackens in scabby chunks.

Arnold Andresen darts among the wreckage with a two-by-four gripped in both hands, jumping from side to side as burning timbers fall, sweat and tears gleaming on his cheeks. He beats each lamb's skull into the pasture, red among the green and gold. His screams grow as theirs die.

Nora is screaming, too, screaming as if she will never stop. The elevator roars its pleasure.

Clark closed his eyes. The past came back so easily, easier every year, easier every hour. He had to struggle to stay in the present as if it were a fetid room. But you have to stay where you are. Unbidden memories will crush you.

Maynard dug an elbow into his side. "You meditating? You turning into one of those sixties Buddhist guys? You're not going to set yourself on fire, are you?"

"I'm thinking."

"About what?"

It was funny how your greatest joys and your greatest fears are in your memories and the black threat that senility will take them away. Perhaps God was a carnival barker working a fixed game: spin the wheel and place your bets; there are no kewpie dolls for you. But you don't lose everything and walk away shaking your head. Dylan Thomas had written, *Do not go gentle into that good night.* A line like scripture. "A lot of things. Nora, for one."

"You've got to quit blaming yourself for that."

"I don't blame myself. It happened, that's all." Clark studied the elevator. He thought of dying lambs; he almost smelled them. "You know what's funny? I can remember what happened forty years ago as if it

17

were yesterday, but I can't for the life of me remember where I put my glasses."

"Hell, buddy. What do you suppose that means?"

"There's no supposing about it. I'm absentminded. I'm old."

Maynard spat into the gravel. "Hell, Clark, all that means is that wherever you put your glasses isn't worth remembering."

"Then a lot of things aren't worth remembering."

"You got that right. I took Helen to a movie yesterday, and I spent the whole time asking myself where Bogie and Bergman had gone. These days you're an actor if you're muscle-bound and haven't dropped the barbell on your head too many times. A woman is an actress if she looks good naked. What the hell is that?"

"I mean important things. I can't remember important things."

Maynard grunted. "We used to have real problems, like World War Two and the Great Depression. Now they have piddly-assed wars in places no one has ever heard of, and you're poor if you don't own a big-screen television. What this younger generation needs is some real problems. The Nips would do them a big favor by bombing Pearl Harbor again." He patted Clark's knee. "It isn't that your memory's going, buddy. It's just getting more selective."

"Sure." Clark watched Maynard smile. Sometimes you can pull a guy out of his moods by giving him the chance to offer reassurance. Clark struggled to convince himself he was being a humanitarian.

The breeze carried away the high school girls' cadence. Clark turned to the football field as he would to a wall missing a picture. They were lying on their backs with their knees bent, straining through sit-ups, an up-and-down rhythm. High, tight breasts, narrow waists, tanned skin as smooth as honey spilled on a table. Giggly voices in the backseats of prewar Fords, soft moans on sweaty nights like the mourning of doves at sunset. Damn. In a cliché-filled world, only one has any meaning. *Those were the days.*

He looked down at the crotch of his pants and shook his head. The hell of age is that it takes the stiffness out of your cock and puts it into your knees, your shoulders, your mind. If only his body had stayed as young as his lust had; if only there were still ways of satisfying both. If only both still needed to be satisfied. Damn.

Clark stood. His long legs required too much leverage for his knees to handle—he couldn't take a step until the clutching pain in them released him. "Let's go."

Maynard pushed his cap back and squinted. "To the Bumblebee?"

"For coffee."

Maynard laughed his dry, lunatic laugh. His belly bounced against his suspenders like a child jumping on a bed. "You're horny, aren't you? Every time you get horny it's time for coffee. What did it today? The talk about naked actresses? Maybe this younger generation has some advantages after all."

"I'm too old to get horny."

"Pray God I never get that old. The only thing that keeps me from being a randy monster is my ticker."

"That's you. All I want is a cup of coffee."

"I doubt that." Maynard grinned and slapped his knees as he stood. His body and breath creaked. "All right, as long as you're buying." He shuffled behind Clark across the feed store parking lot.

They crossed the road. The wind snapped the high school flag. Two paper sacks in an eddy behind the Bumblebee circled each other like boxers. The girls on the football field cheered. Clark resisted looking at them. "You want a Danish?" he asked.

"Just give me coffee." Sweat lay like polish across Maynard's forehead. "Helen's been nagging me to lose weight ever since we left the farm." He hoisted his belly. "She don't know a damn thing. This is one big love handle."

"Retirement will do that to you."

"It didn't do it to you."

"It's hard to get fat on a can of Campbell's."

"Maybe you just need some love."

"Maybe I just need a Danish."

"The last Bumblebee Danish I ate tasted like dust." Maynard took off his cap and wiped his forehead with the back of his wrist. He

19

leaned against the back corner of the café. His thin, white hair flared. "Maybe my tongue died. Does that ever happen to you? Parts of your body die and come back again?"

"No."

"They do to me. Sneak previews of the afterlife."

"You must have connections I don't."

Maynard grinned through his wheezing. "God smiles on me."

A grain truck turned grumpily into the elevator lot. The elevator greeted it with grumbles and groans, the mechanical language of steel and gasoline. "Let's take a break here," Maynard said. "Hot day."

"It'll be cooler in the Bumblebee."

"Let's take a break here." His heart made any walk he took at best slow and at worst precarious. "I'm a little dizzy."

"You're always a little dizzy."

"Ha ha, very funny." Maynard wiped his face. "You should have your own talk show."

"What does the doctor say?"

"About getting dizzy? I haven't told him about it."

"Why not?"

"Because I already know what he'd say." Maynard snorted. "Take aspirin. Do you believe it? With all the money he makes, the best he can come up with is to take aspirin. He's spent too many Wednesday afternoons getting beaned in the head with golf balls."

"Aspirin thins your blood."

"Someone ought to thin Donald Duck's salary. He should go back to chasing Huey, Dewey, and Larry. What a quack."

"It's Louie."

"It's Donald. I know that much."

"No, I mean it's Louie instead of Larry."

"You would know. You got old Donald Duck cartoons at the museum?"

"Not that I've ever found."

Maynard fished his cigarette from his pocket. "You got a light?"

"No."

"Damn." Maynard shrugged. "Maybe Billie will have one." They walked inside with the cigarette between his lips.

Billie Jessup, the Bumblebee's morning waitress, was in almost every respect the size of a child, though her breasts would have looked more proportionate on a taller woman, say ten feet taller. She'd been married to Denny Jessup, a pea-truck driver for the Birdseye plant. They managed to-have-and-to-hold-until-death-do-us-part in an apartment in Waseca for all of three months before they finally divorced. Billie left for Credibull "because," she explained, "Mankato has better men, and Waseca has cheaper bars. By living between them, I get the best of both worlds."

"I saw you two limp across the street," she said as they waited for their eyes to adjust to the sudden shadows. She cocked a hand on a little-girl hip. "Christ almighty, it takes you old farts forever." Her voice cracked like a plate.

"Hot day," Maynard said. "Heart's acting up."

"From the thrill of seeing you." Clark smiled.

"And now I'm all aflutter."

Billie led them to their table down a narrow walkway between a red-linoleum-topped counter and a line of booths growing out of the wall like wood fungus. They smelled like wood fungus, too, and were all empty. Farmers were too busy this time of year preparing for the harvest to loiter, and most of the old-timers spent their mornings at the Burger King on the Waseca side of the Wal-Mart, where the coffee was cheaper. She had her hair tied back today; the sweat glistened on the nape of her neck. As Clark sat he decided he liked her better with her hair framing her face. With it like this her cheeks stood out, and she looked too much like Tammy Faye Bakker already.

Maynard sat across from him. The gold cross around Billie's neck glinted in the fluorescent light, stabbed into Clark's eyes. "Two coffees," she said, "one black and one with cream and sugar. Any Danish?"

"Not for me." Maynard pointed at his cup. "I want a lot of cream in there. Find me a light for my cigarette."

"A little cream and no light," Billie answered. "You're supposed to

21

be on a diet. You're supposed to quit smoking."

"Christ in a hand bucket, does everyone have to know my medical history?"

"In a town the size of Credibull," Billie said, "everyone knows the shape of the mole on your ass."

"Would you like me to show it to you? To confirm your suspicions?"

"Living single hasn't yet destroyed all of my standards. Now, if you were wearing Clark's ass . . ." She nudged Clark with her hip and winked. She slipped behind the counter for the coffeepot.

Another part of the morning routine. Each day dawned with Clark sweeping out his son's hardware store, what used to be *his* hardware store, across the street from the Farmers National Bank. On Mondays, Wednesdays, and Fridays he walked from the store to the Credibull Historical Society, where he served as a volunteer curator, rambling among the exhibits or trying to figure out the microfiche machine. On Tuesdays, Thursdays, and Saturdays he sat for an hour with Maynard at Henry's before crossing to the Bumblebee for coffee and Danish and as much ogling of Billie Jessup as he dared. Old men shouldn't ogle.

Maynard took a gray handkerchief out of his back pocket and wiped the sweat from his face. "Damn this weather. Almost makes a guy wish for winter."

"Yeah." Clark watched Billie fill his cup. For the thousandth time, he wondered how old she was. A late teenager, he guessed, or in her early twenties. Fresh skin covered by too much makeup. She always had the smell of perfume and sex about her.

She took the pot back, then returned with his Danish. "Holler if you need anything."

"Will do." Clark felt an old ache echo as she walked away. He thought of soft moans in prewar Fords, of sit-ups and up-and-down rhythms. What he wouldn't give to be young again, with a cock that gave the world the finger. Something stirred in his pants, or he wished it did. All that was ancient history.

Maynard was stirring what little cream Billie left for him into his coffee. "So what do you think?" he asked.

"Think about what?"

"About going over to see the matinee in Mankato this afternoon. Haven't you been listening?"

"No." Clark felt like dirty water swirling down a drain. "I guess I haven't."

"The Mankato matinee at three o'clock. They're showing something with muscleheads and naked women. What do you think? Helen's and my treat. With you along I won't spend my time thinking about this damned writer. It's hell spending a whole day angry."

"I promised I'd see Nora this afternoon."

"See her some other time."

"I promised I'd see her today."

"Hell, she don't know when you see her. She don't know a damn thing at all." Maynard's face paled gray. "Oh, God. I'm sorry, Clark."

Clark dropped his gaze to his coffee. "Forget it."

"I put my foot in it up to the hip, didn't I?"

"You always do, Maynard."

"I know. I'm famous for it."

"*Infamous* is a better word."

"Yeah, infamous. I'm infamous for a lot of things. But I really am sorry."

Maynard pushed his coffee away, spilling it on the table. His face was still gray enough to make Clark wonder if his heart had skipped too many beats. He felt a burst of cold panic. He didn't want to lose a friend in a café. He didn't want to lose a friend at all. "Are you all right?"

"Yeah. I just don't want coffee this morning. Makes me piss."

"It never used to."

"I think my bladder's petrifying. Pretty soon I'll be wearing those damn adult diapers. Christ in a hand bucket."

Clark watched him pull the spilled coffee into a narrow rill with a fork tine. "Do you want my Danish?"

"No." Maynard sighed. "Say hello to her for me, will you?"

"Sure."

23

"And Helen, too. Helen always sends her regards."

"Sure."

"And why don't you come over for supper tonight? Helen makes too damn much food, anyway. I can't stand leftovers."

"All right."

"Six o'clock. I'll pull out a roast as soon as I get home. You know Helen's roast beef. Melts in your mouth."

"You're right about Nora, Maynard. It's just that I promised."

Maynard set down his fork. He rubbed his face again, seemed to rub the gray from it. "Then just make sure you're on time. Cold beef gravy congeals. Might as well eat boogers."

"I'll be on time, Maynard."

The overhead light flickered in Clark's coffee. Nora used to make gravy, too.

Chapter

2

From the corner of Nora's window in Ambrose's Nursing Home, Clark could see the rocks lining the shore of Crystal Lake; he could just hear the water mutter. Autumn was beginning to ignite the maples on Hotel Hill with scarlet, a color as final as the gasps of many of the home's residents. It was a comparison Clark could not help making.

"I started putting up storm windows yesterday," he told Nora. His shoulders cringed beneath his fingers like dogs about to be beaten. Old pain. Old dogs. "I'm thinking of hiring Maynard's grandson for the second floor. I just can't dredge up the energy to climb that ladder."

Nora stared at a spot on the wallpaper two and a half inches above Clark's right shoulder. He had measured the distance—she had stared at the same spot for the last nine months. If he moved his chair four inches to the right he could almost convince himself that her eyes were raptly studying his. He had quit moving his chair a long time ago.

"I thought of getting our son to put them up for me, but you know Walter. He'd break half the panes and end up in the emergency room twice before he got the ladder against the wall." He laughed quietly, not feeling the humor inside. The gray strands of Nora's hair could no longer hide the scalp beneath them. Her ravenous body consumed itself but had no taste for her loose, leathery skin. Her face spread across the pillow like a wrinkled napkin dropped carelessly over a skull.

It was five o'clock; Clark had been at the home for an hour. He turned toward the hall, watched a nurse walk past, then turned away as if he had seen something shameful. He shuddered as if extremely professional beetles in white staff uniforms were crawling up and down his spine. The biggest travesty of modern medicine is that it makes people live longer than they should; makes them die in places like this. *Home*—what a word. *Institution* was better, or maybe *prison*. It should be *inmates* instead of *residents; guards* instead of *nurses*. We gloss our horror with euphemism. We sugarcoat our pills.

He rose to stretch his legs, to walk the caged feeling from his soul. The pain in his knees flared before subsiding into background noise. He shuffled to the window and looked out onto the west side of town. He studied the back of the historical society, where he would be working in the morning, a temperate redbrick building on Josef Meyer Boulevard that forty years before had been the Lutheran church. Across the boulevard, children challenged one another to jump from bar to bar on the elementary school's jungle gym, the same jungle gym Walter had climbed on thirty years before. A girl squealed as a flirting boy chased her out of sight around the school, butterflies flashing in the light of a setting sun. Young and first love.

• •

"Do you love me?" she asks.

Hannah's eyes are big and blue and beautiful. Until she gets boobs her eyes will be the most wonderful thing about her, and Clark is madly, madly in love with her. He is so much in love with her that he imagines saving her from bad guys and carrying her off on Grandpa's old Percheron like knights used to do in olden days. He is so much in love with her that he thinks that one day he will take all his clothes off and she will take off all of hers and they will lie on a bed like he had seen Dad and Mom do through the cracked-open bedroom door.

"Tell me, Clark. Do you love me?"

Clark makes a disgusted face because Freddy is watching. *"Why would I love you? You're a girl."*

"I don't love you, either." She pushes him to prove her hatred. He chases her into the oak trees to prove his. If he isn't careful, he will catch her where Freddy can see, so he fakes stumbling over a root so she will have the time to get out of sight. Things would be so much easier if Hannah didn't run like a girl.

When it's safe, he sprints to catch up to her. He grabs her around the waist and they tumble together. He acts as if he is mad because he needs for this closeness a manly justification, but when he looks into her eyes, into those big, blue, beautiful eyes, he cannot maintain it.

She presses her lips to his cheek. He knows he should wipe the wetness off—girls' germs—but he cannot. His wiener feels funny against her leg. Squished.

"Clark Holstrom," she says solemnly, *"I love you and I know you love me, too."*

He cannot lie to those eyes. *"I will love you forever, Hannah. Hope to die if I don't, but don't tell anyone, okay?"*

"Okay."

They lie together for years and years until Clark remembers that his dad is taking him out to see his cousin Norman that afternoon. Norman is very wise and very evil. He has naked-lady postcards. He has shown Clark how to use the postcards, how to pull down his pants and yank on his wiener while looking at them and say, *"Oh baby, oh baby, give it to me, give it to me." That makes you shoot your wad, as Norman calls it. Clark has looked and looked and yanked and yanked and even used the "Oh baby" incantation, but all he ever gets out of it is a sore wiener.*

Norman can shoot his wad twice in a row. Clark thinks that maybe the reason he can't shoot his wad even once is because shooting your wad at naked-lady postcards is evil and Clark does not want to do evil. But by Norman's face he can see that evil can be fun. It looks as if it can be a lot of fun. Maybe if Clark keeps practicing he'll be able to do evil things, too. Maybe he'll want to.

"I got to go," he says as he stands.

"When will you come back?" Hannah asks.

"Pretty soon."

She grows solemn again. "Promise me something, Clark Holstrom. Promise me that you will always come back."

"Don't be a goof. Of course I will."

She stands and kisses his cheek again. He tries to kiss one of her big, blue, beautiful eyes but she closes its lid. He can't wait until she gets boobs.

He kept that promise before the war, but it took him ten years to honor it afterward. Hannah had married by then to a building contractor or a landscaper or something. Clark had seen her lugging three overweight children into the corner grocery as he was driving by on his way to his brother's farm. The wide hips, the tired eyes of a family's matron. She was not the same Hannah, and Clark was not the same boy who had made such promises. He'd driven by silently. *Always* is too damned big a word.

Nora was staring at the wallpaper, her wrinkled, liver-spotted hands lying quietly across her hips. The folds on her forearms shone against the sheets like limp sails spread across a desiccated sky. She's only three years older than I am, he thought. Why does she look so ancient? Something roiled in the pit of his stomach like a bad meal. What does this say about how I look? About how old I am?

Three months before, he and Maynard had been sitting on the feed store bench. An ambulance had screamed by, on its way, Clark guessed, to Rochester and the Mayo Clinic.

"What are you most afraid of?" he had asked Maynard.

"Alzheimer's," Maynard had said. "You?"

Clark had paused. He'd known his answer before he had asked the question, but a quick response would hint too strongly at a cold and visceral fear. "I guess it would be ending up like Nora."

"That would be bad," Maynard had agreed.

Ending up like Nora, eyes open but not seeing, brain there but not thinking, made fear drip icily into Clark's throat. Worse yet would be eyes open *and* seeing, brain there *and* thinking, knowing about the stinking diapers, feeling someone roll you on your side, change the sheets, and slam you back down like a car hood, understanding that eating is only a swallow reflex keeping you alive for yet another day of this. Christ. Perhaps God was a puppeteer who cut your strings when he tired of you, who let you fall helplessly onto white linen sheets. He had other puppets.

"No," Clark said softly, a scream inside, *no.* He'd run his car off a bridge first. He'd stick his head in an oven or drink himself to death, a bump of sleeping pills with one bottle of Everclear as fast as he could take it for the chaser. *No.*

Unless your mind goes first, he saw in Nora's eyes. *Or unless it comes on you so fast that you don't have the chance.*

There has to be a way, he told those eyes. There has to be. A man cannot suffer beyond that which he is able . . .

Comes on you as fast as it came on me.

No, he screamed again.

There had been a cold stretch the winter before, nights at thirty below, the air as sharp as shattered glass. He'd fallen asleep listening to the television mutter as Nora watched *The Late Show.* When he awoke at two to use the bathroom, the living room was vacant and the television still on. Her bedroom was empty.

He found her lying near the garage beside a garbage bag stuffed like a turkey and the overturned trash can—she'd slipped and broken her hip. Her frozen legs shriveled to black stumps the doctor amputated in the spring. She never made a sound during the operation; hadn't made a sound since. Comatose, Clark had been told. Brain-dead. Are there any words that can really be believed?

"I'll bring a picture for you, Nora, maybe one with wildflowers. Something to look at besides the wall. You'd like that, wouldn't you?"

A fly crawled in jerks down Nora's cheek to sample the wetness at the corner of her mouth. Clark waved it away. He held her hand. Its clammy touch made him jerk away. He tried to force himself to take it again and failed.

In the hall, Annie Halverson began to cry. The bitch nurse had abandoned her miles from home, she lamented, out in the cold. In the room across from Nora's, Bob Tunnell was complaining about the same bitch nurse as she lifted him off the toilet. Nora's once-amber eyes had faded; her whole face had faded. Her cheeks hung like two wrinkled pouches. She wasn't anyone Clark knew anymore.

He drives the old Model A out to a farm five miles north of town to deliver an air compressor that Mike Caruther said needs delivering. A woman at least five years older than he is watches the truck from the front porch as she shakes dust from a rug. She isn't pretty.

"Can I help you?" From the flat way she speaks, he can tell that she isn't bright, either. Her eyes hold a faint luster. That's something, at least.

Clark checks the sales slip. He smells either the dust or the woman— he is not sure which. "I'm looking for Benny Tupelo."

"He's in the fields."

"Are you his wife?"

"I'm his sister."

"Do you live here?"

"Yes. I clean up and look after the kids. Amy, that's his wife, teaches in Mankato."

Clark nods. She is too old to be living with her brother. "Can you sign for this?"

She drapes the rug over the railing and steps into the yard. She signs the receipt slowly while the tip of her chalky tongue probes her lips. Her signature is big and loopy, like a child's. Nora Tupelo. *"Put it inside the barn door," she tells him.*

He drives the truck to the barn and sets the compressor inside the door. It is heavy, and he is sweating when he drives back past the woman. She is shaking out the rug again, her eyes following him to the road.

As he drives back into Credibull, Clark thinks about this old maid with the rug. He has hardly thought about women since he returned from the war, but the war was a winter now beginning to break. This woman with the rug has the breasts and hips and look of a woman. She's a little on the pudgy side.

He rolls up the window to keep the dusty road out of the cab. He glances at her name on the receipt. Nora Tupelo. *At least she has something in her eyes. Clark has always liked women's eyes. Mirrors of the soul.*

Loneliness breeds illusion. Illusion breeds at best an ill-fated love. He remembered thinking as he watched Nora in white plod down the aisle at St. Luke's Lutheran Church, *God, what am I doing?* and thinking as he stood in the reception line, a smile frozen to his face, *God, what have I done?* He had held Nora in his arms that night, but he made love to a frozen smile and a question. Neither had been satisfied. Neither ever would be.

The fly was on her face again. He waved it away. Walter was born the year Mike Caruther died and his wife sold the store to Clark. Nora eventually surrendered what little vitality she had to the seventeen-inch-diagonal nirvana of television, mankind's latest created god. She wasn't much different now than she had been before her accident—instead of lying on a sofa and staring silently at a screen, she was lying on a bed and staring silently at a point on the wall two and a half inches above his shoulder. Then why did seeing her like this make him feel so bad? God damn, he thought, or better yet, God be damned: it captured more closely his philosophy.

Clark recognized the cumbersome footsteps coming down the hall. Annie Halverson pleaded her case as his son stopped at the door only long enough to nod nervously in her direction. Walter had a habit of avoidance.

"Hi, Dad." Walter was bald and almost as overweight as his mother had been. His face was pitted with acne scars like bad memories; his complexion shone in the fluorescent lighting. He looked older than his forty-three years.

"Hi, son. How was work today?"

"We're hopping." Walter sat in Nora's easy chair; his legs, wrapped in brown polyester pants, looked like two overstuffed sausages gone bad. His eyes buzzed around the room. He could never hold a gaze, making it damned annoying trying to talk to him. "I figured you'd be here, it being Thursday and all. I got an idea."

"Say hello to your mother. You always treat her as if she isn't here."

"Hi, Mom. Dad, I got an idea." He said it all in one breath.

Clark suppressed a sigh. "What?" Walter always had ideas.

"I was thinking, what is the one thing that everyone in this town wants but has to go out of town to buy?"

Clark could think of a lot of things. A decent meal that didn't include beef, pork chops, or potatoes. Farm implements. Movie tickets. A good cup of coffee, the kind where the aroma intoxicated you. A good used car—Lucky Thursten, who owned the lot across the highway from Ambrose's, was known to the locals as the Lucky Lemon. "I don't know."

"Computers." Walter grinned. The scars pulled into odd angled creases; his teeth were yellow and bad. Hadn't Clark bought him braces when he was twelve? A thousand dollars down the drain. The kid never could take care of anything. He used to kill goldfish on a daily basis.

Walter leaned forward, his elbows on his knees, his belly testing the fortitude of his shirt buttons. "The way I see it, we can make a deal with IBM or Hewlett-Packard, carry their line if we promise to do so many dollars in business. Maybe I could learn to fix them, and we could carry software. We'd be the only computer dealer in town. We'd make a fortune." His eyes sparkled, then buzzed away.

Clark shrugged. "I don't even know what software is."

"Software is computer programs, Dad."

"What's the matter with the hard kind? It never did me wrong."

"Hardware's just . . . well, it's just *hardware,* Dad. Computers are the future. Computers are our opportunity."

One quirk about Walter was that he never said what he meant, but he wasn't deceptive enough to hide what he was trying not to say. If he was talking about the store and used the words *we* and *our* instead of *I* and *my,* it meant that business was bad. *We* and *our* made failure not entirely his fault. Walter was a mover and a shaker only in the way he shifted responsibility.

"I don't know why you come to me with this, son. It's your store now."

"I want you to be a part of it."

"I sweep the floor every morning."

"Any moron can sweep, Dad. Is that enough?"

Clark looked at Nora, trying to hide his eyes from his son. Say it, Walter, he thought, say it. Say you have to find something to sell besides hardware before the Wal-Mart drives you out of business. Say that the store I spent forty years building you're going to tear down in less than five. Don't play this game with me.

"So how is business, Walter?" he asked.

"Like I said, Dad, we're hopping. We'll really hop if we get these computers. What do you think?" He propped one hand on Nora's bed. She tipped slightly toward him, her eyes settling on the wall a few inches lower than usual.

"I think," Clark said, "that you should do whatever it is that you think you should do. It's your store now."

Walter pursed his lips and stared at the floor. The fluorescent light reflected off his scalp and cheeks. "So you think computers would be a good idea?"

Clark sighed. "If you think so, Walter."

Walter nodded and stood. Nora shifted back up to stare above Clark's shoulder. "All right, then we'll do it." He stepped toward the door. "Come on, I'll buy you dinner at the Burger King. We'll celebrate."

Dinner at the Burger King was no celebration. "I'm eating with the Tewles."

"Oh? Why don't you ever eat at my place?"

Because your place is a dump. Because I know hogs who can cook better than you. "You never ask me."

"One of these days, I will."

"Fine."

Walter smiled—a thousand dollars down the drain. "Sounds good. See you later, Dad." He rested a clammy hand on Clark's shoulder and stepped out of the room, keeping his back to the ever-complaining Annie Halverson. Her pleading rose as his footsteps faded. He hadn't said good-bye to his mother.

Clark shook his head apologetically at Nora. "You know Walter. Always running to nowhere." What a kid—Clark wondered if anything he had said could be believed. He might try selling computers. He might invite him to dinner. He might not. The success of any plan depended on when the next plan came. "Where does he get that from, Nora?"

You might accept his invitation, Nora's eyes said, *you might not. Where does he get that from? You have to ask?*

Clark rose and looked out of the window. The playground was deserted; the nursing home's shadow stretched languidly across the lawn. He checked his watch—it was going on six. If he hurried, he'd make it to the Tewles' before Maynard could complain about the gravy.

In the hall the bitch nurse, a short woman built like a linebacker, was finally dealing with Annie Halverson, using the cold, efficient technique nurses use when they have been nurses too long. She moved the poor woman as if she were a Monopoly token—roll a three, slam her down, bang, bang, bang, you're on Boardwalk. He pushed through the scrubbed, antiseptic air and was outside spitting his discomfort into the weakening sunshine before he realized that he had not said good-bye to Nora.

Like father, like son, he thought. Like son, like father.

The Tewles lived south of Highway 14 in a small white house on Josef Meyer Boulevard. Clark waited almost eagerly at the door—stepping inside the house's familiarity was like putting on a favorite pair of shoes. They owned no VCRs, no microwaves, no machines that answered their phone or talked to you. Nothing had a remote. The Tewles still lived in a world where nothing came with more than a three-page instruction manual.

"Come on in, Clark," Helen called from the kitchen—they had known each other too long for anything as formal as answering the door. Clark waded out of the evening's coolness into a roast beef bouquet as savory as a Rembrandt masterpiece. Maynard sat on the sofa, his shirt open, steadying with both hands a beer can perched upon his lolling white belly. With his legs spread he seemed to be giving birth to a bouncing baby cushion.

"Sit down, Clark. The Twins game is about to start."

"Thanks."

Helen stepped into the living room, wiping her hands with a dish towel. She still had youth in her eyes, still had auburn traces in her hair—she was eleven years younger than Maynard. Her body was as delicate as window frost. "I hope you're hungry. I hope I made enough."

"He's hungry," Maynard said, "and the day you don't make enough food is the day hell has a hockey team."

Helen slapped his arm with the towel. "You never let anyone speak for himself."

"You always manage to. Gab, gab, gab."

"I know your ways."

"My ways aren't difficult to know. I drink beer and fart a lot." Maynard crushed his can between the heels of his hands as Helen went into the kitchen. He stood carefully, balancing on the strength of his heart like a tightrope walker. "I'm getting another beer. You want anything from the icebox?"

"A Coke."

"Coming up." He nodded at the television. "Keep track of the count for me."

Clark tapped his empty pocket for his glasses, then sat far enough away from the television to minimize farsighted incoherence. He almost knocked over a pile of romance novels stacked up on an end table, the leaning tower of Harlequin. The leadoff batter had stepped to the plate.

He watched the batter take a strike before letting his gaze drift to a wedding portrait of the Tewles' daughter, Barbara, and her husband, Brian Mischke, hanging above the television. Brian looked so frightened that the photographer must have had to touch up the wet spot on his tuxedo fly. Barb was radiant, both as a blushing bride and as an expectant mother—you can't touch up a five-month pregnancy. Relief flashed in her smile.

His gaze wandered from picture to picture, from memory to memory. The baseball game fell into the years, all of the years, so many years here in this room. An aerial shot of the farm hung surrounded by three rows of black-and-white portraits like chicks scrabbling around a hen. The farm bulldozed under, the people in the portraits unknown. Men sat like sepia-stained cardboard while their women stood beside them, their smiles locked to cover the pain of the corset inquisition. All those people were long gone, six feet under, or passed away—they were whatever euphemism you choose to cover your frosty fear of death. People who had lived and loved and been loved now accepted dusting once a week from a woman who probably had trouble remembering their names. Time buries you. It smooths the sand over your face with frigid fingers. He leaned back in his chair and let his head roll to the side. He breathed deeply.

"So, what happened?" Maynard raised his beer to his lips. The Coke he handed Clark sweat coldly. Judging from the angle at which Maynard had to hold his beer, he must have drunk half of it in the kitchen.

"Nothing much." It was the best answer Clark could give.

"Oh." Maynard sat down heavily and stared at the screen. "What do you mean, nothing much? The leadoff batter is on second base!"

The pitcher's cap had a *TC* on it. *Twin Cities*—one of the good guys. Clark shrugged. "I mean nothing much as far as the Twins are concerned."

Maynard grunted. "You got that right. That damned Erickson. You'd think that for ten million dollars a pitch he could put a few in the strike zone that didn't get knocked back into his face."

"You'd think so."

The second batter popped a single into center field. The leadoff man streaked to third. Maynard covered his face with his hands. "Oh, hell. I can see where this is going to end up."

Clark drank his Coke and let his eyes drift back to Barb's portrait. He wondered what the bulge beneath her gown would charge for putting up second-story storm windows. He turned to the farm. Life flowed in its pastures, in its fields, in the trees shading the front of the house. Life flowed so fully that he could smell the manure, could feel the grass beneath his feet, the wind on his face. It must have been taken in the late forties, back when Clark could still walk through that grass without feeling spurs in his knees. In those days he could flex his arms and feel the strength in them; when he planted his feet he could not be moved. He couldn't make a mistake then, but life goes on and one thing you learn is that you make mistakes. Drinking had been one, and there had been others. Hell. He wondered if it were somehow possible to change everything that happens in and after a photograph. Perhaps God was a film editor and life was on a rewindable reel. *God Almighty, A.C.E.* scrolling through the credits.

A sudden exhaustion, weighted with seventy-two years, forced Clark deep into his chair. I'm too tired to rewind, he thought. Leave me here. Make me young now.

Heat from the kitchen caressed his cheek. Helen was taking the roast from the oven, mitts on her hands with embroidered kittens prancing across the knuckles, the roast with its pearl-onion necklace dark and steaming. Clark's stomach growled. It had been a long time since he'd eaten good roast, and Helen made good roast. Seeing her in the kitchen raised an old yearning.

"Dinner's ready," she called. "Turn the TV off."

"You mean turn the TV up," Maynard corrected. "If we turn it off, no power gets to the speaker and we won't be able to hear the game. Think about it, Helen. It's basic electrical theory."

She speared the meat, pulled it onto a platter, and set the platter on the kitchen table—the house was too small for a dining room. "You can live for once without your blessed Vikings."

"It's the Twins. The Vikings are football."

"The Twins, then. For once I'd like a decent meal without you shouting every time someone scores."

"I don't shout, I curse. With the way these pansies are playing, scoring is always done by the other team."

"Turn it off, Maynard."

"I'm leaving it on, Helen."

Helen took a pitcher of lemonade out of the refrigerator. The slap of its door was her only answer. Maynard turned the volume higher than he needed to, then sat at the head of the table. Clark sat beside him, his back uncomfortably straight. Maynard studied Helen, then grunted.

"What the hell." He went back into the living room and turned off the television. "Their season's done anyway." He sat again. "Good night, Helen."

Helen smiled. A glowing warmth filled her eyes that Clark could not remember ever seeing in Nora's. "Good night, Maynard." She slid a slice of roast and one pearl onion onto her plate, then passed Maynard the platter.

Clark shrugged. "I won't ask what that means."

"Something we've tried on and off," Maynard said around a mouthful of beef and potatoes. He swallowed loudly. "We never go to bed in the middle of an argument, so saying good night means the argument's over."

"It sounds strange," Helen said, "but it works."

"As long as it works, who cares how strange it is?"

Clark made a sandwich out of his beef and two slices of homemade bread. The taste made him puddle in his shoes. The last roast beef he had eaten had been in a Mankato fast food joint. It had been sliced thinly enough for a pound to cover a parking lot and was tough enough to substitute for the asphalt. This beef was fresh and sliced two inches thick, bought at a butcher shop on Crystal Lake's northwest shore, where all the meat was local, where reputation still meant something. He bought his own meat there when he felt ambitious or foolhardy enough to attempt cooking it.

"So what are you reading, Helen?" Clark had been pointing out her romance novels' literary decrepitude for months. He'd once bought her a novel by Edith Wharton, but "nice" was all Helen had said when she finished it. The cover of the next book she read had depicted a tanned Goliath clutching a woman with a chest that defied both realism and gravity. He couldn't remember anything else about it, except that both the words *love* and *lust* were in the title. It's funny what people choose to remember.

"The only reading she ever does," Maynard answered for her. "Some big galoot is always stuffing his purple-headed love pump into some gasping virgin's quivering flesh."

Helen stabbed at her beef. "It's better than reading nothing at all."

"I read." Maynard popped an onion into his mouth. "The *TV Guide.*"

"Why do I love him?" Helen asked Clark.

"I can tell you that," Maynard said. "Ask her how well her quivering flesh and my purple-headed love pump get along."

"*Got* along." Helen sipped her lemonade. "Get your tenses right."

39

How she could remain so genteel while discussing such a subject was beyond Clark. Signs of the times, he supposed. They had never talked about things like this in the old days. They'd just done them.

"*Got* along, then," Maynard said, "but one more really good *get along* would be all right with me."

"Your heart couldn't handle it."

"But what a way to go." He belched quietly. "The ticker makes love just like it is in her damned novels—fiction."

"Fiction to you," Helen said.

"Fiction to us," Maynard answered. "I hope."

"Fiction now, but you won't live forever. I'm just waiting, Maynard." She winked.

"When I'm gone," Maynard said, "you're free to find some big galoot with a love pump like an oil well. You have my permission."

"As if I'll need it." She turned to her plate.

Small talk seasoned the rest of the meal, television and weather talk, who was living, who was dying, who was gone. Helen turned to Clark while he sopped up the last of his gravy with the last of his bread. "Someone was saying at the grocery store today that a farm south of town was broken into."

Clark nodded. "It was in the paper. The burglar made off with a VCR."

"Was there anything else in the paper? I haven't had a chance to read it."

Maynard and Clark looked at each other. Maynard pushed his plate away and grumbled something Clark couldn't understand. The color in his face thickened and mottled.

"Hog prices are up," Clark said quietly.

Helen's eyes flitted from face to face. "Did something happen? What happened?"

Maynard rose slowly, pain and anger playing on his face. "Clark, you tell her, but wait until I turn the game on." He went to the refrigerator for a beer and shuffled out of the kitchen, his free hand clenching and unclenching, his feet rasping on the linoleum. "I sure as hell don't need to hear about that again."

Clark waited until the television crowd cheered—either the Twins had scored or Kirby Puckett was up to bat. "A man is coming to Credibull to write a book about Albert Wilson."

"Oh, God." Helen's hands fluttered. "You should have kicked me under the table."

"It would have come up sooner or later."

"I suppose." She set his empty plate on her own, then motioned for Maynard's. "When is he coming?"

"I don't know." Clark handed it to her. "Soon."

Helen bit her lower lip. She rose and went to the sink to run dishwater. "Albert Wilson is the last person we need to be reminded of. Those three years until Father Callahan confessed were the worst in our lives. Do you remember how crazy Maynard got?"

"I remember." He helped her clear the table.

"What are you going to tell him?" she asked. "The writer, I mean."

He leaned against the sink, close enough to Helen to smell her hair. Old memories rose that he forced down like bile. "As little as possible. If he asks where the Wilson farm is, I'll tell him it's on St. Anne's Road. If he asks where St. Anne's Road is, I'll tell him it's up by Minneapolis. If he calls me a liar, I'll plead senility. Old people always have that to fall back on."

"I mean about the murder."

"That Callahan killed him. He'll believe me—the good father was a nut." Father Callahan had been a middle-aged man who'd dissipated his loneliness through adultery with Albert Wilson's wife. After she'd died the truth came out, an argument followed, and murder. "What was that story about him and Mary?"

Helen blushed. She was Catholic, and the subject of Father Callahan embarrassed her. "You know perfectly well what that story was. You'd just rather hear me tell it."

"You won't, will you?"

"Of course not."

A parishioner had walked into the church one afternoon as Father Callahan knelt in front of the Virgin's statue. Not wanting to disturb his prayers, the parishioner stole up a side aisle, to find him masturbating, "Hail, Mary" spurting from his lips like the semen onto his cassock. Poor woman died a decade later an atheist. The priest had been a crazy and lusty son of a bitch.

Maynard belched from the doorway. Clark hadn't even noticed he'd been standing there. "Did you tell her?" He sounded drunk.

"Yes."

"Can we get on with watching the game now?"

"If Helen doesn't need my help."

"Go watch your game," Helen said. "I'd rather do this alone."

The Twins were behind six to four. Tom Kelly had pulled Erickson in favor of a chinless reliever who doctored the ball with either saliva or emery boards, if Clark remembered right. His attention wandered to the pots banging in the kitchen.

Maynard fell asleep in the eighth inning, his head back, his mouth open, his snore an alcohol-scented whistle. Clark turned off the game and went into the kitchen. Helen was sitting at the table. The thumb of one hand worked the knuckles of the other.

"Is he sleeping?" she asked.

"Yeah." Clark sat down.

"I worry about him. He's been so unpredictable lately. Have you noticed his mood swings?"

Maynard had always had mood swings. Clark shrugged.

"When he laughs, he laughs too hard. When he's angry, he's . . ." She looked down. "And then there's his heart."

"What do you mean?"

"You know about his heart."

"What do you mean about him getting angry?"

She began to speak, then stopped. Her thumb rose and fell as it made its way across the back of her hand. "He doesn't hit me. He just shakes me a little."

Clark sat back. He looked briefly into the living room. Huh—a hark back to old suspicions and ugly stories. "How long has this been going on?"

"Only the last few months."

"Why haven't you told me before?"

"It's only been a couple of times. There hasn't been anything to tell."

"Has he hurt you?"

"No, Clark. God, no. He couldn't hurt me now if he wanted to, and he doesn't want to." She wiped her eyes. "He's a seventy-eight-year-old man with a bad heart."

Clark studied her face. He remembered stories whispered in corners, stories of Helen running across the fields, of Helen with a bloody nose or a swollen eye. You didn't talk openly about things like that back then; silence was more a dark shadow than something golden. Maynard's rumored justification had been that she fucked around. Hell, Clark thought, we all fucked around. She wouldn't meet his eyes.

"What do you mean, *now?*" he asked.

"I didn't say now."

"You said that he couldn't hurt you now if he wanted to. What do you mean?"

Her eyes flashed. "That was thirty-five years ago. He's a good man now. He's been a good man for a long time." She studied him with an accusatory silence. "We've all changed, Clark."

He looked down. His hands lay before him like corpses. Blue veins like blue lips, a touch like wet earth, ashes and dust. "I didn't mean to imply anything."

"Clark, look at me." He reluctantly looked up. Tears had flooded her eyes. "To see someone do penance for thirty-five years tears out your heart. Do you think he would have turned that TV off thirty-five years ago?"

"No."

"But something's happened." She glanced at the doorway. "He's more confused now, he forgets more, and he gets more angry."

"Take him to the doctor."

"He won't go."

Clark took her hand. It was small and delicate and nothing like Nora's. "I'm as worried for you as I am for him."

She pulled away. "No one writes books about murders that have been solved for thirty years. Maybe this writer thinks this one isn't really solved. Please, Clark."

"Please what?"

"Please take care of Maynard. His heart. I don't know what he can stand."

"What can I do?"

"Tell this writer whatever will make him leave Maynard alone. What's the difference between Albert Wilson dying and Maynard Tewle? A man is a man."

Clark studied her. Yes, a man is a man, a hammer is a hammer, a murder is a murder. A crazy priest is a scapegoat who wraps our fears in his rosary, who lets us walk down the street at night and only half expect a murderer to be following. "Innocent men are innocent men."

Helen's wet eyes flashed. "What does that mean?"

"It doesn't mean anything."

"What does that mean?" Her voice had risen.

"Nothing, Helen."

"Don't you get suspicious, Clark Holstrom. You know the truth."

"I didn't mean it that way. I just mean that I'm not sure what I can do."

She nodded and relaxed slightly. "I know. People find what they are looking for, if it's really there or not."

A growl came out of the living room. Maynard stumbled into the kitchen, wheezing. He scratched his globe of a belly where South America would be. "What are you two doing out here?"

"Just talking," Clark said.

"Who won the game?"

"The Twins were down in the eighth."

"You didn't watch the rest?"

"It looked pretty much over to me."

Maynard smacked his lips as if his dinner had gone bad. "Damn Twins." He smacked again. "Oh, what the hell. Damn everything." He patted his shirt pocket. "You got a light?"

Clark looked at Helen. Her eyes had fallen to her hands. "No, Maynard. I don't smoke."

"I thought you didn't drink."

"I don't do either."

"Oh well . . ." A yawn finished Maynard's sentence. "I'll see you in the morning."

"Are you coming over to the historical society?"

"What day is it tomorrow?"

"Friday."

"Hell, no. Going to the historical society runs the risk of getting educated. What the hell does a man my age need an education for? I'll see you on Saturday." Maynard hobbled into the living room with his fingers rasping his belly. His footsteps creaked up the steps and slowly padded across the floor above them. He wasn't much of a host.

"I'll do what I can when the writer gets here," Clark said.

"Thank you."

"I should be leaving."

Helen showed him to the door. "How has Nora been?"

The coolness outside hunched his shoulders. "You know. The same."

She nodded. "My oldest sister got that way. It's hard."

"Yeah." The sky was bleeding on the western horizon. "I'll see you, Helen."

"Good night, Clark."

He hesitated before leaving. He felt a deep regret that he had not met this woman before he had Nora. She would have been in high school then. "Call if there's . . . you know, anything you can't handle."

"All right." She closed the door.

The year was just late enough for Clark to shiver, imagine he could see his breath, and wish he'd brought a jacket. He glanced at the upstairs light before following the back alley away from the sun toward home. As he strolled he descended deeper and deeper into thought, into memories falling like the night. He crossed the street into the canyon formed by Sanders Funeral home and St. Luke's. He used to go to that church, but hadn't since he'd retired. It didn't feel right. He did not know who God was, but he did not think of him as a lion tamer. Jump through the hoops and into heaven you go. Religion wasn't all bad, Clark guessed. Just most of it.

The feed store threw its shadow away from the streetlight at the mouth of the alley like a bucket of dirty water. Clark imagined it to be the old Chicago and Northwestern Railroad Depot, the one they tore down when they widened the highway. His uncle had died of influenza at a depot waiting to embark a transport to France and the First World War. Clark's war had been the second. He'd left Hannah like Don Quixote dancing with the hornéd moon and could not have been more misguided. As long as he'd stayed with the pretty English girls and the accents that punched at his loins like the voltage from a heavy-duty battery, the war had been fine, but then came Normandy. Now, standing at the foot of that alley, he was again wading ashore on a foreign beach with the water and the sand both a salty red, and . . . and . . . and he had to close his eyes and shake his head because that was as far as he could think about that. There had been things after that beach, things outside of Paris and in the Ardennes, but that beach had been the worst. He remembered it now only in instances tainted crimson, washed in salt and terror. He remembered it in the tightness in his throat, in a mind screaming with what he forced himself not to remember.

Walter's war had been Vietnam, though he'd never been called up. He'd been a hippie, tuning in, turning on, and dropping out, a domestic war hero, as he liked to say. Clark had never been able to convince him that it just wasn't the same. You can't explain it to someone who hasn't been there. *Qué cosa más mala es la guerra,* Hemingway had written. War is a terrible thing.

The house waited down St. Anne's Road like a faithful and dying dog, as dark and bleak and lonely as the feed store. He and Nora had bought it on a proud spring day in 1953. They had been living in an apartment above what was now Sheri's Craft Nook, across the street from the Bumblebee. Back then, Sheri's had been Swenson's livery and harness shop. The oily scent of neat's-foot used to rise through the floor.

Not much call for that kind of work now. There hadn't been much call for that kind of work then—it was just something Old Man Swenson could do without bothering anybody, something he had always done, like Clark had always done hardware, like Walter was trying to do hardware now.

Software, he reminded himself. Computers. He wished hardware came as easily to his son as it had to him.

In his mailbox he found only sweepstakes junk mail—yes, a million dollars was eagerly awaiting him. Before going up the walk he turned to look at the row of windows above the craft nook. Walter now lived in an apartment down the hall from where he had lived as a baby. It all goes in circles, Clark thought. Wherever you leave, you return. Whatever you've done comes back to you.

His front door was unlocked—until this recent burglary blight, no one in Credibull had had a need for locks. Clark still didn't. He didn't own a VCR—he'd rented one once, but couldn't figure out how to hook the damn thing up—and replacing a broken door or window would cost more than his radio was worth. He tossed his mail into the junk basket he kept beside the door, then adjusted his thermostat to compensate for the living room chill. He sat. Using the remote his knees had insisted he buy, he turned on the television, flipped through its stations, and turned it off again. Clark grunted as the screen stared at him. The damned thing watches you like Big Brother, scooping out your mind in dollops. Nora had spent too much of her life staring back at the thing. He thought about her lying on that bed, her eyes so big in his imagination, and tried to get his mind to follow his eyes around the room. He needed to think of something else.

He willed the clock to turn faster; he tried to catch the minute hand moving. His eyes drifted restlessly from wall to wall, studying pictures and the warp in the paneling. His living room wasn't much different than the Tewles'—fewer photographs, a little less of an "Old McDonald had a Farm" ambiance—except that everything here looked boxier, all straight edges, all awkward. Since Nora had fallen, everything here had somehow shifted three degrees off center—instead of grazing furniture as he walked through his living room, more and more he found that he was bumping into it. Maybe feminine taste leaks out of a room the way taste leaks out of a bag of potato chips left open overnight. Maybe he should advertise in the Mankato State paper for a female roommate. If she would rearrange his furniture, he would only charge her utilities.

He scanned the cluttered book titles on the coffee table for something that might interest him, then picked up a paperback of Sinclair Lewis's *Elmer Gantry,* an old book with a picture of Burt Lancaster on the cover. He set it down again—though his favorite author, Lewis was for tonight too biting. On the bookshelf beside him waited Hemingway's *The Sun Also Rises,* Eliot's *Middlemarch,* Woolf's *Orlando.* All too heavy. He decided if only temporarily that he should develop an interest in comic books. He should don the superhero costume, drink the secret potion, or get caught in a tragic if empowering scientific experiment. *Captain Clark, defender of old coots and toothless women, the man who never ages.* Supergeezer. Hell.

He rose groaning to his feet, having to make two attempts to separate himself from the chair—Christ, sometimes the pain was frightening. He stumbled toward the basement door, his feet grabbing at the carpeting as if he were wearing cleats. He turned on the basement light and slowly descended the stairs. He liked his basement stairs—they were one of the few things he knew of that groaned more than he did. On two sawhorses rested his retirement project—a four-by-eight-foot plywood sheet covered with tiny trees, light poles, and balsa buildings that he intended to one day donate to the historical society. Artificial grass with blades so fine they felt to his fingers like velvet lay across lawns no larger than his palm. Credibull, Minnesota, population 1,273, lay in his basement, its size making Clark feel divine.

Perhaps God was a model maker. Perhaps he created the world because he couldn't find anything to read. In the beginning, God grew so bored he created the heavens and the earth. He created the street signs and the lakeshore, the Farmers National Bank and St. Anne's Road. He created Lucky Lemon's used car lot and the Sunset Motel beside it. He even created the three doghouses in the Haskins' back-yard. As soon as his order came in at Sheri's he'd create the dogs to go with them—a rottweiler and two mixed breeds. All in all, God had quite an eye for detail.

He turned off the light switch at the foot of the steps. He fumbled with and finally plugged an extension cord into the outlet beside it. The Credibull model lit up, each streetlight, each window. Let there be light, and there was light. He smiled.

His eyes followed, across the model, the route over which his day had taken him, a habit he'd developed the day he'd finished laying down the streets. He'd started the morning at home, walked to the store, then over to Henry's to sit on the bench with Maynard. Back home again, from there to Ambrose's to see Nora, then to the Tewles'—he found his glasses stretching from gutter to gutter on Josef Meyer Boulevard. Finally, home again. Like every day, this one reminded him of a yo-yo. He could walk-the-dog or go around-the-world, but he always ended up at the little white clapboard house on St. Anne's Road. The string always winds tight again. You always end up in somebody's fist.

He saw himself walking down the alley, saw the Fords no bigger than Matchboxes rolling down the highway. He turned back time to when the Fords were bigger, before the world had gone crazy with cop-killer music and girls-who-love-girls pornographic rental videos and auto-matic pistols in every schoolboy's lunch box. Walter was walking down the street, his curly hair billowing from his head as if his scalp were smoking, his face blotched, the hem of his bell-bottom jeans mud rimed, a peace symbol pulling heavily on the chain around his neck. Clark turned back time a little more. The cars looked like fat-bodied bugs and all the businessmen wore fedoras. The only paved road in town was the highway. The girls screamed each time they heard Frank Sinatra on the radio, olive oil and static. He could see to the bottom of Crystal Lake now—only in retrospect did it live up to its name. The lone green on its surface was the army-surplus green of painted john-boats and the lighter green of their three-and-a-half-horsepower John-

son Seahorse outboards. He was on the water with Mike Caruther and
Jack Falstaff, the druggist—they were teasing Jack about his name—
fishing for crappies and sunfish off the lily pads along the north shore.
Maynard wasn't with them; he must have been in the fields. A fish
stringer hung heavily from the bow.

Mike died of a heart attack in '49, not even forty years old. Jack
joined him in '74. All that medicine he'd handed out had not been
enough to recompense the Reaper. Time takes you when it's your time.
Jack's came when he was seventy-one. Clark wiped his face. Christ. He
was seventy-two.

He sat impotently upon his workbench stool. His hands trembled as
he gripped the bench's edge; balsa dust pressed into his fingertips like
tiny fangs. He wiped his face again. God be damned. What right did anyone have to do this to a man? *Do not go gentle,* Dylan Thomas had written, but what he hadn't written was that you go. You go. Try to stop it.

Street dances and Fourth of July parades unfolding on the model
became a refuge against this insane futility. He felt strengthened by
the grumble of Minneapolis-Moline tractors trudging reluctantly toward the fields, by the *Caruther's Hardware* sign coming down and his
going up to replace it. Women in knee-length cotton dresses, the slow
funeral trudge for a boy come home from Korea. Voices as thick as
butter with German and Norwegian accents. Pretty girls, no matter
when, always pretty girls. Good times, too, though back then he'd been
too liquored up to tell the good times from the bad. Alcohol had
evened out his highs and lows into an unchanging decline.

He rose and walked to the stairs, his fingers trailing over grass and
gullies. The surface of the lake was as cool as the real lake on a night
like this would be. He felt stronger now. He unplugged the model. The
lights winked out like they do on any night in any little town.

Seventy-two years came back as he struggled to climb the stairs,
wrapping him in the stinks of age, in mildew and camphor oil. On the
highway a car honked its horn, a lonely sound swallowed quickly by
darkness. He stopped. He could almost swear the sound had come
from the model. When he turned, Maynard and Helen were driving

into town from their farm three miles out on St. Anne's Road, bringing little Barbara in to the apartment to play with Walter. They waved at a window above the harness shop. He saw himself hanging out of it, waving back, his hair blond now instead of white, his forearms corded from hauling boxes of heavy brass plumbing fixtures at the store. Early days. Back then he could not be moved.

He wiped his face, wiped the tears and the years away with trembling fingers. Oh, to be young again. To be young and not tired. To live in a world you've made with your hands.

He turned off the basement light and waited for his eyes to adjust to the darkness. He plugged in the extension cord, then sat on the bottom step to watch good memories unfold. Maybe he wouldn't donate it to the historical society after all.

Chapter

3

Clark was so bleary eyed the next morning that he could hardly see the lock on the store's front door. He'd been up with the model until two and up twice after that with his bladder. Clark and his bladder had become over the years constant nighttime companions, as intimate, if not as affectionate, as lovers. Latrine love.

He yawned at the white-ringed horizon, wiped the itchy blur from his eyes, and found the lock. He turned the key, then hurried inside to the burglar alarm as fast as his arthritic spurs allowed. He fumbled with a second key before inserting it into the security lock.

"Now, let's see if I can get this right." He was supposed to press the top button while simultaneously turning the key from *Armed* to *Standby,* then press the bottom button either for five seconds or only after five seconds had elapsed. One would prevent a call to the police and one wouldn't—which did what, he couldn't remember. To hell with the thing, anyway. He turned the key and ignored the buttons. He saw no reason to pay obeisance to a burglar alarm simply to avoid its electronic slander.

Maybe the burglar plaguing the town was over seventy. Maybe he was up at night with his bladder anyway, and figured he might as well try to make his time profitable. Sneak up to a house, piss on the flower bed, break in, and steal a radio. Piss on the flower bed again on the way out. You'd know his victims by whose roses were dying.

Clark turned on the store lights, squinting as the sudden brightness drilled into his eyes. He went into the back. Forty years of preparing for customers had convinced him that Walter was wrong; it *did* take more than a moron to sweep a store, or at least to sweep it right. A moron would grab the first broom he found, but you had to be careful; nylon bristles just didn't do the trick. A moron would raise the broom from the floor while he swept the baseboards, but dragging the broom created static electricity, which attracted and held hair, the store's main debris—what did that kid of his do, rent the place out as a kennel in the afternoons? If it took a moron to sweep a store, it took a pretty astute moron.

Clark found his broom and swept the baseboards. He picked the hair off the bristles and dropped it into the trash bin in back—funny how, regardless of the color with which it began, all hair turned a grungy gray. He walked back to the front of the store with his push broom before shuffling down the first aisle, his age-swollen knuckles interlocked over the end of the handle, his weight driving the broom forward. The lights' glare off the linoleum kept two paces ahead of him like the fiery column ushering the Hebrews from Egypt. Guide us, Jehovah, you great and mighty flashlight.

His mind followed his eyes from shelf to shelf. A lot of his soul was in this store—its voice echoed mutely, its eyes watched silently. He'd sold his first piece of hardware off that shelf there; he'd been reaching into that bin for a faucet washer when he'd smelled neat's-foot and knew that Old Man Swenson was coming with the news that Nora had gone into labor. Each nut, each bolt, each washer held a piece of him. The room was alive with who he was.

"Are you sure that you can handle this, Dwayne?" Clark asks as he hands the boy the store keys.

"Of course I can, Mr. Holstrom." The boy's name, Wilson, is English, though he must have inherited his features from a Scandinavian mother: blond, almost-white hair, a lilt in his voice like poetry. Touch that skin and feel the snow from which it was born.

"Just open as usual and close at four. Leave the keys at the house with Nora."

"Yes sir."

These Scandinavians, my God, they're polite. "I'll be in St. Paul. If you have a problem, call Maynard Tewle."

"I'll call my dad, if that's all right."

Clark nods. He's in too much of a hurry to care who the boy calls. A bus rises over a hill on the highway beyond the train depot. He smiles. "I'll see you . . . when? Next weekend?"

"Wednesday afternoon. Good-bye, Mr. Holstrom." The boy's eyes are as blue and solid as a painted wall. "Don't worry about a thing."

Clark nods again as he hurries toward the depot. Excitement tingles on his skin. He is not worried about the store. He is not thinking about the store. He is thinking about St. Paul.

But, Clark remembered, Dwayne didn't work on Wednesday—his father had been murdered that weekend. Dwayne slipped from an enterprising boy into a distracted oaf who eventually quit the store to be-come a farmhand. He moved from farmer to sympathetic and unsus-pecting farmer until the mid-1960s, when a corn picker plucked off his arms as if it were pulling petals from a daisy—she loves me, she loves me not. He'd died before anyone found him, his blood making mud in the field. Now he was buried out at St. Anne's cemetery beside his fa-ther. Poor kid. That family never had a drop of luck.

He was surprised to find that the broom had bumped into the door—he didn't think his creaky old bones could push it along that fast. He guided the dust into the next aisle and trudged back toward the sales counter. Resting upon it was this week's copy of the *Credibull Weekly Herald,* open to the Ted Lewell article. Lewell's picture stared up at him in a wasted attempt to appear literary. White hair, an annoy-ing little smile, a thick neck like a wrestler's. Anger rose in Clark's throat like bile. Everything about Albert Wilson's murder had been settled or had settled down, and now this son of a bitch was trying to stir it back up. Clark thought of Kenneth Callahan, then, painfully, of Maynard Tewle before looking at the picture again. Even on the yel-lowish paper, Lewell came across as pasty. Someday he'd come calling with questions.

Clark thought of Maynard Tewle again. Between truth and lies and loyalty, where do you draw the line? How much can you bend it before it isn't a line anymore?

Clark finished sweeping by seven-fifteen. He went in the back, made himself a cup of coffee, and settled into the desk chair to wait out the half hour it would take for Walter to arrive. Beside Walter's computer hung a wall calendar, courtesy of some two-bit tool-and-die company. The model for September was riding a five-hundred-piece toolbox as if it were a red metal pony. The only clothing she wore were two dime-sized scraps of pale blue fabric held in place on her chest by what looked to be fishing line, with a scrap of the same fabric between her legs. She was caressing her cleavage with a three-quarter-inch chrome-plated open-faced wrench and smiling as if her greatest desire was to invite him into the picture. Walter's crude attempt at drawing in her nipples flaunted his lack of promise in the fine arts.

Clark studied the model's cleavage. It was funny how the juxtaposition of two oversized glands could stir a guy the way it does. Though a man his age should be beyond it, a body like this body, a body photo retouched and photo enhanced, still tugged at the parts of him the model had been hired to tug at. In the old days when he desired something like this, he would find someone to satisfy the desire. With marriage vows fresh in his mind he had resisted the urge, but marriage had too soon become a duty and the war had left duty as a bad taste in his mouth. At first there had been a few women, then many women, then finally just one, or just one other, and all had been clandestine. Nora had been too dim witted and sofa slackened to discover them. Until.

Too many people use logic not to shape their futures but to justify their pasts, a retrograde logic. He had used retrograde logic for years, though he knew now he had used it only for trivial justifications. He had been during his first eleven years of marriage nothing more than a drunken son of a bitch and adulterer. It was a hell of a thing for him to admit without euphemisms. He felt something like pride at his honesty.

So goes life, or so they said. So goes the final summation of retrograde logic. Its most trivial justification.

He looked at the calendar and struggled to keep from remembering, studied this body hinting with its shadows and its promises. Though he knew he was alone, he glanced quickly around the store before unzipping his pants. He made a few experimental prods at his member; it felt like a loosely stuffed pasta too long out of the oven. He tried to think himself into a sexual state that reached into dim recesses before Nora and marriage, recesses of youth and innocence, sour fantasies gone sour long ago. Yes. To drop fifty years back into innocence. Oh yes. Innocence.

He made a frenzied attempt to bring both this calendar model and himself to life. Think of her as she is, he schooled himself, as she was paid and enhanced to be. His eyes manufactured lust and painted on innocence. Oh yes. Hints of shadow and promise. Oh yes. Do it. Think it. Oh, yes. Do it, damn it. Please, God, please, let there be *oh yes.*

Finally Clark looked away. His attempts had produced only pitiful sweat and a deep frustration. He hated everything about this model and always had. If she were there in anything beyond two dimensions he would have plunged a screwdriver into the grail of her chest. *Oh, Norman, teach me the skills you have learned.* But he had been a child then, and Norman hardly more; life in them both had atrophied. Atrophied, he thought, hell. That justification, like all others, proved to be trivial—you are a man who is meekly succumbing to his fate. Dylan Thomas had written, *Do not go gentle into that good night.* Burn and rave. What exactly is it, he asked himself, that you believe?

Other things, he thought as he zipped up his pants, think about other things. What do old men think about? Checker games, old dogs, older schoolmates. They think about days in the sun. Perhaps there is comfort in knowing life holds more than love and lust and their satisfaction. Huh. Retrograde logic.

His coffee had gone cold. He avoided staring at Miss September by watching two polygons dance across the computer screen like perky gnomes. "A screen saver," Walter had explained when Clark had asked him about it—why the hell he didn't just turn the thing off, Clark could not tell. He grunted and watched it with disgust. Computers are as sinister as he imagined gnomes to be—both promise you pots of gold, but once you're deep in the forest, their smiles turn to evil grins and you end up roasting slowly over an open fire, listening to the flames spit as they gobble up the fat dripping from your behind. Fried ass for the wee people. Never let anything without a soul do your thinking for you.

The Germans had let Hitler do their thinking. Blood on the beach salty red. Fear never forgotten crouched on Clark's shoulder even now. Imagine that little Austrian bastard with a computer.

The front door opened and shut. Walter's steps trotted across the floor like a draft horse's. "You here, Dad?"

"In the back."

"You forgot to relock the door."

Clark winced. "Sorry."

"You always say that. One day I'll walk in to find all the shelves empty." Walter clumped into the back. He stuffed his jacket collar between the chair and Clark's shoulder blades, letting the rest of it drape to the floor. He didn't even nod a hello. "Where's your jacket? It's cold out there."

"I didn't wear one."

Walter's eyes buzzed across Clark's face. "What do I have to do, call you up every morning to find out if you're properly dressed?"

Clark wondered when the point had come when his child became the parent and he the child. "If I think I need a coat, I'll wear one."

"Well, you need one today. The warm weather is flying south with the birds. Excuse me."

Clark slid back so Walter could pull out the computer's keyboard. When Walter tapped the space bar, a calendar replaced the screen saver, Friday the twenty-fourth outlined in red. He hit the *Enter* key. A schedule replaced the calendar. It was as bare as the top of his head.

"Nothing special going on today. I just have to call a few computer distributors." Walter tapped the *Esc* key, and the calendar reappeared. He looked at his father with his *aren't computers wonderful* expression.

"Why do you have a calendar on the computer when you have one hanging beside it?" Clark asked. "A little redundant, aren't you?"

Walter leered at Miss September. Ah, so he could meet people's gazes. "I don't think of that as a calendar." He laughed loudly. "Yee-hah, ride 'em cowboy!"

Clark stared into his coffee. With a laugh like that, with a leer like that, he had no trouble imagining what Walter used Miss September for. Well, like father, like son—Clark's crotch still felt clammy. But you'd think that at least Walter wouldn't glory in it. You'd at least hope he wouldn't.

"It's simple economics, son. That"—he pointed at the screen—"costs a whole lot more than that." He jerked his head at the calendar.

"Yeah, but the computer can keep track of the books."

"A ledger worked fine for me."

"You have to figure everything out for yourself in a ledger. And there's no security. Anyone can know your financial condition with a glance."

"The computer does its job, then. I don't know a thing about the store's financial condition."

"I told you yesterday. Things are good."

Hopping, as I remember, was the word you used. Will the store be hopping when you open at eight? "Are you trying to hide something from me?"

Walter stretched out his arms as if Clark had crucified him. The stench from his underarms screamed like an animal in pain. "Don't you trust me?"

"You have to ask that?"

"You said you were satisfied with sweeping. If you want more, just say the word. The business is as much yours as you want it to be."

Clark waved away his son's suggestion. "I would just like to know how you're doing. I'm retired from the business, but not from you."

"We're doing fine, Dad." Clark must not have been able to hide the skepticism Walter's choice of pronouns produced. "Would you like to see the books? I can show them to you."

Clark shook his head. A father-and-son relationship had to be based on trust, no matter how small a base that was. "Just tell this damned thing that I'm taking a new push broom out of inventory."

"Gotcha. Christ, look at the time." Walter hurried toward the door.

"Every successful businessman knows two key words, son," Clark called after him.

"What are they?"

"Personal hygiene." Walter laughed as if it were a joke.

Clark heard him fiddle with the door, then stop. Angry footsteps strode back into the office. "Damn it, Dad, the security system is blinking!" Walter's face flushed so deeply that his scalp reddened.

"What does it mean when it's blinking?" Ignorance was easier to plead than negligence.

"You know what it means. After you turn the key to *Standby,* you have to hold the second button in for five seconds. Christ, Dad, how many times do I have to explain it to you? It isn't that complicated!"

Clark hated being lectured, especially by his son. Oh for the days when with a single swat he could send him bawling to his bedroom. "Sorry."

Walter glared. "Was Jergen here?"

Jergen Burnett was the night officer on the Credibull police force. He was a large man with the intellectual capacity of a Boston cream pie. "No."

"Damn him." Walter picked up the telephone receiver and punched the number for the police station as if he were crushing ants on a counter. The receiver made tiny digital screams. "Jergen? This is Walter Holstrom . . . I know you got it, my system is telling me you got it. Why didn't you do anything?" His face turned redder. "God damn it, Jergen, what the hell do we pay our taxes for?" He listened for a moment before slamming down the receiver. Even Miss September flinched.

"What did he say?"

"He said he saw you sweeping the floor through the side window."

Clark shrugged. "I suppose he could." The police station was across the street.

"Damn it, Dad, that's not the point!"

"What is the point?"

"What if someone had really been breaking in? Right now they'd be walking away with our inventory. You'd be lying on the floor with a bullet in your head!"

"Then I guess that Jergen wouldn't have seen me sweeping."

Walter scowled at Clark, then at the phone, as if he could somehow hurt Jergen by abusing it again. "You better open, son," Clark said quietly. "You're five minutes late."

The five minutes made no difference—no customers were at the door. Clark and Walter settled back to wait for them, Walter playing with his computer, Clark watching the sleepy cars driving to jobs east

61

in Waseca and west in Mankato. By a quarter to nine the cars remaining zipped by in the reckless way people drive who care more about time clocks than the pedestrians they flatten.

Clark blinked into the morning sun, feeling both its warmth on his face and the coolness radiating from the panes. When the streets were once again safe from the marauding time slaves, a few farmers, former customers, straggled by on their way to the Wal-Mart, more than likely by way of the Bumblebee. He could tell they wanted hardware by the way their hands shielded their eyes from his. What the hell, he thought, he couldn't blame them—from the money they'd save buying at the Wal-Mart they could get a cup of Bumblebee coffee and a half hour of ogling Billie Jessup. Buying from Walter just got you hardware. Only fools and fathers don't get their money's worth.

Elmer Tornquist came in at nine, as wrinkled as a raisin, with Bert Finchley behind him. Elmer had been a farmer—his son, Virgil, now ran the place. The boredom of retirement had driven Elmer to run for mayor. He'd been as surprised as hell when no one ran against him—he'd run only for the electric joy of a mudslinging campaign. He won the election with fifty-two percent of the vote, the remaining forty-eight split among a dozen write-ins; Mickey Mouse and Little Bo Peep combined for two and a half. Elmer had been mad as hell that he'd won. Well, if you play, you pay.

"Howdy, Clark." Elmer liked to look and talk like John Wayne in *Chisum*—cowboy hats and belt buckles, *howdys*, *git 'em ups*, and *yippie-ky-yays*. He smelled like sweat and leather.

"Howdy." Clark had learned long ago to speak the customer's language. Get along, little dogie. "Morning, Bert."

"Morning." Bert Finchley's face was so long and loose that every expression became an anatomical crack-the-whip. He bore the distinction of being the ugliest man in Credibull. He sidled through the door, keeping his hands in his pockets to hide the effects of Parkinson's—a hell of a thing for a newspaper photographer to be stuck with. A hell of a thing for anybody to be stuck with.

"What are you following the mayor around for?"

"Damn it," Elmer complained, "don't call me that. It's not my fault."

"Looking for scandal," Bert said. "Not much news this week."

Elmer hoisted his pants by the belt buckle. "Then you're wasting your time." His belly screamed for suspenders, but suspenders were not John Wayne–esque enough. "I'm a damned cherub."

Bert's chin lagged behind his smile. "Then you'll deny the rumor that you spent last night sleeping in the Sunset Motel with three butt-naked Mankato State coeds?"

"That," Elmer said, "is a bald-faced lie. I didn't get a wink of sleep last night." He laughed; they all laughed. A variation on an old joke. A variation on an old laugh.

"Can I get you gentlemen anything?" Clark asked.

Bert grunted. "How dare you call a politician a gentleman."

"Can I get the damned cherub and the resident muckraker anything?"

Elmer shook his raisin head. "Nothing for me." He'd been coming into the store every other day for forty years, but he'd never once come in with the intention of buying. Bert was more of a customer—he'd bought something at least twice as often. Clark's question was habit. "Just seeing if you were in."

Walter bustled out from the back, sweat on his face. That boy could sweat in an igloo. "Good morning, Bert. Hi, Mayor."

"Damn it, don't call me that."

"Can I get some weather stripping for you? It's getting to be that time of the year."

Elmer shook his head. "Don't need weather stripping."

"Then how about some weather-guard plastic to put over your windows? It's real easy to use—you just tape it up and shrink it tight with a blow dryer. Do you have a blow dryer?"

Elmer gaped. A charge involving three naked coeds was mild compared to the slanderous accusation that he used a beauty aid. No one must have told him that in every movie the Duke ever made he had worn makeup. "Now what in God's name would I need a blow dryer for? What would *anyone* need a blow dryer for?"

63

"Women use them," Bert said.

"But they're women." Elmer tugged thoughtfully on his belt. "All that holding stuff they put in their hair needs heat to harden up. But why would a man need one? If he didn't want his hair wet, why did he wash it in the first place?"

"To enjoy the feel of it under his fingers." Walter ran his hand over his scalp. Clark smiled. Not a bad comeback, for Walter.

"To be a prissy boy, you mean," Elmer said. "The problem with you young guys is that you all want to be prissy boys. You got to have your hair just right, and you got to shower every day." Elmer, Clark thought, are you off the mark on Walter. "If God had wanted us to shower every day, he wouldn't have given us sweat glands. The *sweat* washes the dirt off."

Walter laughed as if it were a joke, then stopped abruptly when he saw that the others knew it wasn't. Business rule number one: know your customers. Clark had been drilling that into him for years, but Walter had never been a quick learner. Almost had to hold him back in second grade—among other deficiencies, he kept reading *know* as *k-now*. He started saying it, too.

Elmer shook his head sadly. "Men doing up their hair and wearing makeup, women letting theirs down and showing their ugly mugs to the world. Men dressing like women and women dressing like men. Good Christ, men screw men up the hinder and women stick their tongues in each other. You never saw stuff like that in the old days."

"It was around," Bert said.

"The hell."

"It's always been around."

Elmer grunted. "It was never around here. Prissy boys and dykes always ran off to somewhere else for their perversions. San Francisco or somewhere. I'll tell you one thing. If what God did to Sodom and Gomorrah was a flick of his finger, he's sure to at least fart on San Francisco. You wait. There's a reason all those earthquakes happen out there."

"Are you saying that if homosexuals lived here we'd have earthquakes?" Clark asked.

"We'd have something. Perversion does not go unpunished." Elmer pointed at the ceiling. "That's one goddamned righteous God up there."

The conversation lulled. No honest man can consider divine retribution without discomfort.

Bert changed the subject. "What do you think about this writer coming to town?" He always assumed that everyone in Credibull read his paper.

"What is it about that?" Elmer asked. "Is he going to make a movie or something?"

"A book," Clark said.

Bert nodded, his face scrunching like an accordion and pulling out again. "A movie would be better for the town."

"It would be better for a reelection," Elmer said. "I hope to hell it doesn't happen."

"He told me during our interview that it's bound to," Bert said. "They always turn bestsellers into movies. He said he has a feeling about this one."

"What can he have a feeling about?" Clark asked. "Father Callahan confessed to the murder thirty years ago."

"I'm just saying what he said." Bert nodded at Clark. Shake his head the right way and you could dance a polka. "I told him to come see you."

"Oh hell, Bert," Clark said. "Why did you do that?"

"Don't you want to be famous?"

"I don't want to dig up Credibull's skeletons." He thought about the promise he had made to Helen.

Elmer pulled a lawn chair out of the harvest barbecue display, brushed the dust from it, and sat. Walter's face flushed—he managed the store with a *don't touch the merchandise if you're not buying* philosophy. If he wanted to keep the Wal-Mart from stealing the last of his customers, he'd better learn in a hurry how to read them. It was business rule number one all over again.

Bert leaned against the shelving beside Elmer. Clark propped his elbows on the counter, his hands hanging over the edge. "So how's the wife, Elmer?"

"Complaining about her feet. You know women. They're always

complaining about their feet." Elmer hoisted his right cowboy boot onto his left knee. The Duke would never have approved of the pain-filled expression it took to get it there. "Sometimes I wish I was you, Bert. Sometimes I wish I had never married."

Bert shrugged. "I'll bet being married has its advantages."

"Women complaining about their feet isn't one of them." Elmer propped the chair on its back legs. "A married man knows more about a female's corns than any podiatrist on earth. Christ, the details a woman will go into! My wife describes the smell of her feet to me. She picks the gray stuff out of her toenails, rolls it into balls, then mushes it down like cookie dough. It's enough to make you puke."

"How about that weather guard, Mr. Tornquist?" Walter's eyes were on the chair, not on Elmer.

"I don't want weather guard. Leave me free to browse."

"You can't browse sitting down. Why don't you put the chair back? I'll show you how the weather guard works."

Elmer turned to Clark. "Why do you let him hound me like this?"

"Everyone has their own way. It's his store now."

"Yeah, well I wish it wasn't. He makes it so it isn't any fun to come in here anymore."

"He has a product he believes in." Bullshit. He wants to make some money and get you out of his chair. "He thinks it will be good for you. Isn't that right, Walter?"

"Right." At least he knew enough to play along.

Elmer looked at Clark and rubbed his chin. "You put this stuff on your windows?"

"It keeps the drafts out and cuts down on your heating bills. It'll pay for itself in a month."

"Do you use it?"

"I do," Bert said. "Every winter."

Elmer slapped his boot. His foot popped off as if it were spring loaded. "All right then, I'll take some. I can borrow a blow dryer from that prissy-boy grandson of mine. You wouldn't believe what he done. You know what he done?"

66

"What?"

"Bert, here's a story for you. The little fairy pierced his ear! Can you believe it? He wears an *earring!*"

Elmer brought his diatribe against the younger generation's effeminacy to its logical conclusion—the certain demise of all the finer aspects of Western civilization. "And scoring in the National Football League will drop like a rock," he concluded. "You wait and see." He shook his head. "I was up in front of some damned group last week trying to explain to them Hotel Hill." Elmer's first project as mayor was to push the state historical society to declare Hotel Hill a Minnesota historical landmark—in the 1800s a popular if mediocre hotel had been built there. "You try giving a speech when you know that everyone in the audience is thinking the same damned thing. That prissy-boy grandson of his wears an earring, they're thinking. Try to get them to listen to a word you say. You just try it." He turned to Clark. "Did you come up with anything on that yet?" Elmer had asked Clark to check the historical society's records for anything that would bolster or discredit his case.

"Not yet. It's awfully disorganized over there."

"Nothing came from that Jesse James story, did it?" The rumor was that Jesse James had slept at the hotel two nights before his raid on Northfield.

"Not that I've discovered. There might be a chance that Henry David Thoreau stayed there."

"Isn't he that nut that lived in a pond out east somewhere?"

"He didn't live in a pond," Bert said. "He lived on the edge of one."

"What the hell was he doing in Minnesota?"

"He came here right before he died," Clark said. "For his health."

Elmer slapped his knees with conviction. "I knew it. A nut. No one comes to Minnesota for their health—that's why you get *away* from here."

"Do you think he stayed at the hotel?" Bert asked.

"No," Clark said. "I don't think he did."

"Good." Elmer wanted his first, and preferably all, his projects to fail. He needed at least one grandiose flop to help him lose the next election. The Credibull mayoral office was as hard to get rid of as a plantar wart. "That's damned good."

As Elmer wiped relief from his forehead, Cletis Meadows stuck his weathered head through the door. His aftershave followed him in—the essences of crotch rot and lilac water. "Hi, Bert. Clark. Hello, Mayor."

"Damn it, don't call me that."

"I saw you in here, so I thought I'd stop by." Cletis was dressed, as always, meticulously.

"Speaking of prissy boys," Elmer muttered.

"Where did you get that chair, Elmer?"

"Right there in the display."

"Don't mind if I do." Cletis dragged out a chair, carefully smoothed his pants, and sat. The only wrinkled thing Cletis ever wore was his skin. "I have a joke for you guys." His voice was a high-pitched whistle.

"Oh?" Clark ambled over to where they were sitting. God be damned if he'd ever heard a joke come out of Cletis Meadows's mouth that he hadn't first heard come out of everyone else's.

Cletis leaned forward. The chair groaned its displeasure—so did Walter. Decades spent sitting behind the clerk's desk at the Sunset Motel had spread his buttocks the way heat spreads a scoop of ice cream. "Do you know how to catch a bear?"

Clark shook his head. You dig a pit, fill it with ashes, and line its edge with peas. When the bear comes to take a pea, you kick him in the ash hole. "How?"

"You dig a pit, fill it with ashes, and line its edge with peas. When the bear comes to take a pea, you kick him in the ash hole!" Cletis bounced up and down, ho-ho-ho-ing. He'd played Santa Claus at the Wal-Mart last Christmas—you could fit twelve kids in a lap like his. "Get it? Take a pea? Ash hole?"

Clark smiled. "Hah. Good one, Cletis."

Elmer planted his hands on his knees. "Heard it before."

"You have not." Cletis was indignant.

"Don't tell me what I've heard and what I haven't," Elmer said. He paused after *haven't*, the way John Wayne would have done. "I could never forget a joke as bad as that one."

"Don't you tell me what I know and what I don't," Cletis said. "I made that joke up just yesterday."

"If you made that joke up, I'll eat this chair."

"Then you better start eating."

"Not until I get my camera," Bert said.

"Can we help you with anything today, Cletis?" Clark asked. Business rule number two: avoid confrontations with or between your customers. The only loud voice in a store should be a laughing one. "How about a rake? I've seen the Sunset's lawn, and frankly, you could use about a dozen of them."

That was a lie. Cletis was the type of man who edged his lawn with scissors, for whom a grass blade a half an inch longer than its neighbor was an outrage. He looked shocked for a second, then laughed. If only Clark could teach Walter how to handle people like that, but some things come only with experience. Walter now had over four years of it. Maybe some things don't come at all. *K-now* strikes again.

"With this crime wave going through town," Cletis said, "I could use a new lock for the lobby door. One of those—what do you call them?—dead locks."

"Dead bolts," Bert corrected.

"Dead bolts. Do you have any, Clark?"

"You've come to the right place. Only Houdini knows locks better than I do." He'd be a safecracker now if he had a criminal disposition and the intelligence to figure out how to turn off the burglar alarms. He already had the bladder for it. "My son will get you one." He nodded at the counter, but Walter was already stalking the shelves like a starving fox after a rabbit. By the time Cletis had shuffled to the counter—good God, his ass looked like two Volkswagens trying to pass each other—Walter had bagged the lock and rung up the price. It took Cletis longer to count out the change from his pocket.

Cletis folded his bag, creasing it carefully with his fingers. He stuffed himself into his chair, making a sound like a wet cork shoved into a bottle. "Hey, you guys, what do you get when you cross a rhinoceros with an elephant?"

Clark sighed. Eleph-rhino. "I don't know, Cletis."

"Eleph-rhino!" Cletis bellowed. "Do you get it? Eleph-rhino? 'Hell-if-I-know.' "

"Hah, Cletis," Clark said. "Good one."

Elmer replanted his hands. "Already heard it."

Bert pursed his lips. "Me, too."

"I've got one I bet you haven't heard," Walter called from behind the counter. "This guy's renting a hotel room, see? Let me see if I remember how this goes . . . oh yeah. This guy's renting this hotel room, and these two nuns are next door. Somehow he gets locked out of his room, see, without his clothes on—I forget how. Anyway, so he's out of his room with his clothes off, and the nuns come out of theirs. He thinks, Jesus, and freezes stiff with embarrassment."

"Is this going anywhere?" Elmer asked.

Walter waved his question away. "Let me finish. So he's outside of his room, naked, and these nuns see him, and they can't figure him out. They've never seen a naked man before."

"It's not going anywhere," Elmer said.

"So he's naked, right? They look him over and yank on his cock, and after a minute or so they decide he's a hand cream dispenser." A grin spread across Walter's pitted cheeks. Merry expectation danced hopefully in his eyes. "Get it?"

Elmer, Bert, and Cletis stared at him, their mouths open.

"I never." Cletis clicked his tongue.

"Huh," Bert said, which was as close to belittlement as he ever got.

Elmer nudged Bert with his elbow. "Sounds like he knows something about pulling on other men's dicks."

Walter's face fell like a cow dropping. Embarrassment burned so hot on his cheeks that Clark could feel it. "Dad, I have work to do on the computer. Do you mind looking after things?"

"I can't, son. I have to be at the historical society by ten."

"Could you look after things until you leave?"

"Sure."

Clark watched Walter hurry away. You talk about someone who had never had a drop of luck. Walter always pushed so hard that he killed whatever he was pushing at, like Lenny breaking the puppy's neck in that Steinbeck story. Sure, Clark would look after customers until he left. The customers would leave with him. Walter would be alone with his computer and Miss September. Yee-hah. Ride 'em, cowboy.

"I'm sorry about that, Clark," Bert said. "I didn't mean to chase him off."

"It's not your problem, Bert."

They waited silently, for what, Clark didn't know. From the back came the tap of fingers on keys, like the scurry of mice. Clark looked at his watch. "Well, fellas, I hate to break up the party."

"I have to be going, too." Cletis stood. "I have to put this deadlock in."

"And think up more jokes you've heard before." Elmer waited until Cletis left before adding, "You prissy boy." He rose slowly as Bert waited by the door. "Before you go, Clark, could you get that weather-guard stuff for me?"

"Walter can get it."

Elmer leaned toward him conspiratorially. "I know he can, but would you? Nothing against your son, Clark, but you know how to handle me better."

Clark found the weather guard and rang it up. Bert and Elmer followed him outside. "I'll keep checking on Thoreau for you," Clark said.

"If you find anything that suggests he was anywhere near Credibull, quit checking." Elmer scowled. "I've got to speak to the Ladies' Auxiliary this morning. Damned windbags. Every time I talk to them I get sick on the smell of farts and perfume."

"Sounds like a story," Bert said. "*Mayor Overcome by Flower-Scented Methane.* Maybe channel four will pick it up."

Elmer nodded. "Gives a whole new meaning to the phrase *toilet water.*"

"I'll see you," Clark said.

71

"Sure."

Clark headed west toward Josef Meyer Boulevard. He glanced back at the shine coming off Walter's head as he watched him through the store window. Bert and Elmer had crossed the street and were arguing in front of the bank. People walked by the store. No one went inside.

Poor kid, he thought again. Not a drop of luck.

I started the day at home, Clark thought that night as he watched the model; I went to the store. I walked to the historical society, to the Bumblebee for lunch, back to the historical society, then home again. Another yo-yo.

Cars whizzed along the highway before him; couples held hands as they strolled beside the lake. Canadian geese honked forlornly in the cornfields, fattening themselves for a long southern flight. Walter came out of the store, breathed in deeply the cool evening air, and smiled at the dusk gently falling. He walked briskly home, not to the apartment above Sheri's Craft Nook, but to a new rambler in the thumping heart of the housing development. He was married to a lovely woman who did not allow her children to watch television until after they'd finished their homework. If they didn't study, she argued, how could they hope to be as successful as their father?

The smell of Crystal Lake's limpid water rose sweetly to his nostrils. General Motors had built a new plant on its shore, with no environmental damage or unsightly increase in the suddenly prosperous Credibull population. Nora was home, knitting, a smile on her young, vibrant, much-loved face. Annie Halverson burst from the nursing home's door with Bob Tunnell on her arm. They danced around the light pole on which the bitch nurse was impaled. It was a perfect world.

Credibull, 1989. A tearing ache inside made Clark's imagination falter. He rubbed his eyes. He tried to recapture a beautiful world, but the model was just a model again. Nothing special.

1989. He thought of all the things he'd have to change to bring the model up to date. He'd have to age everything a little—dirty and chip the buildings, stain the windward sides field-dust gray, and round all the corners. He'd have to put a few cracks and potholes in the asphalt. He'd have to take the old Farmers National Bank temperature-and-time clock down and put up the new one that was always three minutes fast and five degrees too cool. He'd have to take off the Haas farm buildings to make room for the Wal-Mart. For the housing development, he'd have to take off the Haas windbreak, too.

His fingers followed the highway toward the lake. They stopped in front of his store—no, Walter's store—then gently touched the windows, as delicate as spiderwebs. With a snap of my wrist, he thought, I could turn that store into splinters.

He drew his hand away as if from something evil. It hesitated halfway to his mouth. He had a sudden, insane desire to slam his fist down through the store roof, through the plywood, through the floor, pounding the store back through everything it was and had been. He forced his hand to obey his will. His fingertips trembled as they touched his lips.

Might as well do it, he thought. It's just like the Haas farm. I'll have to take it off to make room for the Wal-Mart, too.

Chapter

4

Staring at the walls and dome of the Credibull Historical Society was like staring at the sky. The exhibits on the far side pulsated against the paint like coins dropped on a belly. History and space, Clark thought; infinity in two directions.

"I'll be back a little before two," Agnes Miller said. Agnes was the historical society's president and megalomaniac key holder; she didn't trust Clark to lock and unlock the doors himself. He didn't mind except on winter mornings, when he had to wait for her outside with his nostril hairs freezing together and playing games of tug-of-war with one another. From the way the chill had gnawed at his knees this morning, he knew that soon he would mind.

"What's going on at two?" he asked.

"Roger and I have work to do."

Roger VanRuden was researching his family history. He hoped to write a screenplay, a second *Roots,* but there are only so many ways to depict a long line of drunken pig farmers who spent their lives up to their knees in manure. Part of the script would have to be devoted to a great-uncle named Crazy Howie, who as a kid had been kicked funny in the head by a Belgian draft. At his first postpuberty county fair he'd been caught tenderloin to tenderloin with the grand champion Hereford, happily humping away. Perhaps in Roger's movie Robert Redford would play the lead. He'd always been good in love stories.

"What are you working on today?" Clark asked.

"We're searching the land records for his great-great-uncle Frederick." Agnes served as Roger's secretary and was at least mildly infatuated with him. "Did you know that he might be related to George Washington? It's awfully exciting."

"I'm sure it is." Agnes rolled in Roger's screenplay like a dog in roadkill. Sometimes her eyes misted as if she were seeing her name scrolling through credits—*Agnes Miller, Consultant and Mistress.* She would probably try to talk the casting director into getting Angela Lansbury to play her part. Ernest Borgnine would be more realistic.

Agnes buttoned her jacket over her bosom—if only Ernest had a bosom. "What do you have going on today?" she asked.

"Just holding down the fort. I might work on the Hotel Hill project."

"Do you think you could squeeze in time to work in research on the ice cream sundae?" A reporter from the *New York Times* had written that Waseca was the original home of the ice cream sundae, and Agnes was determined to prove that Credibull deserved the distinction. What was she hoping for, world fame? Perhaps she hoped to fall back on an ice cream sundae amusement park if the VanRuden movie deal bottomed out. They could get some college kid to dress up like two scoops with plastic strawberry sauce on his head. Get your picture taken with

Sammy the Sundae. Ride the banana split coaster. Poor Elmer would be mayor for life.

"Check the city layouts," she said. "Look for anything that might be a drugstore across the street from anything that might be a saloon." The story was that Saturday-night drunks with Sunday-morning hangovers couldn't handle the fizz of soda and preferred the syrup straight up over ice cream. The town's greatest distinction could be due to hangovers. Rather dubious. Let Waseca have it.

"You know," Agnes said, "you need something of interest in your life." The Keeper of the Keys had appointed herself the Director of His Life.

"I'm working on the model."

"Building a model is awfully solitary."

"I've researched the Wilson murder. I had to talk to people for that."

"I know, but that was an awfully ugly thing. So much good has happened here, and making sure the world knows about it is awfully important."

Sure. I'll write a screenplay. *The History of Cow Fucking in Credibull, Minnesota.* "I'll try."

"You should research your family. I'm sure it would be awfully exciting, too."

Everything with Agnes was awfully something. "My family isn't from around here."

She clicked her tongue. "Oh, that's right. You're from Illinois, aren't you?"

"Indiana."

"I knew it was one of those *I* states." She hurried toward the door. "I'll see you at two."

"Good-bye, Agnes."

Clark watched the door open and close before wandering among the exhibits in a futile attempt to discover something he didn't already know. On one side of an antique china cabinet hung a buffalo robe; a ceremonial headdress that must have come from a Black Hills curio shop hung on the other. Behind the cabinet's locked glass doors lay seventeen bona fide arrowheads scattered among myriad Native American junk. Agnes had labeled the display *Sioux Artifacts Found in Credibull.* Clark had joked that a better label would be *Sioux Artifacts Found Incredible:* most of the genuine pieces predated the Sioux or came from the Winnebagos, a hapless tribe that had been forced from Wisconsin to Waseca County to Nebraska like a chess pawn trying to escape the queen. The next exhibit dealt with the 1862 Sioux uprising. Credibull had played no part in it beyond serving as a refuge for the fleeing, frightened settlers and as a wary eye on the peaceful Winnebagos—Mankato deserved the distinction as the blood center, where thirty-eight Sioux warriors had swung by their necks until dead on the banks of the Minnesota River. Well, he thought, they had lived by the sword. It was fitting that they should die by it.

The display's centerpiece was the sepia-toned photograph of a boy named George Calliver, who had carried his baby brother to Credibull over fifty hostile miles after he had seen his mother raped and killed by twenty teenaged blood-drunk warriors. He had a twelve-year-old face wrapped around fifty-year-old eyes. He had a face Clark could feel.

George had stayed in Credibull, too afraid to go home and with nothing to go back to. He got drunk the day he turned twenty and killed the husband of a middle-aged woman he had hopes of seducing. Ten years later he hung himself in Stillwater state prison, across the cell block from Cole Younger. He'd somehow come across a strand of barbwire to do it with. If you've got to go nuts, then get kicked in the head and fall in love with cows. It was both less painful and less bloody.

The baby brother went on to become mayor back when being mayor in Credibull meant something—on an upstairs wall was hung a picture of him dedicating Josef Meyer Boulevard. He grew into a grave little man with a bald head and waxy mustache who served three terms. It was funny how different brothers could be.

The Civil War display leaned against the wall at the same spot where the preacher used to magnanimously plead for lost souls to join his perfected one in heaven. It consisted of old muskets and bayonets, two uniforms, and the war diary of Alonzo Jameson, a Credibull native who had fought with the First Minnesota Volunteers when they were slaughtered at Gettysburg. He'd taken a musket ball in the thigh and died of gangrene in the Andersonville prisoner-of-war camp—the last words he wrote were *God help me, I smell like pigshit.* The rest of the sanctuary belonged to Josef Meyer, a German immigrant who'd built the hotel on Hotel Hill when young Alonzo was still scaring little girls with tadpoles. He'd named it the Inn-Credibull—English was still too new a language for him to know how to spell it or to know what in it was tacky. Despite its name, the Inn-Credibull drew patrons from as far away as Chicago until it burned down, three decades after the war. Credibull's namesake and glory was now reduced to a blackened, weed-grown brick foundation and a reluctant mayor's rigorous attempt to fail at getting it memorialized. Josef Meyer never did learn to spell. Clark had read his letters.

Clark climbed the stairs to the second floor. He stopped at the balcony to catch his breath and leaned on the railing to study the floor below him. In the dull reflection of the varnish he imagined he saw a dead congregation listening to a dead preacher silently extol the virtues of a dead god. He heard a ghostly chorus sniveling hymns of mournful praise. Sing, choirs of angels, he thought; lift your voices to the anonymous Father. Perhaps God was a music critic who sentenced churches with toneless choirs to the torment of becoming historical societies. Perhaps he stuffed them with decades and centuries, with the sad smell of dust, until they were dead and gone. Clark pursed his lips as the scene below him faded. Perhaps.

He wandered into the first Sunday School room, where the history of the railroad in Credibull now resided. In other rooms, displays of the two world wars sat as patiently as sanctified children awaiting their lessons. The rest of the floor was used for storage. On the far wall hung the newspaper articles detailing the Wilson murder.

The Credibull Daily Herald. Monday, January 17, 1958. Fifteen cents. LOCAL MAN FOUND MURDERED ON FARM. NO CLUES OR SUSPECTS.

The headline was a misnomer—a body lying beside a workbench can hardly be called no clue. A bloodhound smelled out the hammer in the ditch in front of the house. Hounds and blood are not much different from people and suspicions. Bert Finchley had been ethical enough not to print the town's suspicions about the Wilson/Tewle land swindle that first day, but ethics be damned when a mob is banging your head against a wall. *The Herald* had been a daily back then, and Tuesday's edition had carried an article about Maynard on the back page. On Wednesday, Bert had printed another just beneath the masthead, with a picture of Maynard taken during one of his nastier moments. Agnes used to display those articles at the top of the stairs. Clark had moved them, and had included the article detailing the Callahan confession. Visitors still managed to find the articles, though—they were the high point of the local history tour. Helen Tewle was right; people find what they are looking for.

He spent the rest of the morning searching the archives for saloons and drugstores. At eleven, in an insurance layout from 1890, he found that a drugstore had once faced a saloon across an alley where the Double-Trouble Bar, at the corner of Highway 14 and Josef Meyer Boulevard, now stood. He sat back from his desk and stroked his chin. Every town in America could make a similar claim, but what the hell, maybe this was *the* drugstore and *the* saloon. Credibull, home of the hangover. Instead of an amusement park, perhaps they could put in a long line of aspirin dispensers. Elmer might like that.

He left the layout on Agnes's desk, hung his Back After Lunch sign on the door, and walked the backstreets to the Bumblebee to avoid Walter's store-window eyes. He began eating his meal of roast beef and mashed potatoes, but the ache Billie raised as he watched her took away his appetite, and he ate only half. The sun was warm on his back as he returned to work, but the breeze licking beneath his collar made him wish he'd remembered a jacket. He touched his breast pocket and was reassured as his fingers moved over the outline of his glasses. At least he'd remembered something. A small victory. The battle, if not the war.

A gray sedan was parked in front of the historical society, and as Clark took down his sign its door slammed. A man with pale hair, pale skin, and pale eyes jogged up the steps toward him. Something had sucked all the color out of him.

"Mr. Holstrom? Mr. Clark Holstrom?" His words flew from his lips like wood chips from an axe.

Clark nodded. "Can I help you?"

"I hope so, Mr. Holstrom. My name is Ted Lewell."

The newspaper had made him look older. He had a mustache, not a harelip. "Nice to meet you," Clark lied.

"I'd like to talk to you about a book I'm writing."

Clark hesitated before nodding. "Why don't you come in?"

Lewell strode casually inside. He examined the exhibits with only a hint of interest. "You've read my work." It was a statement, not a question.

"No."

"I wrote a book about Gacy," Lewell said, "and another about Ed Geen. Have you heard of them?"

Gacy was the murdering clown, and Geen the Wisconsin cannibal. Clark shrugged. "You're from Chicago, aren't you?"

"Yes. While I do my research I'll be staying at that chintzy little motel by the lake."

"The Sunset," Clark corrected. "For how long?"

"For as long as it takes."

"That might be a while."

Lewell smiled. "I've got both the time and the money. Those books on Gacy and Geen made me a fortune."

Ah, the true artist, with the true artist's concerns. Sinclair Lewis had written something about that—Clark couldn't remember offhand what it was. "I suppose they did."

Lewell scanned the Civil War exhibit as if he were searching a bookshelf for his own name. "You know what else could make me a ton of money? What could make *us* a ton of money? Did you read the article about me in the *Herald*?"

"I skimmed it."

"That old codger at the paper told me that when it comes to the Wilson murder, you're the man to talk to."

Clark shrugged again. His legs were bothering him. He wanted to sit down.

Lewell wandered to the Sioux display. He ran his hand over the panes, a snot-nosed kid eyeing licorice whips in a candy store. "You give me a hand, point me in a few right directions, maybe show me around the murder site, and I'm sure we can work out a consultation fee that would make your time worthwhile."

"Instead of doing all that for you, why don't I just write a book myself?"

Lewell glanced at him before turning back to the arrowheads. "I suppose you could, but that won't keep me from doing the same. I have the connections. My book will end up in the stores and yours will end up lying in the bottom of your underwear drawer. The only thing you'll have to show for all your work is the pain of trying to write it." He nodded at Clark's hands. "Typing can't be easy at your age."

Clark shoved his hands in his pockets. He had never before been self-conscious about them. "Are you like this only with certain people, or are you a son of a bitch by nature?"

"There is the way things are and the way you want things to be. I'm trying to teach you the difference between the two the easiest way I can—you're not the first person who has tried to beat me out of a book. I want to save you some heartache."

"Let me worry about my heartache."

"I can see we've gotten off on the wrong foot. Why don't we start over?" Lewell smiled amiably as he held out his hand. "Hi, my name is Ted Lewell. I'm writing a book about the Albert Wilson murder. I understand that you are the best person in town to talk to, and I was wondering if I could have a moment of your time."

Clark reluctantly shook his hand. He might as well be shaking hands with a turd—Lewell's stink shone through his smile. "There's really nothing to help you with. The murder was solved in the sixties."

Lewell smiled. "You mean the priest's confession? Doesn't that seem a bit too convenient to you?"

"Dying men don't lie."

"So they say. Is there somewhere we can talk?"

Clark nodded toward the back office. Lewell followed him. As Clark sat at his desk he noticed with relish that Lewell had picked the most uncomfortable chair in the room. "Go ahead."

"All I know is what I read in the *Minneapolis Tribune* and the *St. Paul Pioneer Press*. I couldn't get a copy of the local paper. Do you have one available?"

"The articles are upstairs on the wall. What do you know?"

"I know that on January twentieth, nineteen fifty-eight, Albert Wilson's son and daughter drove into town, and when they returned, their father didn't answer their calls. I know they found his body in the toolshed, his skull like broken pottery. I know a bloodhound found a hammer in a ditch, and that there was a brief national sensation. I know that no suspect was ever arrested. What can you tell me?"

"The son's name was Dwayne and the daughter's was Rose. It was a Saturday night. They'd gone into town to get a new dress for Rose's first date. When they came home, Rose found the body lying beside a workbench just inside the toolshed door."

Lewell scribbled on a notepad and shifted on the splinters infesting the chair. "Where can I find them?"

"You can't. Dwayne died in the mid-sixties in a farm accident. Rose got involved in the church and left town. She only came back to buy a burial plot beside her father. She's in it now."

"What kind of involvement with the church?"

"A lay nun or something. I don't know what the word for it is."

Lewell nodded. "A good angle, especially with the priest's confession. Was there any evidence besides the hammer?"

Since when is a girl's ruined life a good angle? "Not really. Some unidentifiable footprints."

"Leading where?"

Clark waved vaguely. "All over."

"Any vehicle tracks?"

"They figured the murderer either parked down the road or walked out from town." He considered what he should say and what he shouldn't. "He might have come from one of the neighboring farms to the west."

"The footprints led that way?"

"Yeah."

"Can you take me out there?"

He pointed with his chin at the microfiche files. "I have work to do."

"Can you tell me where the farm is?"

"On St. Anne's Road." He paused. "Up near Minneapolis."

Lewell smiled. "St. Anne's Road runs south from the grain elevator. I know that much."

"Sometimes I get my directions mixed up. I'm an old man."

"How about the priest? What was his name?"

"Callahan. Kenneth Callahan."

Lewell scribbled again. "And he was supposed to have been screwing around with Wilson's wife?"

"That was earlier. She was dead by the time of the murder."

"Have there been any rumors of sexual abuse on Callahan's part? Altar boys, that sort of thing?"

Clark shrugged. "He used to masturbate in front of a statue of Mary." Can't hurt a dead man.

"A nutcase, huh?"

"Seemed to be."

"Is there anything else you can tell me?"

Clark studied Lewell's face. He thought of Maynard. Let this bastard make his own living. "You've tapped me dry."

Lewell sat back, disbelief on his face like a rash. "You must know more than that. You're the local expert."

"Like I said, there isn't much anyone knows."

"I see." Lewell stood with a slight ripping sound that made Clark's heart dance. "Where is that newspaper article you were talking about?"

"Upstairs. End of the hall."

Clark leaned back in his chair and passed his fingers slowly back and forth across his lips. Footsteps echoed in the sanctuary, then creaked up to the second floor. They paused—he must have been at the railroad exhibit—before meandering off to the right. When they creaked on the stairs again, Clark began to search the microfiche file.

Lewell stuck his head in the door. "Who's Maynard Tewle?"

Clark didn't look up. He was busy searching for . . . what? "Oh. I guess I forgot to tell you about him."

"That's a pretty big *him* to forget to tell me about."

"Not really. Nobody ever proved anything. It's all forgotten now." Hell.

"Is he still alive?"

"Yes."

"Where does he live?"

"Down the boulevard a few blocks." Clark looked up. Upon careful study he decided that the harelip was *beneath* the mustache. "I just told you that nobody ever proved anything concerning Maynard Tewle."

"What were they trying to prove?"

"Didn't you read the article?"

"I skimmed it."

You're a liar. You read it and are probing my truthfulness. "Wilson made a land deal that Maynard didn't like." He closed the file drawer. "But there was nothing to it."

Lewell smiled. "They say there was nothing to the Kennedy assassination, either. Writers have been making millions off of that for years."

"Lee Harvey Oswald is dead. Maynard Tewle isn't."

"Do you think that if Oswald were alive, things would be any different?" The smile broadened. "I'm in town an hour, and I already have a couple of leads. This book is going to write itself." He reached in his wallet and flipped a card onto the desk. "My name and number, in case you decide to remember anything more."

The sharp image of Helen sitting at her kitchen table filled Clark's mind. Tears on her face, her voice trembling and forcing from him promises. "Leave Maynard alone." But Ted Lewell was already hurrying across the sanctuary, whistling snatches of a tune Clark didn't know. Clark's jog to the door left him with a pair of screaming knees and a sweaty sheen on his face. Lewell was outside, opening the gray sedan's door.

"Albert Wilson died thirty-five years ago," Clark called. "What makes you think anyone will want to read about him now?"

There came that smile again, that arrogant, infuriating smile. "People always want to read about unsolved murders, especially if the killer might be the nice old man next door or the priest they've confessed to all their lives. It gives them something to talk about over coffee."

"Do you care who's guilty, or do you just care about who would sell the most copies if guilty?"

Lewell shrugged. "I just want to write a book." The slam of the car door ended the conversation. He drove south to Josef Meyer Boulevard, then turned left onto Highway 14. He was probably on his way to St. Anne's Road.

Clark watched the children playing on the school grounds before going back inside. He thought about Maynard. He thought about truth and lies and loyalty, and the line between them.

Chapter

5

A slick dusting of snow fell two weeks before Thanksgiving, like powdered sugar on a doughnut. Clark sat at his workbench painting a four-inch-long lamppost he'd bought at Sheri's. The tricky work around the fixture required a surgeon's touch. Damned if his fingers didn't shake more than they used to—they reminded him of Bert Finchley's Parkinson's-ridden photos. Poor bastard.

A piercing beep from the telephone on the bench corner made him jump and left a blotch on the fixture. It was funny how he'd never reacted that way to the old phones with mechanical bells. *Ring, ring* had been easier to tolerate than this alien bleat. He picked up the phone and cursed all post-1970 technology. "Hello?"

"Clark?" The voice was young and old at the same time, a light contralto. "This is Barb Mischke."

Clark's breath caught—when you're old, you dread calls from the children of your friends. Something must have happened to Maynard. "Barb."

Barb paused. God be damned, Clark thought, something *had* happened to Maynard. He wondered where—he could guess how. Maynard lying on the Tewle living room floor, one hand an inch from a spilled beer, the other clutching his heart. Maynard crossing the street or picking up something too heavy for him or maybe just breathing. Maynard and Helen in bed. *One more really good get along would be all right with me.* Even that was no way to go. Hell, there *was* no way to go.

"It's Mom."

"Helen?"

"Yes."

He had forgotten in the rush that Barb had more than one parent. But it couldn't be Helen, could it? Was this some kind of a joke?

In his mind rose Nora's eyes, cold and staring, watching him like a spot on a wall. *It comes,* they said. *It pounces on you like the cold of a winter night.*

The voice of those eyes echoed inside of him. He knew the truth.

Pressure in his bladder awakens him and makes him sit up in bed. The night is thick, but the moon so bright that through the window frost he can see shadows cast across the driveway. It takes him a minute to recognize the garbage can lying on its side by the car's back fender. That damned stray tom must be foraging again. Normally Clark would be angry, but he can feel only sympathy for any creature out on a night like this. The cold is so deep it is evil.

The noise from the television drifts into his bedroom, a muffled voice followed by mumbled laughter. Nora must be watching The Late Show. *He cannot sleep with this pressure; he rises and goes into the bathroom. Afterward he wanders into the living room; Nora is not in her usual place on the sofa. He glances into her bedroom to find her bed still made. The trash can is sitting in the middle of the kitchen floor.*

A panic grips him. He runs outside. Nora is lying motionless in the driveway.

"Nora? Nora!"

She is too heavy to drag to the house. Her legs are frosted hard, bent at impossible angles; he tries to straighten them, but they will not move. He runs back inside and calls the emergency number, then grabs the blankets off of his bed and hurries back out into the darkness. He tucks the blankets around her frozen limbs. He knows this is useless, but his hands need something to do. The cold is terrific.

The sleepy paramedics can hardly get her on the stretcher. When they finally do, a young stretcher bearer slips and bangs her foot against the car fender. His curse does not cover a sharp, dry crack like the sound of a breaking stick. When they get to the hospital they find that they have broken one of her toes. Nora has made no sound.

It's winter, Clark thought. It always waits until winter. "Did she fall?"

"No, Clark," Barb said, "she didn't fall. She had some kind of a seizure this morning while Dad was uptown. He must have found her when he came home." Another long pause. She bit off a whimper as if it were a carrot, with a snapping sound. "She passed on, Clark."

"She what?"

"She passed on."

The blood rushing through his head roared like an animal. Passed on? Christ, she still had streaks of auburn in her hair. How can someone pass on who still has streaks of auburn in her hair? What the hell was this?

He recovered enough to hear Barb say something about Gerald Goodwin. There were two funeral parlors in Credibull—Goodwin's, which handled the Catholics, and Sanders, which handled the Protestants. Clark shuddered to think of lying on Goodwin's slab—he used the same cold efficiency the bitch nurse used. Clark shuddered to think of lying anywhere.

"How's your dad?" he asked when she finished.

She paused again. A raspy sound came through the receiver—she might have been wiping her nose. "I'm not sure. He hasn't said a word. He just sits and stares."

"Where is he now?"

"At the house. Brian and I are with him."

"Would it be all right if I came over?"

She sighed, and her voice lifted. "We'll be waiting."

He hung up the phone and leaned over the bench. At some point during the conversation he had set his hand on the wet lamppost—it was stuck to his palm. He pulled it off and stared at the mark it had left as if it were a portent. He went upstairs, took his coat out of the closet, then stepped outside into the twilight.

The sidewalk was slick enough and his remembrances of Nora's accident fresh enough to convince him that it would be best to drive over. Clark drove a Dodge long enough to span time zones—he needed a lot of metal around him to feel secure when moving at seventy miles an hour. It had been built long enough ago to inhabit the nether realm between *junk* and *classic*; it was cantankerous enough to distrust on any morning he could see his breath. It took two minutes of soulful pleading, one of threats, and one of hot cursing to get it running.

The only lights on at the Tewles' were in the living room. Barb answered when he knocked on the door, her exhausted face hanging like melting wax. "Hi, Clark. I'm glad you're here." Barb had always been more handsome than pretty and not much of either. She had the wide shoulders and hips, the heavy breasts that any daughter born to Maynard Tewle was destined to have. Her complexion was the color of a rawhide chew bone.

"Hi, Barb."

She let him in. A funny, stale smell pervaded the room. Brian sat straight and awkward beside the television, his face, weathered from fifteen years as a lineman, turned away from where Maynard slouched on the sofa. Maynard sat with his knees apart, his hands between his thighs, and his chin on his chest. He was staring at the floor.

Brian nodded at Clark; Clark nodded back, then sat beside Maynard and gently slapped his knee. "You all right, old buddy?" Maynard didn't answer.

"The mailman called me from here this morning." Barb leaned against the door with her arms folded beneath her breasts. "He found Mom while he was delivering. Dad was on the sofa, just like he is now. Did you see him this morning?"

"We had coffee together, but that was before . . ." He didn't know how to say it. ". . . before this." His hands strayed to his pockets as if to hide.

She began to nod, then stopped, as if a nod was an admission she wasn't ready to make. "Gerald Goodwin said that he'd handle the arrangements." Nonsense could find no hold on Barb's nature. She was a damned good kid. It had always been Clark's hope that Walter and Barbara would end up together, but Walter in the late sixties wandered off long enough to wander back with a beard, beads, and married to a tart, flirt, and all-around whore named Jenny. For ten years she slept with everyone in town who would take her except Walter, then left, no one knows where to or why; and thank God, good riddance. She even tried to seduce Clark once, right there in the bedroom in the house on St. Anne's Road. Right there in the god-be-damned bedroom.

Brian checked his watch. "It's suppertime. Kids'll be hungry."

"I suppose." Barb looked at her father, then at Clark. "Could I ask you for a favor?"

Clark nodded. "I'll stay with him."

She sighed with the same relief he had heard over the phone. "I'll fix something quick and run back. Have you eaten?"

"I had a sandwich." He hadn't, but he didn't want to trouble her.

Barb walked heavily across the room to take her father's limp hand. She searched his face for something she evidently couldn't find, then set his hand gently back in his lap. "We'll be back in an hour or so."

"Take your time. You look as if you could use a break."

She smiled tiredly. "Then maybe a little more than an hour."

Brian stood, long hams and spider fingers. He nodded at Clark. "Awful gooda you."

Clark nodded back. Brian never used a sentence with more than three words—when the situation called for one, he just squashed the words into *shouldas*, *couldas*, and *goodas*. He preferred to view life silently from the top of a telephone pole. "Don't mention it."

After they left, Clark turned to Maynard. He watched him stare at the floor and see nothing. Grief is a room with no windows.

"Are you hungry, Maynard? Can I fix you something?" No answer.

Clark waited until he could no longer bear the silence, then went into the kitchen. In the refrigerator he found the remains of a chicken, the legs cut off and most of the breast carved away. He took it out along with the mayonnaise jar, then cut four slices off the loaf in the bread box. The aroma rose to tease him like a promise of summer. The sandwiches he made ended up larger than he knew was good for him. He had never been able to resist Helen's chicken. Maynard had never been able to, either.

He brought the sandwiches into the living room and set one in front of Maynard. "In case you get hungry." He ate the other slowly, studying the photographs, watching the way the thickening darkness coaxed from the lamp its intensity. When he finished eating, he considered the second sandwich before deciding to leave it for Maynard.

He took his plate into the kitchen and studied the room, trying to pick out of it all the things that made it Helen's. The HOME IS WHERE THE HEART IS needlework on the wall above the sink. Magnets shaped like ladybugs crawling on the refrigerator, holding grocery lists and recipes written in a tiny hand. A flowered dish towel hanging from a wooden ring fixed to the knife drawer. Touches of her everywhere, even the smell of her hair in the air.

• •

*Clark and Nora are at a party at the Tewle farm, celebrating May-
nard's fortieth birthday. They are both wearing black. Dirges play on
the record player; festive mourning is in the air.*

*Clark is alone in the kitchen, leaning against the sink. In the living
room, Nora is listening to jokes and trying to tell a few of her own.
Clark winces each time her laughter brays.*

*Helen comes into the kitchen, carrying an empty snack tray. "What
are you doing in here all alone?" she asks. Her voice sways as she
sways. She has been drinking, he has been drinking; he loves the casual
courage he feels.*

He shrugs. "Waiting."

"Waiting for what?"

"Don't know." He knows.

*"The party's in the other room." The overhead light gives her thick
hair a halo's touch. She is wearing a black dress that clings to her like a
shadow, that shimmers as she moves. Clark has heard stories about Helen, stories of clandestine lust in closets and on couches on hot afternoons. As she moves to the sink he sees a story in her eyes he wants to
believe.*

*He feels the first engorgement of an erection like a slug traveling the
length of a rifle barrel. "The party is wherever you want it to be."*

*She sets down the tray. Her breath is fast and shallow. Good, he
thinks, good. He runs his hand down her back and buttocks. He feels
no need to justify to himself that his lust is love. Lust is enough.*

"Clark."

*He doesn't know if the word is an encouragement or a warning; he
doesn't care. He presses himself into her back, seeking the pleasure of
small movements. She trembles and shifts into him. Her breathing is
hard now, his is hard; the laughter continues in the other room. The
braying is only an impetus.*

She faces him. "What am I doing?"

"You know what you're doing."

93

"I'm drunk."

"There's nothing wrong with that. Let's go upstairs."

"God, Clark, another time."

"I don't want another time. Let's go upstairs."

She glances into the living room. When she looks at him again, he sees in her expression that the alcohol and his nearness are seducing her. Good, he thinks again. Good.

"All right," she says.

He is giddy as she leads him up the stairs and into a spare bedroom. She kisses him as he works his hands beneath the hem of her dress and up her thighs. She kisses him hard as she unbuckles his belt, little noises in the back of her throat that he has never heard from Nora.

"Be quiet," she says. "They might hear us." She reaches behind, unzips her dress, and slips it from her shoulders. Darkness pools at her feet; her body is the sun. She guides him to fall back on the bed. He reaches for that wonderful hair, clutches it so soft between his fingers, glowing amber, and pushes her head toward his waist.

"No."

She crawls up his body, keeping hers against him, sheds her panties, more shadows, sheds her brassiere; no use for a girdle, this woman, no, she is not Nora. They move against the weight of two marriages, his hands tracing up the back of her legs, over her hips, up the ridge and ripple of her rib cage, her breasts and their nipples like diamonds. His fingers trace out his pleasures.

Clark feels the wildness coming too quickly, and with the alcohol he cannot stop it. There is a rush and a silence, then Helen asks, "Do you think they heard us?"

The sweat on her chest dries coolly against his skin; the diamonds press into his flesh. A rich, meaty smell adds to his giddiness. "I don't give a damn if they do."

"I hope to God they haven't." She avoids looking at him as she scampers off of the bed. Nora's laughter rises through the floor.

"That was great, Helen."

"God." She hurries for her clothes. "I don't know what I was thinking."

94

"That was great."

"I was drunk."

"So?"

Her eyes flash. "Damn you, Clark. I was drunk."

He watches her dress. Shadow hides shadow and the glow of her skin, night falling. "Clark, get dressed."

"In a minute."

"Get dressed now. Oh, Christ. If someone should come in . . ."

She slips on her shoes and hurries for the door. She leaves without looking back. Clark lies with his legs apart, listening to the muffled sounds of the party. The erection he holds in his hand is dying like a flower. It is a wondrous thing.

Just such a thing had happened with other women, and always afterward there had been a conspiratorial meeting of the eyes, a half smile hinting at a hidden knowledge, but when Clark had dressed and gone downstairs, Helen had been sitting beside Nora on the sofa and would not meet his gaze.

He sucked bits of chicken from between his teeth and leaned against the sink. He had decided back then that perhaps her way was to avoid her lover's eyes. It became a game to watch whose eyes she avoided. Maynard, naturally—all women avoid their husband's eyes. Albert Wilson once and, incredibly, Bert Finchley, the ugliest man in Credibull. Wedding vows are rules daring to be broken.

Clark had not taken his wedding vows seriously until several years later. He liked now to think that he'd straightened out his infidelity in the same way he had his drinking, but in those few moments when he was genuinely honest with himself, he had to admit that resignation had been at least as strong an impetus as morality. It takes a lot of energy to be anything but a bumbling adulterer. And he had owed something to Nora.

Hell, he thought, let's end that thought there. Nip it in the bud.

95

He walked into the living room. Maynard was sitting as he had been before, but a bite had been taken out of the sandwich. Clark sat beside him and waited. Five minutes later, Maynard rubbed his cheek. "I've been thinking," he said quietly.

"That's what I figured."

"Corn or beans."

"What?"

"The south hundred and twenty. Should I plant corn or beans?"

"You sold the farm to the canning company, Maynard."

"Did I?" Maynard rubbed his cheek again. "Oh yeah. Sometimes I forget." He studied the room. "Where's Helen? I need more for supper than a damn sandwich."

"Don't you remember what happened?"

"What happened?"

Christ. Oh Christ. "Listen, Maynard . . ."

"Is she out with her bridge club? All those old biddies ever do is gossip about me."

"She's not with her bridge club. What happened this morning, Maynard?"

"What does that have to do with anything?"

"Just tell me what happened."

"We sat in front of Henry's and talked about Walter finally getting his computers. What is this about?"

"What happened after that?"

"We had coffee. I came home. Helen was in the kitchen. She was . . ." His face grayed. "God." He tried to stand, but his shaking legs wouldn't support him. "Clark, help me up."

"Where are you going?"

"To the hospital. I have to see if she's all right."

Christ, Clark thought, this is harder than I want it to be. Where's Barb? "Helen's not at the hospital." What the hell do I say? "Gerald Goodwin was here."

"Goodwin always smells money. Maybe he was in too much of a hurry."

"Barb called him, Maynard. He wasn't in too much of a hurry. Sit down."

Maynard struggled a moment before collapsing onto the sofa. Large tears streamed over his wrinkled cheeks, a lifetime of crying released. Clark sat quietly, wondering if his lack of interference was a wisdom deeper than understanding, or if he simply didn't know what to do.

"I was hoping," Maynard said when he could speak again. "When I saw her I figured she was gone, but hoping is sometimes believing what can't be true." He rubbed his tears into a sheen. "I was going to call the ambulance, but then everything went blank. I . . ." His hands dropped and his eyes widened. Color drained so quickly from his face it was frightening to see. "Christ in a hand bucket. Was she alive, Clark?"

"She'd gone, Maynard."

"I mean before. Was she alive when I got home?"

"You stop thinking that right now."

"She would have lived if I had called the ambulance."

"Damn it, Maynard, you stop thinking that right now. She was already gone."

"She'd be all right if I had called."

"No. It was nobody's fault."

His color was coming back; patches of his face were livid with it. "I killed her, didn't I?"

Clark clutched Maynard's heavy shoulders. "Maynard, listen to me. She was dead when you found her."

"I killed her." Maynard shook himself loose and wept into his fingers. "I killed my own wife."

Clark let his hands fall into his lap. Some things are beyond both explanation and condolence. Sometimes you just have to let people believe what they will until they don't believe it anymore.

Maynard wiped his face as if embarrassed. "Who's been in here?"

"I've been in here."

"Somebody else."

"Barb and Brian. The mailman, I think."

"Somebody's taken something."

"Taken what?"

"I don't know yet."

He rose quickly, surprisingly after such a draining. He lifted Brian and Barb's wedding picture from the wall and checked the paneling behind it. "Christ in a hand bucket, Clark, I know sure as hell that somebody's been in here."

Clark's eyes snapped to the clock and pleaded with it. Where the hell was Barb? "I don't think so, Maynard."

"I know sure as hell!"

Maynard strode into the kitchen. Clark heard drawers open and slam shut, the stabbing, metallic clatter of rummaged utensils. "I bet it was that goddamned burglar. I bet he came in looking for a radio while I was gone this morning. The bastard probably stepped right over Helen."

"I don't think anything is missing, Maynard."

"God damn it, Clark, don't tell me things I know ain't true."

Clark rose and wandered tentatively toward the kitchen. Maynard was picking through the garbage beneath the sink. Who would steal something out of the garbage? Who would care if someone did? "Why don't we sit down and wait for Barb?"

Maynard slammed the cabinet door shut. It bounced open; he slammed it shut again. "Christ in a goddamned hand bucket, everything is disappearing on me." His shoulders sagged. He was crying again. "Helen's gone and everything falls apart. I'm all alone."

"You're not alone, buddy."

"No. I share the house with a burglar." He cried harder and would have collapsed if Clark had not guided him to the sofa. He was still crying when Barb and Brian arrived a few minutes later.

Barb hurried across the room and sat with her arm around Maynard's shoulders. Brian stood awkwardly beside the door, closed it only when he saw his breath, and sat beside the television with an embarrassed look on his face. "When did this happen?" Barb asked.

"About a half hour ago."

"Somebody's been breaking in," Maynard said. "It's a wonder I haven't been robbed blind."

"No one's been breaking in, Dad. I've been here all day."

Maynard pulled away from her. "What have you stolen from me?"

"I wouldn't steal from you."

The look on his face was ugly enough to make Clark wince. "You don't have to. Now that your mother is gone, all you have to do is get rid of me and you get everything. You're a goddamned grave robber."

"That's not true, Dad."

"One down and one to go, huh, Barb?" Maynard turned to Clark. "Watch your kids. They'll come at you as sweet as syrup, but all they want is everything you got. Never, ever trust them."

Barb's face twisted. "It's been a rough day," Clark tried to explain. "He's tired."

"Yeah, I'm tired," Maynard said, "but that doesn't mean I don't know a few things."

For the next half hour, Maynard alternated between silence, outbursts, and quick searches of the room. When he saw there was nothing more he could do, Clark let Barb show him to the door. She followed him out, closed it behind them, and crossed her arms. Her goose bumps ran in shadows down her arm in the streetlight.

"Sorry," Clark said. "He's a little confused."

"I am, too."

"I'll stop by in the morning to see how he is."

"I'll see you then. I'm going to spend the night here."

"What about the kids?"

"Brian will be home." She shivered. "Why is he mad at me?"

Clark shrugged. "He has to strike at someone, and you're available. By morning he'll be accusing the mailman."

"I suppose." She looked at the stars, looked a hundred years old, with shadows beneath her eyes and along her jawline. Clark was willing to bet that beneath her hair coloring she was grayer than her mother was. Had been. *Get your tenses right,* Helen had said. He shook his head.

"How are you taking it?" Clark asked.

"I have to take it well, don't I? Do I have a choice?"

Walter, he thought, you were a fool for chasing after Jenny instead of this woman. "My phone doesn't have an *off* button," he said. "Call anytime."

"Thanks." The chill shivered silver on her breath. "Things will be all right. It just takes time." She sounded as if she were trying to convince herself.

He nodded. "You better get inside before you freeze to death."

"Thanks, Clark."

"Nothing to thank me for."

She went inside. The Dodge wouldn't start. He stopped to look in the Tewle living room window as he walked down the alley. Maynard was lifting the wedding picture from the wall and glaring at the spot behind it.

Clark stopped to see Maynard after he finished sweeping the store, leaving Walter alone to guard his lawn chairs and figure out a computer display. A thick odor like mildew hung in the living room. Barb slouched on the sofa, her eyes heavy, her head propped on her hand.

"Where's Maynard?" Clark asked.

"Upstairs sleeping. Finally."

"Tough night?"

She nodded tiredly. "He was awake until about an hour ago. I had to fake being asleep before he would trust me enough to go upstairs. Have you ever had to fight to stay awake while pretending to be asleep? It isn't easy."

"He's taking your mother's death pretty hard."

A sigh fell from her lips like sludge. "He's more concerned with his knickknacks than he is with her. He spent half the night peering out the window for burglars, and the other half accusing me of being a thief."

"Maybe he just needs something else to think about."

"I don't know." She yawned. "He's acting like a crazy man."

Crazy with grief. Clark wondered if he would act that way when Nora died. Hell, no—he'd be relieved. He'd probably have to keep from smiling when he heard of it. Her eyes passed quickly across the back of his mind. "He loved her. There would be more to worry about if he didn't act crazy."

Barb nodded, yawned again, and stared stupidly at the carpeting. "You should get some sleep," Clark suggested.

"I have to talk to Gerald Goodwin. I have to make some phone calls."

Goodwin. Clammy hands. Clark wondered if all Catholic morticians were so coldblooded, and if they had always been. It would explain where the doctrine of purgatory had come from. "I can help with those. I can do them from the historical society."

"Thanks, Clark, but I think they should come from family."

Clark nodded. "Then I'll see you later."

Clark didn't have time for phone calls. A fourth-grade class crossed the street from the school to hear his explanation of the Civil War exhibit—he spent a good part of the morning trying to convince one boy that Stonewall Jackson had not been a fighter pilot. To kids, the world has always been as it is now. Stonewall Jackson in an F-16, Jesus Christ in a music video. George Washington played football for the Redskins and squeezed in founding a country at halftime. In Clark's day, old George would have been popping home runs over the left field fence like Lou Gehrig or the Babe. Our founding fathers were the New York Yankees.

"But," the boy asked, "then who was the ones who were . . . who was the ones up in the sky in the planes?"

"They didn't have planes." The boy's eyes widened. "They rode horses."

"They rode horses in the planes?"

"No." Clark struggled to keep the exasperation out of his voice. *Cute* has time limitations that this boy had grossly exceeded. "Planes hadn't been invented yet."

"How old were the guys who invented them?"

"They hadn't been born."

"But if they hadn't been born, how could they invent them?"

101

Clark crouched, hoping eye contact would be worth the anguish he'd go through trying to stand. The boy's eyes grew wide again and he shied away, glancing first at his teacher, then his classmates. Clark had to think for a moment before he understood why.

You're old. You're dust and ashes with life seeping away like water. You're a grandfather in a coffin, your lips glued together; your knotted fingers no child is allowed to touch; flesh-colored makeup covers your gray. You're old, and you reek of the stink that only old people carry. You're old, and to a child with life still wet on its lips you are an alien chained to a grave. You should be in a horror movie.

He forgot what he had squatted to say. He was afraid that by standing his face would reveal more of the monster lurking within. It isn't true, he wanted to wail, the hell if it's true. But how do you convince children otherwise? And how do you convince yourself?

He took out his handkerchief as he stood and pretended to blow his nose. He hid his anger and fear behind white linen. "They rode horses," he said.

He felt weak until they left, acutely old even after. Before she herded her class across the street, the teacher thanked him in her singsong, *I spend all my time talking to children* voice, patting his hand as if he had just wet his pants. He sat at his desk to recover his strength, himself, and to let his anger dissipate.

Who are you angry at? A child? A child is only a child.

He was angry at this betrayal, this god-be-damned spinning of the world that kept adding days to his life. To hell with it all. To hell with gray hair and sore knees, to hell with these so-called golden years. Fool's gold as false as life itself, as its decaying promise. *Do not go gentle into that good night.* But go ahead, rage. See what it gets you.

He stared at the blank face of the microfiche machine and felt the hot tears come; he thought of Helen lying on her kitchen floor. He'd had enough of this kind of thinking; he had to get out where he could see something and think something else. He slipped his coat over his shoulders, hung his sign in the window, and stepped outside. The class he'd talked to was on the playground; the airplane boy climbed on the jungle gym, defying gravity, the world's hard grasp. Defy all you can, it will hold you one day. You will become what you will. What I am. I am sorry, my child.

He hurried past the school, his head cocked to the side as if to protect his cheek from the wind, or as if he were embarrassed. He walked backstreets to the elevator, then turned south on St. Anne's Road toward the Bumblebee. The café was deserted—like coffee, lunches were cheaper at the Burger King. Paper black cats and green warty witches hung lazily from the walls in a clumsy attempt to celebrate the holiday; black-and-orange ribbons crept in loopy arcs across the ceiling. Billie was dressed in black; she looked up at him from where she leaned on the counter, reading a magazine. She didn't smile.

"Hello, Clark."

"Hi, Billie."

"You want the special? Liver, onions, and bacon."

Try getting that at the Burger King. "Sounds good."

She went into the kitchen. Clark shuffled to his table and waited for her to join him. She sat with her arms resting on the tabletop, her heavy breasts curving over it, casting a shadow. The desire to touch such youth left his fingers trembling.

"Not a good day," she said.

"No, it isn't."

Her dress reminded him of Helen. He was in that bedroom again, a memory sharp with sounds, with smells, with touches. He didn't know if he was with Helen or Billie; he didn't know if there was a difference. My God, he thought, this girl could not have even been born then—her parents must have been climbing a jungle gym. If she can be this age then, why can't he be her age now? Why? Hell. Nobody tells you the rules.

"I heard about Helen Tewle," Billie said. "How's Maynard taking it?"

"Tough. They were married for forty-eight years."

"Two years short of golden." She sighed. "Even if I married tomorrow, I'd be seventy by my golden anniversary. A lot of years."

Memories stabbed into him: the touch of lips, sounds made in the back of the throat, diamonds. "My great-grandfather lived to be a hundred and seven."

"You're kidding."

"So did his wife. She was three years younger, but they died at the same age, to the day."

"Then you have a lot of years left."

He shook his head. "Most everybody else in my family died in their seventies."

"They say that the average is seventy-two. Once you reach it, you're bucking the odds." She nodded as if she had quoted a profound truth. "How old was Helen?"

"Sixty-eight."

"She didn't even make the average."

The cross hanging loosely around her neck glinted brightly, like Bethlehem's star pointing the way to salvation. Salvation is what we are all after, pearly gates, golden streets, a return to youthful, bright-haloed innocence. Bliss. If you can find salvation in mangers, then perhaps you can find it in spare bedrooms or café booths. There is rest for the weary; you can be born again. So they say. So they believe.

A sudden, sharp taste filled the back of his throat, the copper taste of fear and pennies. Once you reach seventy-two, Clark thought, you're bucking the odds.

The cook slid a liver special out of the kitchen—he was a taciturn man who smoked while he cooked, who never left his cloister of stove and spattered grease. Billie rose and leaned over the counter for it, one foot off the floor, her arm stretching, the muscles in her calf and behind trembling like a horse's withers. She brought him the plate. "You want anything to drink?"

"Water's fine."

She fetched the pitcher, set it on the table, and sat again. She watched him eat; the heat of her leg burned against his. She was so young, so young. He remembered the mourning of doves at sunset.

"When's the funeral?" she asked.

Clark swallowed a bite of liver. It was wrapped in memory and desire and was tasteless. "I don't know yet. Tomorrow or Monday, I would guess."

"Will you let me know when? I'd like to go."

"Sure."

She wiped her neck with a napkin. The cross glinted between two undone buttons of her dress like that blessed star. Clark stared at it; he could not break his gaze. *To this we all pay reverence.* "I could take you, if you like."

When he looked up, she was watching him. He wondered how she was interpreting his suggestion; he wondered how he had meant it. Can you call taking a girl to a funeral a date, especially a girl more than fifty years younger than you are? Is that what he was after, or was he simply offering a favor to a friend? The problem with desire is that it clouds your motives.

"I'd like that," she said. "It would get me out of here for a few hours."

He felt a schoolboy's thrill and redemption's young, strong touch. "It will be in the afternoon—that priest out at St. Anne's isn't much of a morning person."

"Father Charlie?"

"You know him?"

"He comes in every once in a while." She rested her chin on the heel of her hand and watched him eat. "I'll take you to lunch first. Call me when you know, or stop in."

"All right." It must have been the late fifties, thirty-some years, since he had taken a woman other than Nora to lunch. He'd forgotten how good it could make him feel. "You know, maybe I will have something to drink. Do you make milk shakes?"

"We have a machine in the back."

He leaned forward confidentially. The sweet smell of youth made him giddy; the cross shone. "Make me a strawberry shake with whipped cream on top."

"Coming up."

She walked to the counter and called the order to the cook. Clark finished his meal with young and strong and manly relish. Maybe Stonewall Jackson had been a fighter pilot, after all.

It was not until he got back to the historical society that he remembered he was married.

Chapter

6

The funeral was Saturday, a cold day shivering beneath gray clouds while the wind muttered threats about a second snow. Clark picked Billie up at her apartment above the bank. They drove west on Highway 14 through a series of towns just as senescent as Credibull—Janesville, Smith's Mill, and Eagle Lake—before reaching Mankato. They ate at an Embers on the city's east side.

Billie picked at her seafood salad. "You'd think that after working all morning I'd be hungrier than this."

"You'd think so." Clark had taken one bite of his chicken salad sandwich before pushing it to the side. Funerals made everything taste of formaldehyde.

She pushed her jacket farther into the corner of the booth, then played again with her food. "Where did you use to work, Clark?"

It was funny how she assumed retirement. Age brings back the leisure of a child, except you're supposed to play with medications instead of dolls and baseballs. "I still work, at the historical society."

"That's volunteer, isn't it? I mean real work."

She had a habit of ending each sentence on an upward lilt that irritated him, but since she was Billie he struggled to convince himself that it was an endearing irritation. "I owned the hardware store. I thought you already knew all this. We live in a small town. No moles on my ass."

She slapped his arm. "That's just café talk. All I really know about you is that you're a sweet old guy who likes Danish."

The heat of her hand lingered on his arm like a scent. "And now you know I used to own a hardware store."

She smiled. "Do I need to know anything else?"

Oh, you do, you do. Possibilities leaped wildly in his mind. He could not bring himself to say what he needed to. "I used to fish a lot."

"A lot of *used to*'s," she said.

"It gets to be that way." He moved his sandwich to a new spot on his plate. "Eventually."

"And your wife?"

"She's in Ambrose's."

"I guess I've heard that." She popped a tiny shrimp into her mouth. Her tongue darted out to lick from her lip whatever kind of sauce it was coated with. "She's in a coma?"

He shrugged. "I've always pictured a coma as a deep sleep. Nora isn't sleeping. She just . . . lies there." He did not want to talk about Nora. "What about you? Seeing anyone?"

"You mean steady?" He nodded—too eagerly, he thought. He didn't want to expose too baldly his need for possibility.

She pushed her plate to the side and leaned over the table. "Denny left a bad taste in my mouth for steady. I can't stand a man for longer than three days anymore. After three days they quit trying to impress you."

The waiter came, a big kid with sculpted hair, a voice like a hinge, and a crotch Clark couldn't help noticing. He filled their water glasses, then asked, "Can I get you anything else?" He talked to Billie, not Clark.

"Not right now." She studied him. "You must play football. Big shoulders. Strong arms."

The waiter smiled shyly. "Linebacker. I got seven tackles in the game against Faribault last night."

"Outstanding." Billie ran her hands down her sweater, smoothing out the wrinkles, accentuating herself. Clark's anger flared as he watched the waiter gape. To a kid that age every tit is a wonder. Take your crotch and your arms and your adolescent voice back to the head cheerleader and let her *you-rah-rah* all over you. Leave Billie and me alone. And more silently he thought, *because I can't compete with you.*

"Thanks." Clark smiled, feeling the glitter in his eyes. "We're fine for now."

"Just let me know if you need anything."

The waiter smiled at Billie. Billie smiled back. "Nice guy," she said as she watched him walk away.

"Yeah." Clark watched her. He remembered slipping strong, young arms around slim waists; he remembered running hands down sweaters to smooth away wrinkles. He needed more than memories. He needed to wrench his leg maneuvering with this girl in the backseat of a prewar Ford, he needed fierce touches and high moans, he needed breath coming strong with sweat fogging the windows. In an age inundated with teenaged models in Wonder Bras and sixteen-year-olds giving phone sex, he needed to be more than an old and sexless man. For a moment he felt impotent, but then remembered that this girl was sitting here with him and not with the table-waiting linebacker, young Thunder Crotch.

You do what you can. *Do not go gentle.* You fight for your life.

109

He stretched his legs beneath the booth, pulling at the arthritis, and let his knee come to rest against hers. Youth seeped into the joint in a spot so warm he thought it might blister. "So you like boys his age?" He emphasized *boys*.

She smiled. "I like boys any age."

Well, perhaps there was promise in that. She did not move her leg away. "You know, Billie, I've been wondering about you."

She was looking at him, smiling at him, the look in her eyes meant for him. "Wondering what?"

Wondering what pleases you. Wondering what you do at night in that apartment above the bank, and wondering what you would do there with a man like me. As he slipped toward his mind's dark places, Nora's wide, leathery face broke through to stare at him from where it rested on his conscience. She managed to mutter, *Till death do us*, before he pushed her away with remarkable ease. If he had remembered earlier how easy pushing her away was, perhaps he and Billie would have been by now beyond lunches in Embers before funerals. It was funny how you forget things.

A memory of Helen replaced Nora, diamonds beneath his fingertips. "Wondering a lot of things," he said to her, or to Billie.

"Oh?" Billie glanced at her watch. "My God, look at the time. If we don't hurry, we'll be late." She dabbed at her mouth with a napkin and stood. As she leaned over to retrieve her jacket, her cross swung like a pendulum marking out Clark's heartbeat. It stopped when she stood.

Clark followed her to the cash register. For a second he saw her short hair long and amber. He rubbed his eyes, and in the pressure upon them saw Nora creep again into his mind, and again he pushed her away. Nora, his wife, his partner in a marriage that had always hung from *until death do us part* like rotting meat from a hook, Nora was dead, or so close to death that the small distance made no difference. I'm the one alive now, he shouted inside, I'm the one still kicking, me and all these god-be-damned too-young people. If I can drink from this girl, then I will drink from her. I am a thirsty man.

"Good luck at the next football game," Billie said to the waiter as he

110

rushed by. He smiled back and almost bounced the fish platter he was carrying off the wall. But, Clark thought, I'll be in the car with her on the drive back to Credibull. Not you.

Billie shivered as they stepped outside. "It's a funeral kind of day, isn't it?"

"Yes." He opened the car door for her, then walked eagerly to his side. Before they reached the little country church on St. Anne's Road he had patted her knee twice, had felt her leg almost rupture with the force of her vitality. She didn't seem to mind his touch. He imagined she liked it.

St. Anne's was cold, always cold, colder with the weather. Old farmers stood in the vestibule, roughened hands in pockets, their corded forearms, straining against the cotton and polyester fabric of their sleeves, pulling open their jackets. Bulging bellies, the smell of their farms upon them. Clark nodded greetings as he ushered Billie into the vestibule and shivered away the cloudy day. Their talk of Helen and Maynard, the weather, and the Vikings died as they nodded back and looked at who had accompanied him. Billie smiled. A little thrill ran through Clark.

He searched for Maynard and didn't find him; the pews were now just filling. The casket at the front of the church was open for the viewing. Helen lay within it, her face molded wax, the white silk that framed her glowing strangely, a beacon in the dull black fog that seemed to be rising from the carpeting. The thrill within Clark died when he looked at her and rose again when he turned to Billie. He didn't know what to feel. What to believe.

"Do you suppose we should pay our respects?" Billie asked.

"I suppose," Clark said.

Clark guided her toward the casket with his hand against the small of her back. He could feel the farmers' stares upon him. Yes, he wanted to shout at all these dead, white, craggy faces, yes, this girl is

111

mine. His hand dropped, and he cursed himself for being so damned narcissistic.

"I don't like looking at bodies," Billie whispered as they stopped in front of the casket.

"I don't either."

He had expected being so close to Helen to carry him back to that night in the bedroom, to other nights, other memories, a vivid montage zipping through his mind with the swiftness of years. It did not come, because this body in the casket was not Helen. The eyes were wrong, the skin was wrong, the way her lips pressed together was wrong, all wrong. Helen never held her mouth like that. Helen was not in the casket. Helen was standing beside him, a younger, more voluptuous Helen, a Helen with heat in her body and life laughing on her lips, a Helen who thrilled him. A Helen who let him touch her knee, let him guide her with gentle pressure to show the world that yes, yes, this girl is mine and there is life in me. God be damned for all of the empty, cold bodies lying in caskets and nursing homes, and glory be to youth and innocence, the gods every damned one of us worship. Every last damned one of us.

"You know," Billie said, "I don't know if I ever met her."

"Me, either."

He did not explain himself; he didn't know if he could. The line forming behind them prodded; he guided Billie stiffly back and they took seats halfway up on the right side. She moved against him as the pew filled. The smell of perfume and sex filled his nose and mind. No formaldehyde. The young are blessed.

Gerald Goodwin stepped forward to close the casket, a heartless man performing a heartless, official, and cold duty. The farmers filed in. A woman younger than Clark but old enough for wattles played the tubercular organ, her neck craned forward, her eyes chasing the notes across the page as if they were playing tag. Billie sat tightly against him. The pew was crowded with Helen's friends—sympathy friends, mostly, some who still held suspicions about Maynard from before Father Callahan's confession: *I'm so sorry you married that son of a bitch what can I do to help* friends. He wondered how many people would show up at Maynard's funeral. Not many, he guessed. Billie wouldn't be crowding him then, unless she had a reason other than too many people. The thrill ran through him again. Love can make impossible things happen, and lust can make you believe they will. Maybe it was the other way around. He thought of Agnes Miller that day in the historical society. *L* words and *I* states. It was so easy to be confused.

Barbara walked solemnly up the aisle, her head back, her shoulders back, her eyes on the crucifix above the altar. By the elbow she held her father, the boys following behind, and Maynard looked an old man. They took their seats in the front pew with Maynard slouched forward and the boys with their heads bowed. The people gathering behind them stared at the backs of their heads and shook and bowed their own. They waited for their shepherd.

The only member of St. Anne's Parish that Clark had ever heard openly question God's existence was its new priest, Father Charles Milton. Father Charlie was skinny and tall and looked about as old as Thunder Crotch. His favorite answer to any doctrinal question was "Who can say?"—his faith was founded on the rock of agnosticism. It was rumored that he came from a rich New York family that had pulled religious strings to get him assigned to the Minnesota backwaters to avoid any, or any further, embarrassment.

"What gets me about this," Father Charlie said during the homily, "is, what happens now?" He rubbed his cheek as if he were checking his beard, though the only reason Clark suspected he would ever need to shave would be for the experience. "We get to some point and we die. What happens then? It gets me!"

Clark was familiar enough with the Polish and Irish history of St. Anne's parishioners to know it had taught them to be long-suffering. As their priest continued, Clark saw in their wind carved faces only a bewildered toleration. They tolerated Father Charlie because he represented the authority of the church, and Father Charlie was not Father Callahan privately thrusting his privates at statues in orgasmic litany. Hail *Mary*, full of *grace*, the Lord is with *thee!* Yes, well, we all have our statues.

"All we really know is that at one time or another we all have to go through it." Father Charlie looked down at the polished walnut casket. So cold it looked, catching the glare of the overhead lighting. "I wish I could offer some kind of hope or promise. I can't." He turned, hesitated as if he thought he should perhaps say something comforting, then sat. From the front pew, Maynard stared blankly at the coffin, his shoulders trembling. Barb cried silently, dabbing quickly at her eyes with a handkerchief. The look on Father Charlie's face struggled between impotent frustration and the pride of a Cub Scout accepting a merit badge for doing his first good deed. Clark grunted. Too much honesty can turn a man into an unfeeling bastard.

The woman with wattles began to work at the organ again. Father Charlie lifted the host toward the crucifix for its blessing. Why go through the motions, Clark wondered, if you don't believe what's behind them? The question was not on anyone else's face—nothing was on any of their faces—as the parishioners rose and slowly shuffled to the front of the church to accept the body and blood. The sign of the cross, knees quickly bent, a head quickly bowed. Transubstantiation. The parishioners in Clark's pew rose, and Billie rose with them. He never knew she was Catholic. He sat where he was and watched her kneel in front of Father Charlie with his fingers in his lap, trembling. He thought many things.

She came back and sat beside him, smiling apologetically. He wondered what she had to be apologetic about. Possibilities raced through his mind. A little wine still wet the corner of her lip and she wiped it off with her finger. He stared at the stain as she dropped her hand to her lap. His eyes caught on the cross hanging around her neck. His heart beating time. He lifted his eyes to the ceiling and wished he could pray.

With the close of the mass, Father Charlie rose to give a benediction as amorphous as fog on water. The pallbearers came forward: Brian, ungainly in a black cotton-and-polyester suit, and five nephews from Helen's side of the family—farm boys with red faces and callused, meaty palms. They carried the casket out to the cemetery plot behind

114

the church, the wind licking at their coattails, the ground wet from a fresh smattering of snow and rain. Maynard stumbled behind them, guided by Barb and Father Charlie. The parishioners circled around a contraption designed to lower the casket into the grave. Sometimes forceps pull you into this world; always they pull you back out. By life's end you'd think you could escape metal's frigid touch.

Father Charlie spoke again, more briefly than in the church—like the precipitation, the temperature was dropping, falling into shivers and foggy breath. The service broke into handshakes and hugs and standing around awkwardly. Clark stayed by Billie's side until he noticed the mud-colored sedan parked by the road and the milk white face behind the wheel.

Anger or apprehension flared inside of him—he didn't know which. "I'll be right back," he told Billie.

"Where are you going?"

"To talk to someone."

He crossed the lot to Lewell's car with gravel crunching beneath his heels. Sleet settled on his eyelashes. Lewell rolled down the window. "What are you doing here?" Clark asked.

"My business is to keep track of the key players."

"This is a funeral. Can't you let business slide for a day?"

"Business," Lewell said through a smile, "is business."

Anger flickered in Clark's chest, then cooled when he remembered he had spent the service thinking about Billie Jessup. Business is business. "You don't have to be so blatant about it."

"We each have our own style."

Clark looked away to keep his anger down. Maynard was staring at the fields as if he were asking them questions. He wandered toward the road, toward where his farm had stood.

"Where's he going?" Lewell asked.

"I don't know. I better check on him."

Maynard crossed the road, his arms hanging loosely. By the time Clark left the parking lot he was in the far ditch and struggling to climb into the field. "Helen?" he called.

Clark hesitated. Could it really be that Maynard did not know that his wife was dead? "Maynard?"

Maynard slipped to his elbows and knees. He gasped, and his face grayed. "Helen?"

"It's Clark, Maynard." The dead, wet ditch grass was as slick as ice. Easy now, he thought. If you fall and break something, you'll never get up again.

"Helen?"

Clark helped him up. "No, Maynard. It's Clark." Maynard's face paled as he stood; slowly his color came back. The people at the church were watching them. "Maynard, do you know what happened to Helen?"

"Of course I know what happened. Where is she?"

Christ. Good Christ. "What happened to Helen, Maynard?"

"She died. I'm not crazy. I know that she died."

"Then why are you asking where she is?"

The rain spotted Maynard's cheeks and glasses. "Because I was hoping it would be like the priest says. Since no one knows what happens, no one can say that she didn't come back here. I was hoping she came back here."

"She's across the road, Maynard."

"I know she's across the road, but . . . *she's* not across the road." The tears on his cheeks mixed with the rain. "When I followed the casket out, I looked over here and saw all the buildings still standing. I thought to myself, Maybe this has all been just a dream. Maybe we're still on the farm and I just dreamed that we grew old."

"The buildings are gone, Maynard."

Maynard stared across the barren fields, black against a gray-and-white sky as stiff as the portraits on his walls. "It was here, but then it all went away." His hands rose, then dropped again. His elbows were stained with the earth's blood. "What happened to it all?"

Oh, Maynard. My friend. "I don't know."

"It was just here!"

"I don't know, Maynard."

116

Helen's nephews were standing on the shoulder above them. They helped Maynard, still crying, onto the road. Clark let them haul him up and was glad to feel solid gravel beneath his feet. He tried to see in the fields what Maynard had seen, and failed. Well. We see only what we want and need to see.

He waited for Lewell to drive past, then crossed the road. Billie was watching him through the Dodge's windshield. "What was that all about?" she asked as he climbed in behind the wheel.

"He just wanted to see his old farm." He studied the way she sat, the rise and fall of her. Her scent recaptured his thoughts. "We might as well go."

"What will happen to Maynard?"

Hell, who knows? "He's spending a few days with his daughter."

The wind whistled dirges on the drive back into town. Clark watched the road, as wet as a tongue, sleet melting on its surface so quickly it might have never been. Billie sat with her elbow on the armrest, her chin in her hand, her narrow hips strapped in tighter than Nora's had ever come close to accomplishing. The belt pulled her skirt an inch above her knee—a nice knee, with just a wash of color. Clark wanted again to touch it, to feel its youth flow into his arm. He felt stronger than he had in years, or he felt the need to be. He felt the need for narrow hips and aching groins, for a gluttonous celebration on a cold Saturday afternoon. Cold ground and cold days meant nothing; molded wax on silk, leather on linen meant nothing, were nothing; we cannot let them mean a thing. The rain falls ignorant to earth, to die in a billion splattering asphalt funerals, but we are not raindrops. We must know where we are going.

Credibull rose on the horizon. There was no color to the town; it was all grays and browns. Clark was tempted to stop at the house, to invite her in, but didn't. Making love to another woman in Nora's home was something that even in his adulterous days he had never done—somehow the right to property had been more sacred than the right to fidelity. A pang pulled at his chest. A pang for Nora? A pang for something.

"Do you want me to drop you off at the Bumblebee?" he asked.

"God, no. I'm taking the rest of the day off." Yes. Oh, yes. Another pang for something.

He passed the feed store and stopped at the highway with the elevator frowning down. He turned left, drove down half a block, then parked the Dodge opposite the bank. He turned to Billie, this child, this girl, this woman. His fingers rested on the back of her seat, an inch above her shoulder, and trembled.

She smiled at him with a puzzled expression. "What?"

Invite me up. For the love of all things sacred, invite me up. "Since you have the rest of the day off, I was wondering . . ."

"You were wondering what?"

The words were thick in his throat. "I have some free time, too, and I thought maybe I could come up for coffee, or . . . something."

"Or something?" She still looked puzzled. A hand rose to cover a smile. Merriment danced like gnomes in her suddenly soulless eyes. "Oh, Clark, what do you want to do?"

"I just thought that we . . . I mean, we've never really gotten to know each other."

"You aren't talking about a movie or something, are you?"

"Not really."

"Oh, Clark. Oh, Clark." Her laugh was a heavy, harsh bawl. Her face was twisted into ugly merriment. "You want to fuck me, don't you?"

"Christ, Billie—"

"Go on, say it. Tell me that you want to fuck me."

The word was a sock in the gut. "Well . . . I just thought . . ."

Her laughter echoed between his ears like flashes of pain. She covered her mouth again to stifle it. "Clark, you're a sweet old guy, but you're an *old guy!*"

He backed away from her as if she had shoved him, feeling his age gnaw his joints, his soul. "Forget it."

"This is a joke, right?"

"I didn't goddamn mean it to be a joke." Only in defiance was there dignity.

118

"Why, Clark, you dirty old man." She slapped his knee. "I didn't know guys your age could even get it *up* anymore! Can you?"

"Forget it."

"Oh God, Clark." She was still laughing. "Oh, God." She studied him with tears in the corners of her god-be-damned little-girl eyes. "I like you, Clark, I really do." She glanced down at his pants and covered a laugh again. "All right. Let's go upstairs. I've never fucked an old guy before."

"No." He didn't want to go upstairs. He wanted this woman out of his car. "I'm no oddity for you to whet your experience against."

She laughed loudly. "But Clark, if you can still *fuck*, you *are!*"

"Get out of my car."

She quit laughing. "I'm sorry. It was just all so unexpected."

"Get the fuck out of my car." Yeah, Billie, I can use that word, too.

Anger flared on her face, as if it were her life, her desires, her expectations that had suddenly come crashing down. As if some little bitch had pulled the years down upon *her.* "All right." She opened the door. "See you at the Bumblebee."

"Maybe."

"Or maybe not?" She leaned inside. The cross dropped on its chain like a lynching victim. "Christ, Clark, I didn't mean anything by it. If you want to fuck, then let's go fuck. It might be fun."

"If I want fun, I'll find some other old fart and play a game of checkers. You want to shut the door, please?"

"Be that way then." She slammed the door and strode angrily around the front of the car, her body bouncing, her breasts butting against her jacket like the horns of an enraged bull, the cross rocking angrily. He waited for her to disappear behind the door beside the bank. Watching her damned little-girl hips made him want to run his fist through the windshield. He'd probably shatter every bone in his hand. Old bones are brittle.

He gunned the engine. The Dodge sputtered and died.

To hell with these god-be-damned too-young people, he thought as he restarted the car and drove away. Dirty old man, she had said. To hell with them all.

Chapter

7

By the Monday before Thanksgiving, what had survived from that first dusting of snow was the consistency of old vanilla frosting. Clark shivered preemptively before he stepped out into the predawn. He was an old man who grew cold easily.

His age had leaped forward since the funeral. It was hard to stand against a storm of years, while young laughter in old cars echoed. You become what you are: gray hair, swollen knuckles, a faltering mind. You drape baggy clothes over a body crushed beneath the weight of a lifetime. Your lifetime, Clark, he said to himself. All those years are your years.

"What's the matter with the Bumblebee?" Maynard had asked that first Tuesday after the funeral.

"Nothing's the matter," Clark had said. "I'd just rather not get coffee there." They'd been sitting in front of Henry's with gloves on their hands, caps on their heads, and cold licking the bare patch of throat framed by Clark's upturned collar. Steam rose from the grain elevator in heaving gasps that disappeared into the heavy gray sky. "The food is better at the Burger King."

"At the Burger *what?*" Maynard asked.

"King. Burger King. The restaurant down the highway from the Wal-Mart."

Maynard's eyes had drifted across the railroad tracks. "Oh, yeah, the Wal-Mart. Sure, let's go to the Burger King." Clark had to show him the way.

It was colder this morning than it had been that Tuesday, though sunnier. The air gnawed at his ears as he walked by the elevator; it gave his nose a frosty tweak. Jergen Burnett drove by in his squad car and parked in front of the store. Jergen was a pillar of the community and was built like one. He was the same heavy diameter from head to foot, as if his mother had been a toothpaste tube and he'd been squeezed onto a bristly world. He had that color, too.

Jergen bumbled out of his car. "Hello, Clark. I thought I'd help you this morning with the security system. I'm getting tired of Walter always calling me a son of a gun."

"Help me?" God, don't help me. Jergen had inherited from Walter the title of Credibull High School Class Boob. "I think I can handle it."

"Don't be silly. I'm an expert in these things." He snatched the keys from Clark's hand before Clark could protest. How do you argue with a pillar?

The key to the Dodge did not fit in the door, as Jergen discovered. He eventually fumbled the door open. The security system cawed. Jergen bustled inside.

"Let's see here . . ." He floundered with the key chain.

"It's the round key," Clark said.

"There's a lot of round keys." Jergen flinched at the cawing, dropped the keys, and booted them halfway across the floor as he bent over to pick them up.

"It's round on the lock end. Here." Clark pointed it out. "You put it in and hold down the first button while you turn it."

"There's buttons? I didn't know there were buttons."

"Two of them."

"Well, criminy." Pillars do not swear. "What do I do with the second button?"

The cawing settled into a long, slow bleat that ended in accusatory silence. "Nothing, now. Our time is up."

"Huh." Jergen scratched his head and grinned. "I guess we're burglars. I guess I'll have to arrest me."

"Hah. Good one."

Jergen grabbed the front of his uniform. "Come on, you. Spread 'em." He jerked himself down onto the counter, knocking over a plastic collection bottle for Jerry's Kids. Pennies fell to the floor like music. "Sorry about that."

"Forget it."

"I better take this guy in before he causes more trouble." He slapped a handcuff over one wrist and dragged himself toward the door. "I'll put him in lockdown. Maybe I'll rough him up a bit."

"Hah. Good one." Clark supposed Jergen would spend the morning trying to find the handcuff key. "See you later."

"See you. Come on, you thug." Jergen managed to get safely outside, but when he opened the car door the cuff banged against it with a sharp metallic clang. Should leave a nice scratch in the paint.

Clark cleaned up the pennies, then swept. When he passed the shelf holding the lock washers he remembered the time Randall Soderberg's son had swallowed one. Randall had always been one of those high-strung types—he'd had the boy's stomach pumped. Tommy, the kid's name was. He'd gone to school with Walter, volunteered with patriotic zeal for Vietnam, and died over there. He'd been a war casualty only in the broadest sense—he'd died of an overdose in a Saigon brothel, lying in the stink of his own vomit. He always had swallowed the wrong things—a lock washer, a drug, the lies about a war. Poor kid.

A computer display with twin monitors like blank, shiny eyes stared at Clark from where the barbecue display had sat—only foolhardy and frostbitten souls barbecue in a Minnesota winter. Hewlett-Packard and IBM had turned down Walter's license application, so he was selling something with the undignified name of Wind River Technologies. It sounded more like one of those high-tech outdoor-sporting-goods stores: mountain computers that used granola instead of microchips, scratch-resistant screens guaranteed to withstand grizzly maulings.

"The security system is blinking, Dad," were Walter's first words when he stepped through the door.

"That was Jergen Burnett's doing."

"You let him in here?"

"I didn't *let* him in here."

"Christ, Dad. That guy is a bull in a china shop. Did he ruin anything?"

"Only his car. He's now at the station, scratching his head and giving himself a bloody nose."

"What do you mean?"

"He locked his handcuffs around one wrist."

"Why?"

"He likes elaborate jokes."

"Christ, he'll never find the key." Everyone knows everyone in a small town.

Walter paid homage to the security god, pushing its buttons, turning its key. He made a quick, angry phone call to the police station, then opened the store. "You'd think Jergen would be too busy tracking down the real burglar to have time to tear my store apart."

My, Clark noticed, not *our.* "You'd think so. How are the computers selling, son?"

Walter walked over to his display, planted his hands on his hips, and smiled. It could have been his child. "Hotcakes, Dad, hotcakes. I sold one yesterday, and two last week."

"It's a good price." Clark had checked competitors' listings in Mankato and was pleasantly surprised—Wind River was considerably cheaper. He had a sneaking suspicion that this was a case of you get what you pay for. He hated himself for having so much trouble being optimistic about his son. "I hope they work for you."

Walter grinned and looked almost handsome. He even smelled good today, or at least not bad. "They already are." He laughed. "Christ, Dad, I thought Christmas came *after* Thanksgiving!"

Clark smiled. One of them was doing well. "I should get to work."

"It's a little early. Something special going on?"

"Field research."

Walter nodded. "I'm happy to say that I'll be much too busy to join you." He rubbed the top of a monitor as if he were tousling hair. "Got to order some more of these babies. I'm going to get rid of the one in the back and go to Wind River."

"Must be a good computer."

"The best-kept secret in the business. Won't be a secret for long, though, if I have any say about it."

Clark went in back for his coat—Miss November was wearing a pilgrim's hat but was in no other way dressed even remotely like a pilgrim. He slipped his coat on with a groan. The pain from putting on storm windows had never entirely dissipated, and now with the cold it flourished. In his younger days he would have hidden a groan like that, but his younger days had ended a half hour after Helen's funeral. "I'll see you tomorrow." He shuffled up front and opened the door.

"Hey, Dad?" Walter asked. "What are you doing for Thanksgiving?"

"Well . . ." He could no longer say he was going over to Maynard and Helen's, not without Helen. He supposed Maynard would be at Barb's. Maybe not. Maybe two old bachelors could get together. Of course, Walter was an old bachelor, too.

What the hell, Walter was his son. "Nothing special. Nothing planned."

"Why don't you come over to the apartment for dinner? I'll cook a turkey with all the fixings."

"You?"

"You might be surprised by what I can do."

Might be—he was doing all right with the computers. "All right."

"Good. See you tomorrow morning."

"See you." Clark stepped outside. The cold pummeled his chest. Christ, he thought. I'm not a bachelor.

He walked carefully down the street, balanced on glass legs, his heart leaping into his throat each time one of his feet slipped an inch. Only at times like this was it still difficult to forget Nora. Sometimes he felt like a child hiding from the bogeyman—don't look, and that nursing home wasn't really out there. But like a child he knew that it *was* out there, that it was now looming over *him*, was breathing its cold, antiseptic breath on *him*, was making the little gray hairs stand up on the back of *his* neck. It was just a matter of time before he found himself lying on one of its beds, watching Nora stare at a wall, feeling his life drain away like water into a rusty pan. He muttered something incoherent, even to himself. He shivered and pushed the home from his mind. It is important to forget what shouldn't be remembered.

The sun was too heavy—he could almost feel it reflect off the grain elevator beside him. He noted with more relief than regret that the high school football field was empty; he avoided looking at the Bumblebee. The old railroad depot sprouted as he crossed the highway, fertilized by memories that were hard to keep down at this time of the year. He thought of all the things that happened or had begun to happen there. He wished he could forget them as easily as he could Nora.

It is a Friday morning. Clark, Nora, and little Walter are waiting at the depot for the Jefferson Lines bus to St. Paul. Walter is making patterns with his toe in the parking lot gravel, whispering loudly. Clark stands with his hands in his pockets and his eyes far down the road. He feels Nora watching him.

"You'll be home Sunday night?" she asks.

He glances at her. "I always am."

On the third weekend of each of the last six months he has been telling her he has a tool convention in St. Paul he cannot neglect. As he glances again at her heavy face, he feels a twinge of unease. He assures himself that it is impossible that she knows. Lying is a skill he needs to work on.

The bus rumbles into the parking lot. Its size and ferocity drive Walter to disappear behind his mother's hips. A weird kid—here he is something like nine years old, and he still pulls baby-shit stuff like this. Bus brakes hiss, tires grind on gravel, and fumes pollute the air. Nora paws at Clark's arm in a clumsy attempt at affection. "I'll miss you."

"You, too. See you Sunday."

He plants a habitual kiss on her cheek and tousles the kid's black, wiry hair. He fishes his ticket out of his pocket and steps on board. His eyes are on the road ahead as the bus pulls away.

Clark has to sit beside a fat man who wears black horn-rim glasses and has his hair cut in a patchy heinie. A bad sunburn has left peeling skin like soot on the top of his ears. He nudges Clark. "I'm a salesman for the Schmidt brewery." Clark does not respond. "Are you a salesman? You look like a salesman."

"I own a hardware store."

"Really?" The fat man smiles. "Now there's a fascinating line of work. Always thought I'd like to go into hardware."

Clark knows that if he can get the man to talk about himself he will no longer have to answer questions. "Brewing has always fascinated me, too. How do they do that? Do they just throw grain and hops in a barrel and let them rot?"

"No, it's a lot more complicated than that . . . ," the fat man begins to explain. Clark ignores his long and windy answer by watching the wind work through the late-autumn fields. They remind him of the sea.

A woman completely unlike Nora is waiting for him in St. Paul. She is tall and small-breasted, with a thin ripple of ribs on her chest like disturbed water. Her long blond hair is black at the roots and tied into a ponytail with a blue ribbon. She is ten years older than Clark. Her name is Deloris.

She waves a hand as loose jointed as a bag of bones when she sees Clark watching her through the window. Clark smiles and flicks his hand in response. The sunlight flashes off of his wedding ring.

"Your wife?" the fat man asks.

"My girlfriend."

The fat man quits smiling. . "Oh." He says nothing more. Clark wishes he had told him that earlier.

As Clark steps off the bus, Deloris brushes her hands over her cheeks like a rabbit washing its face. "The wind," she says. "I'm a mess, right?"

"You look fine."

She takes his arm. "Oh, Clark, I missed you so much. Don't you know that I missed you so much?" Clark knows that she is smarter than her words. She is smart enough to understand that opportunities are greater for a divorced waitress rapidly approaching middle age if she acts a few degrees less intelligent than her lover. Her desperation fills him with power. Power makes him feel good. King of the beasts.

"I missed you, too." He kisses her. "What do you want to do tonight?"

She has a smile that speaks of things that have nothing to do with happiness. "I thought we might go dancing."

He shrugs. "Let's spend the night at your place. Do you have a bottle there?"

"Yeah, but . . ." Her smile drops as she brushes lint from his shoulder. "Can't we at least dance for a little while?"

"Do you have something against spending the night at your place?"

"No, I just thought . . ." She looks away. The first thing you have to do with any woman is break her gaze. "Can't we at least have dinner somewhere nice?"

He ought to at least give her something. He has, after all, already won. "Sure, we'll eat somewhere nice, someplace with dancing. But not for long, okay?"

"We have to go to the apartment first and change."

"We have to go to the apartment first and do a lot of things."

She smiles and kisses his lips heavily. "That's what I've been waiting for," she says, though he can tell that she hasn't. She has been waiting to spend the evening dancing.

He climbed into the Dodge when he reached the house. The snow on St. Anne's Road strobed in sunlight and shadows. The wind over the lonely fields moaned like an orphan.

Last night Clark had called in sick to Agnes Miller, knowing he would be driving this morning out to the Wilson farm. He'd never malingered in his life, until now; it was that damned reporter's fault, Lewell, the way he had of forcing promises made to friends' wives. Clark had seen him drive by the house on Saturday, his smile through his windshield a pale flash like a quick glimpse of wet bone. Clark considered cajoling Cletis Meadows at the Sunset Motel into rifling through Lewell's room to find out what he had discovered, but Cletis was too upright to ever go for it and too stupid to pull it off. Still, pilfering was mild compared to the crime of destroying an old man for a buck. You weigh the efficacy of morality against its consequences. Something needed to be done.

The Wilson house thrust its soiled face into the western wind. The gray faded leeward into a paint-stripped speckle; the outbuildings leaned toward the house with sagging shoulders. The toolshed still stood, forty feet back from the kitchen window.

Clark parked the Dodge in the neglected driveway. Thanks to the soreness in his knees and shoulder, it took him three tries to get out of the car. Everything that had happened here sucked the air from his lungs, left him standing impotently. He recovered enough to cross the yard to the toolshed—he had to steel himself before he could enter.

This was where it had happened. Tools still lay on the bench, unused for thirty-five years. He had figured schoolboys would have stolen them for souvenirs—*You know where I got this? The Wilson farm!* He picked up a pair of pliers, then set them down. Nails lay scattered across the bench; he kicked a few up from the dust on the floor. His fingers strayed over a claw hammer, but they found no ball-peen.

That's what he'd been killed with. Right there. He'd been lying right there.

Clark closed his eyes. The dirt floor rolled; an earthquake or vertigo. He gathered enough strength to open his eyes; he couldn't help thinking of Maynard. Right there, right god-be-damned there, lying right there on his back with one arm thrown across his face, both battered into the consistency of bread pudding. A punctured eyeball dripping down. Broken teeth scattered like the nails—maybe those were the souvenirs the kids were after. Christ. Clark was too close to this. The closeness pushed him out the door.

A bloodhound had sniffed out the hammer in the ditch, halfway into the corrugated-metal culvert running beneath the driveway. The police had speculated that the murderer had been trying to hide it, but you don't kill someone, not like that, then take the time to hide the weapon. You drop it and run. You run as fast as you can.

It was damned cold out there, damned cold. Clark walked around the house to warm himself, then went into the kitchen. He smelled dust and nothing else.

Rose Wilson had said afterward—when she could say anything at all—that when she and Dwayne had returned from town with her dress, she had thought nothing of her father not answering her calls; he was often preoccupied. She had been standing at the kitchen window when she saw the dark, spreading stain in front of the shed door. She'd wondered if her father had spilled a can of motor oil. She'd gone to see.

Rose never did go on the date she'd bought the dress for, never went on any date, Clark suspected. She left town before the sensation had died, and Clark did not see her again until the mid-seventies, when she came home wearing a crucifix and a pained, beatific expression. She made arrangements to be buried beside her father. She was buried there now.

He brushed aside cobwebs before entering the gutted living room. He considered going up to the bedrooms, but his knees and the decrepit-looking stairs persuaded him not to. He needed more air than the broken windows allowed—his chest felt as tight as a rag being wrung out. He went back outside. Across a small, dark field, Father Charlie was stacking hay bales against the church foundation. Clark followed the road to where he was working.

"Hello, Clark." Father Charlie may have been an agnostic, but he was a Catholic agnostic. He always spoke to his misguided agnostic Protestant brethren in somewhat of a condescending tone. "What brings you out here?"

"Nothing much." Clark watched him work. "I wanted to look at the Wilson farm."

"I've heard that you were a local-history buff." Father Charlie heaved a bale from the pile beside the cemetery fence onto the straw wall. A thump and crackle as it landed home. The sweat on the priest's forehead reflected the sunlight as he faced Clark. "Reliving old memories?"

"Huh?"

"Memories of the investigation." Father Charlie never wore a collar—he preferred sweatshirts with the Minnesota Twins logo. This one read *Twins Twice, '87 and '91.*

"Oh. No, just thought I'd look around."

"I suppose you know about the book writer in town."

"He stopped by the historical society."

The priest heaved a big, healthy sigh. "He stops by here occasionally. He asks a lot of questions about Father Callahan."

"No surprise there."

"A few about Maynard Tewle, too."

Huh. "What kind of questions?"

"What do I know about him, what is he like. He asked to look at the church records."

"Did you show them to him?"

Father Charlie nodded. "Honesty and openness are virtues. Of course, if there is no God, then what foundation is there for virtue?"

Clark did not want to be dragged into Father Charlie's agnostic proselytizing. "Did he find anything?"

Father Charlie shrugged. "He didn't look as if he had when he left. What could he find in church records, anyway?" He stacked another bale.

"Did you tell him anything?" Clark asked.

"What could I tell him? I wasn't here at the time of the murder—I wasn't *born* at the time of the murder."

Clark nodded at the priest's sweat-sogged back. He sniffed the wind coming across from what had been the Tewle farm, leaned against the cemetery fence, and studied the tombstones. He had read a story once about what dead people do in their graves. Old women knitting yellow grass into coffee table coasters. Old men smoking dandelion roots.

Father Charlie stopped working to stand beside him. He nodded at the tombstones. "You see all this and it makes you wonder what is going on." He indicated his sense of futility with a shrug of one shoulder and a tilt of his head.

Clark shrugged. Frost had kept the soil from settling into Helen's grave. "I guess no one really knows."

"Oh, Helen Tewle." Father Charlie blushed. "I'm sorry—I know she was your friend. It's just that if there is no soul . . ." The wind carried the rest of his thought away. "Look at the Wilson stones. I've always wondered why the wife's is white and the rest of the family's black." He had no subtlety in changing subjects.

The four squat stones rose hardly a foot above the turf. They sparkled angrily in the sunlight, as if indignant. What do dead people do? "The wife died before the murders. Cancer, I think."

"I've heard something about her and Father Callahan. Some kind of liaison?"

"That's the story," Clark said.

"The husband's is black because of the way he died. And the others?"

"The son died in a farm accident. The daughter, well, no one around here is sure. She got involved in the church. She only came back to Credibull twice—once to buy a plot beside her father, and the other to be buried in it."

Father Charlie silently studied Rose's grave, his tongue working in his cheek. "Then she died at the same time her father did. Poor woman."

Clark nodded. Her tombstone read *Rose Ruth Wilson, 1942–1981.* Nothing more. He imagined her down there, withered more now than she had been even in life, crossing herself with dead fingers, a muddy crucifix on a moldering chest. Her breath coming in quick, cold whispers that smelled only of decay. *Hail Mary, full of grace, the Lord is with thee . . .* Blessed and suffering Virgin, intercede for us all.

An engine whined on the highway. They both turned to see a gray sedan come down the road and park in front of the church. A wet bone face smiled. Clark turned back to the tombstones.

"Hello, Ted," Father Charlie called. "What a pleasure!"

A car door slammed. Footsteps hurried toward the cemetery. "Hi, Charlie. Did you watch the games on Sunday?"

"Giants won," Father Charlie said.

"Bears lost."

"You owe me a beer. Two, because the same thing will happen this week."

They laughed. My, Clark thought, how chummy. What was Lewell after with that? He wasn't the chummy type.

"Hello, Clark." A hand slapped Clark's back.

Clark winced as if he'd been attacked. He wanted to wrench the fence post out of the ground and smash Lewell over the head with it. "Hello, Mr. Lewell."

"I stopped by the historical society to talk with you, but what's-her-name said you were sick. I went to your house, but you weren't home. Somehow I knew you would be out here. What would you call that, telepathy? Is telepathy against the teachings of the church, Charlie?"

"What is prayer, if not telepathy?" Father Charlie asked.

Lewell slapped Clark again. Clark tested the fence post's resistance—it was in there pretty solid. "I was wondering if I could talk to you privately. Do you mind, Charlie?"

"Of course not. I'll be inside, working on my sermon." Father Charlie hustled away. Clark suspected that writing his sermon ought to take all of five minutes. How many different ways are there of saying *I don't know?*

Lewell squinted into the sun. With a jerk of his chin he pointed at the cemetery. "Which ones are they?"

"I think you probably know. I understand you've been out here a few times."

Lewell shrugged. "A few. I just wanted to get the conversation pointed at, how should we say, the meat of the argument." He laughed lightly. "I used to say that in northern Wisconsin, while I was writing that book about Ed Geen. Those hick cheeseheads never did catch the joke." He paused. "Geen was a cannibal, you know."

"I know."

"How about Maynard Tewle? What is he?"

Clark felt his color rise. "What the hell is that supposed to mean?"

"I'm introducing the next point of the conversation."

"You've got a hell of a way of introducing things. Do you insult everybody's friends, or am I a special case?"

"Sorry. People get uncomfortable around me—I guess they're afraid they're going to find themselves in one of my books—so I make light of discomfort right away." He shrugged. "What the hell, sometimes it works." He studied the graves. "You've known Maynard Tewle for a long time, haven't you?" He didn't wait for an answer. "What can you tell me about him?"

He's an old man. I owe his dead wife a promise. "Why should I tell you anything?"

"Would you rather I write in my book that you didn't? Wouldn't it sound like you're covering something up?"

"Covering up what? A priest confessed to the murder on his deathbed. Did you miss me telling you that at the historical society, or do you just hear what you want to hear?"

"How long have you known Maynard?"

So that's the son of a bitch's game—avoid questions. "Since I moved here after the war. I was a box boy at the hardware store. He used to come in for supplies."

"Did he have any problems that you can remember? Marital problems? Problems with his neighbors?"

"You're not very subtle, are you?"

"I don't have time to be. Did he?"

"No."

"I know he did."

"Then why did you ask?"

He shrugged. "What do you know about Arne Sauer?"

Clark studied him. It didn't make a damn bit of difference what he said. If Lewell was asking, he already knew the story. "He was a piss-poor farmer who tried planting flax. You don't plant flax around here."

"Yeah, I heard he lost his shirt on that one. Taxes came due, and he couldn't pay." He turned to the fields. "His farm was around here somewhere, wasn't it?"

"Why don't you tell me?"

"All right. He owned the eighty acres just south of the Tewle farm. Nice land, I hear, just not so good for flax. Maynard Tewle liked that land, didn't he?"

Clark hesitated. "Yes."

Lewell wiped his mouth, his fingers pulling the skin tight at its corners. "It must have really ticked Maynard off when Sauer sold the land to Wilson."

"Sauer had promised Maynard first crack at it. Of course it ticked him off. Wouldn't it tick you off?"

Lewell pursed his lips and nodded. "Sure it would. Almost enough to kill somebody."

"Almost, just like you said."

"Why didn't Sauer give Maynard first crack?"

Because one night Arne Sauer found Helen running across his field with blood running from her mouth and a big red handprint on her cheek. Because she had spent the night in his wife's care, and her sobbing had broken his heart. Because in those days you didn't interfere in family affairs, and all you could do to a wife beater was either beat him yourself, which Arne was too small and timid to do, or get him some other way. "I don't know. I imagine you do."

"Not yet." Lewell rested his forearms on the fence. "There are a lot

135

of angles I could take on it. There are a lot of angles I could take on your lack of cooperation, too. Does Tewle have something on you? Why are you covering for him?"

Anger tasting of bile rose in Clark's throat. "Because the truth is that Maynard and I killed Wilson together. What the hell, we were buddies, and you always help out a buddy, right?"

"Clark—"

"Our biggest problem was deciding who got to swing at Albert first. Maynard insisted I do it, and I insisted he did. We were polite in those days."

"Clark—"

"It's Mr. Holstrom to you, you scrubby little vulture. Did it ever occur to you that I'm being uncooperative because you're an asshole?"

"All right. Mr. Holstrom." Lewell put on a smile that Clark wanted to knock into the back of his throat. If only he were twenty years younger. "I apologize for any implications."

"You're a writer, aren't you?"

"You know that I am."

"Then you ought to understand people well enough to know that I don't give a damn about your implications. What I give a damn about is that your motives for writing this book have everything to do with money and nothing to do with the truth. You can hurt people that way."

"And covering for a killer *is* concern for the truth?"

"Callahan is dead."

"Why are you covering for Tewle?"

"Go to hell."

"I've done a little checking on Kenneth Callahan. Does it seem likely to you that Wilson's wife would have an affair with a homosexual priest?"

Clark stared at him. "What?"

"Kenneth Callahan liked it up the pooper. He was as gay as a daisy."

"How do you know that?"

"How well do you know Bert Finchley?"

"Well. I've known him forty some years."

"I bet you don't know him as well as I do." Lewell smiled at the tombstones. "Bert Finchley has a secret."

Clark didn't like the direction this conversation was heading. "What secret?"

"Come on, Clark. Don't you wonder why in all these years he's never married?"

"No, I don't. Some people are like that."

"I'll tell you what some people are like. Kenneth Callahan was fucking Bert, not Wilson's wife, and as he lay dying he knew that rumors about the two tag-team cocksuckers were beginning to fly."

"I don't remember any rumors."

"Maybe your memory is faulty."

"My memory's fine." Just selective.

"It would be bad in a town the size of Credibull for a newspaperman to be known as a cocksucker, wouldn't it? It's such a conservative community."

Clark couldn't deny that. He didn't answer.

"So Callahan made up a story about him being straight, taking the pressure off Bert. And everyone believed him. Dying men don't lie, right?"

"Speaking of making up stories, who gave you this one?"

"Bert."

"He wouldn't tell you something like that, even if it were true."

"It took a little prodding."

Clark studied the graves. Father Callahan's was in the front and off to the right. Christ. You can bury a lot more than bodies beneath a tombstone. Poor Bert. "I take it you're going to do the decent thing and leave that out of your book."

"I'll put in my book just what I have to."

"It'll finish Bert Finchley."

"Yeah, well, Bert Finchley's problems are Bert Finchley's problems."

"You bastard. You moneygrubbing bastard."

"Well, Clark, I am what I am, as Popeye would say." Lewell's infuriating smile wormed across his face. "I'm sorry, you prefer being called Mr. Holstrom, don't you?"

Clark watched Lewell amble back to his car, open the door, and turn back, standing with one foot on the frame. "This book will get published with or without you, Mr. Holstrom. The only thing up to you is how you'll be portrayed in it."

"Feel free to turn me into a monster. You're still a moneygrubbing bastard."

Lewell got into the car, leaving the door open. "You know, Clark, playing hooky from work is a habit you're going to find hard to break. You only get results with your nose against the grindstone."

He shut the door before Clark could answer, then drove back toward the Wilson farm. Clark thought about truth and lies and the line between them, about loyalty and promises.

Christ, he thought. I've drawn the line.

The *Credibull Weekly Herald*'s office was in a yellow brick building sharing an intersection with the police station, the hardware store, and the Farmers National Bank. Bert and his nephew, Tom, made up its staff. Tom's writing ability doomed each story to third-grade incomprehension, and Bert's Parkinson's disease did the same for the pictures. The paper survived because mediocrity is tolerable when it serves only mediocre needs. Tom was typing at his computer when Clark stuck his head in the door.

"Praise the Lord, Clark."

"Hey, Tommy." Tom was a fervent Pentecostal who spent a good part of his time whooping it up with God and the chosen in somebody's basement church. Anyone who thought they had all the answers always gave Clark the willies. "Is your uncle around?"

"He called in sick this morning. Bless God, he said something about a bad stomach."

"Bless God for a bad stomach?"

" 'All things work together for good to them that love God, to them who are the called according to his purpose.' " The quote did not interrupt his typing. "Romans eight, twenty-eight."

Clark wondered when the last conversation he'd had with Tom had been in which he hadn't had a Bible verse chucked into his face. The kid probably quoted scripture while making love to his wife. *Blessed are the meek,* perhaps, or something about persistence.

"Do you want me to take a message?" Tom asked.

"No thanks. I'll try catching him at home."

"Pray for him, all right?"

"Sure. I'll see you."

Bert lived a block north of Goodwin's Funeral Home in a slate gray house with white shuttered windows. Clark got out of the Dodge and studied the building. It didn't look like the home of a homosexual, if it *was* the home of a homosexual. It should be more feminine.

"Christ, Clark," he muttered as he started up the walk. "What do you know about homosexuals?"

Bert answered on the third knock. He was wearing a housecoat over striped pajamas. "Clark."

"You can't win the Pulitzer loafing around the house, buddy."

"Oh, I don't know. Maybe news will happen here."

"What does that mean?"

"It doesn't mean anything. It was something to say."

"I was wondering if I could take you to lunch."

Bert pulled open his housecoat to reveal more of his pajamas. A purple jelly stain ran along one side. "I'm not dressed for it."

"I'll wait until you change."

Bert's heavy eyes hid in a heavy face, no smile. "I'm not up to it, Clark. I'm really not."

"Ted Lewell told me this morning his theory about Kenneth Callahan."

"He told you about Kenny?"

"Yeah."

Bert nodded slowly. He sighed. "You want to split a tunafish sandwich? That is, if you're not worried about being seen coming in here."

"Rumors are just rumors, Bert."

Bert ran his fingers down his long jaw. "Yeah, well, maybe they aren't just rumors."

So it was true. Clark felt a sudden and intense discomfort—this kind of thing didn't happen in Credibull. Fairies are supposed to run off or be run off to do their dirty deeds in Minneapolis or San Francisco. A cocksucker, Lewell had called him. What the hell—it was true; the word, if not the tone. But, damn it, a nobler side of Clark tried to say, he's still Bert. "Not too much mayonnaise with the tuna, okay?"

Bert held the door open. "Come on in."

The air inside was the same gray as the siding. A television sat in one living room corner, framed copies of the *Herald* surrounded it on the walls. A picture of a couple Clark assumed to be Bert's parents hung beside Kenneth Callahan's obituary. It hanging there shouldn't have been surprising. But it was.

Clark followed Bert into a kitchen lighter than the living room, more alive. He accepted the chair Bert offered. Bert took a can of tuna out of a cupboard and an opener from a drawer.

"He got me," Bert said as the opener bit. "He got me cold."

"How did he find out?"

"Hell if I know—I'm just a small-town reporter, not some hotshot investigator. He came up to me on the street two days ago and spilled everything. Right there on the goddamned street, with people walking by! I thought I was dead where I stood."

"Hell, Bert." It was all that came out. "Damn it, I don't know what to say."

Bert stopped, the can half open. "I've been hiding this for fifty years. I don't know what to say, either." He turned the crank on the opener. A sharp click and the lid cocked and settled into the can. "What did he tell you?"

"That Kenneth Callahan wasn't having an affair with Wilson's wife, but with you. That he had confessed on his deathbed to murdering Wilson in order to protect you. That rumors had been flying." He paused. "I don't remember any rumors, Bert."

"You weren't listening for them. I was." He emptied the can into a bowl, then ladled in some mayonnaise and stirred it. He paused with the fork trembling in his hand. "I'm a flaming fairy, Clark. Always have been. There, I said it. What do you think of that?"

Clark didn't answer. He felt only uncomfortable, as if he'd opened a door and seen something shameful. Cocksuckers. Christ. Words he didn't know stuck in his throat.

"All right," Bert said. "I understand." He tossed a loaf of bread on the table, then sat beside it. "I'm not evil, Clark."

"Hell, Bert. I know that."

"Kenny wasn't, either."

"He couldn't have been, to do what he did for you."

"He died so fast. I wonder if it wasn't some early form of AIDS. I wonder why I didn't die, too."

Clark felt uncomfortable, damned uncomfortable, but he couldn't turn away from that long, sad face, those photographer's eyes. "You were meant to go on, Bert." Christ, he sounded like Tommy. All things work for the good. But first you have to be chosen.

"I loved him." Bert stopped in the middle of spreading the tuna to shake his head. "It would make a hell of a news story. Front page. What do you suppose Tommy would think of it?"

"Not much, I expect." Forgiveness was limited to the chosen, too.

Bert shrugged. "But Lewell scooped him. Kenny and I will be front page in a book. Maybe on a movie screen." He handed the sandwich to Clark. "You want something to drink?"

"Just water. It's nobody's business, Bert."

Bert filled a glass from the tap. "Tell that to the book writer."

The water had a funny taste, like well water, like tears. Bert sat as if collapsing. He pushed his sandwich away and wiped his long face with long fingers. "What the hell, it'll be popular. People like to have their entertainment, and prissy boys make good entertainment."

"Don't call yourself that."

"It's true. Ask Elmer when he finds out."

141

"It isn't true."

"By this town's definition, it is." His fingers rested on lips. Bushy eyebrows tumbled over his eyes. "Credibull will ride me out of town on a rail."

"You're overreacting."

"Then they won't, but they'll think about it. They'll tell their little jokes over coffee, smile their little smiles from store windows as I walk down the street. Ever notice how fairies walk? They're loose in the ass."

"Come on, Bert. In this day and age—"

"Clark, we're not from this day and age." Bert's eyes flashed. "The people who know me here I've known for fifty years, and that is not this day and age." The anger left; despair creaked in his voice. "I couldn't stand to lose their respect, Clark. They're all I have. It would kill me."

"You'll have to wait and see what happens."

"I know what I'll be waiting for. I know what I'll see." He sighed hard through his nose. "Maybe I ought to blow Lewell's head off, though bashing it in with a hammer in this case would be more appropriate." He smiled without humor. "You wouldn't mind doing me that favor, would you?"

Clark couldn't return the smile. "You've got the wrong man for that, Bert."

"I suppose." He studied his sandwich. "You want another one?"

"No." Clark had eaten only half of his. "Something doesn't make sense, Bert. Why did Father Callahan masturbate in front of Mary's statue?"

"Hell, Clark, think about it. That rumor didn't start until after he died. You know why?"

"No."

A flush started in Bert's cheeks and spread. "Because it's easier to believe a guy is a murderer if you can also believe he's a nut. That's why."

"Hell, Bert, don't get mad."

"I'm beyond mad, Clark. I'm well into sorry." He wiped his eyes. "This goddamned town." His heavy gaze pushed Clark against his chair. Clark knew he should say something, but didn't know what.

When the silence became unbearable, Bert did him the favor of turning away. "Finish your sandwich," Bert said.

The tuna had settled queerly by the time Clark drove home. He left Bert standing in his housecoat to close the door on a world grown cold. Clark was sitting in the basement contemplating Bert and the model and that damned Ted Lewell when the phone on the workbench rang.

"Hi, Clark. This is Barb Mischke."

"Hi, Barb." Is Maynard gone now, too? How could he be—he was driving his pickup across the model, moving a load of Holstrom belongings from the apartment to the house on St. Anne's Road. Helen was sitting beside him. "How are you?"

It took her too long to answer. Oh, Christ. "Could I buy you lunch?"

Clark gratefully wiped the crumbs from his lips. You don't offer to buy lunch for someone, then give them news that will ruin their appetite. "I just finished a sandwich."

"How about coffee?"

"What's the matter, Barb?" No one but Maynard ever wanted just coffee.

"Well . . ." Her sigh sounded like static. "It's Dad. Can we talk over coffee? I'll take you to the Bumblebee."

"Not the Bumblebee. How about the Burger King?"

"I thought you liked the Bumblebee."

"The Burger King is cheaper."

"I'll pick you up."

The Burger King was as crowded as always. In the playroom, knee-high children played with a flood of plastic balls, their voices drifting among the smells of grease and tortured meat. It used to be that kids sat in their chairs and ate their meals. It used to be that they didn't run and scream in a room full of giant plastic hamburgers. But it used to be that you could buy a meal worth sitting down for.

"How's the coffee?" Barb asked.

Pig sweat. "All right. Yours?"

She shrugged. "You look awful."

"I've had a hell of a morning. Why did you call?"

She sighed like a deflating tire, collapsing visibly. "Have you noticed how Dad's been acting since the funeral?"

"Shocked."

"It's more than shocked."

"He'll get over it. Give him time."

"He's not getting over it. I'm afraid to give him time." She sipped her coffee and looked out at a Wal-Mart world. Her makeup had settled like dust. "Something is wrong when you're afraid to bring your father over to the house for Thanksgiving dinner. He's been so angry with me."

"About what?"

"About me not arriving three minutes before I said I would. About me not calling when I promised, about me calling when I did. Sometimes he doesn't even know who I am. I swear, Clark, I don't know what to do with him."

Clark winced at his coffee and set his cup down. "Your father has spent his entire life with someone cooking his meals, washing his clothes, and making him laugh when he needed to. After almost eighty years, anyone would need time to adjust to living alone. I think he's doing pretty well."

She sighed. "Yeah, well, maybe."

A child wailed in the playroom. Another child was beating his head with a yellow ball. A heavyset woman shouted once at them before returning to her burger. They stopped only long enough to trade places.

"Maynard has always been a strong man," Clark said. Not like Bert. Hell. That damned Lewell. "He'll be all right."

"I'm not so sure. Would you like to see how he acts?"

"I know how he acts. I see him almost every day."

She wiped her mouth with a napkin, then stood. "Come on."

"Where are we going?"

"To Mom and Dad's . . . to Dad's house. You haven't seen how he acts with me."

144

Barb drove a minivan. Clark savored the weak warmth the sun cast through the windshield. She turned onto Josef Meyer Boulevard and parked in front of her father's house. As Clark opened the door she grabbed his shoulder. "Wait here. I don't want him to see you."

She moved heavily up the walk, heavy hips, heavy steps, her hands swinging like wrecking balls. Just as she reached the steps, a Maynard Clark had never seen before stuck his head out of the front door. This Maynard was a twisted knot, a snarl, an animal that had been beaten too many times.

"What the hell do you want?"

"Hi, Dad."

"Hi, Dad—you always *Hi, Dad* me. And then you come in and steal everything I own."

"I haven't stolen anything, Dad. I just want to see how you are."

"How the hell do you expect me to be? My own goddamned kid is robbing me blind."

Clark flinched at his words. He wondered if what he was seeing had always been there, hidden in closets, behind smiles, shown only to family. A bloody image flashed through his mind of Helen stumbling across an alfalfa field. A bloody and silent Albert Wilson lay beside a workbench. Clark rubbed his fingers over the whiskers sprouting along his jawline.

He doesn't hit me, Helen had said, *he just shakes me a little.*

"You're a bitch of a daughter," Maynard said. "You always have been."

Barb was looking more and more like a frightened child. "Dad . . ."

"A fat, greedy bitch. How your poor bastard of a husband can stand to fuck you is beyond me. Where do those little brats of yours come from? What do you do, use artificial insemination?"

Barb was six again, with tears streaming down her cheeks. "I'm trying, Dad," she whimpered. "I'm trying to do what's right."

"You're a fat, greedy bitch. There's only one way to deal with fat, greedy bitches." He raised his hand and clenched it.

Enough, Clark thought, enough. He opened the door. "Hold on now, Maynard. You don't really want to do that, do you?"

Maynard's glasses flashed in the sun; his voice wheezed angrily. "Who the hell are you?"

"You know who I am."

"Clark? Christ in a hand bucket, you've gotten old!"

"So have you, Maynard. You don't really want to hit your daughter, do you?"

"She's trying to steal from me!"

"All that she's trying to do is ask you to Thanksgiving dinner."

Maynard didn't lower his hand. "Is it Thanksgiving?"

"This week, Dad," Barb said.

His voice hardened again. "It's just an excuse, Clark. She'll get me out of the house so she can come in and take everything I own. Her and that goddamned burglar work as a team. Helen and I see them staring in the windows at night." His fist was still balled. "Why can't you do the decent thing and wait until we die?"

"Do you know what I think, Maynard?" Clark asked. "I think that if you hit her, she'll beat the hell out of you."

Maynard's eyes did not leave Barb's face. They narrowed. "You know, you might be right." He lowered his fist. "You saw it, Clark, you saw it all. She tried to provoke me. You see what she is now."

Barb's shoulders shook. "Why are you like this, Dad? What have I done?"

"It's not only what you've done, it's what you're thinking about doing." He smiled at Clark. "Do you want to come in for a beer?"

"What about your daughter?"

"To hell with my daughter."

Poor kid. "If she goes, I go. She's my ride."

"You trust her more than I do." Maynard scowled. "Well, to hell with both of you, then." He shut the door with a slam that rattled the windows.

"I try," Barb said when she was in the van again, gripping the steering wheel, her knuckles white and shaking. "I try and I try and I try, but you see how he is. What am I supposed to do?"

"I don't know. I've never seen him like this."

"The way he is now reminds me of when . . . I'll tell you something, Clark. You might have been right. If he had hit me, I would have beaten the hell out of him. I saw enough of that when I was a kid."

"I know."

Her eyes were still wet. "So what am I supposed to do?"

"Put up with it?" He was painfully aware of how bad that advice was. Age doesn't bring wisdom. We all stumble around.

She laughed harshly. "Put up with it. That's what they always say, isn't it? Be a good girl and put up with it." A blink forced more tears from her eyes. "Sometimes he can still be like he was before Mom died. I just hate going through hell waiting for those times to come."

"I'll watch him," Clark said. "He's still nice to me."

"He just told you to go to hell."

"He's nice to me most of the time."

She wiped her cheeks. "Thank you." She started the engine, shivered, and turned on the heater. "Do you still think this is just a phase he's going through?"

Clark didn't answer. The van warmed as she pulled into the street. When she drove by the store, Walter's computer monitors watched them. Walter wasn't in sight.

The bank's shadow fell across Clark's face as she accelerated toward the elevator. "A hell of a day," he said.

"A day of hell," she answered.

Chapter

8

Barb phoned Clark on Wednesday to say that Maynard had asked her why she hadn't invited him to Thanksgiving dinner. He hadn't remembered Monday afternoon.

"Maybe it really is just a phase." She had invited her father to dinner.

The past whirled on Thanksgiving morning as Clark climbed the stairs beside Sheri's Craft Nook to the apartments above. How many times had he climbed these stairs, back in the days of hauling hardware, dirty diapers, and Nora's black-and-white, Lucille-Ball-and-Milton-Berle-dominated world? Life had been a struggle between that world and the green and blue and yellow world of sweat and life and an absence of laugh tracks. Love in the day and lust in the night and a simple, deep breath of cool, autumn air. Who would have thought that the black-and-white world would win?

The stairs creaked beneath his feet—the same stairs as then; it looked to be the same carpeting. Their creaking weaved like a thread through the blare of televisions and children, of muffled voices hidden behind scarred wooden doors. How it all comes back.

He had to force himself not to turn toward his old apartment—old habits were harder to break than steel, were still shiny after all these years. He crept toward Walter's apartment, afraid to stir up this fleck of the world that he had abandoned so long ago. Tinny, manic cheering blasted through Walter's door. A sick feeling caught in Clark's throat. He did not want to be here, did not want to see Walter here. He could go home and call back and say he wasn't feeling well. Walter would believe him because men Clark's age are always sick, and men Clark's age are not supposed to lie—the taste of eternity is too strong on their lips. He thought of old lies about adultery and drinking and other things. It was funny how it takes so many years before the truth becomes an advantage.

The door opened before he could leave. Walter stood in the threshold, greasy, heavy, bald head gleaming, shirt untucked but at least clean, pockmarked face spotted with shadows as if he had peppered himself. His eyes buzzed to his father's face, then down the hall. "I thought I heard someone coming up the stairs. What are you doing standing out here?"

"Just thinking about how this used to be."

"Used to be a hell of a lot newer, I'll bet."

"Not really. About the same."

"Come on in."

Clark stopped just inside the door. An odor hung in the air as crisp as dirty underwear. It was a place lived in too long without a window open, and with winter coming on, but at least today the living room was picked up. A sprucing for the holidays.

Walter lumbered through the blare of television football into the kitchen and stirred something on the stove. He stood with his hips thrust forward, his shoulders slouched over them like a question mark. "Don't expect much. I don't do this often."

"That's fine." Clark stood uncomfortably. Why did he feel like a stranger in the home of his son?

"You'll never guess who I heard from," Walter said.

"Who?"

"Amber Goltz. Remember her?"

"Yeah. Jenny's friend." Women like that travel in packs. "How in the world did you get in touch with her?"

Walter laughed. "She called me—she said she figured I'd be in Credibull. She's just divorced and living in St. Paul."

"What's she doing?"

"Nothing that I know of." He grinned into his pan. "I think she has the hots for me." Christ. That's just what you need, another bitch and more abuse. "The last I heard from her, I was working at that bookstore on Snelling."

"I remember."

"I asked about Jenny."

Hell. "Oh?"

"She's living with some guy in San Jose. A loser, Amber said. Some kind of an addict." Walter slouched more, and the smile disappeared. If God had an ounce of decency, he'd make forgetting easier. "She should have hung around, Dad. She would have seen. Things are picking up."

"Some women are like that." He wasn't sure how much or what he should say. "Some women just . . . they just have to roam around. Don't get started on it, Walter."

"I can't help it." His eyes were wet, as if from the steam rising from the pan. "Jesus, Dad, once you're married, it's so damned hard to not be married anymore. I just wanted it to go on, like you and Mom."

No, Clark thought, not like me and your mom. He didn't say anything.

Walter wiped his eyes and smiled. "Why don't you sit down? You look like an oaf standing there."

"All right." Clark crossed the room and turned down the television.

"Leave that up, Dad. I can't hear it in here."

"Who's playing?"

"The Bears and the Lions. It's just about to start. Should be a hell of a game."

"Sure." God, what a stupid sport. Spoiled, oversized babies popping steroids like jujubes and trying to kill each other. Give them guns and get the damned game over with.

Strange, queasy smells wafted from the kitchen. "Dinner's ready," Walter said. "Why don't you get the TV trays out, then come load up your plate?"

"The trays are in the closet, right?"

"You betcha."

Clark stripped off his coat, laid it over the sofa, and went in search of the trays. It took him three tries to set the first one up—thinking of the strain his poor back would suffer as he struggled to reach his plate from the sofa distracted him. The game began; Clark went into the kitchen just as the crowd began its kickoff roar. Who the hell spends their Thanksgivings at football games? Damned fools.

Walter stood with his hands on his hips, smiling down at the stove. "Turkey with all the trimmings. Stuffing, potatoes, and cranberry sauce. I hope you don't mind turkey roll—I don't trust my cooking enough to roast a whole bird."

"It'll be fine." The turkey roll wallowed in a tinfoil pan, pooled in grease, struggling against the twine that defined it. Instant potatoes, boxed stuffing, and canned cranberry sauce. Clark hated cranberries. "Looks good."

"The pop is in the fridge."

Clark filled his plate only out of respect for the holiday. He cracked open a cheap, supermarket brand of cola as he lowered himself onto the sofa. A stink rose from the can like the smell that blew across Crystal Lake, like the smell of the apartment. He pushed it to the far corner of his tray. His fork caught on the gristle spiraling through the turkey. He pushed his slice over next to the can.

Walter pointed at the screen with his fork. "Look at the arms on that big fucker with number ninety-three on his back," he said around a mouthful of potatoes. "He'd rip his mother's head off if she were carrying a football."

"Sounds like a nice guy."

"You can't play defensive end and be a nice guy." Walter slurped a beer. His eyes never left the screen. It had a gaze he could hold.

It used to be we'd go out to Benny's farm for Thanksgiving dinner, Clark remembered; it used to be we'd sit down to a twenty-four-pound turkey with real trimmings and a glass of red wine. We'd talk about the farm and listen to one of the kids bungle a knock-knock joke. We'd sit around and fart in the living room while the women did dishes, Benny in the corner with his cheek against his guitar, twanging feebly on its strings. We'd go outside and play horseshoes, or cards around the kitchen table in cold weather. Clark looked around the apartment. No horseshoes here.

"God damn!" Walter shouted over the suddenly wild crowd. "That poor son of a bitch! Got his clock cleaned! That's what you get for playing quarterback, you dumb fucker!"

Clark turned to the screen. Big number ninety-three was dancing a weird dance over his crumpled victim. Clark tried to get his eyes to wander around the room, but there wasn't much to wander to. A couple of photographs, one of Jenny lounging in a stringy red bikini beside a pool, peeking through the frazzled hair blowing over her eyes, her legs spread, her chest thrust out to the camera. A black-and-white photo of Clark in baggy pants and Nora in a flower print dress standing in front of the store, taken on the day they'd bought the place. He saw big smiles on those long-ago, alien faces, big dreams in those long-ago, alien eyes. Nora's face still held something—it wasn't just wrinkled leather on linen. He saw a young couple still in as close to love as they had or would ever be.

Walter cheered something guttural, an attempt to shout two different snatches of profanity at once. Turkey grease ran in a shiny line from the corner of his mouth; his bulging belly threatened to overturn the TV stand. All those dreams had boiled down to a failing store and an overweight son sitting in a dumpy apartment watching a football game. Clark felt a sudden and heavy sadness.

Beside Jenny's picture, Walter had tacked a white ribbon he had won in the second grade. Clark shook his head. Christ. What kind of a man displays a childhood ribbon?

The kid jogs toward Clark and Nora, his chubby cheeks flushed, his eyes wide and happy. "Did you see it?" he asks. "Did you see what I done?"

In the fifty-yard dash, the boy has placed fifth in a field of ten. "You did great, Wally." Clark is relieved he did not finish last.

"I got a ribbon and everything!"

"We saw." Nora squats to give the boy a hug. The fabric stretches audibly over her hips. "We're so proud of you."

"And this ain't nothing," the kid says.

"Isn't nothing," his mother corrects.

"And this ain't nothing. I'm going to run and run and run, and next time I'll win it. And then I'll run and run and run, and pretty soon I'll be just like Jesse Owens. You watch and see!"

Clark tousles the boy's wiry hair. In his mind he sees a sleek young man with arms outstretched, mouth open and gasping, a victory tape stretched across his chest. He smiles inwardly as he remembers his own desire, long forgotten, to run like Jesse Owens. The things we believe.

Walter did not run and run and run. He never won another ribbon; he never ran like Jesse Owens. A week after the track meet he wanted to be a cowboy, then a fireman, a singer, a clown, an architect. After high school he said he wanted to just *be*, like the rest of those drug-intoxicated spooks from the sixties. After the war he tried to be the new Hemingway, to write of this most recent lost generation, and failed. He tried being an environmental activist and failed. He tried a dozen different things. If he had not failed at them all, he certainly had not succeeded at any of them, either.

For a couple of years he worked at a socialist bookstore in St. Paul, then quit when Ronald Reagan made liberalism unfashionable. He cut his hair, began spouting the merits of Milton Friedman, Robert Mundell, and supply-side economics, and waited like a beggar for the wealth to trickle down into his empty golden bucket. Without a college degree he couldn't get a job in the jet-set world of fucking the poor, so he worked as a stock boy at a discount store on the north side of Minneapolis. He chased Jenny, succeeded somehow in marrying her, then failed in the marriage after coming home to run the store when Clark retired. It's funny how people spend all their time searching for themselves and none of their time finding. We chase static.

"Touchdown!" Walter's arms shot into the air as the crowd roared its frenzy. "Touchdown! Take that, you fuckers! Yes! Oh, yes!" He pushed his tray away and danced in his chair like a crippled St. Vitus. A beer commercial rolled onto the screen as the football players prepared to do it to each other again. Walter wiped the sweat of vicarious exultation from his face. "I'm going to take a piss, Dad. Holler if I'm not back before the kickoff. What a goddamn game!"

"Sure, son. All right."

Walter jiggled off to the bathroom and shut the door. Urine rumbled against porcelain. On the screen, young models flaunted themselves and extolled the virtues of imbibing. Clark pushed his tray away, then leaned forward and rubbed his face with his hands. No beer bellies on that screen; no bald heads. Tanned, beautiful faces and happy, beautiful smiles. They knew who they wanted to be.

"Walter," he whispered. "Walter."

His heel kicked something protruding from beneath the sofa. He reached down, felt a corner of a magazine, and pulled it out. The back cover advertised rum; he flipped the magazine over to reveal a fat teenaged girl with huge breasts and bleached blond hair, small hands covering what had to be enormous nipples. Legs spread; a black leather strap between them. *Gash Magazine,* the masthead read, *for Cunt Connoisseurs.* Christ, Walter, where did you find this?

The sound of Walter's urination still filtered through the door. Clark tried to open the magazine, but found the pages stuck together. A nausea spread from his stomach into his throat. Yee-hah. Walter was bringing his work home.

Christ, Clark thought, he probably lay right here on this sofa with the magazine balanced against his thighs. Christ. What kind of life was this for a son of his? You dream of Jesse Owens and you get a thin, white ribbon tacked to a wall, you get a bald guy alone in a dirty apartment yanking on his crank, you get a cunt connoisseur. Perhaps God was Don Juan, seducing us with fantasies and leaving us sore and destitute in the morning. To hell with that. To hell with it. We don't need to feel like whores.

The bathroom door clicked, hinges sighed. Clark shoved the magazine beneath the sofa. He hid from his face what he felt in his soul.

"Have they kicked off yet?" Walter asked.

Clark looked at the screen. Another beer commercial was playing—two young men in expensive suits drank their elixirs and bragged about their children. "Not yet." What we want is what they will advertise—the commercial was a classic example of supply and demand. Little supply and intense demand. If God was not Don Juan, then perhaps he was a tycoon, cornering the market to keep up the price of his wares.

"Hell of a game, isn't it?" Walter sat.

"Hell of a game, Walter." Clark watched his son's eyes devour the screen, the same look he probably had while he paged through *Gash.* Cunt connoisseur. "You know, son, you shouldn't be up here all alone."

Walter drained his beer, then went into the kitchen. "I'm not all alone," he called from the refrigerator. He came back in time for the kickoff with another beer in his hand. "You're here."

"That's not what I mean."

"I know what you mean. If I can't be with Jenny, I don't want to be with anyone."

Clark sighed. "That didn't go well, son."

156

"It went all right." Walter ran his hand over his scalp. You build walls around what you don't want to remember. You cultivate selective memory. "But she's gone now, and I like being single. There's a lot of women out there, Dad. I like playing the field."

Clark searched for the magazine with his heel and found it. He still felt sick. "Still—"

"Do you mind if we get back to the game? It's about to start." Walter turned to the television. In that instant he reminded Clark too much of Nora.

"Walter—"

"Please, Dad. I want to watch the game."

Clark sat silently on the sofa. He watched the television and his son. Thanksgiving is too much of an irony.

Clark walked over to check on both Maynard and Bert Finchley late in the afternoon—both were about the same as they had been the last time he'd seen them. He spent Thanksgiving evening painting spots on a plastic dog. His fingers trembled; the spots jumped into zigzags. My son, he couldn't stop thinking, living like that, my son.

He set down his brush to wipe his eyes. He followed the reflection of the overhead light off the glass surface of the lake to the bright spot it made on the wall. A point to be measured.

Something inside him shouted what he did not want to hear. *Credibull, 1989* was as much an investment in lonely fantasy as Walter's magazines, as a two-bit tool-and-die calendar hanging beside a computer. Clark set the dog down and stared at the model. Like father, like son, he thought. Like son, like father.

As he stood, anger brightened the edges of his vision. He held in his old, feeble hands a life as wasted as Walter's, and he was too old to do a damned thing about it. "To hell with this." Something hot and wild pushed his voice from his throat. "To hell with this all. To hell with this all!"

His hands gripped the edge of the plywood. Rage bubbled in his mind and spun his sight around. When he could think again, he heard a crash and saw the model rebound off the wall to the floor, knocking over one of the sawhorses. No flame, no screams, only whimpers. A crunch of bone and metal.

Tiny people struggled over the ruined streets. The old life, the lonely fantasy still beckoned. To hell with it, he thought. To hell with a life ending in frustration's sunset. To hell with a life filled with too much god-be-damned surrender. I am an artisan of waste who has passed his skills on to his son, but what right does God have to keep us from redressing our failures? What right? What right?

When he calmed, he was straddling the highway's remains. Downtown Credibull lay shattered; the elevator had again exploded. He'd crushed the bank; both funeral homes were damaged. Crystal Lake's cracked surface flashed his face in a split and grotesque image. What memories had survived scuttled out of sight like cockroaches.

His rage died slowly—he had not allowed himself to get that angry in years. He wanted to both laugh in triumph and cry in despair. His fists had been clenched so tightly his fingernails had broken skin.

Credibull, a life, 1,273 lives, lay scattered around his feet in bits of balsa and plastic.

Can't fix this, he thought. He laughed softly and covered his face. What am I supposed to do with my time now?

Strange dreams fluttered against Clark's sleeping eyes. Billie Jessup was wearing black leather panties and serving him coffee the color of lead; a dead Helen mourned her living husband; Nora rose from her pillow to join her. He was a tiny man walking through a devastated world when a telephone ring awoke him.

He fumbled with the receiver. A dead animal smell from his dream haunted him. Can you smell in dreams? "Hello?"

"Clark?"

"Yes?"

"Clark, you got to come over here."

It was Maynard. Clark propped himself on his elbow. The sudden ache in his shoulder made him roll onto his back. "What?"

"Christ in a hand bucket, Clark, they've surrounded me!"

"Who's surrounded you?"

"Barb and her burglar ring. They're trying to break into my house!"

Clark rubbed his eyes. What the hell was this? The pressure of his fingers made brief and brilliant flashes, like the dreams. "Did you call the police?"

"They're a part of it."

Damn you, Maynard, you wake me up in the middle of the night for this? "You're talking crazy."

"I called Jergen. He said he'd check it out. When I called back, he said he didn't find anything."

"Then maybe he didn't find anything."

"He never drove by, Clark."

"Maynard, I really don't think—"

"Christ in a goddamned hand bucket! I can see their goddamned faces in the goddamned windows!"

Clark sighed. "Do you want me to call Barb?"

"What difference would that make? She's out there with them."

"Do you have any idea what time it is?"

"It's two-thirty. Come over."

Clark sighed. "I'm going back to sleep, Maynard. I suggest that you do the same."

"They'll rob me blind. They'll kill me in my bed."

"Good night, Maynard."

"But Clark—"

"Good night."

Clark managed to close his eyes before the phone rang again. "Clark, come over. They're all over the goddamned house!"

"What am I supposed to do about it?"

"Drive up. If they see a car, they'll leave."

"Just drive up and drive away again?"

"Drive up and stay."

"Maynard, I'm tired."

"So am I. See you in a few minutes." The line clicked.

Clark quietly cursed in the darkness. Well, he thought as he climbed out of bed, the only way to handle this was to handle this. He thought of Barb and a burglar ring, then grunted. A bird brushing the window, maybe, or a branch scratching a pane. Imaginations can hide so much more than darkness can, especially an imagination like Maynard's. He wasn't getting better.

Clark struggled into his coat at the front closet. Old people heal slowly, and maybe this was still only a case of time—after all, Clark's shoulder still hurt. It was funny how things take so much more time when you have so little of it left. Perhaps God was a game show host with his finger itchy on the buzzer. Too bad, time's up. Sorry, no consolation prizes. Thank you for playing the game.

The late-November early-morning air was shockingly cold; the ground sucked greedily at the warmth in his feet. For half a second Clark saw Nora lying in a bank and that garbage can skittered into the driveway. Don't slip, he reminded, he pleaded with, himself. Please. Don't slip.

As he listened to the Dodge's baleful *chuh-chuh-chuh*, he realized that the one driving force that had gotten him this far from his bed was the hidden knowledge that a cantankerous automobile would within minutes put him back in it again. He made the mistake of giving the key one more turn—the engine turned over and sadistically sputtered to life. Well, that's what you get for giving second chances.

He backed onto the snow-packed road, silver in the streetlight glare, and accelerated slowly toward the alley. The air was clean and cold, the stars were fireflies dancing a foot in front of the windshield. The exquisite beauty of a northern night—he could almost convince himself that seeing this was worth getting up for.

The houses, the alley, the church, and the funeral parlor huddled into themselves. The Tewle windows were dark. Maybe the game was over, maybe Maynard had gone to bed. Clark toyed with the idea of going to bed himself, but he'd come too far and it was too cold to have done all this for nothing.

He saw no movement outside of the house—hell, as if he had expected any. The front door was open. He stared through the screen. "Maynard?"

He saw no movement, but heard a sharp click as cold as the night, a click like an ice pick driven into his chest. Maynard's shotgun hammer. "If you fucking move," Maynard said, "I'll blow your goddamned head off."

Clark's throat went dry. Old fear climbed out of an old and hidden lair. Water and sand, red and salty. "Maynard, it's Clark."

A faint silver line ran from a shadow crouching on the other side of the door toward Clark's chest. "You goddamned thieves. You think I'm going to just let you in here?"

"It's Clark, Maynard." Cold fear, rosy red, dripped into the pit of his stomach. I am not ready to die. I am only seventy-two. "Please."

"I'll kill you. Damned if I won't."

A brief flash of Albert Wilson lying on the toolshed floor, and Clark was looking at the rifle barrel again. "Maynard, you just called me. Don't you know who I am?"

Time took a breath. "Clark?"

"Of course it's Clark." The silver line lowered. Clark felt a little stronger, the coldness crawling out of his lungs and over his skin. He had come too close to finally understanding God. "At this time of the morning, who else would it be ?"

A hand beckoned Clark, grabbed his sleeve when he opened the screen, and yanked him inside. "They're out there, Clark. You must have seen them."

"I didn't see anyone, Maynard."

"Get down." The hand forced Clark into a crouch—his knees screamed. He could see Maynard's eyes in the streetlight, the loose, cratered skin at his throat silver like the moon. Maynard jerked his head toward an open or broken side window. "There was one over there just a minute ago."

"Have you been shooting out your windows?"

"I broke it with the stock. I don't want to shoot at reflections."

"How long have you been doing this?"

"Since sundown. They only come after sundown."

Clark shivered. Christ, if a salesman had come to the door, or a neighbor delivering leftover turkey, they'd be lying dead on the steps. A Girl Scout selling cookies. Clark himself, if he had come unexpectedly. Christ.

"Why don't you give me the gun, Maynard?"

Maynard's fingers slipped up and down the barrel, then tightened just above the chamber. "Why?"

"I can shoot them, too. You're a little jumpy. You don't want to put a hole in the living room ceiling, do you?" He hated himself for saying what he knew he had to. "What would Helen say?"

"Helen is dead." Maynard's thumb traced the hammer. His eyes narrowed to black slits. "You're one of them burglars, aren't you?" The barrel shifted to point over Clark's shoulder. Clark had seen that very same barrel drop a pheasant as quickly as a flick of an eye, as casually as a glance. "You came in here to take my gun away, and then the others will follow. Christ in a hand bucket, Clark, I never thought you would turn on me, too."

Clark couldn't stop looking at Maynard's eyes. Drop that barrel an inch and Clark would be a pheasant pinwheeling above a cornfield, his life spinning away in crazy circles. His only chance was to duck under the muzzle, push it up and away, and wrestle it free from Maynard's grip. He swallowed. Who the hell are you kidding? A geriatric Dirty Harry.

"Maynard, we've been friends for almost fifty years. I wouldn't turn on you."

The barrel dropped an inch. "The hell. Helen told me about how you tried to fuck her in the kitchen."

Oh, Christ. To be killed for a forty-year-old seduction. "Maynard—"

"I should blow your head off. I should beat you to death, like Albert Wilson."

162

"Maynard, I was different then."

"The hell."

"You were, too."

Maynard paused. His eyes widened to reveal a light beginning to flicker. "Yeah," he said. "Yeah, I guess I was." The barrel dropped to point absently at Clark's genitals.

"I'd never turn on you, Maynard."

"No," Maynard said, "I guess you wouldn't."

Clark's hand snaked out to close over the barrel's freezing touch. Easy now. Easy. "We'll watch for these burglars together. Let's set this to the side until we need it."

Maynard's hands were two limp rags. He stared at the sofa. "Yeah. Sure."

Clark took the gun, opened the chamber, and removed the shell. It sat like a toad in his palm, its red casing glowing dully in the streetlight. Thank Jesus or Allah or whichever divinity happened to be on duty. "Do you want some coffee?"

"Sure."

Clark set the gun outside the back door, then tossed the shell into the cabinet beneath the kitchen sink. He turned on the light and waited for his eyes to adjust to its stabbing brilliance. An open peanut butter jar sat on the counter, and a stack of dishes tottered in the sink. Garbage littered the floor; only the HOME IS WHERE THE HEART IS needlework was as it was supposed to be. He filled the coffeepot and set it on the stove to percolate. When he went back into the living room, Maynard was slouched on the sofa. The end table light was on. Glass shards sparkled on the floor.

"I miss her, Clark."

"I know."

"I miss her so much that sometimes I think that just the missing will kill me. It wouldn't take the heart, it wouldn't take old age, it wouldn't take anything else. Just the missing."

"I know, buddy." Clark sat beside him.

"I miss her so much I get crazy sometimes."

"Everybody gets crazy sometimes."

"What scares me the most is that sometimes I think I'll go crazy permanent. And what scares me the most about that is then I'll quit missing her."

"No you wouldn't."

"I would. Some things I know." His body collapsed on itself like Nora's. His skin was too loose. "I wouldn't have done it, you know. I wouldn't have shot you. I mean about you and Helen in the kitchen."

"I know, Maynard. When did she tell you?"

"Must have been in the mid-sixties, after I calmed down." He rubbed his chin. "If she had gone upstairs with you, would you really have done it?"

So, she hadn't told him. "I don't know, Maynard. I did a lot of stupid things back then."

"You and me both." He shook his head sadly. "Forty years is a long time."

"Doesn't seem long, sometimes."

"No," Maynard said, "it doesn't."

Clark stuffed an old quilt into the broken window. He poured two cups of coffee, then refilled them fifteen minutes later. He knew he'd be with Maynard the rest of the night. That was fine—he wouldn't be able to sleep after what had just happened, anyway. Fear is caffeine.

The sky in the east cast a half-light into the kitchen. Maynard was asleep on the sofa—Clark had stretched him out on it with a pillow and blanket. He sipped coffee as he leaned on the counter and numbly watched the morning grow.

"We have a problem." Clark had called Barbara from the historical society. The back of his neck ached with a tension like spikes driven into the muscles.

"Oh?" In the background, two young, belligerent voices rose above a backdrop of Bugs Bunny music. "What problem?"

"Your dad."

"I've been meaning to call you about him. Could you get him out of the house for a few hours? I need to clean the place up, and I can't do it while putting up with his tirades."

"You need to get him to a doctor. I spent all last night with him."

Apprehension rasped in her voice. "What happened? Is he all right?"

"He spent a good part of the night crouched by the front door with his shotgun. When I showed up he thought I was a burglar. He almost blew my head off."

"Oh, God." The space of her pause filled with more Bugs Bunny music: violins and xylophones climbing maniacally over scales. "What's wrong with him, Clark? It goes beyond Mom dying."

"That's why you need to take him to the doctor."

She laughed harshly. "Can you see him sitting with me in my van? I can't."

"Maybe Brian can take him."

"He's getting as bad with Brian as he's been with me."

"You set up the appointment, and I'll take him."

She paused. "It was bad, huh?"

"Yeah."

She sighed. "All right. Are you at the historical society?"

"Yes."

"I'll make an appointment and call you back."

"All right."

It took a week to get Maynard into Dr. Donaldson's office. Dr. Donaldson had abandoned Credibull for a position at the Mankato clinic—his idealistic, country-doctor dreams had worn themselves dull on farm accidents, unwanted veterinary work, and twenty-four-hour call. His warm personality clashed with his hands—Clark wondered every time he shook one how his wife reacted when he touched her. He should have been a mortician.

165

Clark waited in the lobby as Maynard went back into the myriad examining rooms. He watched the children sniffle their first winter colds into the back of their throats. A boy of about sixteen was slumped in the corner chair, his hand conspicuously covering a bad case of acne. His face was more red than white, purple in spots, pussed. His hair dark and oily. Heavy stomach. His chest every schoolgirl's dream. He reminded Clark of what's-his-name in Salinger's *A Catcher in the Rye,* the kid who always wandered into Holden Caufield's dorm room.

The woman beside the boy was tall, stunning, and striving silently to communicate the lie that she was not this boy's mother. When the receptionist called the boy's name, Raymond Acton—Clark remembered then that *The Catcher in the Rye* character was named Ackley—the boy skulked to the desk with his mother's eyes only occasionally glancing up from her copy of *Cosmopolitan* magazine. The boy glanced at her before moping after a nurse into the medical maze. His lonely eyes held no sadness. He had probably gone beyond that.

Clark couldn't help thinking of Walter. We don't like to admit that our children are not what we want them to be, successful and beautiful and forever young. They are not supposed to be dumpy and bald with pockmarked faces, masturbating to magazine pictures of horrible vaginas horribly spread. They are not supposed to be cunt connoisseurs. But a dropped rock falls and we ruin our ruined children. So go the ways of the world.

Clark's eyes dropped when the woman's rose to meet them. He studied his hands until Maynard and Dr. Donaldson walked into the lobby. He rose to meet them, abandoning his thoughts to his chair. Another disease in a disease-ridden room.

"Hello, Clark. How's the store?" Dr. Donaldson's voice still held a touch of small-town congeniality, still held an attempt to recognize his patients as something beyond medical riddles with wallets and insurance policies. Well, they'll break him of that soon enough.

"Fine. Walter's selling computers. He's doing a fine job."

"That's good."

"That's good." Maynard's Donald Duck mimic was a running joke on

Maynard's side, a running sore on Dr. Donaldson's. The doctor's eyes promised that he would use less Vaseline during the next rectal examination.

"How's Nora, Clark?" Clark shrugged and smiled a half smile. The doctor nodded. "Could I speak to you alone for a minute?"

"Whatever you have to say about me, you can say in front of my face," Maynard said. No duck voice this time.

"It isn't about you. It's about Nora."

"It's about Nora," Maynard mimicked. "Then I'll wait over here." He waddled away, quacking. A kid with snot hanging from his nose in two thick ropes laughed and called him silly.

"What is it?" Clark asked.

"How long has Maynard been confused?"

So it wasn't about Nora. Ah, deception—the country boy was picking up a few city ways. Clark shrugged. "I started noticing it right after Helen died."

"Was it sudden or gradual?"

"Sudden. Your wife's death will do that to you."

"I didn't mean to imply that it wouldn't." Dr. Donaldson pursed his lips and studied Maynard. Maynard had Little Snotty in stitches, but was staring over the boy's shoulder at the Acton woman. "Has he ever complained about motor, speech, or sense impairment? Nothing that lasted long, maybe from a few minutes to an hour?"

Clark nodded. "He said once that parts of his body die and come back again. He called them sneak previews of the afterlife."

Dr. Donaldson pinched his lower lip between his fingers. "Do you know what a TIA is?"

"I've heard the term. Transient something or other."

"Transient ischemic attacks. They're mini-strokes that leave no permanent damage. Has he ever complained of vision loss, especially just in one eye?"

"No."

Dr. Donaldson pinched his lip again. Maynard quacked. Little Snotty bellowed. "Do you know what multi-infarct dementia is?"

167

"It's stroke-induced senility." Clark thought of Maynard on the sofa the other night. He'd been so frightened, so frightened. "Maynard isn't crazy."

"I'm not saying that he is."

"You said that as if to imply *not yet*."

"Did I? Then I guess I did."

Anger licked Clark's chest. He wasn't sure who or what it was directed at. "We're talking about a friend of mine."

"Relax, Clark. In a twisted way, we're talking about a friend of mine, too."

The Acton woman put her magazine on the corner table and strode toward them, as if she wanted to punch Clark in the mouth. She spoke a few quiet words to the receptionist, then went out the front door, looking at her watch. The receptionist spoke to her son when he came out. He followed his mother like a twig in a current, on his way out to the BMW, Clark supposed. He'll sit in the backseat without having to be told. The ways of the world.

"I'd like him to see a specialist in Rochester," Dr. Donaldson said. "He needs an MRI. I think he's had a little clotting in his heart that broke loose when his wife died and resulted in an embolism. I think he'll have more."

"And that's what's making him . . ." He did not want to use the word *senile. Do not go gentle into that good night*, Dylan Thomas had written. "Confused?"

Dr. Donaldson nodded. "The strokes can be so mild that in many cases no one will know he's had one. The effects are cumulative."

"What can you do for him?"

"I've prescribed anticoagulants, but I'm not sure how much good they'll do." He nodded at Maynard as he would at an old car. "There's a lot of damage in that body." He rested his hand on Clark's arm. His touch was cold, even through the shirtsleeve. "I could be, and I hope that I am, wrong. It could just be the shock of his wife's death. An MRI in Rochester would tell us that."

Clark's throat pulled tight. He saw Nora on the sidewalk, legs in the bank. Something happens to everyone. Everyone. "What can I do?"

"Don't let him smoke or drink. Keep an eye on his diet."

"I'm not always with him."

"That's something his family might want to consider. He has a daughter, hasn't he?"

"Barbara."

"She should think about putting him somewhere with full-time care."

A nursing home. A stiff, sterilized smell, a smell to claw through, suddenly dazzled Clark. Annie Halverson and Bob Tunnell's keening voices echoed in his ears, bound his words in his chest.

"If I'm right, Clark, he's going to get worse. I'll call Rochester. Do you have his daughter's number?"

"Try the book. Barbara Mischke."

"One nice thing about small towns," Dr. Donaldson said, "is that it only takes a second to look up a number."

Maynard was as quiet as the dark fields around them on the drive back to Credibull, as brooding as the wind moving over the furrows. Clark's thoughts stretched forward and backward like the railroad tracks running alongside the road. A lonely sight in winter, railroad tracks. They reach for the horizon as if they're hungry for it. What does the future taste like?

"You and Donald Duck were talking about me, weren't you?" Maynard asked.

"We were talking about Nora." Big city ways. Clark sighed. "He thinks you should see a specialist at the Mayo. He thinks you should have some tests done."

Maynard grunted. "He can't figure a damned thing out for himself. What a quack." He stared out the window, his eyes watery.

"You're quite a crowd pleaser," Clark said. "You and that voice and the kid."

"Oh. Yeah." Maynard turned to Clark. "What's wrong with me?"

Clark glanced at him, then studied the road. His eyes kept drifting to the railroad track. "Nobody knows anything, Maynard."

"Not yet, but that's what the tests are for, aren't they? What does he think I have? Is it something with my heart?"

"No," Clark admitted. "Not really."

"Then what?"

"He's worried about you being confused."

Maynard's breath wheezed. "That's a polite way to say I'm going crazy, isn't it?"

"He just thinks you ought to check it out. Fix it now, and you won't have to worry about it later." A small, white lie. Clark's hand tightened on the wheel. The hell if it was. It was a lie as big and black as they come.

Maynard watched him silently. Clark could hardly stand that gaze. "Is it Alzheimer's, Clark?"

"No." But it might as well be.

"Tell me the truth. Is it Alzheimer's?"

"It isn't Alzheimer's, Maynard."

Maynard blew out a hard sigh. Clark hazarded a look at his face. It was lined and pale, and his eyes were filmed. He looked like an old man, older even than seventy-eight. "Good. Give me the palsy, take away my arms and my legs. Break my hips. Don't take my mind." He wiped his mouth with trembling fingers.

Credibull climbed the horizon. The trees on Crystal Lake's western shore lay in a line like a brush stroke. The bank's third story rose in a little brown square above the smudge of downtown buildings.

"When I go," Maynard said, "I want to know it."

Clark took Maynard to his appointment at the Mayo Clinic on Monday, December 6. He drove Barb's minivan, not trusting his Dodge to the cold. It was a long morning of lobby waiting, of polite, smiling receptionists shuffling them around like chessmen.

"He's got it," Clark told Barb over a late lunch. "He's had some brain damage, and he may have more. The specialist said he'd call you this afternoon."

Barb stared into her coffee. Only her eyes betrayed emotion. "Why did this happen, Clark?"

That was a hell of a question. Clark shrugged. "Who can say?"

"You try to do what's right by everybody, and in the end it doesn't mean a thing. I mean, you bust your ass . . ." She smiled ruefully. "Dad used to beat the hell out of me for swearing in front of his friends. I still flinch when I find myself doing it."

"I remember once walking by Walter's room. You two were in there practicing cusswords. You must have been around ten."

"I don't remember that." Her hand rose to her cheek, apparently to cover a smile, actually to wipe a tear.

"You do more than your share," Clark said. "Of busting your ass, I mean."

"Do I?" She stirred her coffee, looking down. "Dr. Donaldson suggested a home for Dad."

"He told me he would."

"I can't do that. All those people out there just waiting to die, it's like a big coffin. Dad isn't ready to die. He isn't—" She cut herself off. "I'm sorry. I forgot about Nora."

"It's all right. I think about the place the same as you do."

"I can't leave him alone, though. Can I?"

Gun-barrel memories, silver lines in moonlight. Cold, cloudy breath drifted through Maynard's living room like a newly departed ghost. "No."

She sighed, either in resignation or in decision. "I'll take him in with me."

"Can you live with him? I mean, with the way he is?"

"I don't have much of a choice, do I?" Her face fell; she looked ancient and tired. "He's streaky. Sometimes he's too addled to be bad."

The home or your home, Clark thought. Hell, Barb, you can beat yourself to death against a rock or a hard place. Either way, you beat yourself to death. "When would you do it?"

"I'll talk to Brian and the kids. Maybe in a week or so." She looked at him for the first time since he'd told her what the tests had confirmed. "It's not quite as urgent as you think. I took the guns out of his house the last time I cleaned it."

"He'll fight like hell, you know. If he imagines for no reason you're stealing from him, what will he think when you move him out of his house?"

She shrugged. "Maybe he won't know what's going on."

"What will you do if he does?"

"Deal with it," she said.

In the back corner, a pregnant woman with stringy red hair loudly scolded a small boy wearing a Spiderman T-shirt. He had just doused her cigarette with his strawberry shake. The sugary stink of sizzled ice cream and tobacco didn't help Clark's appetite.

"Can I count on help from you?" Barb was looking at him. Makeup covered the pores on her cheeks. Her whole face was hanging.

"Maynard is my friend. I'm not about to abandon him now."

"Thank you." She turned briefly to the woman and the boy, then toward the window. "I've often wondered about you and Dad. After what happened with Albert Wilson, why is it you stuck by him when no one else would?"

"All I remember hearing then was gossip." He paused, not sure of what he should say. "If only we knew all the things we want to know."

Barb's fingers tapped the table absently. "What a horror that would be."

Either it took Barb a few days to convince Brian about the need to move Maynard in with them, or it took Maynard a few days to grow complacent enough to move. Not until the following Friday did she call Clark. That morning they packed Maynard out of his house on Josef Meyer Boulevard. Maynard rode with Clark in the Dodge; Barb followed in the van.

"Where we going?" Maynard asked.

"Over to Barb's." The sun through the windshield was a warm kiss, a hard stare.

"Who's Barb?"

"Your daughter."

"Oh." Maynard wiped his face. He stared out the window at nothing. "You know, Clark, I was looking at the fields the other day. I can't for the life of me figure out why I seeded them all with alfalfa."

"You're living in town now, Maynard."

"Sometimes I get tempted to cut the wire on Wilson's damn holsteins and let them wander into those fields. Ever see a cow bloat on fresh alfalfa? Kills them." He chuckled. "That would teach the bastard."

It was hard to watch this. It was hard to listen to it. "You're in town now, Maynard. We're going to Barb's house."

"Let's stop at the Double-Trouble," Maynard said. "I could use a drink."

Me, too. Clark shook his head. No. "Maybe Barb will have some lemonade."

"She sells that stuff in one of those stands out by the road," Maynard said. "No one's around to buy it, so I have to drink the whole damned pitcher, glass by glass, doling out a nickel for each one. Christ in a hand bucket, that's god-awful stuff. Gets to the point where all I have to do is think about the color yellow and I spend the night pissing."

"How old is Barb, Maynard?" They were passing the grain elevator.

"I don't know. Forty-something."

"Do you know you're going to be staying with her?"

"She and that husband of hers going on vacation? Do they need someone to look after the kids?"

Clark grabbed on to that. He had to grab on to something. "I don't know about the vacation. Maybe the kids are just too much for Barb."

"I'll whip them into shape."

They turned into the development, followed two deserted streets to the back corner, and parked in front of a gray rambler with a dead flower bed beside the door. A black-and-white collie bounced across the yard to greet them; a young boy with an open zipper joyfully followed. Barb and Brian had the fourteen-year-old, this one, and another somewhere in the middle. All boys, all piss and vinegar. Clark's chest panged as he watched the child bound to its grandfather and not to him. God be damned, Walter, we were meant for more than what we have.

"Gampa!" the boy shouted.

"Hi, kid." Maynard pulled himself wheezily from the car as the boy raised his arms.

"Gampa, up!"

"Let me catch my breath." Maynard's blanched face raised an anxious lump in Clark's throat. "Grampa's a little tired today. Why don't you run into the house and watch some damn cartoon or something? Take this damn dog with you before it starts humping my leg."

Brian's mother held the door open as the boy bounded inside, a gray woman wearing a gray sweat suit and bright, shiny sneakers, as if jogging had shaken all her color into them. She silently watched the two men through the screen before shutting the door. Clark pursed his lips. Well, we know what she thinks of this.

Barb parked the van in the driveway, then climbed out, carrying a battered brown suitcase. Clark shuffled toward her as Maynard followed the walk to the house. "That went smoothly," he said.

"As smoothly as I could have hoped."

"Are you sure you have everything?"

"Everything he'll need for now. Will you get the other suitcase?"

Clark fumbled it out of the van, his knees loudly protesting, the pain in his shoulder dancing with its weight. He set the suitcase just inside the door and caught his breath as he straightened.

The boy was sitting on Maynard's lap in front of the television, watching a sappy purple dinosaur sing about flowers. Brian's mother was in the kitchen, chopping carrots with evil vengeance.

"I'll see you, Maynard," Clark called.

"Sure." Maynard waved toward the door. "Don't forget what I said about cows and alfalfa," he added, as if this were a cryptic truth.

"Will you be all right?" Clark asked Barb.

"We'll see." Barb nodded. "We'll be fine. Go on and enjoy your day."

Maynard's decline had pulled the spirit out of Clark, left him depressed and listless. The last thing he wanted to do was work at the historical society—he stopped at the Burger King and called Agnes. "This move is taking longer than we expected," he told her.

"Oh?"

"Nothing was packed. Would it be all right if I took the rest of the day off?"

"Take as much time as you like, Clark," Agnes replied cheerily. "I'll take care of things."

You'll take care of things, all right. Roger VanRuden was in today, and without Clark around Agnes would feel freer to conduct her mild, middle-aged, Midwestern seduction. "Thank you, Agnes."

He drove to Mankato. He studied the gauntlet of fast food restaurants, car dealerships, and discount outlets lining the highway on the east side of town. No more mom-and-pop places, he thought, we're all after that nationally recognized name. Famous brand, famously bland. He grunted as he descended the riverbank. We've been strip-mauled.

He followed the Minnesota River to the downtown mall, where he wandered for an hour before driving up the bank to the state university. He passed a cinema, then turned around and pulled into its lot. The marquee advertised something he had never heard of, called *Henry and June*. It didn't sound as if it had anything to do with southern Minnesota or friends on the decline. He was in the mood for something he had never heard of.

A woman with silver hair was fumbling with her purse in front of the ticket window. The attendant, a blond girl wearing an oversized college sweatshirt, waited with exaggerated patience on the other side of the glass.

"I have a quarter in here somewhere." The woman was tall and thin and at least a decade younger than Clark. "I *know* I have a quarter in here somewhere."

The girl popped her gum and busied herself with displaying Gandhian fortitude. The woman finally snapped shut her purse. "I guess I don't. Could you give me my two dollars back?"

"Keep the money," Clark told the girl. "I'll cover the quarter."

The woman turned to him. A network of fine lines etched her near-translucent skin. She could have been crystal dropped just hard enough on the floor. "That's very kind."

"It's only a quarter."

The woman waited as Clark paid for the tickets. "I could have sworn I had a quarter," she apologized. She was almost as tall as Clark. "Age is making me forgetful."

"Your memory is just getting more selective. Where you put a quarter isn't worth remembering."

"That's a wonderful way to look at it." The woman smiled. "My name is Emma Richard." She held out her hand.

"Clark Holstrom." Her hand was porcelain left out in the sun. "Do you know what this movie is about?"

"Henry Miller and Anaïs Nin. It's wonderful."

They walked into the lobby. Clark tried to distract himself from her touch on his arm by studying the blur of refreshment-stand prices. He tapped his pocket for his glasses, found them, and left them where they were, suddenly vain and embarrassed. Her touch was so damned warm that her fingers could have been embers. Why is it nowadays you can only buy popcorn in tubs the size of garbage cans? Why do you have to mortgage your house to afford one? Christ, her hand felt good. It reminded him of faraway summer. "June was Henry's wife, right?"

"Yes." She released his arm. "Do you know Henry Miller's work?"

"I read *Tropic of Cancer.*"

"A wonderful book, don't you think? Henry Miller was a genius."

No man who had written a book with as much sex in it as that one had ever lived in the Midwest. God strikes down such people. Hell, he seemed to be striking down everybody, except this woman. "I couldn't understand it."

"Then you may not be able to understand the movie."

"Then I wasted two bucks and two bits."

She smiled again. She had a very nice smile, Clark thought, a smile that used her whole face. "Two bucks and two bits on Henry Miller, whether you understand him or not, is never wasted."

She was watching him, her thin body straight, her shoulders back, her pale hands contrasting with the dark purse she carried. The wedding ring she wore sunk into his feelings. Hell. He tried to shake clear his head. What was he thinking?

"I'll take your word on that," he said. "Would you like some popcorn?"

They sat together beside the aisle, the popcorn bucket filling Clark's lap like a beach ball; it pressed into his thighs each time she reached inside. The theater darkened for the previews. Clark winced at each exploding car, at each exploding building, at each exploding muscle-head, at the women as naked as a G-rated preview would allow—it wasn't Bogey and Bergman anymore.

The film opened on a watercolor world. "France," Emma whispered. "Have you ever been to Paris?"

"During the war," he whispered back.

"What did you think of it?"

She was leaning close to him, whispering conspiratorially. He could smell the perfume on her neck, and the salt and the sweat, and in the darkness the cold channel fear. He could hear bullets zinging and blood-soaked voices; he could see beach barricades and boys exploding with no G rating. "It wasn't a good time to be there."

"I suppose not." She reached into his lap for popcorn. "I try to get there as often as I can. I don't have that tainting." She nodded at the narrow streets and water-stained buildings on the screen. "I've been down those streets. They don't look that way anymore."

"How often is often?"

"Every few years. I invent tours—the Henry Miller tour, the Ernest Hemingway tour, the James Joyce. The Gertrude Stein begins at twenty-seven rue de Fleurus."

"There's not a lot of women around here who read writers like that."

"There's not a lot of *people* around here who read writers like that, you mean. No, there aren't. Do you?"

"I read *Tropic of Cancer,* didn't I?"

An elfin woman in the movie was writing in her diary. An actor stepped out of an old car and struck a match on the sole of his shoe—Clark remembered him from some action-adventure film. He'd shaved his head to play the role of Henry Miller. As he slid the top of a soufflé onto his plate, the elfin woman giggled. So did Emma. Oh, those uncultured Americans.

Memories came too easily for Clark to concentrate. Scenes of Paris and its countryside, of whorehouses and lesbian bars, of sex between women and sex between women and men trotted playfully past his eyes. This was not France. France was starving girls selling themselves for rations. France was GIs raping farmers' daughters in haylofts and outhouses, anguished screams and throaty laughter; France was German snipers putting bullets into the same laughing throats the next afternoon. France was Clark's buddy losing an eye to the splintered cheekbone of another buddy who had taken one in the face. France was not artists' garrets filled with naked contortionists. France was not café celebrations. France was not playful.

"What did you think?" Emma asked when the lights came up.

Clark shrugged and felt the tense shadows thrown up in his mind recede. "Is that how Paris is for you?"

"I wasn't there in the thirties."

"Me either."

They stood. Clark had been sitting too long and became dizzy—the only focused part of him was the crystal pain in his knees, the memories in his mind and in his senses. He stood in the aisle and gripped the seat in front of him and waited out the swirling. Emma busied herself with negotiating the popcorn bucket past Clark's seat and did not notice. Thank God for that. Getting old means you have more things to hide.

"I know a wonderful little restaurant, if you're interested," Emma said. "I'd love to discuss the movie with you."

178

Clark's watch read five o'clock. He figured he might as well settle this business of the wedding ring right now. "Won't your husband be wondering where you are?"

She glanced at her ring. "I've been a widow for almost a decade." She nodded at the band on his finger. "And you?"

Should he give her the dictionary definition of a widower, or the emotional one? "Same thing, but only for a year."

"I'm sorry."

"I am, too." Well, that was that. Nora's heavy eyes forced his shoulders into a stoop. He resisted. "It can't be helped."

He followed Emma up the aisle. Her legs were thin and pale beneath her skirt hem; she was wearing high heels. She had young legs for an older woman. He suddenly felt very lonely. "What kind of restaurant is this?" he asked.

"Oriental. It isn't a restaurant, really—it's a little food booth in the River Hills Mall. I go there to watch people and eat with chopsticks."

"Sounds good." The only Oriental food he had ever eaten was the canned stuff he'd heated in a pan. Beef like bits of his shoe, bean sprouts like phlegm. Don't they put dogs in Oriental food? Rat meat?

"Do you know how to use chopsticks?" she asked.

"Sure. You carve them into forks."

Emma laughed as they reached the lobby. The sky outside was slate; the streetlights glowed, still only dully. Little Miss Gandhi leaned on an elbow, studying a textbook. "Did you drive here or walk?" Emma asked.

"I drove. I'm from Credibull."

"Would you like to follow me?"

"If my car will start. It gets temperamental in this weather."

"Driving cross-country in a car you may not be able to drive back in is a little risky, isn't it?"

"Call me a daredevil," Clark said.

With the sun so low the air was turning frigid, but the Dodge still held enough warmth from his earlier puttering to start. He made a few quick turns, drove down a long stretch of highway, and crossed High-

179

way 14, following the taillights of Emma's big Buick like a firefly searching for a pulsing, electrical dream. The River Hills Mall squatted long and low behind an asphalt desert. Long lines of cars had been parked like caravans. The entrance was a green glowing oasis.

"Could I take your arm?" Emma asked as he met her. "High heels and icy parking lots have their disagreements."

"Of course." The cold made Clark's joints so stiff he might have been walking on stilts. Still, it felt good to have a woman depending on him. A tall woman with a slight touch of perfume. A thin, straight woman with silver hair, her skin sunlit porcelain. A woman with life in her eyes.

My eyes have life, too.

Nora lay on his conscience as if it were a pillow. He tried to push her away but failed. Her gaze was so heavy.

Inside the mall a carousel twirled a Lewis Carroll nightmare of grimacing horses and giant rabbits; lusty goats chased zebras in circles. Little legs splayed over saddles, fright and wonder propped open innocent eyes. Calliope music wound through the Christmas throng. In restaurants like tents in a medieval market, food sellers bartered their wares.

"It's over there." Emma pointed across a cluster of mauve tables at a glowing sign Clark couldn't read. She spread her arms and spun in a circle. She was joy in the season's insanity and insanity in the season's joy. "This is why I come to this place. Don't you just love carousels?"

Clark watched the people watching her. Scandinavian and German faces as bland as bread dough hid their contempt behind layers of politeness. Nora's eyes watched her enviously from his shoulder. "I suppose."

He followed her through the tables, past the heavy faces, the dank smell of wet boots in pasta sauce, and the packages piled around feet like treasures. Mouths slurped, children cried, and faces betraying nothing looked up, then fell again. He and Emma were just another old married couple—nothing special, or nothing more than special. He wished he hadn't thought of marriage.

A line wound in front of their restaurant counter like a snake about to strike. The menu on the wall behind the counter was indecipherable, as much from the infiltration of foreign words as his eyesight. Maybe *kung* meant *lung* and *pao* meant *paw*. He didn't want to think about *subgum.*

"What are you going to have?" Emma asked.

He studied the food pans, nestled into the counter in long, stainless steel rows. Open your mouth and close your eyes, and you will get a big surprise. He searched for the closest thing to familiarity. "That chicken stuff looks good. That is chicken, isn't it?"

"Chicken and cashews."

Minnesota cuisine does not mix the products of trees with the roosting animals that shit from them, but what the hell—it was either that or lungs in toenail sauce. "Then chicken and cashews it is."

"I need something tangier. Sweet-and-sour pork," she told the scrap of Oriental girl behind the counter, "and an egg roll. Fried rice, please." The girl nodded, then spooned onto a plastic plate portions large enough to give any American-born manager ulcers. She couldn't have been fourteen. Baby hands.

Clark got his chicken and ordered an egg roll—everyone seemed to be getting one, and it had been a long time since he'd had eggs. He reached for his wallet.

Emma waved his hand away. "They're together," she told the woman at the register.

"No," Clark said. "Please."

"I asked you. You didn't ask me."

They wandered for a few minutes before finding a table close enough to the carousel for Emma's liking. Large tropical plants near the front windows played absurdly against the snow outside. Attendants in long-sleeved green turtlenecks and blue aprons scuttled like multicolored beetles. The carousel operator struggled to hide his boredom.

Emma poked her food with her chopsticks. Clark opted for a plastic fork. The food was good, God, it was good, until he bit into the egg roll. He groaned.

181

"What?" Emma asked.

"Cooked cabbage. If there is anything I cannot stand, it's cooked cabbage." It had always reminded him of leeches rolling around in his mouth, looking for a place to hold.

"It's an egg roll," she said. "What did you expect?"

"Eggs." He sighed. "I don't eat this kind of food very often."

"You could have said something."

"Actually, I didn't want you to think. . ." He shrugged.

She smiled that wonderful smile, then laughed. "I'm sorry. I'm not laughing at you."

"Yes, you are."

"Yes, I guess I am." She wiped an orange-colored sauce from her lips and snorted into her napkin. Clark laughed, too. He had never enjoyed coming across as a hick so much. It was easy to be comfortable with this woman.

I'm still here, Nora said.

"So what did you think of the movie?" Emma asked when they had gotten back to eating.

"My honest opinion is that no one could fuck as much as they did and still be able to walk." He blushed—it was *too* easy to be comfortable with this woman. "I'm sorry. My language."

She smiled. "One thing the Anglo-Saxons were good at was coming up with strong, simple words. *Fuck* is so much better than *intercourse.* I have never been able to understand why it was relegated to profanity. The influence of the church, I suppose." She studied his egg roll, then lifted it from his plate. "So you think they fucked too much?" she asked before she bit into it.

"Too much and in too many ways. It didn't make any difference how many or what sex or what color—"

"Up to now, Clark," she said, "you haven't impressed me as a racist."

"I don't mean race. I mean they were fucking while they were painted blue. Is that how the world is now?"

She smiled. She had strong eyes, a strong gaze, like Nora's had suddenly become. "That film was set in the thirties. That's how the world was for us."

Clark finished his meal without speaking. He watched Emma eat his egg roll. The lights reflected off her silver hair in a glow almost divine. Athena sat across from him—no, more than likely Venus, if she could use the word *fuck* so easily, if she had analyzed *why* she could use it so easily. He propped his elbows on the table. "So," he said.

"So?"

"So all I really know about you is that you're short on quarters."

She wiped her mouth as she shrugged. "I'm a seventy-three-year-old widow. I just retired from the directorship of the Minnesota Valley Arts Council."

"You're interested in the arts?"

"I worked with music and writing, mostly. I got John Hassler down here for a reading a few years ago. I love modern dance the most, but try to get dancers down here and you get the pigheaded minority screaming pornography." She lifted her chin. Her hands rose slowly, like birds taking flight.

"You look like a dancer," Clark said.

She laughed. "I'm too big and clumsy. I tried it once at the university and nearly snapped the back of the poor boy who lifted me."

"Did you go to Mankato State?"

"The university in Minneapolis. I met my husband there. His dream was to be the next Thomas Wolfe. He ended up an insurance salesman."

"So goes life."

"Life goes any direction you want it to go. I loved him enough to finally admit to myself that he simply lacked the courage." She pushed her plate away and crossed her arms on the table. "And you?"

"You want to know about my courage?"

"I want to know about your past." She waved her sentence away. "I hate that word. What is the past but a bunch of stuff you can't do anything about? Tell me about your future."

"It's easier to talk about my past." There's so much more of it. "I was thinking about college when the war came along and never got back to thinking about it. I guess that afterward I didn't have the heart."

"You grew up in Credibull?"

"No. Indiana."

"How did you end up in the frozen North?"

"That's a long story." He paused. "I wandered around after the war, trying to sort things out."

"And Credibull provided the answers?"

He laughed. "Credibull is where I ran out of money."

"Has it provided any answers since?"

"Could any place?" He shrugged. "You never really know anything, do you?"

She propped her chin on the heel of her hand. "I do."

"I'd love to learn what you've discovered."

She raised her voice above the thickening calliope music. "I know that in the world there is beauty and pain. I know that the very best thing you can do is live the very best way you can."

"You sound like a youthful optimist."

"I *am* a youthful optimist."

A middle-aged attendant scurried up, grabbed their plates, and scurried away again. "I don't mean to sound so negative," Clark said. "I'm not always this way."

"It's your wife." Emma smoothed her hair; her ring flashed in the light. "Did you say she died last year?"

He couldn't remember. "Yes. She slipped on the ice and broke her hip. She froze."

"I'm sorry. How long were you married?"

"Forty-five years. Almost forty-six."

She nodded. "It takes time to adjust. You'll eventually find that life goes on."

"I suppose." He stretched his legs toward the carousel. A goat the size of a Shetland pony leaped toward him as if hungry for his throat. It went around the wheel and leaped at him again. Everything always comes back. Another yo-yo. He thought of his model, lying in pieces on the basement floor. "It's getting late."

"We don't have to talk about this."

"It's not that. It's . . ." It was that. "It's just that it's getting late."

"All right." She slipped her coat up over her shoulders. "Well, thank you for the movie."

"It was only a quarter. Thank you for dinner."

"It was only a meal."

"Then thanks for showing me this place. I'll be back."

"But not for the egg rolls." She looked as if she were waiting for him to ask a question. "Perhaps sometime . . ."

Sure, Nora said. *Sometime.*

Her dead eyes stared as he lifted his coat from the back of the chair. To hell with you, he thought, to hell with you. He didn't know if he was cursing Nora or himself. By the time he had buttoned his coat, an attendant had wiped the table.

The air outside felt ten degrees colder than it had before they had eaten. The frost on the asphalt glittered beneath the lights as if the parking lot had been dusted with stars. The Dodge's handle burned his fingers. He cursed silently and wished he'd worn gloves.

"If you're ever in Credibull, stop by the historical society," he called to Emma over the hood. He hated the fact that she was so far away from him. "I do volunteer work there."

"I'll make a point of it." She smiled at him as she climbed in the Buick. She revved the engine once, then waited as it warmed.

Clark lowered himself into the Dodge. You're a fool, he admonished himself, a damned fool. Here is a woman like the ones you've always dreamed of, the opposite of Nora . . .

There's that name again.

Her hard eyes smiled. They stared blindly at a wall but saw all there was to see. Hell. Hell, bloody hell, as those Londoners used to say. He sighed and resigned himself to calling a lost moment morality.

He could keep his sense of futility out of his mind, but not out of his actions as he jammed the key into the ignition. The Dodge responded with an *if that's the way you want to be, then to hell with you* silence. He pumped the accelerator, then held it down three-quarters of the way, using all of the tricks he knew. If it didn't go now, it wouldn't. It didn't.

The wind blew car exhaust past Emma's window. She mouthed something in the exaggerated way people use who want you to read their lips. He couldn't make it out. He slapped the Dodge's steering wheel, cursed, and opened the door. The damned thing always had a way to get even. Now his hand hurt.

Emma rolled her window down. "A daredevil, isn't that what you said?"

Clark shrugged. "You win some, you lose some."

"Maybe you should call for a tow."

"A motel would be cheaper. It'll start in the morning, after the sun warms it up."

"Would you like a ride back to Credibull?"

"I couldn't ask you for that. A motel would be fine."

She nodded through a shiver. "Get in. It's cold out there."

Clark glanced at the star-littered sky. Perhaps God was a joker, and this his practical joke.

She opened the door for him. He slipped inside while pondering his theology. A new-car smell and leather seats more comfortable than any easy chair he'd ever owned greeted him. A brace of air from the heater warmed his face.

Emma smiled. "Do you believe in fate?"

"Only fate in hindsight. Do you know of a good motel?"

Being so comfortable with her before made being uncomfortable with her now all that much more of an agony. She watched him, but he saw only Nora's eyes. "It's only late if you were planning to drive back to Credibull. Since you're not, it's early."

"I guess you could look at it that way." He shifted and tried to concentrate on the air blowing across his face. He wanted to tell her that Nora wasn't dead; but that deception, like a jump off a cliff, had gone too far.

You, Nora said, *are so full of shit.*

186

"Do you like coffee?" Emma asked. "Have you heard of Jamaican Blue Mountain?"

"No. I mean, no, I've never heard of Jamaican Blue Mountain. Yes, I like coffee."

"It's the best in the world. I have a bag of it back at my apartment."

She was watching him. He shifted again. He didn't know what he wanted to say.

"Some people call me forward," she said. "That's what you're thinking, aren't you?"

Clark shrugged. *That's* what he wanted to say.

"When my husband died, I realized we all have only so many days. Not using them wisely is sort of a sin, don't you think? Now how about the coffee?"

She was watching him intently. What the hell do you say? What is a sin and what isn't? "I like coffee."

"Do you like Beethoven's Sixth?"

He tried to place it, couldn't. He'd always wanted to know classical music better than he did. "Yes, I do." A joke, he thought. God's up there laughing.

"I have a recording. On a night like this we need to be reminded of summertime."

We need to be reminded of something, Nora said.

Yes. Well, he thought, we all have only so many days. Emma put the car in reverse and backed out of her parking spot.

Emma lived in a retirement complex two blocks west of the college. A black leather sofa contrasted so sharply with the white walls that its edges seemed to vibrate. A crudely carved ebony panther prowled across a glass coffee table; a black-and-white print of two French models kissing each other in front of a fountain blazed on the wall. Clark was afraid to sit down—his clothing was an intrusion of color.

"Very nice. Quite a bit different than mine."

"Let me guess." Emma reached into a cupboard and set a plump burlap sack on the counter. Whatever was in it settled with a sound like a chuckle. "Grandchildren's school pictures on the wall, an oak veneer coffee table, and flowered sofa cushions."

"No flowers," Clark said. "A solid green."

"My second guess."

"And no grandchildren."

She glanced at him as she rummaged among pots and pans. "How about children?" She took out a black plastic gadget and a clear pot with a plunger in it.

"A son. The coffee table you got right." He felt color rise to his cheeks, a further intrusion. "Pretty Midwestern, huh?"

"Didn't you say you like to read? Hemingway, Fitzgerald, and Cather were all Midwesterners. So were Sinclair Lewis and Theodore Dreiser. Being a Midwesterner puts you in good company."

"They all moved away."

"But they never left it behind." She put on a kettle, then slid the gadget, the pot, and the burlap sack across the counter toward him. "Do me the favor of loading this up while I locate Mr. Beethoven."

"All right." He wondered which *this* she was referring to.

He watched her walk across the living room to a black stereo in a white cabinet. He picked up the sack and found it held only coffee beans. He'd never bought coffee like this before—coffee was supposed to come in cans that go *whoosh* when you open them. He opened the gadget—it must have been the grinder—and stared at its two halves staring back. The kettle mumbled like an impatient audience barely tolerating an incompetent magician. Soon it would be howling and throwing tomatoes. Not only did he have to figure out what to do but there was a time limit on his figuring. He felt as if he were in school again.

"A little full," she said when she came back. He had filled the business half of the gadget to the rim. "If you make our coffee that strong, we'd be up all night." Her eyes smiled. "Clark Holstrom, what are you up to?"

Yes, what are you up to?

188

He avoided the question by studying the living room. "Nice music." It sounded familiar, perhaps only because he needed it to. "What orchestra is this?"

"The Cleveland."

"Oh." Cleveland has an orchestra? "Nice."

She closed her eyes. "Quiet now. This is my favorite part."

Her hand bobbed an invisible baton to conduct an invisible orchestra. Her fingers floated like birds dancing in a sunset as she hummed a soft contralto. Wind tasting of the earth swept through Clark's imagination, dripped down to lick the corners of his mouth, his eyes. He was standing alone on the top of the world, gazing across its domain.

"Beautiful," he said.

"Yes."

He studied the thin lines on her face that spoke of so many things he had never known. He wished he were inside her head, looking out of her eyes, hearing the music with her ears. How would it be to know the world as she does? Are the sounds subtler, the colors different? How would it be, Emma, to live with your past instead of mine?

Her eyes opened with the singing of the kettle. Her slight smile hinted that it might spread across her face. He was so close to her that if she were an open door, with a twitch of his foot he could step through.

"What?" she asked.

He broke his gaze with difficulty. "Nothing."

"I'll get the kettle." She left her reverie for the stove, leaving him still in his. She put the ground beans in the pot, poured in steaming water, and pushed the plunger down just far enough to hold the beans under the water. She came back with the pot and two cups.

"So," she said, "you never did tell me about your future."

"You never told me about yours, either."

"My future is Paris and music and bringing beauty to this little cow town. And love."

"Well, we always hope for love." It sounded so damned sappy. He felt he should be wearing a purple dinosaur suit.

189

He looked from her to the clock above her head. Seven-thirty—a lot of the night left. He imagined Emma's bedroom, black bed frame, white walls, white linen sheets. A hell of a lot of future could happen before morning.

Clark Holstrom, Nora asked, *what are you up to?*

He saw sterilized sheets and a face spread like leather across a stiff pillow. It was funny how someone who could only stare could get around.

Emma pushed the plunger to the bottom of the pot, poured out two cups of dark, earth-smelling coffee, and handed him one with questions still in her eyes, her blue, living eyes. "Your future?" she asked.

He accepted the cup. "I really should be going."

"You'll at least drink your coffee."

"All right. But then I really should be going."

"Fair enough." Her hand brushed his. A quick touch, a warm hand. She'd covered the age spots on the back with some kind of cream.

"You'll like this," she said.

A twirling sensation began in his stomach, then tumbled into his groin. He pushed Nora away by clinging to the hope of possibility. It died when his hand strayed as casually as he could muster into his lap to find nothing, nothing at all. God be damned. On that last day we will stand before the judgment seat and get our asses fried—perhaps God was a short-order cook, and *hallelujah* simply means *over easy.* Only Clark's crotch would survive the fire, because not even God could bring it back to life. Some things are beyond omnipotence.

Well, he thought, so goes life. You have nothing tonight, but you always have what memories you dare to muster. Emma was wrong; life at our age is not in the future but in the past, in good memories plucked ripe from trees like apples. Not even God can take that away.

Sour grapes,

"What did you do for a living, Clark?" Emma asked.

"I owned a hardware store. My son owns it now."

"That continuity must make you feel good."

"I don't think it will be hardware for long. He's doing better with computers. Sign of the times, I suppose."

"And your wife?"

"I met her when I moved to Minnesota."

"What was she like?"

He shrugged. Nothing like you. "She liked green sofas." Keep sharp and keep it short. When you're talking about Nora, avoid the present tense. "I don't want to bore you."

"You're not boring me."

He sipped his coffee. Its vapors steamed his lungs. The taste was as rich as the music. He watched her hands, then glanced at her face over the cup. "This is good."

"It is, isn't it?"

Her gaze was too heavy. By the time his coffee was half finished he knew he would not stay beyond reaching the bottom of the cup. Face reality, old boy, he thought. For a moment he felt comfortable.

"You have a nice life, Emma," he said.

"I suppose that in every life there are things missing." She looked as if she were struggling to remember something. "An old widow and an old widower don't owe anyone a damn thing, Clark."

"I suppose not." He sighed. "It has nothing to do with you. Call it conservatism." Call it Nora. Call it age. Call it a howling darkness, call it a scream against everything and everyone and *do not go gentle into that good night* and, damn it, why not stay here? Why not? A last flash of Nora's eyes stained the black-and-white of the room, stained the delicate color of Emma's face, the silver of her hair, even the smell of her, as if he were wearing tinted glasses and had rancid cotton stuffed up his nose. *He simply lacked the courage,* Emma had said. "Call it a Midwestern upbringing."

She set down her cup. She smiled slightly, with no danger of it spreading. "All right. I would still like to see a movie with you sometime."

"Of course. Listen, maybe in time . . ."

"Of course." After the coffee she went to the closet for their coats. "There's a nice motel on Highway 14. I haven't stayed there, but that's what I've heard."

"I'm sure it will be fine."

191

She drove without speaking. Headlights flashed in his eyes; he felt depressed, defeated, and foolish. He looked at her once in the glare and guessed that she was feeling the same. He thought about Billie Jessup and wondered why Nora had not crept into his mind with her as she had with Emma. That hot, lusty taste had been so much more overwhelming with Billie, that rotting feeling in his chest so much more overpowering. Perhaps they had driven Nora away. By the time they reached the highway, he knew that he was giving himself too much credit.

The reason you didn't think of me while you were pursuing Billie is because with Billie you knew that you had no chance at all.

Emma pulled into a motel parking lot across the highway from the mall. "I expect a guided tour of the Credibull Historical Society," she said as she parked in front of the motel office.

"Of course." He lifted the door handle, but held the door shut. He wanted to savor this last moment. Another memory.

"Is there any history in Credibull?"

He forced a laugh. He needed to end this with something light. It felt only terrible. "Not much."

"Are you familiar with the Mankato Historical Society?"

"Not really. I stopped in once, years ago. A lot on the Sioux uprising, as I remember."

"Yes." She paused. "Well, good night."

"Good night." The cold worked at his knees as he got out of the car. He shut the door with a *whap* like the sound of a meat cleaver against a cutting board. The end of that.

The office clerk was a thick woman wearing a wig slightly askew. Orange makeup caked her face; her eyes were bleary from staring at a black-and-white television squatting on the end of the counter. "A single?" she asked.

"A single." It was funny how easy it seemed for her to make that assumption.

Clark took the key, paid its price, and went to the room. He lay in the darkness, his back against the unfamiliar mattress, the unfamiliar sheets and smells huddled around him. He listened to the traffic on

192

the highway. Headlights passed through the window and across the ceiling. Light and dark. Black and white. He thought about contrast and felt he would cry.

· ·

Clark kept his room key until after he had crossed the highway and started the Dodge. He banged its steering wheel again when the engine turned over. "Why couldn't you do that last night?" He drove home across glittering fields between snowbanks that reflected the sun into his eyes.

As he passed the store Walter came out, waving his arms. Clark parked in front of the bank. Walter crossed the highway, rubbing his naked gooseflesh. He had already opened.

"You didn't sweep," he said as Clark rolled down the window. "I tried calling you, and you didn't answer. You drove in from the wrong direction."

Clark wondered how many more obvious facts his son could point out to him. Yes, and I'm wearing pants. I have a shirt and coat on. You'll notice I'm not wearing scuba flippers. "The car decided I was going to spend the night in Mankato."

"Broke down?"

"It wouldn't start." As a lot of things wouldn't.

"A wild night on the town, huh?" Walter smiled, his teeth as yellow and crooked as kernels in a stunted ear of corn.

"A wild night," Clark said.

Chapter

9

Credibull hung its Christmas lights only a week and a half before Christmas—someone on whatever board it was that decided such things must have made the stunning realization that Christmas decorations were not for Thanksgiving. Green tinsel and red-and-white lights curled around the telephone lines. Scraggly plastic trees hung like lynching victims in a snow-blown ghost town, their green strips flapping loosely in a balmy cold, temperature in the low twenties. Winter's tanning weather.

Clark had bought a tree the Saturday before at a lot on the Credibull side of Janesville. He'd done his Christmas shopping at the Wal-Mart. He hated shopping there—you could get lost in the aisles for days and have to live off the discount dog food—but when you have no idea what to buy, it's best to go somewhere that throws so many things at you that something is bound to stick. He'd had no idea what to get Maynard—what do you buy a seventy-eight-year-old man? He found him a pair of gloves.

The girl who worked in the electronics department talked him into buying Walter a game for his new Wind River home computer, a knights-and-damsels-and-dragons thing—save the princess and gain her undying love. Digital romance seemed hardly better than the two-dimensional glossy kind Walter hid under sofas or hung on walls. But hardly better was a step above not better at all.

It was late in the evening, the Monday before Christmas. He had just finished rereading *A Christmas Carol,* a tradition dating back to when Walter was a child. On his way to his bedroom, Clark noticed that he'd left the light on in the basement. He shoved his hands in his pockets as he went down the stairs, as if to protect them from the model's devastation. He figured he ought to fix the damned thing—perhaps what was done really wasn't irrevocable. He stared impotently at the lake's cracked surface before shutting off the light and climbing the stairs to the bedroom.

He lowered himself in the darkness onto the bed with the slow nobility of a tumbling statue, then stared at the window frost glowing in the streetlight. It raised literary images—he saw in its patterns the divinely glowing Beatrice leading Dante on the guided tour of heaven, wipe your feet before entering, please, you came by way of hell. Was hell all fire and brimstone, or was it Dante's freezing cold? Perhaps God was schizophrenic—Christ, how could he deny it?—and used both. Clark had always been a fire-and-brimstone man, but his views had changed since that cold snap last winter, since . . .

He shivered. It was too cold in the bedroom—what Dante could write about this. Clark's feet were always cold enough now to shock him when they grazed a calf or ankle. His blood had lost its heat by the time it reached them—it meandered instead of pulsed. It clotted more quickly now into little curds that one day were bound to break loose from the damn aches in his knees and shoulder and work their way up to his brain. Why the brain, he thought, and not the ass? He could handle multi-what-the-hell dementia of the ass—a return to a seven-year-old ass would be desirable. Why can't diseases take you where you want to go? Why aren't there any good ones?

Brains and asses. It was funny how he found himself thinking about things. Clots. At seven, bogeymen hide in closets; at seventy-two, they hide in your blood. A sudden fear clenched his chest, and he thrashed his legs beneath the covers, gritting against arthritic pain. He had to get the blood moving. He stopped, exhausted, with heat rising from the quilt's edge. I can't thrash all night, he thought. What the hell do I do? I grow old until it gets me, that's what I do. God be damned.

He was still breathing hard when he heard tires crunching on the old snow on St. Anne's Road. He rose to a knock on the door, slipped on his slippers, and pulled back the curtain. Barb Mischke's minivan waited wretchedly at the curb, Brian slumped at the wheel as if he were melting. Pluming exhaust wrapped his silhouette in white shadow.

Clark cursed himself for making light of dementia. Something bad had happened to Maynard and that joking had called it down upon him. Beatrice had whispered stolen thoughts into a sniper God's ear, and the sniper God had shot clots instead of bullets into the back of his best friend's head. He pulled his housecoat over his pajamas and hurried into the living room.

Barb was a lump on the other side of the door. She stared at him from puffy eyes and a puffy face; she looked ten years older than the last time he had seen her. Her breath billowed, as if she'd been running. "Clark," was how she greeted him.

"What happened to him?"

She pointed at the alley, a quick lifting and dropping of her arm. "He said he was going to walk home. We couldn't get him in the van. He's out here in pajamas and slippers."

197

Clark was already reaching into the closet for his coat and boots. "He'll freeze to death."

"Or his heart will kill him. He was walking fast."

Clark's coat was on, his gloves were on, his hat settled upon his head. He'd shucked his slippers off and was standing barefoot in his boots with the rubber sucking at his skin. "I'll follow you."

"Just get in the van."

The cold slammed into his chest like a hammer. Wind-driven snow shone on the sidewalk. Brian was opening the van's side door, the streetlight reflecting eerily around him. Clark got in the front seat while Barb climbed in behind.

"I've had about enough of this kinda thing." Brian's eyes flashed at Barb, as bright as the stars, as bright as the winter moon.

"I know you have," Barb said.

"About enough."

He slammed shut the door, then stomped around the front of the van, his orange hunting jacket brilliant in the headlights. Barb waited until he was behind the wheel before answering him. "I can't put him in a home while he knows he's going into a home."

Brian put the van in gear. "The sonabitch thinks he owns the damned house. Can't even sit in a chair without him hollerin' about something. He threatened to beat my kids. Nobody, and I mean god-damned nobody, threatens to beat my kids."

"I know," she said.

"We gotta goddamn spot for him all lined up at Ambrose's. What're we waitin' for?"

"I can't put him in while he knows it," she repeated. "He has feelings."

"I've had about enough of his feelings. Like having a two-hundred-pound baby running the place." Clark had never heard him say so much. "Then he pulls shit like this."

Brian turned into the alley. Tires ground angrily on snow and gravel. The house was dark—either Maynard hadn't arrived or he wouldn't ever. Anxiety licked Clark like an ice cream cone. He saw Nora in the driveway, then Nora in a nursing home bed; he smelled her sweet-and-

198

sour stinking. Her legs had been gangrenous stumps the doctor amputated in the spring.

"He's not here yet," Clark said. "You didn't see him on the road?"

"Only in front of our house," Brian said. "Serves the sonabitch right
to be stuck out in this." He fell silent as he pulled to the curb. They all
did. "Sorry, Barb. Didn't mean that."

She put her hand on his shoulder, leaving it there only until the van
stopped. She opened the door and climbed out as quickly as her fatigue allowed. Clark followed her up the sidewalk.

Shouting came around the house with that ineffable tone that snow
can give it. "Good night! Damn it, Helen, good night!"

"Out back," Barb said.

Brian nodded. "I'll go round the far side."

Deep footprints violated the bank beside the walk. The icy crust
pushed up Clark's pajama legs and rasped against his shins. Big crystals
like burrs fell into his boots and nestled with a touch like pain against
the hollow of his heel. He ignored them as he plodded after Barb.
"Maynard?" he called.

"Damn it, Helen, don't lock me out! I don't care about the goddamned television! Good night!"

"Dad!"

"I won't hurt you, and you know it. Good night!"

The snow receded below Clark's boot tops. It melted around his
heel and worked beneath his instep. The neighbor's lights came on;
red-and-blue flashes reflected from the street like weird lightning in a
fantastic dream. "Maynard?"

"I'm not that way anymore, Helen. I'm not that way! Christ in a goddamned hand bucket! Open the door!"

Maynard stood in the backyard, staring at his second-story bedroom
window, his chest heaving like a character's in a cartoon. The kitchen
window was shattered. A shadow covered his right hand and dripped
into snowy, smoking divots. Barb stopped abruptly, her mouth open,
her eyes on her father's hand. Brian stood at the far corner. Clark
worked his way around Barb.

Be forceful now. "Good Christ, Maynard, what the hell did you do?"

Maynard looked at Clark, his eyes wolf wild. "Who the hell are you, and what the hell are you doing in my yard?"

"You know damn well who it is." Does he? "It's Clark, Maynard."

"Clark? Christ in a hand bucket, you've gotten old!"

"What are you raising all this commotion for?"

"The damn woman won't let me in! We had a fight and she won't let me in!" His eyes flashed in the darkness and howled at the moon.

"Do you really think that breaking a window will help any?"

Maynard shrugged, his hands splayed open at his sides, blood dripping from his right set of fingers. "I got mad. Sometimes when I get mad I do crazy things."

Heavy footsteps behind Clark grew louder. He turned to see Jergen Burnett in some kind of police cap with earflaps. Barb hurried toward her father. "Let me see that, Dad."

Maynard shrank away. The blood fell more thickly. "It's that lady! Keep her away from me, Clark. She won't let me come home!"

"Dad, it's Barb. Let me see your hand."

Maynard flailed with his damaged hand. Blood flecked her coat. "Damn you, keep away! Clark, make her keep away!"

Clark took Barb's shoulder, pulled her back without saying anything, then stepped around her again. Blood had spattered everywhere— good Christ, Clark thought, I hope he didn't cut an artery. Clark was suddenly, curiously glad that this was happening in a midnight world and not a full-color one. He couldn't handle salty red. "Maynard, let me see that."

Maynard held out his hand like a child. "Christ, Clark, how did you get so old?"

"It happens, Maynard."

"But not so fast!"

The meat below the thumb was deeply gashed, with other gashes between his fingers and across their pads. Dark blood welled and dropped and covered Clark's hands in a warm, sticky bath that steamed in the moonlight. A long line running down Maynard's index finger

200

sparked with glass splinters. Electric man. "Jergen," Clark asked, "do you have a towel in your squad car?"

"No, but I got a first aid kit." Jergen bustled forward. He slipped in the snow and pinwheeled his arms wildly for balance, almost clipping Barb with a hard right uppercut. Damned dolt. "Maybe you better let me take a look at that."

Good God, no. "Why don't you use your radio to call the Mankato emergency room? Tell them we'll be coming in."

"I think I ought to take a look at that."

"One of us has to call," Clark said, "and you're the only one who knows how to use the radio."

Jergen stopped. "Good point. Be back in a jiffy." He trundled around the corner.

"Can you get a towel out of the house?" Clark asked Barb.

"Brian has the keys." She nodded at her husband. Brian disappeared around the far side of the house. She stepped toward her father.

"Damn it, Clark, keep that lady away!"

Clark looked at Maynard, then at Barb. How much of who you are goes away when your father no longer recognizes you? "Maybe you ought to help Brian with the towels."

She looked away before turning. "Yeah," she said, "all right." A lonely, dark lump faded into the shadows. Poor kid.

Maynard stared at his bleeding hand in astonishment. "What did I do?"

"You ran your hand through the window." Clark packed a handful of snow over the wound on Maynard's thumb. He had no idea if it would do any good.

"Why won't she let me in, Clark?" Maynard's face was ghostly in the shadows; it should have had more color to it. "I haven't hit her or nothing. I'm not that way."

"I know." What was he supposed to tell him? "She went away. Don't you remember?"

Maynard tried to close his hand and winced. "When's she coming back?"

"Well—"

He jerked away. The wounds bled freely. "Don't tell me she isn't coming back, Clark. Don't tell me that."

"She's coming back, Maynard." He thought wildly. "She's only gone for the weekend."

Maynard let Clark take his hand. "Why am I staying at that lady's?"

"You can't stay in your house, not with the work going on in the basement. Don't you remember?"

"Oh yeah. Something to do with the furnace, isn't it?"

Lying is sometimes a convenience, but this was no convenience. "Yeah. The furnace."

"Good. Damn thing never worked right, anyway."

Brian came back with an armful of towels. Clark took the thickest and gently wrapped it around Maynard's knuckles. "You know what this reminds me of?" Maynard asked.

"What?"

"I don't know if you've heard this yet. Do you know what I heard?"

"What?" Clark raised Maynard's arm above his chest. He expected the bleeding to stop quickly now. That heart can't pump uphill.

"I heard that the Wilson kid got his arms caught in a corn picker. You hear that?"

"I heard something about it," Clark said.

"I mean the Wilson kid that used to work for you. Not the girl, but the other one. Remember him?"

"Yeah," Clark said. "I remember him."

"Killed him. It's in that family to die in bad ways."

"Yeah."

"Wife died of TB, didn't she?"

"Cancer, I think."

Jergen came around the corner, exuding his own special brand of incompetent authority. "It's all set up," he said. "We just have to load the old guy in the squad car, and I'll buzz him on over."

"I'm not going nowhere in no squad car," Maynard shouted. "I didn't do it. You've got nothing that says that I did. Damn you people."

"What the dickens is he talking about?" Jergen asked.

"The Wilson murder, I think."

"I didn't do it! To hell with you if you think I did!"

Jergen studied Maynard with a condescending, *you crazy old fart* expression. "Sure you didn't, Gramps. I just want to run you over to get your hand looked at."

"I ain't going nowhere in no goddamned squad car!"

"You will if I tell you to," Jergen said.

Jergen, Clark thought, you giant walking ass. "Maybe it would work better if we took him over in the van."

Jergen shrugged. "Suit yourself. I'll give you an escort."

"I don't think we need an escort."

"I think we do. Let's get him on back to the van. Come on, Gramps."

Maynard shrank away again. He dropped his hand, the towel came loose, and fresh darkness spilled from his fingers. "You stay the hell away from me! I didn't do it!"

Clark waved Jergen off. "Get your escort ready. We'll meet you out front."

Clark and Maynard followed Jergen around the corner; Brian and the towels brought up the rear. They hadn't reached the front walk before the bleeps and blips and whistles from Jergen's siren sounded experimentally. More neighborhood lights came on.

Barb was huddled against the side of the van, her arms across her chest, the blood streaks on her coat like cracks in a doll. She'd been crying. She opened the door as they approached.

Maynard pulled away from Clark. "I'm not going with that lady!" His towel was loose and sopping. "The hell if I'm going with that lady!"

"Why don't you and Brian ride with Jergen in the squad car?" Clark struggled to hold Maynard, struggled to keep from slipping on the snow. Thoughts of Nora lit up his mind like lightning flashes. "If you don't mind me driving your van."

"That'll work," Brian said.

"Go around to the other side of the squad car, Barb," Clark said. Where your father can't see you. "I'll get Maynard into the van myself."

Clark wrapped another towel around Maynard's bloody one before helping him into the front seat. More lights came on as Jergen pulled away from the curb, his siren like a cat fight. Ass.

The ride to Mankato was quieter than the scene in the yard had been. Janesville was a ghost town after sunset; Smith's Mill and Eagle Lake dropped into the darkness like rocks down a well. Maynard sat with his hands in his lap, humming tunelessly.

"A nice night, isn't it?" he asked near Mankato's city limits. "With the stars and the moon and everything?"

"A nice night," Clark said.

"So, are you jumping in the sack with that Tupelo woman?"

"What?"

"That Tupelo woman. What's her name."

"I married her, Maynard."

"Oh yeah, in the late forties you did, didn't you?"

"Yeah."

"Hell of a long time ago." He hummed for a minute. "I saw a girl at the high school I wouldn't mind jumping in the sack with. Ellen or Helen or something. Don't know her last name. Do you know her last name?"

"Tewle, Maynard," Clark said. "Helen Tewle."

Maynard laughed loudly, his voice high and breaking: "Hell, that's my last name! What, you think she's my sister? I'm not about to jump in the sack with my sister." He leaned toward Clark confidentially. "Have you ever seen my sister?"

"No, Maynard."

"She looks like me. Would you jump in the sack with a woman who looks like me?"

"No, Maynard."

"No, Maynard, is right." He smiled into the darkness. "A nice night, isn't it? With the moon and stars and everything?"

"A nice night, Maynard," Clark said.

The emergency room personnel took Maynard in with quiet and tired proficiency; the rush of their starched uniforms rustled like gulls taking flight. Clark, Barb, and Brian waited in the lobby—Jergen waited in his squad car. A young doctor with a deeply tanned face came out once to speak with Barb. She sat again with no expression.

"Thirty-four stitches," she said. "They're bandaging him up now. The doctor is worried about him not having professional care."

"Hell," Brian said. "I've been worried 'bout that for a long time."

"He thinks that a social worker should evaluate him in the morning."

"A social worker?" Clark asked.

"It's required for nursing home admittance." She had to bite off the words and spit them out.

"You know what the social worker will say, don't you?" Brian asked after a silence.

"I know." Barb looked at him from a heavy face that had seen too much for one night. "We could still take care of him."

Brian shook his head. "I'm sorry, Barb, him being your father and all, but enough is enough. I won't have him in the house."

"Please, Brian."

"Enough is enough." He leaned toward her and took her big hand. "At the home, there's people who can take care of him. They're there full-time, and they know what they're doing."

They know, Clark thought. They pick you up and slam you down with an efficiency you can feel like a chill. He wished it was his place to say something.

"How will we pay for it?" Barb asked.

"The county will take his house in exchange for the home's expenses."

She stared at him coldly. "You've checked all of this out, haven't you?"

"Somebody had to, Barb."

"It's a pretty high price to pay, isn't it?"

"Believe me, we come out ahead."

"He won't want to go."

"He won't have a say." Brian sighed. "He'll get three squares a day

205

and be with people his own age. They'll have things for him to do . . ."

"Don't try to justify it to me. I know what a home is and I know what I'm doing to Dad." She rubbed her eyes quickly. "Maybe we should wait until Monday. Think it over."

"It's supposed to get colder tomorrow. What if he pulls this stunt again and we don't find him?" He watched her from stern but loving eyes, eyes that were not frightened, like in the wedding picture; eyes that saw something that had to be done. The cruelest kind. "Is that how you want him to go?"

She hardly had the strength to shake her head. "No."

"I'll call the home right now, see if there's a bed open. If the social worker can see him early enough, we might get him in before noon." He rose before she could protest and walked to a pay phone across the lobby. He stared at it, then came back. "You know the number?"

She didn't look at him. "No."

"They must have it at the desk." He walked to the desk, spoke quietly, and carried a Credibull telephone book back to the pay phone.

"What do you think of this, Clark?" Barb asked.

He shrugged. What do I think? Rock and a hard place, that's what I think. He saw in his mind a scene out of Steinbeck, an old farmhand crying because he did not have the strength to shoot his decrepit dog. But Maynard wasn't a dog, and he cursed himself for thinking it. "It's not my place to think anything."

A heavyset nurse wearing a polyester uniform walked by, her legs rubbing together. Brian was trying to balance the book on his thigh, his finger pressed against a number. He picked up the receiver, cradled it on his shoulder, and dropped a quarter down the telephone's throat. Barb watched him punch the numbers, but turned away when he began speaking. She had wet eyes and silent tears.

"Are you all right?" Clark asked.

"I wish he didn't have to be in such a damned hurry." She wiped her cheeks with both hands, pulling the skin tight, creating deep furrows in front of her ears. "Why is it that while you're a kid you never stop to think about times like this? It's not like you don't know they're coming."

"Probably because you're a kid."

"It makes growing up hardly worth it." She took a deep breath, then stiffened. She watched her husband nod at the phone. Her eyes were firmer now, the tears a film over stone. "I should be over there. I should be making that call."

"You don't have to do everything, Barb."

"It should be my responsibility. I don't want this to be anyone else's."

The doctor motioned Barb over. They spoke quietly as she filled out forms. Clark sat alone until Brian came back. They looked at each other. Brian nodded.

Barb shook the doctor's hand, then walked back to where Brian and Clark waited. "They're keeping him until morning. They had to give him a sedative." She paused to study the darkness outside the main entrance. "I ask you for too many favors, Clark."

"What is it?"

"If the social worker gives the green light, they'll examine him tomorrow morning, and if there's room at St. Ambrose's, that's where he'll go."

"There's room," Brian said.

She didn't acknowledge him. "I was wondering, Clark, if you would drive him over."

Hell, Clark thought, we all gather there, like the elephants' graveyard. "He won't like going to the home."

"The doctor said they could give him something if it looked like he would be a problem." She paused. "I'd do it myself, but—"

"I know." He'd have to call Agnes, have her fill in at the historical society for an hour or two. He did not want to do this. "All right."

Barb's gaze struggled mightily not to waver. "I'll meet you there with clothes and things."

"All right."

"Thank you."

"Nothing to thank me for."

Clark found it funny how they all knew what the social worker would say. He had a fleeting thought about how Walter would handle this when it happened to him. *If,* he admonished himself, *if* it happens to me. Assumptions become self-fulfilling prophesies. Do not go gentle. *If, if, if.*

Barb called the next morning just as Clark was coming out of the bathroom. He had slept from the time he returned to Credibull until almost ten without his bladder once awakening him. He had forgotten how good a long, hard piss could feel.

"The social worker said we should put him in Ambrose's." Barb's voice was flat and dry, like a chalk floor.

"And everything at Ambrose's is ready?" he asked.

"They're waiting for us."

"I'll be on my way."

The sky was a lid of gray. The frozen fields stretched away on each side of the highway, the battered stalks remaining distinct in the frigidly clean winter air all the way to the horizon. It was big out there, it was empty. It was lonely, too, with the fields like faces and the wind so breathlessly still. Clark tried to remember each time in his life that he had been lonely, tried to fill this empty time between Credibull and Mankato with emptiness. He had a sudden desire to turn the car around and head back east to Indiana. It was not much different there, though. A little less cold.

He thought about Maynard.

Maynard was sitting on the edge of his big, professionally made bed, humming as he had been the night before. His face was a gray lid, too, his eyes a billionth of a degree out of focus. Clark saw only cloudy comprehension.

"Who are you?" Maynard's voice was a jackhammer.

"I'm Clark, Maynard."

"Oh yeah, Clark. Hell, you've gotten old."

Clark leaned weakly against the door frame. The words held a deeper sickness than they had held the night before. "I know." His knees ached; his shoulder hurt. His friend of more than forty years had died during the night, but his friend was sitting before him on the bed, humming. How can this be? How can this be?

"You know what I done?" Maynard held up his heavily bandaged arm. "I ran my hand through a window."

"I know, Maynard."

"Damnedest thing. Helen locked me out of the house, said I had bashed her. Hell, I hadn't bashed her. Do you have any idea when the last time I bashed her was?"

Clark saw Helen in the fields, blood running from her mouth. He saw blood flowing across the furrows, across St. Anne's Road, into the toolshed of a neighbor with an English name. He saw salty red; we all know or will know the truth. "Not in a long time," he said.

"A couple of years, anyway. She locked me out and I cut up my hand. Do you suppose she'd hold a grudge that long?"

"I don't think so, Maynard."

"Hell of a woman. Died a few months ago. She's out in the Catholic cemetery. Wanders around the farm."

"I know, Maynard."

"Hell of a woman. She locked me out of the house last night because she said I bashed her. I cut up my hand breaking out the kitchen window. That's how I cut up my hand." He held his arm up again. "Do you know how long it's been since I bashed her?"

"Let's go, Maynard."

"It's been a hell of a long time. Couple of years, anyway." He laughed his high, demented laugh. "I cut my hand last night because she locked me out of the house."

The pain of seeing this ripped Clark deeply, much more deeply than the pain he had felt the night that Nora had slipped. He wanted to scream and cry and rage. He wanted to climb the silver ladder to heaven and spit in the face of God. What right did he have to allow this? "Let's go, Maynard."

"Where are we going?"

What do you say? Does it make a difference? "We're going home."

"I broke a window there last night. Ran my hand through it. Helen said that I bashed her."

"Let's go home, Maynard."

"Wanders around the farm."

"Sure, Maynard."

"Cut my hand up, though. Make it tough to plow."

"Yeah."

"Cut it up last night. Ran it through a window."

"Yeah," Clark said.

At the desk he signed whatever papers they shoved at him. His mind drifted through Maynard's wanderings like a lost child looking for a warm hand. He thought of Emma Richard. He saw her hands float before him, nice hands, hands riding gently on the air, birds dancing in a sunset. He cursed himself for not staying with her that night, cursed Nora for perching that night on his shoulder like a diseased parrot. Morality is fine until you come right down to it, come right down to holding a warm hand, to holding someone warm in the night. Warmth outweighs all the tenets and doctrines and stone tablets that muster history into its rigid, moralistic lines. He wanted nothing more desperately than to crawl to her door and plead forgiveness for all he had done that night that dull eyes and god-be-damned morality had told him was laudable. But Maynard was sitting beside him, humming blankly, a friend for more than forty years. Clark concentrated on the road and tried to forget Emma. No, damn it. The hell if he'd forget her. The hell if he could.

"Hurt like hell," Maynard said. "Ran it through a window."

The drive back was longer and lonelier and harder than the drive there had been. Snow began to fall just west of Janesville, large flakes that melted as they scuttled across the windshield. Clark's thoughts wrapped around him as if they were barbwire; when he extricated himself he found his knuckles white and aching on the steering wheel and the speedometer at seventy. He forced himself to slow. As they approached Credibull, he began to think about the nursing home, about

210

Nora and Annie Halverson and old Bob Tunnell, about starched sheets and bedpans and sterilized air. About Maynard. When he came back from thinking about them he was driving forty-five with a line of vehicles building impatiently behind him. He forced himself to speed up.

"Gonna put alfalfa on the back forty, oats for cover," Maynard said. "Corn on the front. But I ran my hand through the window. Cut it up pretty bad. Hard to plow."

"I have to tell you something, Maynard."

"Maybe go fishing after work. Helen won't like it, but Christ in a hand bucket, I can only stand that damn kid's crying for so long. Helen died a few months ago. Wanders around the farm."

"I'm not taking you home, Maynard."

"Ran my hand through a window. Cut it up pretty bad."

"I'm not taking you home."

"She says I bashed her, but I haven't bashed her. Haven't bashed her since that damned Wilson got his. Son lost his arms in a picker. Cut it up pretty bad."

Clark pulled onto the shoulder and let the cars behind him pass. "Listen to me, Maynard."

"Who the hell are you?"

"I'm Clark Holstrom, Maynard. Listen to me."

"Clark? Christ in a hand bucket, you've gotten old!"

"I'm not taking you home, Maynard. I'm taking you to Ambrose's. You can't take care of yourself anymore."

Maynard's bloodshot eyes seemed as impenetrable as the little red clots in his mind. "Got fields to plow. Be tough, though. I ran my hand through a window."

"I'll look after your fields for you."

"I ran it through a window. Helen locked me out. Said I bashed her. She's dead. Wanders around the farm."

"Just until your hand gets better." How impenetrable is futility?

Maynard smiled. "Ran my hand through a window." He hummed his tuneless song as Clark pulled back onto the road.

"Helen thinks I bashed her, " Maynard said. "She's dead, you know."

211

"I know, Maynard."

"Wait until I tell her I haven't bashed her. Won't she be surprised?"

Barb was waiting at Ambrose's front desk, staring through the window across the gray ice and fishing houses covering Crystal Lake. Her eyes darted trepidly as Clark walked Maynard to the desk and took his arm to keep him from walking beyond it. Maynard didn't seem to recognize his daughter.

"Is everything ready?" Clark asked. He felt the walls gather around him, those damned sterilized walls, an army, a coffin. Whatever it was that they emanated caught in his throat and stuck.

Barb only nodded. A tall, dried weed of a nurse nodded, too, an efficient jerk of a nod. Mrs. Trodahl, a woman Clark had met once and had quickly tried to forget. It was funny how often that happened in a place like this. "Everything is ready," she said. "Come along, Mr. Tewle."

"Tough to plow," Maynard said. "Said I bashed her."

The Weed Woman led Maynard down a starched, sterilized hall as if she were pulling a wagon. Clark and Barb followed. When Maynard began to wheeze, Barb jumped forward and took the nurse's shoulder. "Not so fast. His heart."

The Weed Woman gave her a calm, condescending look, a look you would give a child. "I've reviewed his file. I know his condition."

If Clark had had the nerve, he would have punched her in the mouth. Don't you realize, he raged inside, what Barb is going through? What we're going through? You and the bitch nurse must be buddies—you probably spend your Friday nights kicking out the walkers from under your patients.

"Here we are," the Weed Woman said, as brightly as a bellboy at the Ritz. She probably expected a tip.

The room was small and white and horribly clean. Barb had brought in the living room chair and Maynard's bedroom curtains to lend a familiar air. A new portable television sat on the dresser, angled toward

212

the empty bed. An old man Clark did not recognize watched them from the second bed like a lizard in a terrarium.

"This is Jonathan," the Weed Woman said. "He's been with us awhile." The lizard just lay there like Nora until he turned silently to the wall.

"I cut my hand up, you know," Maynard said. "Be hard to plow."

"Of course, Mr. Tewle." The Weed Woman patted his arm. "I know you'll be happy here." She turned to Barb and Clark, so dried out that her bones creaked. "I'll leave you alone for now. Walk around, get acquainted with the place."

"I am acquainted with the place," Clark said.

"Oh, of course. You're Nora Holstrom's husband, right? We all love Nora around here."

"I suppose you do." She can't complain.

The Weed Woman looked at her watch too quickly to read it. "Well, there are other residents. Please feel at home." It was a purely mechanical action followed by purely mechanical words. She disappeared into the hall.

Maynard wandered slowly around the room as the words coming out of his mouth tumbled over one another. Barb tethered him by the hand away from the lizard. The pressure of the place was two hands around Clark's throat slowly squeezing. Only in Ambrose's did he ever feel so trapped. Selective claustrophobia. Survival instinct. He thought of Emma Richard again.

"I should get over to the historical society," he said. I should get out of here.

Barb nodded. "Thanks for bringing him over. If I had known he would be like . . . this . . . I would have done it myself."

"That's all right." He turned to Maynard. "You take care, old buddy."

"Got to plow," Maynard said. "Ran my hand through a window."

Clark patted his arm, a yielding, heavy, directionless thing. He turned away to find himself staring at the lizard's back. A desperate tightness bound his chest. The pain of five sharp crescents on his palm forced him to unclench his fist. God be damned. Got to get out.

"I'll sit with him until he's comfortable," Barb said.

"Yeah." Clark turned from the death on the mattress to the death in Maynard's eyes. Frying pan to fire. Got to get out. Got to get out.

"Christ in a hand bucket!" Maynard shouted wildly. "Got to plow!"

Clark hesitated at the door. "Are you sure you'll be all right, Barb?"

"Yes." She still held her father's hand. It jerked hers like a dog on a leash. A sadness filled her eyes, but no tears. She was in control now. "Are you going to see Nora?"

Hell, no. "Maybe this afternoon. I have to get to the historical society." His throat pulled to the point of asphyxiation. Got to get out. "See you, buddy."

"Says I bashed her. Ran my hand through a window. Wanders around the farm."

Clark left without answering. If he'd been capable of running, he would have. He hesitated at Nora's hall only momentarily before hurrying for the lobby door. He did not breathe again until he was outside.

The sky the next morning was a cold, pale blue and the air as crisp as an apple. Clark's breath floated before his eyes like a dream from which he could not awaken. The elevator across the highway was silent; the football field empty. It would stay that way until spring.

He sniffed the air and looked down at the paper that lay unread in his lap. The type swarmed—he tapped his pocket for his glasses, but didn't have the strength to take them out. The sweet scent of feed swirled in and out of cold-rimmed nostrils, there and gone and there again. In the Wal-Mart parking lot a woman dragged a child bundled to look like an obese munchkin toward the front door. Clark turned to make a comment about her, but no one was sitting beside him.

Finally he rose, fighting tiredly the decades dragging him down. He dropped the newspaper onto the bench as if it were a dead thing; through eyes wet even in the frigid breeze he looked across the road at

214

the Bumblebee Café. He shuffled south toward his house. Maybe he'd go see Bert this morning. Maybe he'd spend it reading.

Life goes on until it doesn't go on anymore. The hell of it is that each change reminds you of that. It was the surest sign of mortality. He missed Maynard.

Chapter

10

Wednesday brought warm weather with the snow melting and the earth seeping and the streets shiny beneath the sun. The car tires sputtered with the snowmelt. The air was like a warm breath that could not quite tempt Clark into believing that one day spring would return. Too much winter remained for fantasies.

He swept the floor in the morning, then walked to the historical society. The old Lutheran congregation rose from the sanctuary floor before him like fumes from the varnish. From the office door, Agnes smiled through its transparency. "Have you done your Christmas shopping?" she asked as she slipped her coat over her shoulders.

He shook his head clear. The congregation receded. "As much as I have to do."

The back of her arms hung loosely from the bone as she struggled to find her coat sleeves. "I left something for you on your desk. I won't see you until after Christmas."

Clark felt a guilty twang; he hadn't thought to get her a gift. He'd have to pick up something over lunch and leave it for her. Maybe a picture—he wondered briefly how much Roger VanRuden would charge for posing nude sprawled across a table cluttered with genealogy books. "That's very nice of you."

"Yes, well, Merry Christmas." She bustled to the door, buttoning up as she went. "I still have the ladies' group to shop for. It gets awfully crazy this close to the holiday."

"Where are you going?"

"To Mankato. To the mall on the hill."

That would be the River Hills Mall. Tropical plants, buzzing attendants, grotesque monsters dancing to calliope music circled in his mind. He remembered the subtle tastes of chicken and cashews and thought again about Emma Richard. He wondered what she was doing now. She was probably listening to music with her eyes closed, her fingers dancing upon the notes or tracing images in the steam rising from her coffee. She was probably dreaming of the future.

Quaint images, Nora's eyes said. *You bastard.*

He forced her from his mind, and out of spite thought of Emma again. Fingers riding nightfall; birds dancing on the sunset. Sweet Emma. The longing for her returned.

Agnes was standing at the front door, smiling back at him. He wondered what he had just missed her saying. He spread his smile to match hers and said, "Merry Christmas."

Agnes nodded and shut the door behind her. It boomed heavily like a safe door closing, the latch rattled and clattered as it found its lock, and a cold wash of air ran across the floor and up his shins like seawater. The silent congregation rose to offer their silent prayers to their deaf and silent God. Clark stared up into the dome and lost focus in the blur of incomprehensible depth, like staring into the heavens. There must be a trillion dreams in the air. They are what makes the sky blue.

He stepped into the back and saw upon his desk a small blue wrapped package. He slowly opened it, hiding from himself the eager anticipation that as a child had turned him into a paper-ripping maniac. Christmas and birthdays had been big days back then. Now they came at him as fast as a flurry of punches.

He thought at first that Agnes's gift might have been a set of historical society keys—it was that size and shape. What came out of the wrapping was a cigarette lighter. He turned it in his fingers. It was a nice lighter, but what the hell was he supposed to do with it? Agnes knew he didn't smoke.

He tried to think of a gift for her as equally useless and thought again of Roger VanRuden. His creativity waned, and after working for an hour he called the only florist in Waseca who would deliver as far away as Credibull and ordered for Agnes a half dozen roses. He halfheartedly checked a few diaries he hauled out of storage for any mention of Henry David Thoreau and found nothing. He wandered around the ground floor, reexamining all the exhibits he had examined a thousand times, before stopping in front of Alonzo Jameson's Civil War diary. What a final Christmas he must have had, freezing in Andersonville, life dropping from his bones like snow from tree branches. He thought of the boy who had asked about Civil War airplanes, who had grown so frightened by Clark's alien features. He was probably dreaming of a Nintendo game for Christmas, one of those "kill as many as you can" games—digital blood and video death by the thousands. At that age Clark had dreamed of BB guns, but, he guessed, such violent aspirations were no longer allowed.

He wandered up the stairs into the choir loft, then looked down on the silent congregation. Agnes had left him no work, and with three days until Christmas, no one would be in. Now he knew the lonely stagnation his son had grappled with before the computers had kicked in. He thought about Miss September and her two-dimensional glossy love. He traced through his mind the web of all the times he had been in love, which were few, and all the times he thought he had been in love, which were many. He thought of the promises he had made to Hannah in the backseat of his father's car, of the promises he had made to English girls in the backseats of English cars, of the promises made to French girls who spoke no English at all. He thought of Nora, and he remembered promises broken.

He was standing in front of the Albert Wilson article, studying the photograph of the toolshed, with Maynard Tewle's farm in the distance. Clark remembered when he had first seen that story as clearly as he remembered Pearl Harbor or the day JFK went down, as clearly as he struggled to keep from remembering Normandy. The times, he thought, I've lived through. The Depression, the war, Hiroshima and Nagasaki. Little brother Bobby lying on the pantry floor of the Ambassador Hotel. King taking us to the mountaintop and getting buried there. Armstrong leaving a footprint on the cheek of the man in the moon. Korea and Vietnam and Watergate. The things we are capable of: bullets and blood and love and laughter and dancing in moondust like pixies.

Nora is in the kitchen, making breakfast. Clark is sitting at the table with the paper spread before him, but he is watching her work. He is no longer angry.

Little Walter comes in with a schoolbag over his shoulder. "Goin' to school now," he says.

"All right, son," Clark answers. "Have a good day."

When he tousles the boy's hair, Nora stares at him strangely. She does not speak and he wants to ask why, but instead he picks up the paper. He reads shocking headlines and sees Maynard's name mentioned only in passing. He ponders that.

"You see this?" he asks. "They put it in here."

"I figured."

She does not say more. He watches her heavy hips as she shifts from burner to burner. She is fixing bacon and eggs. Coffee. The clatter of the spatula against cast iron sounds like short, frightened cries.

"Nora," he says.

She does not answer him. In her movements he sees a resignation to sadness that breaks him like glass. He wants a happy family and to be a happy man, and he has and is neither. From now on he will be a good husband; from now on he will leave the liquor, the infidelity, and the anger behind. In his hands he holds what anger can do.

"Nora," he says again.

She still does not answer. She reaches into the cupboard for a plate on which she slides his breakfast. "Here." She fills his cup with coffee.

He hadn't thought about that in a long time. He didn't want to think about it now. He pushed it deeper into his mind than his memory reached and studied the nail holding the newspaper frame to the wall. Pull it out and it all comes tumbling down; the plaster crumbles and the glass cracks. All things fall into ruin—maybe even memories. Babylon is dust.

He was so resigned to a day of solitude that the door's clatter startled him. Footsteps too quick to belong to Agnes hurried across the sanctuary.

"Clark? Where the hell are you?"

It was that damned Ted Lewell. Clark looked at Maynard's farm before forcing himself back to the choir loft. He looked down from the railing. All the color Lewell possessed seemed to be gathered in his face. His lips were so red he might have bloodied them.

"I thought you'd be back in Chicago for the holidays," Clark said. He'd been hoping, anyway.

Lewell tucked a moldered book beneath his arm. "I got it," he said.

"Got what?"

"What I was looking for. You yokels didn't know a damned thing."

"Got what?" Clark repeated.

"The daughter's diary."

Fear rushed through Clark, and more thoughts of Maynard. His trembling hands sweat on the railing. His promise to Helen, how he would do what he could, bellowed in his ears. Thinking of her brought a sadness that moved with the fright as if making love. "Where did you find that?"

"Come on down."

"Tell me where you found it."

"Just come on down."

By the time Clark reached the sanctuary, Lewell was in the back sitting at Clark's desk, paging carefully through the book. Clark had to sit on the splintered chair. "Where did you find it?" he asked again.

"I had to think like the kids would," Lewell explained in words as meticulous as a kindergarten teacher's. "I thought like the boy but came up with nothing. But girls, hell, girls keep diaries. Where would a girl as private as Rose keep a diary?" He didn't wait for an answer. "In the back of her closet in a hole she probably knocked in the wall herself. She kept it from nineteen fifty-six until the murder." Lewell turned a page. "Listen to this, from December twenty-second, fifty-seven: *'I finally got to see "The Bridge over the River Kwai." I went to see it in Waseca with Mary and her older brother, the one with the big adam's apple. Randy, I think his name is. Anyway, it was kind of keen but too sad to see again. Why Alec Guinness kept William Holden from blowing up the bridge, I can't figure out, especially when he ended up doing it himself.'*"

"That's groundbreaking stuff," Clark said. He relaxed a little.

"Let me finish. *'When I came home that smell was in the air, the same smell that was in it a few weeks ago, like perfume. Dad was the same as he was then, too, and the house was the same, neater somehow. Dad says nobody's been here, but I don't know. I bet someone has.*

" 'I baby-sat the Tewle girl last night. What a brat! I made two dollars and stole a handful of jelly beans.'"

Lewell looked up with a jackal smile. "Well?"

"Is killing someone over a handful of jelly beans considered justifiable homicide?"

Lewell was too impatient for the joke. "Having an affair with somebody else's wife might be. She said she smelled perfume. How many widowed farmers do you know bathe in lilac water?"

"Not many." Clark shrugged. "So maybe Albert Wilson was seeing someone. Why do you think she was married?"

"Because he wouldn't admit to his kid that he had someone there. It wasn't Callahan fucking Wilson's wife. It was Wilson fucking someone else's."

"That's a leap."

"But it's a logical leap." Lewell snapped the cover shut. "What do you know about Maynard Tewle's wife?"

Clark thought of that night in the kitchen, in the bedroom. Lust flashed. On his fingertips he felt the touch of diamonds. "She died a few months ago."

"I heard she got around. Have you heard that?"

"She was an attractive woman. If you're asking me if she had an affair with Albert Wilson . . ." He shrugged. Don't ask what I know you're going to ask next. Please, don't ask. "A lot of people get around."

"Did she ever get around with you?"

God be damned. "No."

Lewell smiled. "Come on, Clark, a woman like that and a handsome guy like you? And you seeing her as much as you did? She never slipped a tongue in your ear or a hand down your pants?"

"No." Oh, to hell with it all, anyway. "And what if she did? I'm not Albert Wilson."

Lewell leaned back in the chair. Resolve glowed in his eyes. He'd jumped to a conclusion and landed firmly upon it, like a tiger. "Things are coming together."

"You don't know that."

"Maybe I don't. But I know what to do next. I'm going to find out it was her—"

"That's conjecture."

"You didn't let me finish. I'm going to find out it was her, or if it wasn't I'm going to find out who it was." He bounced to his feet and slapped the diary. "A gold mine," he said as he picked it up. "A god-damned gold mine."

Every time Clark talked to the bastard he wanted to jam his fist down his throat. "Now that you have your motive, you can leave Bert Finchley alone." I'm sorry, Helen, he thought, but when promises come tumbling down, you grab the closest thing you can. You've got to save something.

"Bert is too much a part of the story."

"You're a writer. Write around him."

"He's too interesting a part of the story." He smiled his infuriating, god-be-damned smile. "What if there's a movie deal?"

He patted Clark's shoulder as he hurried out of the office. Clark listened to his footsteps echo across the sanctuary floor, to the front door clatter open and shut. He sat with his elbows on the armrests, his fingers touching his lips, his palms pressed together as if in prayer. He thought of Maynard and Nora, of Bert Finchley in his pajamas, his long face pulled longer by exposure's fear. He thought of Helen, young and sweet and dressed in the black of a shadow. He tried to picture Albert Wilson's rough farmer hands clutching her buttocks. How easily the image came didn't surprise him. If nothing else, it made everything believable.

What the hell are you doing? he asked himself. What the hell are you going to do?

Tom Finchley was shrugging his coat on when Clark walked into the *Herald*'s office. "Hi, Tommy. Bert around?"

"I was about to go check on him when this call came in. Do you know Norm Unger?"

"Of course I know Norm Unger. He farms north of the lake."

"He's going to try raising llamas, bless God." Did using a phrase like profanity make it profanity? "The first one is supposed to be delivered in half an hour. I'd better get a move on."

"Why would anyone in Minnesota want to raise llamas? The wool? The meat?" Maybe they used them in Chinese cooking. He pushed that image away. It wasn't the time to think about Emma.

Tom smiled as he pulled on his gloves. "Norm's probably raising them so he can see his name in the paper." He glanced at his watch. "I wish Bert was around. We need photographs." He closed his eyes and bowed his head.

"You run to the llama. I'll check on Bert."

Tom opened his eyes and smiled again. "You're an answer to prayer, Clark. Get him out to the Unger farm as fast as you can. It would be nice to get a couple pictures of them unloading it. We're short on news this week, and photos fill out a page."

Clark could not remember ever being God's instrument before. "Like lightning," he said.

Bert's house sat in his yard like a top hat sitting on a frosty, smooth skull. Clark sensed a hint of snowman magic as he stepped out of the Dodge. Christmas in a little town is as bright as snow in sunshine.

He knocked on the door, then studied Goodwin's Funeral Home. He couldn't help but think about Helen in there, a mortician's cold hands, a murder victim's cold hands, crawling over her body. Helen and Wilson seemed too unlikely, but a slap across a face, the taste of blood raised by a husband, can drive a woman anywhere. He wondered if on that night of Maynard's fortieth birthday a slap had driven her into his own arms. He wondered why one had never driven her into them afterward. *He doesn't hit me,* she had said. *He just shakes me a little.* It made a guy wonder.

He pounded on the door again. "Bert," he shouted at the wood. "Bert!" He stepped off the porch and walked around to the living room window. He cupped his hands to shield his eyes, the windowpane cold against the edges of his palms, two icy smiles. He saw just an overturned chair on the floor, newspapers on the wall, and something large and heavy hanging beside them, struggling like a hooked fish. A long-fingered hand clawed the air.

"Bert," he whispered. The cold spread up his wrists into his forearms, into the pit of his stomach. "Oh, good Christ. Bert."

He hurried back to the walk, his body shaking a little looser with each jolting step, his knees sending up shocking little sparks. He tried the door and found it open. A heavy, acrid odor of sweat and urine choked him as he went inside. Bert hung from the wall by his belt, the tongue nailed near the ceiling, the buckle looped around his neck. His toes just reached the floor, and he bounced upon them like a child reaching for a cookie jar.

"Bert! Oh, Christ!" Clark ran to him and clutched him around the hips. The dark stain on Bert's trousers seeped into his shirt. He tried to lift him. How can one man weigh so much? Bert's face was blue, his eyes cocked at a crazy angle, his mouth pulled into a thick, purple grimace. He'd somehow managed to trap the fingers of his left hand beneath the belt. He pushed with his free hand on Clark's shoulder as if he were trying to drive him into the ground.

Clark gathered his legs beneath him and pushed down on the spiking pain in his knees. He watched Bert's toes and failed to see them rise. He stepped back as Bert flopped against the wall.

"I'm going to find a hammer," Clark shouted through the panic in his throat. "Where do you keep one?"

Bert stared goggle eyed, the elbow of his trapped arm flapping like an impotent flipper. What the hell do you expect, Clark asked himself, an answer? He ran into the kitchen, opened drawers and cupboards, and scattered silverware on the floor with a sound like music. Where the hell was a damned hammer? He ran back into the living room and found one lying on the sofa—of course, do you think he drove the nail in with his fist? He set the chair on its feet beside Bert's struggling body and clawed with the hammer at the nail head. He found and pulled it, squealing, out. Bert tumbled to the floor, clutching with his free hand at the belt, his face still struggling, his lips twisted silently. Clark's knees buckled when he jumped from the chair, and he fell beside him. They both clawed at the belt, Clark's fingers finding the buckle first and slipping it loose. He rolled on his back and bit off his pain in short, hot chunks.

"Why the hell," Bert said when he could, "didn't you just put the chair under me?"

"Do you think I had time to think about what I was doing?" Pain flashed with each inhalation. "I didn't know what the hell I was doing!" He rolled on his side and gasped into the musty carpeting. Christ. Christ. "What the hell were *you* doing?"

"Killing myself, what do you think?" The buckle had chafed his throat, raising blood. It stained his fingertips.

"How long have you been hanging there?"

"Too long. My toes were touching the floor. I should have used the second notch instead of the first."

Bile rose thickly in Clark's throat. "Oh, Christ, I'm going to be sick."

"You know where the bathroom is. Don't puke on the carpeting."

Clark crawled past Bert until he reached the wall, then pulled himself to his feet. He hurried into the bathroom to spew Cheerios and orange juice into the toilet bowl. Hell, he thought as he stared at his breakfast, as the smell of it rose to challenge him to puke again; hell, was all he could think. He flushed the toilet and watched the mess swirl away. When he tried he found he could stand, though he had to work his way back into the living room with his hands on the walls. Bert was lying on his back, gasping at the ceiling.

Clark collapsed on the sofa. "You pissed all over yourself."

"I couldn't exactly jump off the wall and use the toilet, could I?"

"What were you doing on the wall in the first place?" Clark dropped his head back to rest on the sofa, to steady this world. The belt lay powerless on the floor. "What the hell?"

"What do you mean, what the hell? Don't you dare ask me why I did it."

"I know why you did it."

"Then what do you mean, what the hell?"

"What kind of a reason is that?"

227

Bert gasped deeply. He rubbed the raw spot on his throat. "I woke up this morning with that book on my mind and thought, Why hang around? It was a spur-of-the-moment decision."

"Christ, Bert, couldn't you have had a cup of coffee first? Couldn't you have taken some time to think about it?"

"I did have a cup of coffee first. Why do you think I pissed all over myself?" He held out his hand to Clark. "Help me up."

"To hell with you. I've helped you enough this morning."

"Help me up."

Clark leaned forward, took his hand, and pulled the pain from his knees into his shoulder. Bert crawled across the carpeting to sit heavily beside Clark. They both stared at the nail hole marring the paneling.

"You smell like piss," Clark said.

"You smell like puke."

"Christ, Bert, you were going to kill yourself over a book?"

"Like I said, it was a spur-of-the-moment decision." He looked at Clark. He was still gasping. "Have you ever tried to kill yourself?"

"Hell, no."

"It hurts."

"What did you expect?"

"That's not what I mean. I mean it would hurt no matter how you did it. It hurts just knowing you could do that to yourself."

"So why the hell did you do it?" The pain was lessening now toward a dull throbbing.

"Christ, Clark, I didn't know it would hurt until I kicked the chair out. My feet dropped and I said to myself, What have I done?" He gasped again, and coughed. The purple was leaving his lips. "Why did you come by?"

"Your nephew wants you out at the Unger farm to photograph some llamas."

"Fuck the llamas."

"Sure, fuck them now. If I had known that I'd find you doing this, I would have told him that myself." He rubbed his shoulder. "Didn't you even leave a note?"

"Yeah." His voice was husky, belt whipped. "It's on the coffee table."
Clark reached for it, but Bert stopped him. "It's not a very good note.
It doesn't explain anything."

"You try to commit suicide and you don't explain anything?"

"It wasn't like I had time to think about what to write."

"You had time to drink a cup of coffee. Christ, you stink."

"You don't exactly smell like a bed of roses." He reached for the
note and handed it to Clark. "You might as well read it. I at least owe
you that much."

Clark unfolded the note, read it, then tossed it on the table. "*'Fuck
it'?* All you have to say is *'Fuck it'?*"

"I'm a photographer, not a writer."

"But *'Fuck it'*?"

"So I'll mail it to the llamas. What do you want from me?"

They stared at the wall, then at each other. Their breaths slowed;
Clark's pain shuffled into the back of his mind. The shock of what had
happened wore thin enough to expose the shock of why. "The book is
still there, Bert."

Bert nodded heavily and rubbed his throat again. "I know."

"You're not going to try this again, are you?"

"If you do it wrong," Bert said, "it gives you a hell of a lot of time to
think. But all I can remember now is that it hurts too much."

Clark patted his knee. You old fairy, he thought. We put ourselves
through the damnedest things. "So what are you going to do?"

"Hell if I know."

"Dealing with it won't be easy."

"You think I would have tried to kill myself if I thought dealing with
it would be easy?" Bert rubbed his face, then patted Clark's hand patting his knee. "You're a good guy, Clark, but you're as dumb as hell
sometimes." He sighed. "At least with this book people will know
Kenny wasn't a murderer. There's good in everything bad, right?"

"Sure," Clark said.

Bert withdrew his hand from Clark's. He stared at it for a moment,
then let it fall into his lap. "I wasn't hitting on you, you know."

"I know."

"Good." Bert breathed deeply. "Which Unger?"

"Norm."

"What the hell is Norm Unger doing trying to raise llamas?"

"Chinese food, maybe."

"They put llamas in Chinese food?"

"Hell if I know."

"He always was a crazy bastard."

"Always was." We all are sometimes. "He must be making a spur-of-the-moment decision."

"You have to watch out for those," Bert said.

Clark slept late on Christmas morning because he was in no hurry to go to dinner at Walter's. He wished he was making Christmas dinner himself so he could have invited Emma Richard over, or maybe Bert Finchley. He shuffled from the bed to the bathroom, rinsed his face, and stared into the mirror with his razor blade poised at his neck.

When the first stanza of "Silver Bells" came over the radio, he rushed into the bedroom to turn it off. If he had to listen to that song one more time, the radio was going out the window. Maybe it would land on Santa's head as he made a late delivery. Maybe it would send him to the hospital, where the doctors would refuse to operate on an uninsured fat man in a funny suit. They'd give him a Band-Aid and a bill for $2,000 and leave him befuddled outside the lobby door. The jolly old elf would somehow end up on the streets of Manhattan with that jolly old ass a semen depository for perverts living in cardboard boxes. Mrs. Claus would be frantic for all of a day and a half before she announced she'd had a secret lover for decades, the filthy-rich elf accountant who'd been embezzling from the old man's toy-construction budget. As Rudolph searched for the sex slave Santa, a Patriot missile would blow him out of the sky, and the Republicans in Congress would point out the need for increased defense spending. Christmas in the real world.

Christ, Clark admonished his reflection as he drew down the razor, what a Scrooge you've turned into. He wondered what had happened to that glow he used to feel as Walter tore the wrapping off the Tyco train set. Yeah, well, it used to be that Nora wasn't lying as limp as a slug. It used to be that Helen was alive and Maynard wasn't wandering through a nursing home. You never used to find friends tacked by a nail to the wall.

Christmas was supposed to be the celebration of a miraculous birth, but, Clark told his face in the mirror, you are seventy-two and too far away from births to attach any miracles to them. You know where they inevitably end—Good Friday is just around the corner. Dead at thirty-three, he was.

He finished shaving. When he pressed the towel against his face he saw in the pattern on his eyelids an image of Emma Richard on Christmas, listening to Handel's *Messiah,* a big turkey on the table. She was sitting there in that black-and-white apartment with her grandchildren all around her, steam rising from the knife blade her son-in-law was using to carve the bird.

Clark couldn't remember if she had told him about grandchildren, or children, for that matter. Maybe she was alone listening to Handel, her life as monochrome as her apartment, tears dropping onto an empty table like Christmas glitter. He had an acute longing to see her. He could not force that longing away as he lowered the towel and stared at his reflection. Even Nora's heavy eyes perched upon his shoulder could not drive it away. A struggle between the image and the eyes ended with Nora turning away. *I set you free,* either she or his anticipation said. *In defeat and blessing, I set you free.* Nora, he thought, ah, Nora, my lifelong unloved love. Thank you for this gift.

Clark splashed on a sting of aftershave and stepped into the bedroom. In the closet he found an old man's clothes. As he pulled on his pants he savored both his liberation and the freshness of thinking about Emma without guilt. He smiled through the ache slowly pulsing in his knees—he decided he would go over and see her today. He'd have to see Walter first—it was Christmas, after all—but he'd cut that short if he could. He whistled as he tucked Walter's computer game beneath his arm and left the house.

He felt too alive for driving; he walked to Walter's apartment. He climbed those threadbare steps and knocked jauntily on the door. When he opened it, Walter looked older than Clark felt, though he still looked younger than Clark had seen him in a while. His suddenly steady eyes flickered with success's electronic spark.

"Merry Christmas, son."

"Merry Christmas, Dad. Come on in."

A small balsam fir perched precariously on top of the television, a small, rectangular present lay wrapped in green beneath it. Ham swam in a shallow pan on the kitchen counter; two pineapple slices caramelized black lay upon it like shingles. Mechanical cheers leaked from the ever-present television football crowd.

"I've been busy this morning." Walter's shirt and pants were clean, though his zipper was down. An almost edible scent fought with the balsam aroma in the thick air.

"I guess you have. Where do you keep that computer?"

"In the bedroom."

"You'll need it for this." Clark tossed the present to Walter with a flick of his wrist. "A game the salesgirl said you would love. Merry Christmas. Again."

Walter turned the present over in his hands. "You shouldn't have told me what it was. You've ruined my anticipation."

"I was thinking about your anticipation this morning. Not now—I mean when you were a kid."

"You know what my favorite Christmas present you ever gave me was? That red bicycle."

"That was your birthday, son. Why would I buy you a bicycle in the middle of winter?"

Walter shrugged and tore the paper off the game. "After a while they all run together." He studied his present with delight in his eyes. "Hey, I've heard of this. It's supposed to be good. I'll try it as soon as I get a chance."

He set his present on the television, catching the tree as it toppled backward like a quarterback getting his clock cleaned. The crowd cheered. "Here's mine for you." He picked up the green present and caught the tree again. "I know how you like old books. I stopped in at a used place when I was in the Cities last weekend. They had this."

Clark accepted the present. He studied it with his fingers and smelled it through the paper. Dusty sweet, petrified ink. Nothing beats the smell of an old book. "What is it?"

Walter just nodded. A smile twisted the pocks on his face into weird creases and crazy angles. Clark carefully removed the wrapping paper. He held in his hands a battered old volume with a torn and half-missing dust jacket.

"It's Sinclair Lewis's *Babbitt*. First edition."

Clark carefully turned the book over, carefully opened and read the cover page. God, oh God, the hell if it wasn't. In Walter's face he saw his own smile reflected. To hell with the Manhattan Santa—Christmas never really goes out of you. "This must have cost you a fortune."

"Not too bad. The jacket is ripped."

Clark searched the book, turning gently the gossamer pages. He found and read the quote he had tried to think of when he first met Ted Lewell:

> In other countries, art and literature are left to a lot of shabby
> bums living in attics and feeding on booze and spaghetti, but
> in America the successful writer or picture-painter is indis-
> tinguishable from any other decent businessman.

You had eyes that saw into our souls, Mr. Lewis, he thought. You must have been a son of a bitch to be around. He closed the book and turned it over again, concentrating on the way it felt in his hands. Make sure, he warned himself, you know its touch. If this is a dream and it goes away, you'll want to remember at least its touch. "Thank you, Walter." He felt embarrassed by his own gift. He should have gotten him something nicer. "Thank you very much."

"It's nothing, Dad." Walter thrust his hands into his pockets. His face held a smile pleased at giving pleasure. "Are you hungry?"

"I'm starving."

"Then let's dig in."

Eating was not as awkward as it had been at Thanksgiving. Clark's back did not hurt as much. The food was better and Clark was happier and no magazines poked from beneath the sofa. The only thing that was the same was football's vitiate idiocy, and if he had to, he could live with that. He looked around the apartment at photographs and mementos. It all looked different, somehow. A new day.

"I didn't tell you why I went to the Cities," Walter said around a mouthful of ham.

"I thought it was to get the book."

"Yeah, well, I had two reasons. I had a date with Amber Goltz."

Clark looked at his son. Oh God, another Jenny. He swallowed the rising dread with a chunk of pineapple. "Oh?"

"We went to some Shakespeare thing at some little place in downtown St. Paul. She's into that sort of thing now."

She used to be into strange and very drunken men's hotel rooms, Clark recalled. The day had filled him with enough clemency to believe that anyone could change. He had. "What is she doing?"

"She works for Films in the Cities, or Film in the Twin Cities, or something like that. One of those artsy things. Secretarial work."

Well, good for her. "How did you like the Shakespeare?"

"Couldn't understand a damn word of it. Too many *thees* and *thous*." He paused to watch the game. "It was nice having her explain it to me, though." He waited until his father looked at him before he continued. "I like her, Dad."

"That's nice, son."

"No. I mean I really like her."

Clark paused in his eating. Walter was talking of liking a woman who was not Jenny. He glanced at the picture of Jenny flaunting her crotch. A new day. "That's good, son."

Walter leaned forward to reach into his back pocket, his belly working the tray like toothless gums working a cracker. His scalp flushed with the exertion, and the slight smell of him drifted over to the sofa. He smelled like ham. "I got a picture of her and her daughter."

"She gave you a picture?"

His flush turned to a blush. "Well, not exactly. I wanted a picture of her, but didn't think I should ask."

"So you stole one?"

"It was lying in a desk drawer with a bunch of others just like it. I'll give it back one day." He set his tray to the side and handed a photograph to Clark. It showed a nice-looking woman, a young middle age, and trim. She had dark hair and very soft eyes, reformed wisdom within them. The girl had hair the color of her mother's but long and flowing, with a ribbon in the back. She was wearing a dress with frills, the kind they wore nowadays only for pictures, weddings, and funerals. Neither was pretty but both were handsome. Clark could see plainly that Amber was no longer the Amber he remembered, the user who liked to be used. Either she'd changed or his memory had grown faulty. Selective, Maynard would say.

"I wish you the best, son. I sincerely do."

"Thanks, Dad." Walter took the picture back, brushed a crumb from its surface, then set it on his tray. They ate pumpkin pie for dessert, Walter's eyes drifting from the football game back to the picture as if he were in a boat and had a need to constantly check the anchor. Clark felt very, very good inside. He thought of Emma and saw in his mind her crying in her apartment. He wished he was not enjoying this visit with his son so much.

"I hate to do this to you, Walter, but I need to leave."

"Are you going out to see Mom?"

A sudden dread rose at the risk of giving Nora a chance to pop back into his conscience. "Among other people."

"Will you say hi to her for me?"

He nodded in relief—without Walter stopping by there would be no pressure to see her. It felt good to have her off his mind, his shoulder, his conscience. It felt like crawling out from beneath a very stuffy blanket.

"I need to be running, too," Walter said.

"Where are you going?"

Walter smiled at the picture. "Up to see Amber. I bought some presents."

"What presents?"

"Her daughter is into Barbies. I bought Amber a necklace. Cost me a damn fortune."

Clark stood. "I don't want to keep you."

Walter stood, too, his bulk requiring the use of both hands upon the armrests. "I suppose I should try out the computer game first."

"It can wait. Let's get these dishes done and go do the things we have to do."

"The dishes can wait, too."

Walter turned off the television, then bussed the dirty dishes into the kitchen. Joy permeated a hurried grabbing of coats and gloves. Clark held Lewis's book like a fragile child.

"You know, Dad," Walter said as he shut and locked the apartment door, "this is the best Christmas I've had in a long time."

"Me, too, Walter," Clark answered. "Me, too."

Bright lights reveled in Mankato, reds and greens and blues. The air held just enough cold to be bracing, to be Christmas. The River Hills Mall vestibule glowed against its snowy backdrop like an emerald on cotton. The motel he had stayed at the night he had met Emma had managed only a halfhearted attempt to do homage to the season—one string of dismal lights and a cardboard reindeer taped to the office door. I should never have stayed there, Clark thought as he passed it. He forgot about it immediately.

He did a quick drive through the campus to buttress his courage. Good Christ, he thought, you're acting like a nervous schoolboy. He remembered the first time he'd taken out Hannah, how he'd kept walking by her house, too frightened to open the gate, until finally her father shouted from the living room window, "For Christ's sake, come on in." Love or its promise does the damnedest things to you. The tickle of a giggle in his chest surprised him. When was the last time he'd giggled?

He drove by the theater. *Henry and June* was no longer playing. Too bad—the more he thought about it, the more he realized he had enjoyed that movie. There weren't many cars in the parking lot of Emma's apartment complex, but her Buick was there. He couldn't get over what a lucky day this was turning into.

He parked beside her car, his heart beating so hard he could feel it, life's rhythm renewed. He went up the stairs with his new book in his hand, into the ammonia-smelling warmth of the hallway. He bounded up one more flight, adrenaline fifty proof in his veins, in the slightly acrid smell of his breath. He felt almost drunk, a condition he had not experienced for thirty-five years; he had forgotten how much he had enjoyed its pure simplicity, how it curved all the lines. He was at her apartment door. She opened it to his knock before he realized that his mind was completely blank. That was just like the first time he had dated Hannah, too.

She had not been crying. She was dressed as if she were going out. He hoped she always dressed that way.

"Hello, Clark," she said, with only a hint of surprise.

"Hi."

They stared at each other. Clark's heart sent out surges that pulsed in his knees and shoulder. He was too caught up in Emma to notice anything more than a distant ache, a thunder over a horizon. *For Christ's sake*, Hannah's dad had said, *come on in.*

"Hi," he said again.

"It's so good to see you." She stepped away from the door.

As he walked by her, he caught the scent of her perfume, of flowers, of the promise of the almost-forgotten summer, of love. The season's colors spangled the black-and-white in her living room, a lifetime of red-and-green knickknacks released from their cardboard prisons for this one week of the year. He felt like a fool. Who was he? A seventy-two-year-old bumpkin. He was as devoid and clear of what he wanted to be as the sunshine coming coldly through the window.

"I want to show you my present." He held out the book gawkishly. Good Christ. It was something a schoolboy would do.

She smiled. He could get lost in that smile for the rest of his life. "It looks like a marvelous present." She was looking at him, not the book.

"My son got it for me. It's a first edition of Sinclair Lewis's *Babbitt*." Her hands reached delicately toward the book. "May I?"

"That's why I brought it." He watched her open the cover. He marveled at the delicacy of her fingers, the set of her wrists and shoulders, her narrow hips, the gentle rise of her breasts. He watched her lips work silently as she read. The creases running down her cheeks told stories more real even than the one she was reading. He had to force himself not to touch her hair.

"You must have a wonderful son," she said as she handed it back.

He stood with the book awkwardly in his hands, wondering if setting it on the kitchen counter would imply a stay longer than she wanted. "He is." He held her eyes. They were blue, with streaks of amber like Helen's hair. He saw no other eyes around. "I don't remember if you told me about your children."

"We were never able to have any. They're the joy of old age, I've heard."

Clark shrugged, but did not answer.

"Don't you agree?"

"I don't want to open a can of worms."

"It is a can of worms I've opened and emptied a long time ago." She sat on the black leather sofa and motioned for him to sit beside her. The young French couple kissed upon the wall. "Hence the business of writers and music and the arts council directorship, I suppose."

He sat, still excited, still uncomfortable. "I hope I'm not interrupting anything."

"Does it look like you're interrupting anything?"

"I'm not keeping you from an appointment?"

"I have something in a half hour or so. Some young friends from work, exercising their compassion on the old and lonely widow." She touched his arm lightly. He wanted to fall into the warmth of her fingers. "But that's not for half an hour."

She sat with her arm extended along the back of the sofa. "So," she said after a minute, "have you seen any good movies lately?"

"Not since the one I saw with you."

"I thought you didn't like that movie. Too much fucking, as I remember."

"I've reconsidered."

"Henry Miller would be proud." She smiled. He imagined heat radiating from her fingertips to penetrate his shoulder. The ache in it dropped away like petals. This woman is Lourdes, he thought. This woman is the touch of Christ.

"I've been thinking about you, Clark."

"You have?"

"Why did you come to see me today?"

"Wasn't the book convincing?"

"No," she said, "the book wasn't convincing."

Her laughter made him laugh, and the screen between them dropped. He settled into the sofa. "I guess I came to see you because I was thinking about you, too."

"Oh? Then I hope I didn't interrupt *your* plans."

"No. I was at my son's and he was telling me about his new girlfriend—"

"And that made you think of me?" Her fingers poked playfully at his shoulder. "Do you want me to be your girlfriend, Clark? Can I wear your pin? Maybe we should put on Sammy Fain and neck."

"You're making fun of me."

"No, I'm not. This is the way I am. If I offend people . . ." She shrugged. "Well, I'm too old to give a damn about that now."

"You don't offend me." He was not surprised to find he meant it.

"I thought that was why you left that night."

"No. That was because . . ." He kept looking for Nora's eyes, and kept not finding them. "That was because I was a little confused."

"And now you're not?"

"And now I'm trying not to be."

Her gaze ripped him open. He had the strange and terrifying sensation that this woman could see all his shadows. She turned to her watch. "Oh, damn."

"The people from work?" he asked.

"The people from work."

He felt as if he were reading the first words on the last page of *Alice in Wonderland*—the marvelous fantasy was about to end. Well, he thought, was all he could think. "Would you mind terribly if I came along?"

She smiled again. Her fingers touched him, not poking or playful this time, but a touch meant to touch. "I would like that."

"I'm not dressed for a party."

"You're dressed fine." She stood, waited for him to stand, then walked to the closet by the door. She opened it, stared at her coat, and closed it again. "No."

Clark wavered. Everything felt ready to tumble down. "No?"

"No, you don't want to go to a party. I don't, either. Why don't we just stay here?"

"Sure," he said. Yes, oh yes, he thought.

"I have some wine in the refrigerator. We can have a more intimate party."

"I don't drink wine."

"Come now, Clark. It's Christmas."

"You don't understand. I *can't* drink wine."

"Oh." Her brow furrowed. "Would you like a shot at the coffee again?"

Who would have thought when he woke up this morning that such a day awaited him? He could not help but smile. "Sure."

"Why don't I start the kettle while you find some music?"

"Anything but Christmas music. I'm sick to death of it."

"Then jazz or something. The blues. Do you like the blues?"

"Do you have Billie Holiday?"

"Somewhere. And then you can read to me from your book."

"I knew I brought it for a reason," he said.

He turned toward the stereo. Her footsteps clicked sharply on the kitchen floor, then softened; when he turned, she was crossing the carpeting toward him. She put her arms around his waist; her warmth encircled him. Her face was close to his and he was wandering through those eyes, through that smile. The scent of her perfume made him giddy.

"I'm glad you came back, Clark."

"I am, too." Emma's lips pressed against his, a quick touch, a circle as round and warm as her arms. She walked away toward the kitchen. He placed his hand on the stereo cabinet to steady himself.

He found a compact disk of Billie Holiday; as small as a baby album. Billie Holiday, he thought as he studied the cover, dark hair piled high, flowers like a crown, the only lady who could ever really sing the blues. He remembered listening to pale imitations of her voice in smoky St. Paul bars during the fifties. Deloris beside him had been as hungry for whatever it had been that she had wanted as Billie now sounded. The last night he had spent with Deloris, he'd listened to Billie Holiday's music. He shook his head. That was a weekend he didn't care to remember.

He thought instead of the other Billie, Billie Jessup, of that dark day sitting in his car in front of her apartment. How horrible the word *fuck* had sounded coming out of her mouth. Emma, he thought as he watched her move around the kitchen, you are right. Such a word should never have been relegated to profanity, but with Billie Jessup, its relegation was inevitable. The act would have been profane, and he realized now that on that day he had wanted to commit sin. There is no return to a golden age, but perhaps there is no need. He felt sinless now, or almost sinless, sanctified by Emma's circles.

"Ooh, ooh, ooh, what a little moonlight can do."

Emma was dancing lightly toward him, singing along with the music. Her contralto failed at meeting even a fifties singer's limited success and he didn't give a damn. She pushed a tiny overweight elf to one

241

side of the coffee table, then set two cups with coasters upon it. "The water will be ready in a minute."

"It will be a struggle," Clark said as he stepped toward her.

"What will be?"

"Billie Holiday versus Sinclair Lewis."

"I'll turn the music down." She lifted a black control from the table and pressed a button that reduced Billie's voice to a whisper. "I want to hear you read."

He picked up the book from the counter, sat on the sofa, and opened it. She held up her hand before he could begin. "After the water is done." They sat together comfortably until the water boiled. Emma chased it down. No arthritis in those joints, Clark thought admiringly.

"So now we're ready," she said when the cups were steaming and the kettle back on the stove. "Read to me of Mr. Babbitt."

He read to her as he would to a child, with different voices for different characters, shaping the story with the rise and fall of his words. He skipped through the book, also like a child, to capture as much of the story as he could. He read to her of George Folansbee Babbitt, the Realtor and town booster, the large, pink-faced go-getter who did not realize he was trapped in who he was until he realized too late. Clark did not notice when the music ended. The struggle had been won.

He finished with George speaking to his son. "Don't be scared of the family," he read. "Nor of yourself, the way I've been. Go ahead, old man! The world is yours!" He closed the book and looked at Emma's face, something he had only glanced at for an hour and a half.

"Well?" he asked.

"Well." She sighed.

"Didn't you like it?"

"I loved it." She moved against him, a delicious warmth he could not ever remember feeling. She took the book from his hands and set it gently on the table. " 'The world is yours.' Do you believe that?"

He tried to pull her full warmth into a body aching for it. He thought of Hannah and Deloris and Billie Jessup, but their warmth was not this warmth. This warmth had only the vitality remaining after seven slow-burning decades, and he knew that if he did not capture it now he perhaps never would. He felt very good, very comfortable, but he felt he was grasping at something that could dissolve in his fingers.

"I am beginning to believe," he said. But suddenly he was speaking from an intense comfort. He was speaking from a world that sometime soon would grow cold in a bed in the house on St. Anne's Road. Sometime soon that world would grow even more fragile with the knowledge that the people he had spent his life with were falling away one by one, dropping to the earth like raindrops, a splatter and gone. He knew that sometime soon he would be lying in that bed and kicking his legs desperately, dreaming of clots migrating toward his brain. He dreaded its coming. In that bed, the world was far too large for anyone to take. That world wasn't fiction.

She took his hand and examined its palm, then the thick veins running along its back. "I refuse to believe that anything is impossible." She raised his hand to her lips and kissed it. He cupped her chin, raised her lips, and kissed her with a weathered passion. She returned his embrace, ran her hand around his waist, pulled him toward her, inviting him to do, he guessed, what he would. A thought of impotence tightened his body—he hated being an old man. If she noticed she gave no sign.

She stood and held out her powdered, liver-spotted hand. An old hand that still moved as delicately as a child's, that still danced on sunsets. "Come on," she said.

"Where are we going?" He was reeling in all that was happening and was afraid to understand.

"Just come on."

She helped him to his feet. At the stereo she put on more music— someone playing a saxophone. She led him down the hall.

Panic touched him, a fear of giving disappointment. "Emma, I don't know."

"Go ahead, old man," she said softly. "The world is yours."

Light filtering through the drapes softly lit her bedroom. He knew she was waiting for him to kiss her, but that was something he found he could not do. She pressed her lips against his, the touch of her hand on his chest as light as a breath. She stepped away, stepped forward, wrapped her arms around his waist, and kissed him again, then stepped away to the dresser to rummage in a drawer. She took out something white and turned toward the adjoining bathroom.

"I'll be back in a minute. Make yourself comfortable."

She shut the door behind her. Clark looked about the room as if the walls were ready to topple. Well, he thought, you have believed for too long that sex between people your age is the stuff of frustration and fantasy. You have believed for too long that some things should and do die before the body. So now it is time to quit believing.

He rubbed his crotch, then his chin. It is hard to quit believing— sometimes it is impossible. Perhaps there is comfort in knowing life holds more than love and lust and the satisfaction of them. "Hell." He spit the word. Retrograde logic.

As he hesitated over fleeing or staying, she came back into the room. She was wearing a white negligee cut low and dropping only halfway down her thighs. Her legs were so thin that her knees bulged, so pale that blue veins showed thickly. Her breasts were small and withered. The sight of her shocked him because he had always pictured her beneath her clothing as young. The strength of her spirit had always seemed the cure for aging.

She smiled almost shyly. "I haven't worn this in years." When he didn't respond, she asked, "What's wrong?"

"I don't know." His hands rose, then fell limply. "I don't know about this."

She sat upon the bed. He saw from the shape of her toes that arthritis had not left her completely unmarred. "I once told you that people our age don't owe a damn thing to anyone," she said. "Do you believe that?"

He shrugged. "I guess so."

"You believe so many things," she said. "Do you ever live what you believe?"

244

Her words were a slap, a punch in the gut. The flashing years and all their empty tenets made him sway—creeds carved in marble and ignored, promises spoken to and dying upon the air. It all flashed by in a swirling rush like water down a toilet. Eternity's black hole is haunted by a Tidy Bowl man in a little boat singing about your failures. God be damned. There are just too few days to live a life of both conviction and repose. Especially now.

Do not go gentle into that good night, Dylan Thomas had written, Dylan Thomas now screamed. *Do not go gentle into that good night.* But Clark could only listen in weakness. He was, after all, an old man.

His hands rose and fell again. "I don't know what I can do."

"Let me worry about that." He let her guide him to the bed. He had no strength for resistance.

He sat beside her. She kissed him, placed his hand on her thigh, then unbuttoned his shirt. She slipped it from his shoulders before kissing him again.

"Do you want to take your undershirt off?"

"No." The room was not dark enough for exposure. His body soon would be causing him enough embarrassment.

"All right." She worked his belt loose and unhitched his pants. Her fingers crawled inside his open zipper. He felt nothing with her touch but a cold sadness.

"Lie down," she said.

She held the covers back for him—his pants fell rumpled to the floor. She took off her panties, her buttocks ropy, a blurry thatch of gray. She pulled the negligee off over her head, her ribs in ripples, her stomach lined as if she had walked through a spider's web. She possessed a boy's anatomy beneath an old woman's skin.

Clark watched as she lifted the covers and slipped beneath them next to him. His frustration was so acute it brought tears to his eyes.

"Don't worry," she said softly, "don't worry." She kissed him while running her hands down his chest, stopped kissing him when they reached his waist. "Let's get your underwear off."

"I don't know. I'm still uncomfortable."

245

She watched him for too long. "Would you rather not do this?"

She had a way of throwing questions at him as heavy as the world. How was he to answer? "Not now. Not yet, anyway."

She nodded, then raised her hand to rest upon his chest. "Is it all right then if we just hold each other?"

"I'd like that." Damn. Damn.

They lay beside each other, silent in the room's shadows. Somewhere outside church bells played Christmas music. Sunlight leaked around the drapes.

"I'm sorry," he said.

"There's no reason to be sorry."

He put his arm around her and felt guilty that this was the only act of which he was capable. He closed his eyes and stared at the darkness behind them. A creaking laugh crawled like a worm out of the back of his mind. A laugh of triumph.

I knew all along you wouldn't get it up, Nora said. *Do you really believe I would trust you?*

His frustration layered over him like a quilt. It reached the sky.

Emma called Clark three days later while he was taking laundry out of the dryer in the basement. They talked about Sinclair Lewis and *Babbitt,* about music, about her philanthropic young friends she had forsaken on Christmas. They did not talk about the bedroom; they did not talk about love. They were warm and clever and overly polite.

"So they weren't upset about you not coming over?" Clark asked.

"They were more worried than upset. They thought I might have slipped on the ice and broken something."

Clark thought of Nora. On the ruined model, she was moving box after box through the front yard's wreckage into the house on St. Anne's Road. The windows were shattered, a hole gaped in the roof; it was a warm, spring morning. He and Maynard sat near the driveway in lawn chairs, drinking beer and wiping the sweat of moving a sofa from their foreheads. They stared at the broken pieces of the lake on the horizon.

"Clark?" Emma asked.

Clark rubbed his eyes. "What did you tell them?"

"That I had unexpected company. An old and treasured friend." She paused. Music filtered through the receiver, classical and light. Clark thought about her hands, about fingers dancing delicately. "They asked if I would like to come over for New Year's Eve. I was wondering if you were busy."

What do you say? Clark thought. He wanted desperately to be with Emma but he did not want to repeat what had happened at Christmas. "I'm not sure."

"It wouldn't be long," she said. "We could make an appearance and leave, if you like."

"We ought to at least stay until midnight."

"Then you'll come?"

He had given an answer without realizing it. "I guess so. I'm not busy." What the hell was he thinking? What the hell was he saying?

"Don't be so enthusiastic."

"It's not that. It's—"

"I know what it is." She paused. "There is no reason anything has to be rushed. That was my fault."

Maybe it was. Maybe it had been the rush, but hell, when you hit this age all things must be rushed, all life lived in a desperate panic. That was as far as he wanted to think about that. "Do I need to dress up?"

"Just be yourself. That's all anyone can ask."

They talked a few minutes more, banal talk, Clark staring out of the window, avoiding the model, because he dared not look at the model, watching a bundle of winter clothes trudge along the sidewalk. He was surprised to hear the sharp, pulsing buzz the telephone company used to tell you to, damn it, get off your butt and hang up the receiver; he could not remember saying good-bye. He glanced at the model only long enough to see Nora.

He went to the front closet, dressed for the weather, and went outside. The cold was like stumbling through acid. He walked up the street to the elevator, then by the Craft Nook, the store, and the police station. The wind on the west side of town was stronger; only open fields and a frozen lake inhibited it. It worked under his hat to swirl in his ears; it nibbled his eyes, as icy as death and as deathly as cold. Dante had been onto something.

On Ambrose's front walk a wall of cold abruptly stopped him, but not the cold of the winter. It was a cold thrown out by the building itself, a white and sterile cold of leather faces and mindless friends, of old women wailing in wheelchairs and old men crying from toilets. The heavy, icy cold of heavy, icy eyes. It seeped around his neck; it clouded his vision. He had to tell Nora to her face exactly how things were and exactly how things had to be, but he couldn't do it; he couldn't take another step. Hell, he thought, that body on the bed had eyes that saw everything, anyway. Blind eyes see absolutely.

He turned away and searched for some excuse for venturing outside on a day like this. The Lucky Lemon was standing in his parking lot with his hands on his hips, shaking his head at a decrepit pickup. He paced, then came back to shake his head again. In his parka and fur-lined hood he looked like an Eskimo who had just beached a whale and didn't know what to do with it.

It was too cold to be watching a shyster contemplating his latest shyst. Clark crossed the highway to the Sunset Motel. Cletis would be working—he usually was. Clark couldn't help but think of Henry's feed store. He hadn't sat there for a long time. He missed Maynard. He needed something to do with his time.

The wind worked hard against his cheek. Clark paused before going into the office only long enough to see that Ted Lewell's car was not in the parking lot. Good—that would be one less aggravation to contend with. He stood gasping in the lobby with the cold still hovering around him while tinny game-show music buzzed around his head. Cletis was sitting behind the desk, his little toady face and immaculate shirt making him look like a character out of *The Wind in the Willows*. The counter hid his ass. No easy feat.

"Clark?" Cletis adjusted his glasses. "It is you! I can hardly tell with you wearing all that stuff."

"It's cold outside, Cletis." He pulled off his hat. The warmth gathered superficially on his cheeks and lips.

"What brings you out on a day like this?"

He didn't want to tell him the truth. "You've stopped in so many times at the store that I figured I owed you a few visits."

Cletis stood, his hips pushing against the chair arms. "It's Maynard Tewle, isn't it? I know how you two used to pal around together."

Clark looked at the ceiling panels, at the prints on the walls, at the cheap carpeting. He felt a longing for old friends, feed store benches and seed caps, for coffee and Danish in empty cafés. "Yeah, we did."

"I never really cared for the guy, but you can't wish something like that on anybody."

"Sure, Cletis."

"I mean it, Clark."

"Sure."

"Hey, I've been praying someone would stop by. Can you look after things while I run into the can? I drank too many Cokes."

"Sure. What do I have to do?"

"If anyone comes in, take their money and give them a room." He pointed at the key rack. "Pick a room, any room. Any open room, that is."

"Is that writer around today?"

"He's out at St. Anne's, I think."

Cletis waddled into the apartment behind the counter; Clark leaned over the registry to watch the television. A Coke machine in the corner quietly contemplated whatever it is that Coke machines contemplate. On the wall beside the registry a rack had been bolted and lined with keys. A frosty front window looked out onto a frosty world.

Cletis came back smiling. "I have a joke for you."

Oh God. The dread of hearing a Cletis Meadows joke so overwhelmed Clark that he missed the first line. He only managed to comprehend that it had something to do with a dog in a bar pissing on John Wayne, and that he'd heard it before.

"Hah." He wondered how silent the world would be if laughter wasn't socially conditioned. "Good one."

"Well, you sit here long enough and you have time to come up with some jokes."

"I suppose."

This was starting to feel too much like a desperate search for friends. "I ought to mosey along, Cletis."

"Already?"

He shrugged. "Life moves on."

"Stop by again."

"Sure."

Clark bundled up and stepped outside. That had been nothing like sitting on the bench in front of Henry's feed store; nothing like it at all. He walked by the Lemon, his shoulders hunched, hardly even glancing at him. It had been nothing like being with Emma, either.

By the last day of the year, the snow packed on the streets was gray where tires had run, mottled black where motor oil had dripped, and speckled brown where gravel had been spread. The fields slept beneath a deep white blanket whipped by the wind into crests and valleys. Tree branches bent beneath their loads, benevolent giants offering wondrous gifts to the passersby on the sidewalks, but by the end of a Minnesota December, snow was no longer a gift, and few accepted. It was not yet a curse, but it was no longer a gift.

Clark was standing in front of his mirror, preparing for the party, the sun already setting through the window beside him. The preponderance of Emma's call was making shaving difficult. It had been three days since he'd talked to her. Many things can change in three days; a man can die and come back to life in three days. A man, though only a part of his mind dared admit it so baldly, can come back to life and die.

Over the last three days, Clark had buried his apprehension about being with Emma beneath resigned acceptance. You are who you are, he thought as he ran the razor over his throat, and there is wisdom in knowing of what you are capable. He would go to the party with Emma. At midnight he would kiss her comfortably as an old man should. He would wish them both the best year possible. He would sleep in the white clapboard house on St. Anne's Road, she would sleep in her apartment, he would call her in the morning. They would joke, they would laugh. He would not expect from himself that of which he was no longer capable. All inevitabilities are comfortable, he reasoned, if we give ourselves time to accept them.

As he combed his hair he thought about football fields and high school girls exercising upon them. He thought about Billie Jessup, and was amazed that he had actually thought sleeping with her was a possible or even a desirable thing. He thought about Emma. He had to smile at this old man smiling back at him from the mirror. He'd been such a fool over the last several months. Such a fool.

In a brief moment of clarity he studied his face, his eyes. Age and wisdom, he knew, are not necessarily handmaidens. The deepest part of his mind burned with a wisdom that the rest of it equated with foolishness. He knew in that deepest part that in fleeing this foolishness he was becoming a fool. He shrugged and buried the wisdom. Life can only be happy in forgetfulness. Ignorance is bliss. A selective memory uses survival tactics.

"What the hell," he muttered. "The ways of the world."

He put his comb in the medicine cabinet and studied his smile in the mirror. He slicked his hair back along each side of his head with palms wetted by the drip of the faucet, then went back into his bedroom and dressed, pulling his tie to only a slight discomfort. He went back to the bathroom mirror to admire himself. Not bad—there are not many people who look this good at seventy-two. He had always viewed himself as, if not handsome, at least not ugly, though his looks in the last three decades had become too much weathered. He'd worried about them until age, this thing that had evolved in the last three days into a cozy friend, had explained to him the truth. So goes life, or so it said. Or so he had come to believe.

He felt comfortable with this wise denial. Dylan Thomas's poem was a faraway, alien thing. There is nothing wrong, he knew, with going gentle.

He let the Dodge idle in the darkness until the interior warmed, then pulled onto St. Anne's Road. He glanced at Billie Jessup's window as he drove by and smiled at his former foolishness. He'd have to go into the Bumblebee for a Danish sometime.

The nursing home glowed in this new, sober light. Many people his age ended up there, and there was nothing wrong with that. In this world, that was the way things worked, and he was a product of this world. He shrugged. Things seemed so simple that he marveled that he had not come to think this way before. Life is easy if you let it be.

Emma was ready when she opened the door, her hair tied tightly back, a turquoise broach at her throat, her black silk dress reaching to just below her knees. Helen had dressed like this. He shook his head.

"What's wrong?" she asked.

"Nothing. You look beautiful."

"You look handsome."

He smiled as he smoothed down his coat. "I try."

She returned his smile, but kept her distance. He found himself anticipating her closeness keenly; it would provide him an opportunity to tell her what he had learned.

"Why don't you come in?" she asked.

He checked his watch. "Do we have time?"

"Only a moment."

He stepped inside the door. The living room was the same as it had been at Christmas, the same knickknacks, the same red-and-green spangles. A dirty coffee cup rested on the counter; a smell in the air betrayed the presence of Jamaican Blue Mountain. Music played as always. He glanced at the hall to the bedroom for only a moment before turning to the stereo. All good things come to an end.

"Aaron Copeland," Emma said. "Symphony number one."

"I've heard that on a car commercial."

"One of our society's greatest sins is that its members only hear great music on commercials or in cartoons."

"I suppose. I like a good cartoon, though."

Their eyes darted around the room, glanced at each other, then darted again. *Nothing to fear but fear itself,* FDR had said. Of course, FDR had never fought, had never waded ashore on anything but a private beach. Clark had voted for Dewey in '44 and wasn't even a Republican.

"Any resolutions for this year?" he asked.

Emma studied him with an unidentifiable something in her eyes. "A few," she said.

They drove to the party in Emma's car. It was at an art patron's house on the high western banks of the Minnesota River, a house hidden like an eye behind a lid of bare maples, blinking lights. Emma took his arm as they walked up the driveway. He could feel her strength through his coat, could feel how she grasped for something more elemental than his arm. Well, he thought. All good things.

The temperature had risen throughout the day so that now the end of the year seemed to anticipate renewal. Emma rang the bell; Clark stood expectantly with his shoulders back, his gloved hand resting upon the fingers gripping his arm. The great white door swung open; a boy with a shaved head and little round glasses tinted the color of a turd stood before them. He had four earrings in one ear and none in the other and was wearing shorts and sandals. A ratty old vest hung loosely from his shoulders and cut off the angles of a swastika on his T-shirt. Clark stiffened. The nerve of some of these little bastards. A god-be-damned swastika. You always know who's been there and who hasn't.

"Emma," the boy said. He might have been twenty or twenty-five or ten; ages that distant all ran together.

"Hello, Alex." Emma smiled warmly as if this little shit was the kind of thing she saw every day. "Happy New Year."

"Yeah." People swarmed inside the door, a few like Alex, but most dressed in black ties and glittering dresses. None were dressed like Clark. "You know the crowd."

They stepped inside, and Alex shut the door. He nodded at Clark while his earrings glinted. Instead of asking for their coats, he disappeared into the mass of anarchy-flecked sophistication.

"Who the hell does he think he is?" Clark asked.

"He's a poet," Emma said.

"He's wearing a swastika."

"It's a form of rebellion, I suppose."

"Good Christ, it's a goddamned swastika."

"It doesn't mean as much to his generation."

"It means a hell of a lot to mine."

"To ours."

Clark made room in the closet for their coats. "That little Nazi doesn't own this place, does he? Starving artists have come up in the world."

"God, no." Emma handed hers to him. "He works at a Laundromat, I think."

"Then who are the host and hostess? Are they Nazis, too?"

"Nobody's a Nazi. I'll introduce you."

The host was a little man named Willett with wide hips and tiny feet he kept pressed tightly together. He reminded Clark of a thumbtack. His wife was a round, merry woman with hair dyed the color of used motor oil and diamonds too big to be real dangling from her ears.

"Patrons," Emma said. "Be nice."

"I'm always nice," Clark said. He was glad Alex was out of sight.

A quick handshake up and down from the both of them, a shake as if they were Amish. "So," Willett said, "what game are you in?"

"I'm retired. I used to be in hardware." He'd never thought of it as a game.

"I never much cared for hardware. We've got to have it, I suppose."

Try to get along without it, bozo. "I suppose."

"I'm in the shipping game, myself. Grain."

"Got to have it, I suppose."

Another poet went by. She looked like a poet, anyway—a wispy girl wearing a circus tent. "How did you get mixed up in this?" he asked.

"The wife." Willett nodded at the merry woman as she jounced away like a perky forest gnome. She looked as if she'd eaten a lot of fried ass in her day. "It keeps her busy. You?"

"I'm with Emma." He looked around to find her gone. He felt as if he'd been pinned to the modern, head-shaven, tent-wearing world by a thumbtack. "I've never mixed with a group like this before."

"Drives me nuts, but what can you do? You've got to keep the women entertained, right?" Willett leaned toward Clark conspiratorially. "Do you want to know the truth?"

"Sure."

"All these guys dressed like they are? That's all business. You've got to look the part, no matter what business you're in. *Comprende?*"

"Sure."

"More business will go on tonight than I do in a week at the office." He scratched the top of his head. He was bald, though he could not have been much over forty. "Shit like this makes the world go around."

Clark thought of shabby bums in attics living off booze and spaghetti, bums like Hemingway and Faulkner and Dostoyevsky. "I thought love was supposed to make the world go around."

Willett's snort was his only answer. "So what did you do with hardware?"

"Sold it." But Willett had been pulled to the side by a man in a suit much nicer than Clark's—business, no doubt. Clark wanted only to again feel Emma's hand on his arm, to again be sitting on the sofa in her apartment reading Sinclair Lewis. He thought he caught a glimpse of her in the kitchen. He waded through the noise, the clinking glasses, the funny smell coming down the stairs that reminded him of Walter long ago. He was surprised that a straitlaced Babbitt like Willett would allow such a thing in his house. Maybe his wife did; maybe that was the way he kept her entertained. It was part of the game.

The glimpse of Emma turned out to be a woman in her mid-thirties with hair bleached almost colorless. Two straps over her shoulders supported a black fabric tube cut low across her deep, freckled chest. Her hemline was high enough up her thighs for the deep part of Clark's mind to nudge the rest of it. If he were to take a picture of her, he was sure Walter would draw nipples on it.

She smiled at him. "I haven't met you before, have I?" She held her drink as if she were pointing her chest out to the world. Her nails were long enough to render her fingers fit only for rending.

"Probably not."

Her smile was as bleached as her hair, though she was probably not a bad sort, in spite of her obvious circumstances. She lived in a jet-set world. "Are you with that older woman I've seen around?"

"Emma Richard?"

"I don't know her name."

"Yeah. Have you seen her lately?"

"Here and there." She rested her free hand on his forearm. She leaned toward him, her drink almost spilling into her cleavage. Her chest was as spotted as a leopard's. Clark had read somewhere that leopards were the only animals that tortured their prey. "Are you a folk artist or something?"

"No."

"You're the right age for it. I bet you know some pioneer secrets."

Give me a break, lady. "I used to be Thomas Jefferson's butler. When he'd finish in the outhouse, he'd bend over and I'd wipe his ass. That's where the first three drafts of the Declaration of Independence ended up."

"You're joking."

"Of course I am. The pioneers were long before me."

She laughed. He laughed. It was best to take such things lightly—he reminded himself to be accepting of his age.

"You know," the woman said, "you and . . . what was her name?"

"Emma."

"You look good together. You make a cute couple."

Ah, yes. Cute. That word reserved for babies and octogenarians. "I'm seventy-two."

"Can I get you something to drink? I'd really like to talk to you about your folk art."

"I'm sorry. I don't drink."

"Then water or something." She lifted her drink to his lips. Her hem lifted with her shoulders—he saw through the curve of the glass her bare thighs distorted as if in a dream. "This is just mineral water and lime."

Oh, so you're this goofy when you're sober. Don't, he reproved himself, don't. You're here to have a good time. "I promise I'll talk to you later. Right now I'd like to find Emma."

"All right. Save me a dance."

What kind of dancing, he wondered, did a crowd like this do? The patrons waltz while the artists slither oiled and naked to the beat of African drums. He'd like to see this leopard woman buttered up and ready to fry. No more of that, he thought. Remember your age. "All right. I'll see you later."

"It was so nice meeting you. Don't forget the dance."

He had gotten lost in the crowd before he realized that he did not know the leopard lady's name. Admonition flared inside of him—in the fifties he would never have bungled such an opportunity. Well, he thought, it was no longer the fifties. He really was going to save her a dance. A two-step, maybe.

He found Emma in a back room lined with paintings in a style he didn't recognize—he thought it best that in this company he keep his preference for Norman Rockwell secret. He stood awkwardly at her shoulder as she conversed with a blond woman in her mid-thirties, not dressed as a poet or a patron, but as a respectable Midwestern middle-class woman. She wasn't bad looking, but she was no match for the leopard lady's savage sexuality.

"Oh, Clark," Emma said. He could not remember ever being so pleased to feel someone slip an arm around his waist. "I'd like you to meet Loretta Hapsburg, the director of the Minnesota Valley Arts Council."

He took the woman's hand. The Hapsburgs, rulers of empires. He thought of heavyset anemic women and men whose words could slaughter thousands, now sitting across desks from swastika-bedecked launderers. The mighty have fallen. "It's nice to meet you, Loretta."

"You, too, Clark. Emma has been telling me so much about you."

"Oh no." He laughed politely. This woman had the most disconcerting eyes, almost as devoid of color as the leopard lady's hair had been. "So you took Emma's job away from her, did you?"

Loretta mimicked his laugh. "One thing you will soon learn, Clark, is that no one takes anything from Emma. She gives it to you or you don't get it at all."

Soon, Clark thought. The word held an implication he liked. "I stand forewarned."

Emma's arm slipped from his waist to his shoulder. "I'm sorry," she whispered in his ear, "I have to make the rounds." She spoke more loudly. "Don't disappear on me. I want to show you off." She walked away. Her warmth lingering around his waist reminded him too much of her warmth that night lying in her bed. He wished he were twenty-five years younger.

"Emma tells me you're from Credibull," the woman said. "You used to have the most wonderful hotel there, right on the lake."

"I've heard that."

She laid her hand lightly on his arm. "I'm sorry, I don't mean to be telling you your business. Emma said you're the historical society curator."

"I dabble at it."

The woman began talking about history, but he couldn't hang on to the conversation. He couldn't remember her name, either—Loni, or something. His gaze kept wandering from her bizarre eyes to the tangle of reaching arms, smiling faces, and glasses of alcohol into which Emma had disappeared.

"Ah, the young Miss Hapsburg! I've been looking all over for you!"

Willett came into the room, balanced on the pinpoint of his feet. Clark was surprised he didn't leave holes in the carpet. "Hello, uh . . . uh . . ."

"Clark," Clark said.

"Right. Hardware or something, wasn't it?"

"Or something." Clark stepped back and smiled. He let Willett draw what's-her-name into his net even as he extricated himself. He kept backing away, kept trying to become invisible. What's-her-name waved at him through Willett's words as he stepped into the living room.

The people around him were dancing a modern, devil-possession dance, a witches' dance, the Salem shuffle. Uncomfortable heat seized him, loud music smacked him between the eyes like the business end of a ball-peen hammer. He saw Albert Wilson stretched there on the hard dirt floor, stains like shadows running beneath the door. It was funny how one thing reminds you of another. He thought of Maynard.

Clark retreated until he was sitting on the sweet-smelling stairs away from the clutch and scramble that had pulled his chest too tight. He stretched his legs; it felt good to be off his feet. Well, Emma, he thought, you'll have to find me here. I won't go in there.

On the living room television flickered midnight in New York. Few of the partygoers paid any attention—midnight in Mankato was still an hour away. A ball descended like a failing sun into that chaos called Manhattan, into taxi drivers and drug pushers and hard, asphalt streets. Somewhere wandered a lost and buggered Santa.

Footsteps came down the stairs, a step echoed by a slap of leather on skin. Clark smelled the sharp stink of sweat-salted leather and turned to see a sandal framing long toenails stained almost yellow, stuffed black at their corners with a gook he didn't want to think about. White knees bent, pale legs rimed with black hair slithered into loose Bermuda shorts. Alex was smoking a small brown cigarette he offered to Clark.

"No, thanks." Alex nodded an answer and inhaled sharply on the cigarette. Clark refused it a second time. "Emma told me that you're part of the poet crowd."

"I'm not part of any crowd. I hate being classified."

Clark nodded at his T-shirt. "You don't seem to mind being classified as a Nazi. Do you have any idea how many people died because of that thing?"

Alex pulled his vest back for a better view. "I'm not a Nazi."

"What, you wear it for no reason at all?"

"I don't do anything without a reason."

Hell. The son of a bitch was too young to know he was stupid. "Then what are you wearing that for?"

"Maybe it has something to do with keeping friends close and enemies closer. What are you?"

"If you're wearing that, I'm no friend."

"That's not what I mean. You seem to get off on boxing me in, so I'm going to box in you." He sucked on the cigarette. "What the fuck are you?"

An old man. Clark shrugged. "I'm sure as hell no Nazi." He watched Alex snuff out the cigarette, then put it in a vest pocket. The party raged. "You look like you're a Ginsberg fan."

"Ginsberg is shit. The Beats did nothing but muddy the waters."

"Huh?"

" 'Poets muddy their waters in order to appear deep.' Read that somewhere. Nietzsche, maybe."

"You read?"

He nodded. "If Marx were alive today, he'd call *Wheel of Fortune* the opiate of the masses. But what the hell. You got to do something with your time."

They studied each other, then studied the party. Alex pointed to the orgiastic dance floor. The leopard lady fed in the middle of it all, blood and sweat shining on her cheeks, fangs exposed and glinting. "They come here and poison themselves with the firewater and pretend that they're having a good time."

"Speaking of poisoning." Clark nodded at Alex's vest.

Alex shrugged. "Pot is illegal. I smoke in protest." He fished out the cigarette, then put it back. "A crowd like this mixes with us lower lifes to pretend their lives aren't jokes. They can go back tonight to their BMWs and their Jacuzzis and feel vindicated."

Ah, tones of the self-righteous, the pulse of the world. "Sounds pretty hypocritical for you to be here."

"These are the people who pay my wages. They gave me a two-thousand-dollar grant last summer to write poetry they can't understand. What the hell."

"That doesn't make being here any less hypocritical."

Alex shrugged. "You're right. But you don't see me out in *that*, do you?"

The party grew beyond noise into an oppressive silence. Emma floated on the far side of the room, on the far side of the continent. She smiled at Clark and lifted her chin in acknowledgment. He waved.

"You banging her?" Alex asked.

"I beg your pardon?"

"I asked if you were banging Emma Richard."

Sudden, indignant anger rose in his chest. Indignant, he thought, about what? "What business is that of yours?"

"None. Just curious. I wouldn't mind."

"Well, thank you for your permission."

"I mean that I wouldn't mind banging her."

"A little old for you, isn't she?"

"She's a sharp-looking woman."

"A sharp-looking woman who's a little old for you."

"When it comes to banging, age doesn't mean a thing. Age doesn't mean a thing about much of anything."

Clark grunted and studied the party. Wisdom from the mouths of children. Wisdom that does not mean a damned thing because this young poet and launderer has never walked on knees stiff with arthritis, has never watched his friends fall away, has never realized the certainty that he would fall away, too. Well, it will come to you one day, my young, sanctimonious, swastika-bedecked friend. It will come to you hard. The young are immortal, but only while they are young.

"We all have our opinions," Clark said.

Alex responded with a "What the hell" and fished out his cigarette again. The party swirled like sweet, dizzy smoke. Clark watched Emma move so professionally through the crowd, as if this was how she made her living. Or had.

Someone lifted his hand. He looked up in surprise to see the leopard lady. Her chest glistened, her hair at its roots was wet. She was panting, and her teeth were bared. "Come on. You promised."

"Sometimes I say things I don't mean." But he was on his feet with a helping shove from Alex, and she acted as if she had not heard him, anyway. She pulled him toward the dance.

"Don't forget what I said about banging," Alex called before going up the stairs.

Clark was in the crowd, bodies jostling, discomfort rising in his throat, flung like a space-age Crusoe into this alien world. The leopard lady raised her arms, swayed her hips, a smile he saw as a snarl crawling across her face. She bumped her hip into him hard enough to knock him into a man dancing with a champagne glass. Champagne spilled, the bubbly drops on Clark's hand like little cold teeth, the first time he'd touched alcohol in thirty-five years. He tried to crawl out of the crowd but could not find his way through its swirling. The leopard lady spun him around. He tried to dance with her like a sane person but she would have none of it. He tried to dance as she was dancing but his knees, his mind, wouldn't allow him. He stood in a pool of panic and swayed as the crowd swayed him, a puppet on a string, a monkey in a suit, a damned and frightened fool. Clark felt suddenly very lost, very terrified. Abutment against this youth showed only how ghastly his years had become.

The crowd was smiling, laughing, pulling the strings that jerked his arms and legs, that tweaked the corners of the ghastly smile that had opened like a wound on his face. The leopard lady stepped away and smiled, her arms snapping like bullwhips. He was breathing harder than his exertion called for, sucking on vertigo, screaming into his soul like a child into its pillow. The woman swirled, the people swirled, the music swirled him. When it stopped, he did not. He gasped and clawed for something he could not reach.

The leopard lady was kissing his cheek. "You're a wonderful dancer! You're so cute!"

He was too dazed to acknowledge her. A sudden anger mixed with his confusion and terror. He was surprised to find that it was not directed at this woman. How, he thought, could I have allowed myself to become what I am?

"Again," she said.

"No."

"Please?"

"I'm an old man."

She submitted to the one answer that ended all pleading. The emotions in his chest were cold slime he had to crawl through as he fled toward the front door, slipping in despair, screaming silent cries into the night, the tears hot and eager in his eyes. The music was playing again, the people dancing, as he stepped outside into the crystal clearness of the night.

Breathing came easier as he stood on the sidewalk, tears wet on his face. The stars had not changed, but they were anchors too distant. The sky was black, the Mankato lights below him glittering, glow-worms swarming like maggots. There are a thousand parties going on down there, he thought, a thousand bells ringing in the new year. Thirty thousand people lived down there in an overwhelming world he now frighteningly knew he did not understand, 30,000 people who did and did not care that age had left him lost and frightened and spinning. He wanted to scream and cry and rage, he wanted to shake his fists at the heavens, because the hell if he would ever accept this. His gentle knowledge had only been resignation. He was old and powerless, but to hell, *to hell* with the coming of resignation.

Do not go gentle into that good night. Dylan Thomas's words penetrated beyond good and evil and right and wrong to simple statement. Perhaps God was a mathematician: we grow old and die as inevitably as two plus two equals four, but damned if we have to like it. The only heat in the heavy darkness was the tears rolling down his cheeks, and they cooled far too quickly. He wanted to rip God's eyes out. How dare you do this to us? he screamed silently into the sky. To me.

The door behind him opened. Emma came out with her coat over her shoulders, his in her arms. "Are you all right?"

He wiped his face, but could not stop crying. Hell. He hated being seen in weakness. "No."

"What happened?"

He turned away from her, his breath in clouds made indistinct by the tears. He turned back. He was so frightened.

"I got old," he said.

She came down the stairs and took his arm. She held him in a long, silent touch as steady as the stars' slow movements. "Hell, Emma, by the time you're seventy-two you'd think you'd have a few things figured out. But the only thing I know is that I don't know a thing. Why the hell does it have to be this way? Who is the bastard who makes the rules?"

"Let's go home," she said.

She led him toward the car. She opened the door; he climbed in and wiped the tears off his cheeks as she slipped in the other side. The air from the heater when she started the car was cold and blew like the years around his throat, constricting it as they did.

"I'm sorry," she said as she pulled away from the curb. "This was a bad idea."

"I just don't fit in with that crowd, Emma. I don't understand it."

"I'm not asking you to fit into anything."

They rode in silence toward the river. They crossed the bridge and drove up the hill on the east side toward the university and Emma's apartment. She pulled into her parking space, beside his Dodge. The last thing Clark wanted to do was to leave her tonight.

"It's so cold out here," he said. "I don't think I've ever been so cold."

"Come inside."

She led him into the building, releasing him only to search for the keys to her apartment door. They went into the apartment, lit by the glow of an electric Santa squatting on the kitchen counter. She stripped off his coat, tossed it to disappear in the sofa's blackness, and tossed her own after it. She led him down the hall into the bedroom, helped him take his clothes off, then took off hers. It was black on the bed; he could not see her and could only feel her as she slid beneath the covers beside him. Warmth followed the slight, cool touch from the winter still lying against their skin.

Nora's eyes if they spoke were lost in the cacophony around him, this crazy dance. "I can't do anything," he said.

"I'm not asking you to."

Emma kissed his lips, settled tightly beside him, one arm around his chest, one leg over his, her breasts in his side. They lay in silence until Emma's warmth worked loose the ice in Clark's soul, the confusion, the fear. When he knew, genuinely knew, that neither of them expected anything, the last cold chunk of it fell away. He did not feel young, but he did not feel as old as he had.

He turned toward her, worked one arm around her shoulders, then used the other arm with his hand on her buttocks to pull her to him. The warmth was growing into a passion both fierce and shocking. Something stirred between his legs.

"God," he whispered. "God."

She kissed him hard on the mouth. "Clark," she whispered, then he rolled her onto her back, kissed her lips, her neck, her arms, her breasts, working up again as she spread her legs to receive him, her heels against the back of his thighs. She guided him inside and they began moving very gently, her hands on his hips pulling him into her and releasing again. Harsh breathing, warm touches, Clark going much faster than he wished, coming and growing flaccid in heartbeats, in a very few rapid and simple heartbeats. He collapsed on top of her.

"I'm sorry," he said. "I just don't have any more in me."

"There are no expectations," she said.

"I want to do something for you."

"All right." She placed his hand between her legs. "Please."

"You want me to—"

"Please."

He worked his hand against her, her arms around his shoulders. He worked his hand against her until she clutched him tightly with her breath coming hard, arching against his fingers. She made a soft, high moan, like a girl.

My God, he thought later as he held her. A church bell somewhere tolled—it must have been the same church bell that had played the Christmas music. My God, he thought again.

265

Chapter

11

He awoke to the sunlight highlighting the curtains. He did not feel as he had ever felt before—if he felt love, it was not a love he remembered. It was not so much something there as something that was no longer there. A dread was gone.

He was alone in the bed, with the blankets loosely around him. He heard a muffled scratching coming from the bathroom and turned to see Emma brushing her hair. It reached almost to the tips of her shoulder blades and was as colorless as the sun.

We were made to wake up to mornings like this, he thought. He remembered the party and knew it was not coincidence that in the night the darkness lies. Days dawn on new worlds.

He is lying in her bed. The cracks in the plaster ceiling above him are puttied with a darker plaster, like scars showing through makeup. His head throbs with each beat of his heart. He can remember only pieces of the previous night: too many drinks and the blues poorly sung and Deloris's drawn and leering face beside him. He remembers that the leering had enraged him; he cannot remember why.

She is sitting at her vanity, combing her blond hair, black at the roots, which reaches to her shoulder blades. Through her negligee he sees her ribs and her thin, corded muscles. Her eyes in the mirror are devoid of a familiar uncertainty he has always relied on.

"What was with you last night?" he demands.

"What do you mean?"

She looks so old in the mornings. Old and tired. He wants to believe that he can do better than this. "You and that guy."

"What guy?" She smiles into the mirror as she ties back her hair. "Oh, that guy."

He remembers now. Deloris and that son of a bitch at the bar, all bones and hair oil, eyes on each other like groping hands.

"He was a nice guy," Deloris says. "Nicer than you."

"You belong to me." He puts into each word a facade of the dominance he knows he should be feeling. "You belong to me."

"No," she says, "your wife does. Poor woman."

"You bitch."

"Funny. We sat alone together for five minutes, and that guy at the bar never once called me that. For you that would be a record." She sets her comb down and turns in her chair to face him, her legs as skinny and pale as a chicken's. "I think that a guy like that would treat me better than you do."

Her arrogant certainty snaps whatever high, moralistic thoughts he has to keep from beating the fuck out of her. He climbs naked out of bed, thrusts his hand into her hair, and throws her to the floor. It feels good to see her there, to be standing over her, but it is a hollow goodness. He struggles to convince himself that she is simply too shocked to be sobbing, that she is hiding her fear from him behind the heat in her eyes. He realizes that she has always hated him.

"You whore," he says.

"A guy like that wouldn't call me a whore, either."

He wants to kick her, but her eyes drain away his will. She should not be able to do this to him.

She laughs. "You look ridiculous."

He clenches his fist. "I could kill you."

"No you couldn't." She laughs again, damn her. "I don't need you. Get out. Get out and don't come back."

"No whore will ever tell me what to do." But as he is speaking he is pulling on his shorts, his pants, throwing his shirt over his shoulders. She watches him from the floor with a smile on her face. He does not leave so much as flee.

"The hell if I'll come back," he shouts defiantly.

"The hell if I want you to," she shouts back.

He hurries down the street, searching for a taxi. He feels humiliated and enraged. He fears women with strength in their eyes.

My God, he thought, how what I used to be frightens me. But the fact that he had become what he now was encouraged him—it was almost as if somewhere over the years he had been converted to a great and nameless religion. If he could change that much, then he could change more. He would no longer be an old man living alone in the house on St. Anne's Road. He had never lived and now he must, and he must with Emma. To die without living is the worst death of all.

He felt very good lying on his back on the mattress, the gentle softness of the rumpled sheets caressing his chest each time he breathed.

The goodness withered as his wife of forty-five years opened her heavy eyes and said, *So you got laid last night. You can drop these rationalizations.*

What rationalizations?

I believe the words you used when we were married were "until death us do part." Correct me if I'm wrong.

He was staring at Emma's back but seeing Nora lying upon that white linen pillow. That is what I said, he thought. But aren't you dead?

Ask yourself that question. She fell silent as he struggled with the answer.

Emma came back into the bedroom. Her robe was tied at the waist, open enough to just show the age lines pulling at her chest. "Happy New Year." She smiled.

"Happy New Year." He did not smile.

She lay beside him and smoothed back his hair. He smelled on her either soap or skin cream. "What's the matter?"

Yes, well, he thought, that's a hell of a question. "I'm just thinking about all the things I have to do today."

"What do you have to do?"

"Family things." Nora. He felt a hot emotion inside him that he could not name. One way or another, this was going to stop.

"Would you like some company?"

He sat up, saw his shirt on the floor, and reached for it without standing. He did not want Emma to see him naked. "They aren't the kind of things you would like." He spoke brusquely, though he had not meant to. His tone was still aimed at Nora.

Neither spoke as he buttoned his shirt. He swore silently when he had to stand to reach his shorts. He dressed with his back to her. When he turned she was no longer smiling.

"What's the matter?" he asked.

"Was I just a quick fuck? If so, I can recommend some women to you who don't mind being treated like dirt."

"Emma." To hell with you, Nora, he thought. To hell with you for hanging on me all these years. To hell with you for tying me to you with empty obligations.

Empty?

He took Emma's shoulders and kissed her. I am not going to give this up. I am not. "God no. These are really things you would not want to do."

"I don't want to be a quick fuck, Clark."

"I'll see you tonight."

"I'm busy tonight."

He released her, pulled away, and looked into her eyes as she refused to look back. "Emma, let me see you tonight."

She looked at him. Still no smile. "All right." She shrugged. "I was hoping you'd read to me today."

"I wish I could."

"How long have I known you?"

"A few weeks."

"A few weeks." She gripped his shoulders and kissed him hard. "All this in a few weeks. God damn me."

He held her close, trying to pull her being into him. Oh, Emma, he thought, if only I could tell you how much I do not want to surrender you to a dead woman's eyes. You have no right to do this to me, Nora.

Don't I?

Emma used him to pull herself to her feet. "Do you have time for breakfast?"

"If it involves coffee," he said defiantly.

The breakfast should have been good but wasn't—Nora was a wooden taste in his mouth. Clark stirred up all the anger within him. Her constant spying had to end. He'd go back to Ambrose's and confront her. He'd tell her that if she was not dead she was certainly no longer alive and to leave his life alone. His life was his, not hers.

He kissed Emma before he left. "Meet me for dinner?" she asked. "There's a good prime rib place down the street."

"Sure." By then his food would have taste, because this would finally be settled.

It was warmer outside than it had been even the previous night. If the new year imitated March's lion-and-lamb syndrome, then he figured he'd be dead by the end of it. I've got to quit thinking like that, he scolded himself as the Dodge almost cheerfully started. They say that today is the first day of the rest of your life. It was a nice platitude. He shook his head. Seventy-two years left too little time to believe in nice platitudes. It was so much easier to believe in things when he was with Emma.

The snow in the fields shone beneath a soft pastel sky and bit like teeth into his eyes. He thought about a lot of things and tried not to think about Nora. Emma, he thought, oh, Emma. She was an exquisite woman, and God bless America, he still had it in him to rise to the occasion. He prodded his crotch, felt a slight reawakening, and reveled in their lovemaking's afterglow. It had been the most exquisite thing of all. Exquisitest. He laughed at his new word and decided he liked it. He decided he liked it a lot.

Credibull was a long, low smudge on the horizon, a raised place like a scab about to be sloughed. He drove into town feeling like the guy with the white hat in an old western: his back was straight and he could feel his eyes flashing. In his arms he possessed the strength to sweep all the buildings away, just as he had on the model.

He drove home first to wash and further bolster his courage. He showered, then dressed with the meticulous determination of a soldier preparing for combat. The air outside against his damp skull was shocking—even a January warmth in Minnesota was frigid. He climbed in the Dodge just as Walter's Pontiac pulled into the driveway.

Walter had walked halfway to the house before he saw Clark. He huffed over to the driver's side and leaned on the door when Clark rolled down the window. "Where have you been? I tried calling last night and got no answer. I stopped by earlier this morning. You weren't here."

"I was at a party."

"You went to a party?" His voice held a touch of skepticism. Old people don't go to all-night parties. "Where?"

"At a friend's house in Mankato."

"I didn't know you had any friends in Mankato."

Surprise, surprise, Walter, Clark thought, you don't know everything about the old man. "I thought you were going to spend the night in St. Paul."

Walter shrugged. "I left early. There's crazies on the roads after midnight. Where are you heading?"

"To see your mother."

"Mind if I come along?"

Yes, I do, but how do I explain that I want to be alone so I can have a silent fight with a comatose woman? "I guess not."

"Let's take my car. Who knows if this old rust bucket will start?"

Clark climbed out and walked to Walter's passenger door. He dropped onto the seat. Walter tucked his sweaty reek behind the wheel.

"How's that computer game I got you?" he asked as Walter slowed at the elevator.

Walter shrugged. "I can't get it to work."

"Why not?"

"Sometimes Wind River computers aren't a hundred percent compatible. Every once in a while you come across a program that won't run." He waved nonchalantly, as if he were brushing away a fly. "All computers are that way."

He drove past the bank and the store. The gaudy plastic flags adorning the used car lot hung limply. A young couple meandered through the lot, obviously from out of town and ignorant of the Lemon. "So do you think Mom will have a good year?"

Clark grunted. She was having a hell of one so far.

Walter turned into Ambrose's parking lot. Clark studied the tiny ice-fishing shacks that dotted Crystal Lake and the dirty brown road tethering them to the shore like balloons. His resolve wavered. This home held no mysticism—Nora did not really know about Emma, Clark's conscience was simply his conscience, and arguing with her was ludicrous. But those damned eyes, those god-be-damned staring eyes, he

273

could feel them. He struggled to convince himself that just because you feel something doesn't mean it's real.

"This place gives me the willies," Walter said as they went inside.

"Me, too."

The nurses were holding a party for the residents in the lounge: old people spritzed with evergreen, their wheelchairs rigged with sleigh bells that jingled whenever they turned to remind an attendant they needed to piss. Clark glanced across the hall when they reached Nora's room to see that Bob Tunnell's bed was stripped. His personals were gone.

Hell, he thought, poor old Bob. There would be no dancing with Annie Halverson around the light pole impalement, not in this life. Clark knew this happened every day, but that didn't mean he wanted to see it. He didn't even want to think about it.

Nora lay with her hands clasped over her hips, her head to the side and staring. She caught Clark's eyes as he sat. He knew beyond any doubt that mysticism existed, that she had been in Emma's apartment, that if he didn't stop this now then she would haunt him for the rest of her life. He hated her for what she was doing, and for what she had always done.

They say that dead souls become angels, he told her, but your soul is too vengeful for that. You'll have bat wings, snake hair, and a dog's head. They'll name you Alecto. You are a Fury, a haunting Fury, and the hell if I'm going to let you do this to me.

I always loved, she said, *your literary allusions.*

Her chair made a heavy, flatulent sound as Walter sat in it. Clark glanced at him before turning to Nora. "Say hello to your mother," he said in words as measured as blows.

"Hi, Mom."

Hello, Nora. Hello, you grasper, you deadweight.

Hello, Clark, you adulterer, you—

Walter began talking about something that got lost in Clark's confrontation. You never lived. You wasted your life staring at a television and now you want to waste mine. You always were a vengeful, cold-hearted bitch.

Not without reason, she said.

"So, who do you like in the Rose Bowl?" Walter asked. "I think Wisconsin is going to take it."

Leave me alone, Nora. You don't own me.

Don't I?

Those staring eyes, those dead, cold, staring eyes, like the eyes of those sharks he had seen on television. Eyes that rip you to pieces without shedding a tear.

I'll fight you.

It's not hard to fight a comatose woman. You always were a coward, Clark.

You damned bitch.

You rutting brute; you, my husband, my wasted love of a wasted life.

"You damned bitch," he said aloud.

"What?" Walter asked.

Clark looked from her eyes to his son's, then back again. Well, if she wanted a fight, he thought, we'll have a fight. We'll see who's standing when the dust settles. "Nothing."

"So, do you like Wisconsin?"

"Yeah, I like Wisconsin." He wondered what he was talking about.

"Funny how they couldn't kick the shit out of the Gophers."

"Yeah. Funny."

"The Girl Scout junior varsity could kick the shit out of the Gophers."

"I guess." You will not destroy me, Nora.

You've already destroyed yourself.

If dead eyes can smile, then her eyes smiled. Clark clenched his fist and felt the urge to jam it into each one of those damning eyes, closing them forever. No, he thought as he forced his hand to relax, doing such a thing would be the culmination of her argument. Hah. I win, Nora.

He relaxed and enjoyed the sweet taste of a victory he knew, more deeply than he dared to probe, was temporary. He smiled and turned to his son. Walter was telling some joke about the Gophers. Clark did not hear the beginning and he did not understand the end, but he laughed anyway. He wanted to laugh. It felt good.

275

Damn you, Nora. He did not let her answer.

"What do you have planned for today?" Walter asked when they stood to leave, when Clark turned his back on his wife and closed the door behind him. Walter spoke with familial hope, a puppy asking for a walk, leash in mouth and tail wagging.

I'm going to drive to Mankato, Clark thought. I'm going to make long, slow love to a woman in her seventies. I'm going to have dinner with her, I'm going to read to her, and I'm going to fall asleep with her in my arms. "I have some people I promised to see."

Walter nodded. The corners of his mouth dropped. "Oh."

"I thought you'd be heading to the Cities."

"Yeah," Walter said. "Maybe I'll do that."

As Clark glanced in at the lounge party, a booming voice reverberated down the hall. Maynard shuffled toward him in pajamas buttoned one button off, his belly protruding from a tattered robe like a tongue lolling out of a mouth. He was shuffling and wheezing, his hair flaming out from each side of his head.

"I'll wait outside," Walter said.

"Sure."

Clark wondered if this was a good day for Maynard and dreaded that it wasn't. Maynard laughed his high, maniacal laugh. "Clark!"

Clark smiled. How can such a lunatic cry seem so sane? "Hello, Maynard."

"Christ in a hand bucket, how have you been?"

"Good." He walked toward his friend, shook hands, and clasped shoulders. Maynard smelled of antiseptic and sweat—as strange a combination as Clark and Nora. "And you?"

"Well, hell, Clark, what you expect? That damned Jonathan just lies there like a turd. Can't get him to do nothing." He wiped his cheek and reached for the bill of a nonexistent seed cap. "And then there's the damn kid."

"Barb?"

"The damn kid backed the truck into the barn door. Ought to be a law against women drivers."

"Barb?" Clark asked again.

"Who else do you think? I was wondering if you had some of those big old hinges somewhere in the back. Something I can use to fix the damn door. The damn kid backed the truck into the barn door. Ought to be a law against women drivers."

Clark's spirit tumbled. This was not such a good day. "I'll look, Maynard."

"Could you look for some of those big hinges? The damn kid backed into the barn door. Ought to be a law."

"I'll look."

"For those big hinges."

"Sure," Clark said. "I'll look." He squeezed Maynard's shoulder, checking for life as if for a tomato's freshness. Maynard, he thought, my old friend, where have you gone?

"The kid backed into the barn," Maynard said.

"I know, old buddy." Clark released his shoulder and smiled as much as he was able. "I'll see you."

"Check in the back for some of those big hinges."

"I'll see you."

"Ought to be a law."

By the time Clark reached the door, Maynard was retreating down the hall, his robe hanging limply, his heels flapping out of his slippers. Clark had an awful thought about Maynard and the murder that he firmly pushed away. He thought of Ted Lewell instead, and anger flared. What had happened way back then didn't make any difference to anyone now—what was done was done. What will be done will be, and what had to be done, Clark knew in the baby breath of a new year and the warm afterglow of a new love, he had the strength to do.

He stepped outside into the fresh, cold air, the sun bright in his eyes, but cool on his face. The Pontiac was running; Walter watched him from behind the steering wheel, his breath making a frosty circle on the window. Clark looked up into the sky and tried to focus his eyes. He couldn't. There were a billion dreams up there, and a thousand of them were his.

• •

That afternoon, Clark did not make love to Emma. There was no need to, beyond that satiated by the room's darkness and the warmth of their bodies, by the halo leaking around the curtains. They had dinner together at the prime rib restaurant. He read to her from Hemingway's *The Garden of Eden* before he went home. No mindless passion raged, only a slow, comfortable warmth that they both knew would last until they saw each other again.

They spent the next two days together, then did not see each other until the weekend. They were lying together in her bed; she had lain her head upon his chest. They had just finished a casual love and were both staring at different points in the darkness. Clark felt very tired, very good. He felt his age.

"I'd like to see where you live sometime," she said.

"You wouldn't be impressed."

"I'd like to meet your son."

Well, Clark thought, what do you say to that? How do you introduce a love who does not know she is extramarital to a son who thinks you're being faithful to your as-good-as-dead-but-omniscient wife? Why are there no easy questions?

She propped her chin on his chest and studied his face. "We should have a dinner party, just me and you and your son and his wife."

"He's divorced."

"Does he have a girlfriend?"

"A new one, yeah."

"Then his girlfriend. What do you think?"

"I don't know if that would be a good idea." Now, he thought, how do you explain why? He sighed. "I don't know if you'd care for Walter."

"Are you embarrassed by him?"

"No."

"Then you must be embarrassed by me."

"God, no."

"Then what is the problem?"

278

He sighed. I'm embarrassed by me. He couldn't turn her down, but he couldn't acquiesce to her, either. He decided he'd rather risk Walter's wrath than risk losing Emma. He decided he'd rather do almost anything than risk losing Emma.

"If you want to," he said.

"Next Sunday?"

"Sure."

She laid her head again on his chest. He thought about the mess he had suddenly thrown himself into. Maybe he could play sick, but some kind of dinner was at some point inevitable. Maybe he could pass Emma off as just a friend, but he would have to keep her from touching him to pull it off, and Emma touched him all the time: little hugs, little pecks on his cheeks and lips, hands running softly over his chest like bathwater. He liked those little touches. He didn't want to pass off anything.

He stared at the spot in the darkness. Nora stared at a spot on the wall. Things would be so much easier if she were dead.

Emma called on Wednesday with her plans. The dinner would be at the house on St. Anne's Road, where Clark and the Dodge could avoid struggling with the predicted colder weather. She asked him to tell Walter. Clark had grunted at the phone and felt it sweat coldly in his hand. Tell him what?

When he called Walter, he invited him to meet an old friend. Clark suggested that while Walter was at it he might as well bring along that new girlfriend. Walter hesitated. Hope flared in Clark, then died when his son accepted. There are times we take too many chances.

The historical society was closed that week for repairs—the furnace had failed over the weekend, and the water pipes had frozen and burst. The blank whiteness of the landscape and the heavy, entrapping cold left Clark free for a week of thinking about Maynard and cursing Ted Lewell, and for reading. He tried not to think beyond the words, because the cold reminded him too much of his most brutal winter. He had been in the Ardennes after the Bulge had bled them dry, and not all the bodies had yet been discovered. As the snow began to melt, like false innocence it uncovered things that used to be people, things blackened now and hardened, twisted, limbs frozen into unnatural angles, mouths open and crying unnatural cries, eyes as opaque as playground marbles. But at least there had been no stink. They say there is good in everything bad, but not stinking is not much of a good, and it was the only good in that hellish nightmare. The things he had seen had twisted and frozen Clark's soul, had bent it into unnatural angles, into frozen cries. He had deadened with alcohol all he had seen, all he had done, all that he had been before coming back to the States, where all was summer. His soul began to thaw, and it had not had the subtle goodness of not stinking. He ran from Indiana to escape a stink that ran with him. He settled in Minnesota because his running had emptied him of money, and the stink was still with him. He tried to kill it with a steady job, a marriage, but propriety offered only empty promises. He tried to kill it with alcohol again, but his soul was genuinely rotten now. When it all exploded in his face he realized that the only way to kill a stink is to breathe it deeply until it is gone. He had breathed it deeply for many years and it was almost gone now, though the hint of a scent still raised ugly memories. He still had to fight sometimes to keep from thinking.

He wondered as he sat in the house on St. Anne's Road if he was fooling himself again. Maybe sins are tattoos that souls hold indelibly. Maybe the Bible was right; maybe there really is a Book of Life to be opened on that last and terrible day. Maybe each page of that book is a soul printed with its sins in fluorescent letters. Blessed be the name of the Lord. Blessed be the Great and Eternal Copy Editor. May he be liberal with his eraser.

It occurred to Clark while he was reading that perhaps escape was the only reason why he was a reader. We all seek our escapes, he knew. Nora's had been television, Walter's had been his magazines, perhaps Emma's was the arts. He wondered what she had in her life to escape from. He'd have to ask her that one day, if such a day would come.

How the hell are you going to handle this dinner party? he asked himself every time he turned a page.

Emma came over on Sunday with a grocery bag cuddled in her arm like a nursing child. She had called Clark for directions; he had given them to her before scrambling as madly as his knees allowed him to straighten the place up. He had put away the dishes and socks and left only enough books lying around to appear scholarly, but he was not able to add to the house a woman's touch, to eliminate that three-degree shift. He watched her eyes as they wandered about the living room. He wondered what she was thinking.

"What's in the bag?" he asked.

She smiled. "The makings of chicken Alfredo."

"I always thought that dish sounded cannibalistic."

"I skin my Alfreds first."

"Leave the dirty underwear on, if only for seasoning."

She laughed and kissed him. His cleverness surprised him. Well, the right woman will do that to you.

She wandered about until she located the kitchen. She set the bag on the freshly scrubbed table. Fifteen minutes before, it had been caked with dried ketchup.

"When is Walter coming over?" she asked.

"He has to pick up Amber in the Cities."

"Her name is Amber?" Emma walked back into the living room.

"Amber Goltz. If they can't find a baby-sitter, we'll have her daughter as a guest, too. Her name's Betsy, I think."

"I love children." She threw her arms around his neck, her weight into him, her lips tightly against his. She smelled good, like some kind of peppery flower. He put his arms around her. That felt good, too. He couldn't have this after Walter arrived.

"I don't think you want to do that today," he said when she allowed him. "I'm coming down with a cold."

She pulled an inch away from his face. "You don't sound like you have a cold."

"It starts in my chest and works its way up." He hacked dutifully.

"Then I've already caught the bug." She tried to kiss him again. He pulled away.

"It's best to be on the safe side," he said.

She smiled as she released him. She studied the room with neither displeasure nor delight. He was suddenly very aware of just how bad it smelled in there. Stale, like Walter's apartment.

"So this is where you live," she said.

"I told you that you wouldn't be impressed."

"On the contrary." She walked about the room, then stopped to look at a photograph of Clark and Nora standing in front of the store. "Was this your wife?"

Clark nodded. Remember, he thought. Past tense.

"She looks like a nice woman."

Nora had never looked so plain. "The Midwest is known for nice."

"Do you miss her?"

Well, he thought, there is the truth and there is the right thing to say. "Sometimes." There is also compromise.

"Is she buried here in town?"

Buried here in my heart, he thought, in my soul, a cold, hard thing plunged into the living like a dagger. He felt Nora rise and swallowed her bitter taste down. Not tonight. I'll have enough trouble as it is tonight. "Yes. She's from here."

Emma's face softened as she studied him. "It's hard, isn't it?"

"Yeah." He sought sanctity in the face of his watch. It stared back only blindly. "We should probably get started on dinner."

Emma orchestrated the subtle tastes of cream and chicken and Parmesan cheese as if the meal were music. She delicately cooked the pasta. Clark set the dining room table while marveling at her. God bless lonely December days at Mankato cinemas. God bless a woman's shortage of quarters. God bless the touch and feel of a woman, the smells and the subtleties, all the hidden things that make a woman into a woman like Emma.

God bless us every one.

Nora planted herself on his conscience. He knew from the solid echo of her words that for all his efforts she would not be moved. For a moment he hated her, but only for a moment. Perhaps his mind worked its strategies beyond his consciousness; perhaps somewhere in its recesses it had allowed Nora to rise because rising would keep him from being too responsive to Emma. Emma was, after all, only an old friend. For tonight.

Got you, he said to Nora.

You've got nothing, Nora replied.

An engine whispered into the driveway; tires muttered on snow. Clark and Emma looked at each other as car doors opened and closed. Emma straightened her hair. Clark walked to the door.

He opened it to Walter and a small woman with bright eyes and cheeks bitten by the weather. It bit Clark's cheeks, too—it was genuinely cold now, with the sun down. Their breaths mingled thick in front of their faces.

"Hi, Dad," Walter said. "This is Amber."

"I remember Amber." But not like this.

"I remember you, too, Mr. Holstrom."

She held out her small, gloved hand. He took it, smooth leather like cold lips, and pulled her into the room. "Please, call me Clark."

"All right. Clark." She was small, almost petite, with no rough edges to her at all. She was so much different than he remembered.

"And this must be your friend," Walter said.

Emma stood expectant and beautiful in the kitchen doorway. Yes, Clark thought, friend. Friend and lover. "This is Emma Richard. Emma, this is my son, Walter, and his girlfriend, Amber Goltz."

A look flashed between Walter and Amber. A smile dropped. "It's nice to meet you," Walter said.

"You, too."

Walter hung his coat in the closet and took Amber's. "Dad has all these friends I don't know about. It's like he's leading a secret life."

"Perhaps he is," Emma suggested.

Clark was acutely terrified that that statement might contain more than he wanted anyone to know. He relaxed when they smiled in a way that they would not have been able to do if they had understood. Life would be so much simpler without that damned Nora. I want her dead, he thought, I want her dead. And suddenly, it wasn't just words.

"I hope you're hungry," Emma said.

"Starving." Walter was wearing a clean, pressed shirt, the creases softened only where they stretched across his belly, new jeans zippered and buckled tight, with some kind of hiking boots on his feet. The smells of sweat and shaving lotion battled. He was still greasy, still Walter. "I'm always starving. Just ask Amber."

Amber shrugged. She was wearing a maroon sweater with a ski design dancing across her chest and wool pants. The warmth she raised within him made Clark want to throw his arms around her like a daughter. "I'm hungry, too."

"Then let's eat."

Emma led them into the dining room and turned on the light. Clark had forgotten candles—he and Nora had never had candlelight dinners. He did so many things with Emma that he and Nora had never done.

"Dad must have set the table." Walter held Amber's chair. She sat in it without looking at him. She was such a petite woman that Clark wondered if sitting down her feet reached the floor. "He got the forks on the wrong side."

"No, Walter," Amber said. "He did fine."

"They're supposed to be on the right."

"On the left, Walter."

"Really? Oh." Walter sat beside Amber. "Shows you what I know." He smiled and nudged her with his elbow. She watched Emma bring in the food.

They ate in near silence with Clark's hopes continually rising. Unless a football game was televised, Walter concentrated during meals on keeping words to a minimum and stuffing it in. Amber sat beside him with a pleasing smell and manner; she ate too politely. He remembered the evening he had watched Walter walk across the model to his home behind the Wal-Mart. It felt good to think that this woman might be the one who had been waiting for him, scolding Betsy about her study habits. It was funny how memories could warm you, could restore your appetite. He raised a forkful of Emma's chicken to his lips.

"So what do you do . . . is it Amber?" Emma asked.

"Yes. I work for Film in the Cities." She shrugged. "Nothing special. Clerical work."

"I was the director of the regional arts council," Emma said. "I know how special clerical work is."

Walter was scraping the side of his fork along his plate for the last of his sauce. The porcelain howled as if he was skinning it. "Hell of a filer. You should see her file."

Amber glanced at him. "You've never seen me work."

"At the house I have."

"When?"

Walter didn't answer. He poured the last of the sauce over the last of the pasta and continued eating, his lips rimmed with cheesy cream. Amber turned to her plate.

They took their coffee into the living room, where they shared pleasant talk about art and film and filing and hardware. Clark sat in his easy chair, Walter and Amber on the sofa, Emma in a chair of her own, seeming to sense Clark's wish for distance. The night through the front window brightened with a million stars, hope glinting in each one of them. When Emma returned from taking the cups into the kitchen, draped her arms over Clark's shoulders, and kissed his cheek, the stars winked out one by one. She sat again in her chair, smiling.

"I don't think I'll catch a cold from your cheek," she said.

Walter stared at him, at Emma, at him again. His eyes flitted down to dance upon his hands. The top of his skull reddened. "So how did you two meet?" he asked, his voice as flat as slate.

"At the cinema in Mankato," Emma said. "I didn't have change for a ticket, and Clark made up the difference for me. We saw *Henry and June*. It's a good movie for couples." She smiled first at Walter, then Clark.

285

Got you, Nora said.

The conversation grew stilted; it was mostly between Amber and Emma. Walter's eyes flashed at his father; Clark avoided them. He knew he was energizing the bold, bright letters spelling out *adultery* across his face, but he was helpless to do anything but feel the winter's cold move into the room and the sinking pain of Nora's glee. What do you want me to do, he silently screamed at his wife and son, spend the rest of my life rotting in this damned house building a damned model?

I don't want much, Nora said, *just what you promised. That and your goddamned life.*

When I made you promises you weren't lying in a nursing home staring at a wall. When I made you promises . . .

Bullshit, Nora said.

All right, he thought, so it's bullshit. It's better to live in a bullshit world than to live in the one to which you're condemning me. She did not answer because she did not have to. Her answer was written in the fading stars, in the faces around him.

Walter's expression said he would accept no explanations. "Well, maybe we should be going."

Amber was on her feet before his words had left the air. "There is the baby-sitter," she explained. "I hope you understand."

"Of course," Emma said.

Clark showed them to the door, Walter's eyes still buzzing around him almost audibly. "I'm glad you came by, Amber."

"Thank you for having me."

Amber donned her coat; Walter shrugged into his. They left quickly, Walter not saying good-bye. Emma went into the kitchen. Clark was about to shut the door, but left it cracked open when he heard them begin to speak.

"What was that about?" Amber demanded in a voice as hard as the cold.

"What do you mean?" Walter asked.

"About me being your girlfriend. How dare you tell them that I'm your girlfriend."

Clark could see their shadows cast upon the snow, could see Walter's shadowy arm slip tentatively toward Amber. "It was just a little white lie."

She slapped the arm away. "The hell if it was. Damn you, Walter, you write me that pathetic letter and pester me and pester me, and . . ."

"I like you, Jenny."

"My name is Amber."

"I like you, Amber." His voice whined pitifully. It was a whine designed for sympathy that only left you feeling raw. "I was hoping you might like me."

"Like you?" Amber laughed sharply. "I've never liked you. Do you think Jenny ran out on you for no reason? She had a reason, Walter. She had more than one."

"Don't be like that, Amber."

He slipped his arm around her shoulders. Her hand cracked sharply across his face. "Take me home. Don't say a word to me while you do. If you ever call me again, I'll call the cops."

Walter continued pleading while Clark eased the door shut. Footsteps hurried away; Walter's Pontiac rumbled. Clark felt drained to the point of weakness. So, he thought, it had all been a fantasy manufactured by a pathetic son. Perhaps God was a craps player and we the dice, and half of Walter had bounced off of the table. There were no second chances. What kind of God doesn't give second chances?

He felt as if his arthritis had worked into his chest. He felt as if his whole body was turning to granite. Why is it that everything I touch turns to dust? Everything, he thought, except Emma. Oh, Emma. God, Emma. Everything so far.

Dishes clattered in the kitchen. Emma was too quiet. Clark had a childish urge to hide under the bed until she was gone. Well, he thought, I am not a child. Too bad—children are forgiven many things. He walked heavily into the kitchen.

She was standing at the sink washing dishes, soap suds on her hands, plates clattering as sharply as Amber's voice had. As he began to put his arm around her, he remembered Walter putting his arm around Amber at the door. Clark pulled away. "That didn't go too badly," he lied.

"Why haven't you told Walter about us?"

Hell. Clark had lost perhaps everything with his son; he suspected that now he would lose everything with his lover. He felt that only by bringing the whole world into light was there any hope of forgiveness. Not the whole world, but enough of it. "His mother . . . ," he began.

"He's having difficulty dealing with Nora's death?"

Perhaps Clark was a lucky seven. Tonight God was giving some of us second chances. "It isn't the right time," he said. "He's not used to seeing his father in love with somebody." He paused. "Somebody else."

When he tried to put his arm around her, she settled into him. He kissed her neck, smelled her peppery aroma. There was pain and laughter in the lines on her face. Pain and laughter and understanding.

"To one's children," she said, "all other love appears misdirected."

"Sure." It wasn't how he would put it.

Chapter

12

The next morning it was thirty-five below. Clark bundled himself in long underwear, two pairs of socks, mittens instead of gloves because they were warmer, and a scarf over his nose and mouth to protect his lungs. Nothing moved outside; nothing dared move—the air lived and breathed and hunted its victims. The early morning darkness did not even hint at a sun. Trees cracked with pain. The lake in the distance and the snow beneath his boots both moaned.

Clark only shook his head at the Dodge before walking north on St. Anne's Road. He stared up at the dark bulk of the elevator, trying and failing to draw from burning lambs a memory to warm his soul. He turned into a breeze that worked at the skin around his eyes, the only skin he could not keep from exposing. Watery eyes viewed the suddenly impressionistic world as if he were Renoir. He thought of Dante's hell, of the truly damned buried in ice as cold as this. He shook his head. Christ.

When he reached the store, he fumbled with the keys and dropped them. He stared at them on the sidewalk as if they had fallen into another world. The air worked down his collar as he bent over to retrieve them; he could feel his skin turning purple and frosty white. He couldn't pick the keys up without removing a mitten; as soon as he did his fingers turned as stiff and numb as sticks. His knees, his damned knees, wouldn't let him stand up again. He crouched, staring at the sidewalk as his tears gathered and froze in his lashes. Hell, now he couldn't even blink.

I am a blind man, he thought. My ass is to the street, and I am mooning the world. In a few hours his frosty, defiant, and very dead buttocks would be telling all those former customers on their way to the Wal-Mart exactly what he thought of their betrayal. By then his feet would be frozen to the ground and they would have to leave him as he was until spring. I am a wooden Indian doing what every Indian would like to be doing to the white man's conquering world. Take this, paleface. He smiled.

But winter has no sense of humor. As the painful cold gave way to numbness, he realized the danger he was in. He fumbled the key into his palm, the metal burning dully against his skin, and viewed with fascination the slow working of torpid muscles as if he were watching a distant predator. With his free hand he reached for the doorknob; he pulled himself upright with a pain that left him shocked and gasping. He rubbed the ice from his lashes, then with his breath warmed his fingers enough to insert and turn the key. He went gratefully inside.

Walter had taped instructions for the burglar alarm beside it, making Clark's and Walter's and the burglar's jobs all that much easier. Clark turned the key and pushed the buttons, his fingers tingling in the warmth. He went in back for the broom.

Everywhere he turned he saw the look of betrayal in Walter's buzzing eyes. It was in everything he thought about. It took the taste out of everything that had happened the night before, out of the food, the talk, the kisses. It left the evening tasting like dust. His eyes had looked just like Nora's.

He went to the back for the dustpan. You knew that this would come, he thought—Walter isn't about to go away, and the hell if you want Emma to. Two worlds were going to collide, and you knew you'd be at the point of impact. Bug on a windshield, rain on a road. Splatter and gone.

He sat in front of Walter's new Wind River computer after making himself a cup of coffee. Miss January was wearing a short fur parka and nothing else, holding it open just enough to make him wish she would hold it open a little more. There must be a science to that; there must be a guy behind the photographer computing angles. Lust is numbers.

He turned away, not wanting or needing to go through that again. He sipped his coffee. Two Wind River computers waited against the wall, boxes open, packing removed. Clark wondered what that was all about.

Walter came in a little before eight. He draped his coat over Clark's chair without saying anything. His fingers trembled against Clark's shoulder blades.

"Good morning, son." Walter didn't answer. Well then, this is how it is going to be. "What's going on with the computers?"

"They don't work. They're incompatible. We fucked up, all right?" Walter leaned over his computer, pushed a button on the keyboard, and watched the screen saver disappear. When he tried to call up the daily schedule, the screen went blank.

"God damn it!"

He slammed his fist down on top of the monitor. The screen flashed a blip like a soul departing. He slammed his fist down on it again. His face flushed, a desperate wildness came into his eyes. "God damn it! God damn it!"

"I doubt the warranty covers physical abuse," Clark said quietly.

Walter's eyes flashed at him. His face was blotched as if a fire was burning through the thin spots. "What do you care?"

"Do you think I don't care?"

"You don't care about Mom. You must not care about much."

"I care about your mother."

"You care about your whore."

Clark felt the muscles in his jaw knot tight. "Emma is not a whore."

"Then she's a home wrecker."

"Walter," Clark said, "there isn't any home to wreck."

Walter's eyes were wet, his face red and shiny around the tiny pock-marked shadows. "Mom is still around, Dad. She's lying in a bed just a couple of blocks from here."

"Maybe she is, and maybe she's not."

"She is."

"You don't know that." You don't know anything. You believe in a mythology, in a good mommy, a good daddy, a happy little boy. The truth was that there had never been any of that. There had been a mommy and daddy fighting, then a silence worse than fighting, and finally a daddy trying to overcome what could not be overcome. Wake up, Walter.

He looked at the calendar, then at his son. "All I know is that I'm here, Walter."

"All I know, Dad, is that Mom isn't in the ground. All I know is that you're fucking someone else."

Why, Clark thought, you insolent little shit. "Don't use that tone of voice with me."

"Or what? You'll take me over your knee? You'll beat the hell out of me? Come back to the real world, Dad. Mom is alive and your threats don't mean a damn thing." He walked to the counter and stared at the cash register. His knuckles whitened as he gripped its edges. "You can't really believe I'd approve of this."

I don't give a damn what you approve of. Son or not. "I'm sorry you feel that way."

"How the hell else can I feel?" His trembling body oozed over his belt. "I can't stand you sitting there being so goddamned smug, not without getting mad."

"I'm not being smug."

"The hell if you aren't." He didn't look up. "Maybe you shouldn't come in to sweep for a while. Maybe not anymore."

Clark's breath caught. He felt as if Walter had kicked him in the chest. "What?"

"It's not like I can't do it myself." He laughed harshly and shook his head; a shiny spot moved across his scalp. "Hell, it's not like it will even need it."

"What does that mean?"

"I don't know what that means. I don't even know why I said it." Walter walked to the front of the store, looked out the window, then came back again. "Damn it, Dad, why do you have to do this?"

Clark felt as he had not felt in decades—his feet were planted and he would not be moved. There are risks worth taking, things worth not losing. Walter, I love you. You are my son. But. "It's not something I'm going to stop. I love her."

Walter smiled. "You get fucked and you think you're in love. Christ, you sound like a hard-up schoolboy."

Clark stood as he clenched his fists. What did this fat, greasy bastard know about love? "Isn't that why you married Jenny?"

"You leave Jenny out of this."

"Didn't you marry her because she fucked you?" Words were coming that he feared to speak, but he couldn't stop them. "Who's really the hard-up schoolboy here, Walter? Did you know she once tried to fuck me? Yeah, right there in the house, she tried to get me in the bedroom. Do you see me pining for her?"

Walter stomped back into the office, his face livid, a fearful rage in his eyes. He stopped close enough for Clark to see his pores, to smell the stink of him rising. He jammed his finger hard into Clark's chest, backing him up. "Damn it, Dad, leave her out of this!"

The anger in Clark consumed him. It was frightening, unstoppable. He was a little boy cowering somewhere deep inside this angry, old man. "Cunt connoisseur."

"What?"

"Cunt connoisseur. Isn't that what it says on your magazines?"

293

"How do you know about those?"

"Maybe I should lie on the sofa and masturbate onto a picture of some fat bitch with her legs spread. Maybe I should jerk off onto this calendar. Should I go your route?"

Walter snarled, grabbed his father by the collar, and shoved him against the wall. His face was in Clark's face, his breath hot in his eyes. He was finally able to hold a gaze.

"What are you going to do, Walter? Beat up your old man?"

Walter glowered, released him, and strode to the front of the store. His shoulders rose and fell, his fists clenched and unclenched. He exuded a formidable anger. Like father, like son.

Oh Christ, Clark thought. What have I done? "I'm sorry, Walter."

"To hell with you, Dad."

"I'm sorry. I said things I shouldn't have said." God in heaven, I wish I could control my anger.

"To hell with you, Dad. And to hell with that old bitch of yours. You could at least have picked someone worth fucking."

He strode out the door before Clark could answer, walked by the window in front of the computer display, and was gone. Clark waited for him to come back for his coat. He didn't.

He leaned heavily on the counter. Is it love to dredge up for a woman a rage you don't want to admit you own? He studied the shelves, the hardware, the open computer boxes. The store was suddenly lifeless—anger had stripped away all his memories, his soul. For the first time in almost five decades he felt that this store was no longer his own.

With this loss, the anger flared again, grew so alive that he couldn't help but embrace it. Well, Walter, now you've taken away my store. God be damned if you think you can take away what life I have beyond it. It isn't my store anymore; it isn't even ours. It's your store, Walter, *your* store. *Your* store and *your* failure. I will not let you blame me for this.

He slipped on his overclothes. The walk to the front door seemed so foreign that he thought he might become lost. He came back only to throw his keys on the counter.

"Sweep your own damn floor," he said.

The weak winter sunrise had turned the eastern horizon silver. Walter had disappeared. Clark slammed shut the door and made up his mind to go over to Emma's apartment and make love to her as vigorously as he was able—he'd show that leather-faced bitch and her pockmarked son exactly what he was capable of. He hurried through the cold toward St. Anne's Road, then remembered that the car wouldn't start and he had to work this morning anyway. He decided that today was the day he would tell Agnes Miller to take her historical society and her megalomania and shove them as far up her ample ass as she, or perhaps Roger VanRuden, could reach. He didn't need or want that job, or its aggravations. He had better things to do.

He walked past the store, the police station, toward the Double-Trouble on the corner. His anger cooled toward rationality. A gray sedan with a face behind the wheel as white and cold as the snow around him warmed it up again. The car slowed, a hand waved, a mouth smiled. That god-be-damned Ted Lewell—to hell with him, too. That son of a bitch needed to get what he deserved. Clark didn't acknowledge him, and finally the car sped away.

The *Closed* sign was in the window at the historical society. The thought of waiting in the cold for Agnes did not improve his mood. He pondered dropping his pants and freezing to death on the doorstep, just for spite. When he tried the door, he found it unlocked.

The cool sanctuary compared to outdoors was a furnace. He took off his mittens and unbuttoned his coat. From the back drifted moaning.

"Agnes?" He wondered if she had fallen.

The moaning stopped, and a quick scuffling replaced it. Clark was close enough to distinguish the moans of both sexes. "Agnes?"

He stuck his head into the office. Agnes was buttoning the second button on her blouse; the top one was undone. Roger VanRuden was standing with his back to Clark, his hands around his zipper. A thick, meaty smell hung in the air like an accusation.

Agnes cleared her throat. "Hello, Clark. You're early."

So, she had finally done it. The Ernest Borgnine look-alike had seduced her desire. Now *this* would make a good movie.

"A little research?" he asked.

He could see the uncertainty on her face—was he joking, or just naive? "Yes."

"Did you accomplish anything, Roger?"

Roger turned, but did not look at him. "A little."

"Quite a lot, perhaps."

The color in Roger's face, unlike his erection, did not die. "I guess I should be heading to work."

"Maybe you better." Clark was thoroughly enjoying himself.

"Good-bye, Roger," Agnes said, her voice shaky, as he hurried by. "Will I see you this afternoon?"

"I don't know." Roger had grabbed his coat from Clark's desk and was already in the sanctuary.

"Stop by," Clark called after him. "You can never get in enough research."

The front door clattered open and shut; cold washed across the floor. Agnes busied herself telling Clark what needed to be done, though nothing needed to be done. Her blouse's top button was still unfastened, as if she had meant to leave it that way when she had dressed that morning. She grabbed her coat and hurried for the sanctuary.

"Agnes?" he asked as she bustled by him.

"Yes?"

"We all fuck."

Her glance said that the word, if not the act, was anathema. Clark smiled. It was a wonderful word, so much better than *intercourse*.

The mixture of rage and sour amusement enervated him so much that for two hours he did not remember that he was going to tell her he was quitting. Well, he had always been rash in anger. He thought it might be fun to hang around.

He had no work to do: no school tours, no history to research—Thoreau was dead and the great sundae controversy would, it seemed, forever lean in Waseca's favor. He wandered the first floor before climbing to the balcony, where the heat had gathered like the choirs of old. He studied the Albert Wilson articles and thought about Ted Lewell. That damned diary. He wished he could read it more closely; wished he knew what the girl had known, how it could be interpreted. He thought about Maynard wandering around out at Ambrose's and knowing nothing about it—knowing nothing at all, really. He stared down at the polished sanctuary floor, watching the ghostly congregation beginning to rise. One day, he knew, Ted Lewell would come to the historical society again, would stomp across that floor, this time knowing something. What do I tell him? Either nothing, or I confirm his suspicions, or I do something else. He rubbed his chin thoughtfully. Or I do something else.

He lifted the articles from the wall and slipped them from their frames. The old paper was too brittle to crumple; it disintegrated into dust so fine that it tickled his nose. Powdered memories. He didn't think he had it in him to blame their destruction on the old standby senility when Agnes found out, not with Maynard the way he was. He decided he would tell her Ted Lewell had stolen them. She would call Jergen Burnett. Jergen would arrest Lewell, tie him into the VCR and radio burglaries, and break one of his arms in a clumsy arrest. You can kill many birds with a stone the size of a pillar.

He skipped lunch, not wanting to walk in the cold all the way out to the Burger King. He sat at his desk as if waiting for something. Emma came in at one o'clock.

"So, this is where you work." Her heels clicked hollowly on the floor, beating out time.

"Yes. A former church, then a historical society, now a bordello."

"What do you mean?"

He told her about Agnes and Roger, managing to leave out their names. She smiled. "On the desk?"

"I guess. They wouldn't have wanted to do it in a chair."

"Too crowded."

"Too many splinters."

"I never was much of a desk person, myself," she said. "Comfort has always been a big part of passion."

"I know what you mean."

He took her in his arms. Something was wrong—he felt as uncomfortable as if Nora and Walter were watching them from the balcony. I ought to just tell Emma the truth, he thought, I ought to get it out and get it over with. There had been too many surprises in their relationship, too many close calls. The problem with lies is that they so rarely come in the shape of the truth they are meant to cover.

"Show me around," she said.

He looked at her face, at her eyes. I ought to tell her now.

"What?" she asked.

He sighed, then nodded. There would be time. "I'll give you the grand tour."

He showed her the Indian exhibits. He told her the story of the Calliver brothers. The telling after all this time was automatic and left him either free to think of Nora and Walter, or condemned to it. He kept glancing over his shoulder, kept expecting to see someone dart into the shadows. He wanted to tell Emma the truth.

He showed her his office. He led her up the stairs and explained Credibull's history with the railroad. She studied him more than she did the exhibits. He always felt her eyes.

"Wasn't there a famous murder here?" she asked. "It seems to me I heard something about a murder."

"Yeah, well, we don't have anything on that."

"You don't like your dark past?"

He shrugged. "Does anyone?"

"I heard that a man was writing a book about it."

Clark shrugged again. "Yeah."

"You don't sound pleased."

"My best friend was the prime suspect."

"Oh." She nodded and looked at the train pictures.

He addressed her unasked question. "I met Maynard long before the murder. Nothing was ever proven. You don't drop friends because of suspicions."

"But you admit you have some."

Hell. He wiped his face to cover his expression. "Suspicions don't mean anything."

She put her arm around his waist, making him uncomfortable. "You're as loyal as a puppy."

He thought about Albert Wilson and Maynard. He thought about Helen, too, then about Nora. He ought to tell her the truth. He ought to.

He looked over the balcony. Below him, standing in files, was the ghostly congregation, organ music rising like mist. He rubbed his eyes. When he looked again he saw that it was not a congregation but a hanging jury. They looked up at him from desiccated faces, bloody mouths, black evil in their eyes. Men in stiff black suits with collars like nooses, women masked in death shrouds. All the dead were down there, the world's dead, his dead, all were looking up at him, faces like old bone, at him. His father and mother. Freddy with his arms in the air, defying fear and gravity. Nameless soldiers in ripped and bloody uniforms, beach water dripping from rotting noses, bullet-mangled faces, scabby smiles. Mike Caruther, Jack Falstaff, and Arnold Andresen, grinning maniacally with a red-stained two-by-four in his hand. Josef Meyer and George Calliver, his ripped throat grinning, and Dwayne Wilson with black blood pumping from arms severed at the elbows. Rose stood beside him, crossing herself with her breath frosted white upon her lips; Albert smiled his broken smile from his broken face. Helen's hair had gone completely gray, and she was muttering pleas for promises from bloodless lips, from black and bloodless eyes. Nora and Maynard danced around the dead's fringes to a dirge played by Bob Tunnell and the nursing home's bed- or grave-ridden band. They had smiles on their nodding, wrinkled faces. They were beating out the time.

He had an almost irresistible urge to dive over the rail into their midst, to drive them through the floorboards as he had wanted to drive his fist through his Credibull model, to destroy their world. But you cannot destroy the inevitable. Dive and you only join their ranks.

"What's the matter?" Emma asked. "What are you looking at?"

He tore himself away and fell into the incredible living blueness of her eyes. There were no death shrouds there. "Nothing," he said. That was the word for it. Nothing. Perhaps God was a vacuum cleaner. Sing, choirs of angels, play your funeral dirges, pour out your praises into the sucking void. He felt suddenly very weak, very mortal, very afraid. He leaned on Emma, pulled himself away from the rail by hiding in the strength of the breath in her lungs, the warm potency of the blood surging through her heart. He clung to the vivid and inescapable power of fingers like birds in a sunset. The only strength the dead have is the strength they draw from the living. The strength we give them. Well, he thought, the only strength the living have is the strength they draw from the living, too.

"What's the matter?" Emma asked again.

He forced a smile. "I was just thinking about how much I'd like to close up shop early today."

"Can you do that?"

"We were down all last week for repairs. Anyone who stops by will think we still are."

"Won't your boss be angry?"

He smiled. If Agnes could talk Roger into stopping by this after-noon, they would enjoy the privacy. "Is she going to fire a volunteer?" He guided Emma away from the railing, away from the eyes and the faces. He found that he didn't have to lean on her anymore. When he stepped into the sanctuary, it was just the sanctuary.

He went to the office for his coat and boots. As they left the build-ing, he hung up the *Closed* sign and found himself out in the bright af-ternoon, the bowl of the sky pale blue as if the color had condensed in the cold and drained down its sides. The air was alive. Clark felt stronger with his feet on the ground.

"A movie?" he asked.

"Sure," she said.

"What's playing?"

"*A River Runs Through It.* Have you heard of it?"

"I don't hear of much."

She drove down Josef Meyer Boulevard to the highway, then turned right toward the nursing home. Hotel Hill stood beyond it, its naked trees clawing at the sky like dirty fingers. Through Ambrose's walls he saw Nora lying on her bed, perspiration from her dance still glistening on her forehead. Her blind eyes slammed into his chest. He felt her hatred.

You bitch, he thought.

Do you think I asked to fall? Do you think I asked for this bed?

You spent your life on a sofa in front of a television. If we'd had a bed in the living room, you would have lain in it.

And you know why that was.

He rubbed his chin. Maybe I do. Parts of it, anyway. Part of it was Deloris. Part of it was just the bastard I was, part of it was other things. But I changed. You never changed. You were always afraid to.

Some things, she said, *never change.*

"What are you thinking about?" Emma asked.

He turned from the home, from the eyes. It was such a loaded question. "Nothing. Did you say you've already seen this movie?"

"I read the book."

"Will the movie be worth it?"

"If it's like the book."

They drove past the white, sleeping fields, dazzling in their blankets, through Janesville, Smith's Mill, Eagle Lake, and on to Mankato. The red letters on the cinema marquee spelled *A River Runs Threw It*. The cold takes casualties; one is concern for spelling on the part of hapless and frozen cinema employees. Emma parked. They went inside.

It was a film about fishing, or about life and fishing. The river was the Big Blackfoot in western Montana; it served as a metaphor for memory. The film ended with an old guy fishing in the river, haunted by the waters. Clark should have felt good when they left, but he didn't.

"Didn't you like the movie?" Emma asked. The night had fallen. The cold was deep.

"I loved it. That's the problem."

They drove to her apartment without either of them suggesting that they should. They walked up the stairs past an old man carrying a grocery bag, a Campbell Soup can peeking over the top, bean with bacon. He smiled at them, wiped his red-rimmed nose, then went quietly into

301

his apartment. Clark guessed that enough rumors about him and Emma were floating among the residents to keep the bridge clubs busy for years. He ought to tell her.

"Would you like pasta for supper?" Emma asked.

"Sure. In the old days we called it spaghetti."

"Times are changing."

They went inside. The Christmas knickknacks were gone—it was a monochrome world again. Clark found himself wishing he could stay in this apartment forever, a black-and-white world with no grays. So many easy answers. But this apartment had raised so many questions, too.

He smelled his own salty nervousness as she lifted his coat from his shoulders. "Emma," he said, "I have to tell you something."

"What?"

Oh, what the hell. He figured he should at least eat a good meal first. "What kind of sauce are we having?"

"That isn't telling me something. That's asking me something."

"I meant to say that I'm hell with sauce."

"Then you can help me make it."

In a moment of panic, Clark had talked himself into a corner. He had never made sauce in his life; the extent of his culinary expertise was holding jars beneath hot water if their lids were too tight. Well, he thought, you'll have to bullshit. Life in its most irreducible form was simply an attempt at perfecting that art.

He watched her take cans of stewed tomatoes out of cupboards, peppers from the refrigerator, a garlic clove from a basket beside it. "What do you put in yours?" she asked.

"Let me see how you do it. I'll let you know if you do anything wrong."

"A backseat cook." She handed him the tomatoes and pointed at the can opener. He opened the can with a flourish any Italian chef would have been proud of, though he took his time doing it, letting her work ahead of him. She was boiling water for the pasta. He studied her technique. You fill a pot with water, then set it on the stove. You turn the stove on. Not much to it.

"Oregano?" she asked.

"Sure."

"Cumin?"

What the hell was cumin? Wasn't that one of the gifts the three Wise Men brought to Bethlehem? He shrugged. "Sure."

She smiled. "You don't know what you're doing, do you?"

"No."

"Why don't I take care of this? You can wait in the living room."

"All right." He retreated from the kitchen. So much for bullshit.

"Put on Billie Holiday," she said as the odor of fresh garlic punctured the air.

"That I can do."

He found the disc and put on the voice that always made him weep. He sat on the couch, relaxing just enough for his tightness to recoil when Emma asked, "What was it you wanted to tell me?"

"It was nothing." Christ, he thought, it's hot in here. It must be the stove.

"It must have been something. You've gone to such lengths to avoid it."

He stared at the couch, at the carpet beyond his feet. All he saw was black-and-white. No compromise. "I don't know how to say it in a way that will keep you from tossing me out the door."

"Oh?" Her heels clicked on the tile. Out of the corner of his eye he saw her come around the counter to sit beside him. "I won't throw you out. You weigh too much."

"This isn't a joke, Emma." He sighed. She put her hand on his shoulder, then withdrew it when he tightened even more. "Remember what I told you about my wife? About her slipping and freezing to death?"

"Yes."

"She slipped, but she didn't freeze to death."

Silence grew like a weed between them. The water on the stove gently gurgled. Damn, he thought, it's hot in here.

"What happened to her?" Emma asked.

303

"She suffered hypothermia. She isn't really alive. I mean . . ." He was plummeting away from his wonderful, new life. He tried to grab for the sides, but was moving too fast to find them. "I'm married, Emma."

The water boiled. Garlic's sharp scent rose from Emma's fingers where they rested on the sofa back. "You mean, you're still married."

"Yes and no." There had to be a way to justify this. "She's in a bed in the nursing home. She just lies there, staring. She hasn't even spoken for a year." He paused. Was that true? Why the hell do words weigh so much? "Sitting there, I'd never know if she was dying."

You'd know, Nora said.

For a long time Emma didn't answer. Her hand strayed to his shoulder, to the back of his neck, her warm fingers against it, the smell on their tips strong and acrid. "I know all this," she said.

He stared at her. "You know?"

"Your son called me this afternoon."

He tried to shake the confusion loose. The black-and-whites around him swirled. "He told you?"

"I think he was trying to scare me away."

The room stopped spinning with a thud, stopped by hot anger. That fat, god-be-damned snitch. "What did he say?"

"Just what you told me." That fat, shit-eating bastard. "It doesn't matter."

He stared at her again. "What do you mean?"

She slipped her hand to his far shoulder and rested her head beside his chin. "Is she dead?" He felt her words warm on his chest.

"I don't know how to answer that."

"Is she dead to you?"

Yes, Clark, am I?

That was a hell of a question. He struggled to convince himself that she had been dead for years, that he was only hearing the voice of a ghost.

Of a conscience.

"Yes, she is."

"Then she's dead for me, too." Emma gripped his shoulders and stared into his face as if she were admonishing a schoolboy. "There are some things I care too much about to give up."

Oh, Emma, he thought as he pulled her to him. Would you feel this way if you knew the truth? She's not dead. Demons don't die. "I love you." He was surprised to find himself saying it.

"Do you?"

"Yes." It surprised him a second time. He was not surprised to find that it was true.

"I love you, too."

They sat that way until the pasta boiled over. Emma leaped to her feet with a smile on her face, with no trace of forgiveness in her eyes, nor any trace of a need for it. She kissed him quickly, then rushed into the kitchen. He sat as he had been sitting before she left, his arm on the back of the sofa, his hand in the air as if he were still caressing her. With the absence of her scent and touch, anger about Walter rose like a blister. It was funny how anger was always there, waiting for opportunities. Like Nora.

He didn't eat much of the meal—it was flavored only with the heat in his blood. He was too angry to read after it. It had been a long time since he'd packed so much anger into one day—he hadn't been like this since his drunken days.

"Would you like me to take you home?" Emma asked around eight. "You're distracted."

He rubbed his face, his eyes. On the inside of his lids he saw Walter on the telephone, spilling secrets. The god-be-damned snitch. "I guess I am. I'm sorry."

"There's nothing to be sorry for."

They drove to Credibull in silence, the darkness heavy, the cold as intense as the stars. The store was dark; Clark couldn't see Walter's apartment lights from the street. Well, he thought, I'll find out if he's home soon enough. Clark's own house was dark, too, when Emma pulled into the driveway. It looked cold. It looked dead. The historical society's congregation rose into his mind. The jury stared from grinning faces.

He needed something to grab on to. "Will you marry me?" he asked in a blurt of a sentence, like a child asking for a cookie. "After Nora's gone, I mean."

Emma smiled at him a smile that given enough time could melt this frozen world. "We'll see, after Nora's gone. Good night, Clark." She kissed him.

"Good night."

The cold could not match the warmth of the car, her smile, or her kiss. He walked slowly toward the front door until she disappeared around the corner, then hurried to the state highway. What's-his-name, the cook, was sweeping the Bumblebee's floor like a character out of a Hemingway short story. The windows of Sheri's Craft Nook stared like two black eyes. The door leading up to Walter's apartment creaked as he opened it.

Television noise almost echoed as he climbed the stairs, harsh canned laughter. No light leaked from beneath Walter's door. He pounded on it, feeling the wood give slightly beneath his fist.

"Walter? Walter!"

He pounded again, then looked out the window into the parking lot. Walter's Pontiac was gone. He hurried down the hall, down the stairs, and out into the indigo cold. He strode to the elevator, then down St. Anne's Road, with his breath coming back to wrap frostily around his cheeks. Something had been stuffed into his mailbox—the lid was cocked open, as if the box were howling at the moon.

He removed from it a folded stack of computer printouts as thick as a slice of Helen's beef. Three notebook sheets fluttered from its crease to the road like feathers. The cold worked at him as he picked them up; he had to use the lid to pull himself back upright. He stepped into the orb cast by the streetlight and tried to read the papers, seeing only a blur. Hell. His glasses were in his shirt pocket, his shirt pocket was hidden behind so many clothes it might as well have been buried under three feet of concrete. He could only make out rows of numbers. He took them into the house.

He turned on the light and shrugged off his coat, shifting the papers from hand to hand as he did. He slid the books to one side of the coffee table, set the papers down, shivered, and turned up the thermostat. He put on his glasses. The printouts were accounting records; the three sheets a jumble of numbers, a reject from the eternal monkeys eternally seeking to type out the script of *Hamlet*.

"Christ," he muttered. He saw figures for hinges, nails, and lawn equipment. He shook his head. "Walter, what is this?"

It was an incredibly primitive system—hadn't he taught the kid book-keeping when he turned the store over to him? Debits and credits, income and expenses, pluses and minuses, all in a jumble. What had they been doing in his mailbox? Then he studied the numbers, and he knew.

"Christ," he said again.

The expenses and credits grew as he flipped through the pages, the income and debits shrank. The gap between them jumped on the last page of printout, when computers were first mentioned, and, as nearly as Clark could figure, became an impassable chasm toward the middle of the second notebook sheet. A few big jumps there were marked *Returns*. The figures on the bottom of the last sheet exploded and rained upon Clark's fingers like glowing embers on burning lambs. He dropped the pages to the table.

"Walter," he whispered, "what have you done?"

Somewhere Clark had a key for the apartment—Walter had given one to Nora when he and Jenny had first moved to town. Clark searched the kitchen drawers with no luck. In Nora's room his frantic fingers flew through her top dresser drawer, through panties like silk balloons and brassieres designed to carry bowling balls. He pulled out of a back corner a tangle of house keys, car keys, and keys he could not name. On one a piece of masking tape had written across it *W&J* in Nora's childish hand. He shoved it into his pocket, then hurried out of the room and front door. The cold instantly corroded his knees and throbbed in his shoulder. He had no time to worry about it.

He had reached St. Anne's Road before he remembered he'd left his mittens and cap on the coffee table. He strode to the elevator as fast as he dared with his hands in his pockets, his eyes watering. The tip of his nose and the tops of his ears were burning dangerously by the

307

time he reached Sheri's. The television music jangled as he climbed the stairs, having to use the handrail, his breath coming as heavy as Maynard's. A fearful burst of exhaustion, an eternity, left him standing at the top, shaking. He had been in too much of a hurry.

He leaned against the wall, his head back, staring up at the brown, water-stained ceiling, and waited to catch his breath, the air painful in his lungs. When he checked for light beneath Walter's door he again saw none. He fit the key into the lock and opened the door onto darkness.

The reek of armpits and underwear assaulted him. He turned on the light. The couch was still there—well, he wouldn't have had time to move it. The television was there, too. That was an encouraging sign; Clark couldn't imagine Walter without one. Smut magazines lay scattered across the floor as if in mockery.

You old fool, he admonished himself, you're just imagining things. Walter must be in Mankato or St. Paul. Yes, St. Paul—perhaps he and Amber were this very moment patching up their argument. He looked for the picture of Jenny on the wall and found it missing.

Everything inside of him tumbled. "Walter," he said aloud. "Walter, where are you?"

He turned on the bedroom light. The bed was unmade, a spot in the center of the mattress was stained to the point of darkness. The air was as pungent as the living room, and more magazines were scattered on the floor. The computer had been thrown down to rollick among them as if in orgy. A crack ran diagonally across the monitor's face. The game Clark had bought Walter for Christmas lay neatly on the nightstand.

Clark opened the dresser drawers and checked the closet. Underwear gone, shirts gone, pants gone, too. One small, open suitcase had been shoved carelessly halfway beneath the bed, one of a set that he and Nora had given Walter and Jenny on their wedding day. The rest of the set was gone.

"Oh, Walter," he whispered as he sank onto the bed. "Oh, Walter." His son's odor was there, too. It and the stain were all of Walter that remained.

Chapter

13

The next morning, a warm southern wind killed a bit of the cold. Clark walked to the store wondering if he was wasting his time in doing so and hoping that he wasn't. He fished in his pocket for his key before remembering that the day before he had thrown it on the counter. The door was locked. He cupped his hands and stared through the glass, feeling it suck the warmth from his nose and lips. His breath clouded his view, but not before he saw that the store was empty. So much for hope.

He crossed the street. On the other side of the police station door a linoleum-and-tile world awaited him. Jergen Burnett dozed at his desk with his feet up, a half-eaten Bismarck beside him, purple jelly oozing onto the *Herald's* front page. A teenager with long, dark hair and his arm in a sling sat in the cell behind him.

"Jergen," Clark said, and got no answer. The stained headlines of the *Herald* read, STATE TO DECLARE HOTEL HILL A HISTORICAL SITE. Elmer Tornquist was in for a bad day. "Jergen," he said more loudly.

Jergen started, swung his feet off the desk, and dropped his elbow into the Bismarck. "Clark."

"Hi, Jergen."

"What can I help you with?"

"I was wondering if you'd heard anything from Walter."

Jergen checked his watch. "I figure to in about forty-five minutes. That's when he calls to complain about his burglar alarm." He wiped a paper napkin over his elbow. "Is there a problem?"

Hell. "No. I was just wondering."

Jergen nodded as he tossed the napkin at his wastebasket. He missed. "See what I got?" He jerked his head toward the cell. The boy rubbed his shoulder, but didn't look up.

"Who is it?" Clark asked.

"That burglar. I caught him last night." A proud smile slid across Jergen's face, a Gene Autry, a Roy Rogers smile.

"What happened to his arm?"

Jergen reached for the napkin. "Well now, there's a story."

Clark nodded and backed toward the door. You can find Cletis Meadows's jokes in any mouth and Jergen's stories on any cop show. "Well, I'll see you—"

"There I was," Jergen interrupted, "in the squad car, patrolling. Then the call came in. A neighbor had seen a flashlight in the Miller place. Well, you know how my mind works. The first thing I thought was *burglar.*"

"Sure." Clark looked over his shoulder. Cold had never seemed so inviting.

310

"So I raced out there with the siren going and the lights flashing and roared up into the driveway. I burst through the front door just as he was bursting out. I had to subdue him."

"You knocked me over with the door." The kid's voice was high, moaning, and pitiful. "I hit my shoulder on the coffee table."

"You didn't get up again," Jergen said. "I'd call that subdued."

The kid's eyes flashed. "I think you broke it. I ought to sue."

"Cry me a river." Jergen threw his napkin at the wastebasket again. It bounced on the rim and fell to the floor. "He had the Millers' VCR under his arm. A piece broke off when he fell." Jergen smiled like Gene Autry again. "But I got him. Bert's coming over for my picture."

The kid's head was down, his good arm cradling his bad. An end to a burglary spree, Clark thought, an end to an era. "Let me know if you hear anything from Walter."

Jergen nodded. "I'll stop by the store before you leave."

"I don't think we'll be open today."

"Oh." Jergen shrugged. "I'll let you know."

Clark nodded. He looked at the kid, at the mutilated Bismarck, at Jergen's beaming face, then went outside with a dread as cold as the morning crawling through his chest. He wondered where his son had gone.

He spent the day at the house, feeling chilled and fretful. He called Emma at noon; she agreed to come over for supper. He tried to read in the afternoon but failed. He wondered briefly if the store's financial loss had shifted now to his shoulders, but at his retirement he had signed everything over to Walter. *We* did not exist in the legal sense. Only in every other.

"He'll be back," Emma said as they lay in bed that night. "Sometimes people just have to get away."

Clark stared up into the darkness. Like the sky and the dome of the historical society, it would not focus. "Sure," he said.

Force of habit awoke him too early the next morning. He needed to sweep. Instead he shared a pot of coffee with Emma while staring at darkness through the kitchen window. Oh, Walter, he thought painfully. Walter.

Just before nine, Emma kissed him good-bye—she had volunteered to spend the day preparing for an evening with pretentious poets and their indulgent patrons. He'd planned to call in sick to work, but he did not want to be left with nothing but his thoughts. He walked to the historical society.

He spent the morning searching through old insurance records that did not need to be searched through. Ted Lewell came in at one, his face flushed. An excited smell exuded from him.

"I know." Lewell leaned over the desk, his fists planted on it like stumps. "God damn you, Holstrom, I figured it out without you."

"You know what?"

"I know the truth. And you do, too. Damn you, Clark Holstrom. Damn you for hiding it."

A feeling grew in his chest so congealed that he thought his blood was freezing. The truth. Fear squeezed from his pores so thick he could smell it. Maynard danced in the spots in his eyes, a demented Maynard dancing maniacally, his laughter echoing off Clark's eyelids. Clark thought of all the years since Albert Wilson's murder, all the days, all the seconds. "Get out of here, Lewell." His words were too drenched in lies and broken promises to carry any conviction.

Lewell smiled that damned infuriating smile. "Sure, I'll get out." Color drained from him. He looked dead again. "I know, Clark. It'll be a hell of a story." He left.

Clark listened to Lewell's footsteps punctuate the silence of the sanctuary, a staccato rhythm. A sudden and desperate idea left him searching for something heavy. In a corner he found a wrench left behind by a plumber from the week before. He hefted it. The fear was still thick, but no longer a burden—he'd been vivified by a calculating anger. It danced in his eyes as lightly as Maynard.

He hurried out of the office and across the sanctuary on bootless, silent feet. Ted Lewell's back faced him from near the front door. The wrench was almost light in Clark's hand—he felt within it an orgasmic power so complete it burned even the smell of sweat off his body. He was reveling in it as Lewell went through the door, as the cold came in.

The latch clattered shut with the wrench still poised in the air. It grew heavy, and his hand dropped limply to his side.

He winced at the arthritic shoulder spur and the sharp, aching jolt in his elbow the falling wrench had inspired. He found himself staring at the Sioux display. Through his mind flowed the Minnesota River, with thirty-eight sepia-tinted bodies swinging lifelessly from a gallows on its bank. They had lived by the sword, and they had died by it. Lewell, he thought, lived by the pen, and the pen, they say, is mightier. With a sword or even a wrench you cannot destroy a man who values a pen as completely as you can with words, or with the destruction of them.

He let the wrench fall to the floor and studied his swollen knuckles. Thoughts whispered quietly in the air around him. He thought of Maynard and especially of Helen. He thought of Cletis Meadows working as the clerk at the Sunset Motel, where Lewell had a room.

He walked slowly back to his office while his muffled steps mixed with the whispers. Or, he pondered, with the destruction of them.

One distinction of the seasons is the way they allow night to begin. Twilight in summer descends, but in winter it wells from the ground. It bubbles up in bits of blue and gray so fine that at first it can be seen only through miles, but like coffee boiling down it thickens, becomes bitter and impenetrable. Winter nights can be tasted most keenly on the back of the tongue.

Clark walked west past the Bumblebee Café. He wondered briefly if he should have taken the Dodge, but this was too heavy a deed for him to risk even a hint of unreliability. He looked up at the silver television glare lighting the bare window of Billie Jessup's apartment and wondered mildly if anyone was up there with her. He was not surprised to find that he didn't give a damn.

He walked by the store, unopened now for two days. He could not afford distraction, so he pushed enough of his worry about Walter deep enough into his mind to leave behind only an uncertain melancholy.

He passed the police station and thought about the boy sitting inside, arm in a sling, head down, listening to Jergen Burnett's gloating. He was a burglar. We are what we are.

He felt Nora's eyes as he passed Ambrose's, felt their coldness claw him. She knew what he was doing; she knew. The shadowy icehouses pocking the lake made him again think of Walter. The Sunset Motel's neon sign glowed garishly against the quiet darkness. Ted Lewell's car was not in the parking lot. He was probably out celebrating his latest discovery. Good.

Clark opened the office door, went in, and shook the cold from his shoulders. Cletis was sitting behind the desk, watching his portable television. "Hi, Clark," he said as he stood, his ass, no longer confined, spreading like a geisha fan in an Oriental movie. His creaking joints spoke with subtitles.

"Hi, Cletis." Three empty soda cans sat on the counter. That was good, too.

"What brings you out tonight?" Cletis asked.

"Just figured you'd like company."

"I can always use company." Cletis's glasses amplified his eyes to almost frightening proportions—a protozoan's view of a scientist. The gods of microscopic worlds are gigantic pupils. "Have you seen Maynard Tewle lately?"

"Not in a couple of days."

"I heard he's not doing too well."

"No," Clark said, "he isn't." He didn't want to talk about Maynard. He nodded at the television. He felt a certain level of comfort now that what had to be done had begun. "What's on the boob tube?"

"I don't know. Some sit-com. Boobs." Cletis sat again. Air whimpered through a crack in the chair's vinyl upholstery. "Got a joke for you, Clark."

Oh God, Clark thought. "You do?"

"Seems this guy hears this beautiful music coming out of a bar, so he goes in and asks the bartender where it's coming from, and the bartender takes him out back. A midget is playing a piano. The guy asks where the midget came from, and the bartender hands him a magic lamp. When he rubs it, an old genie with a hearing aid pops out. The guy asks him for a thousand bucks, the genie nods and says it'll be waiting for him in the bar. When the guy goes back in the bar he finds a thousand mallards wandering around. 'I asked for a thousand bucks, not a thousand ducks!' the guy says, and then the bartender says, 'You think I asked for a twelve-inch pianist?' "

Well, hell—Cletis had finally told a good joke. Clark laughed as much from relief as anything. "Not bad, Cletis, not bad."

Cletis beamed. "I thought of that just yesterday."

Clark almost believed him. He looked over his shoulder into the night and wondered how much time he had before Ted Lewell came back. "Can I buy you a pop?" he asked.

Cletis nodded at the cans on the counter. "I've already had three."

"That joke deserves another."

Cletis beamed again. "All right."

The Coke machine hummed tunelessly in the corner. Clark walked to it, digging in his pocket. Good God, fifty cents each. He could remember when pop had been a dime. He used to buy it sitting on a stool beside Hannah at a fountain. He used to let his pennies and nickels slip through preteen fingers so he could follow them to the floor and peer up under her dress. Christ, that had been a long time ago. When in life does lust begin?

"Diet something or other," Cletis called. "I got to keep my weight down."

Down around your hips, Clark thought. He dropped in the coins and watched the machine cough up two cold, sweating cans. In a vending machine world, we live on expectorate. He carried the cans to the desk.

Fifteen minutes later, he'd managed to get through both a grape soda and a sit-com, though he couldn't stand either. Laugh tracks echoed the pressure building in his bladder. He wished he didn't have to watch for Lewell or wait for Cletis, but you do what you have to do. You follow the plan.

Clark suffered through a commercial, then ten more minutes of the sit-com. Good God, that Cletis must use his ass as a reservoir. Clark's foot tapped and his sore knees jostled as urgent electric signals crackled in his groin. Finally Cletis stood. "You mind looking after the desk for a minute? I have to use the toilet."

Clark nodded. "Go ahead."

Cletis sidled through the back door into his apartment. Clark stepped casually behind the desk as if not to betray his intentions to the television's thirteen-inch-diagonal eye. Urine mumbling against porcelain left his bladder ready to explode.

He found Ted Lewell's name in the registry. If a weasel could write, this would be its handwriting: small letters with points on them like teeth. Room 110. Clark gauged his time by the intensity of Cletis's pissing, then lifted the spare for room 110 from the key rack and slipped it into his pocket. He backed away from the counter. He was seriously considering urinating in his can when Cletis stepped into the lobby.

"I'll tell you, Cletis," Clark said, "it's been fine."

"You leaving already?" Cletis didn't sit down. He didn't look at the key rack, either. He was either a trusting soul or a fool.

"It's cold out. It'll only get colder."

"I suppose." Cletis pursed his lips, then let them fall into a frown. "Well, you take care."

Clark buttoned his coat. He had never noticed before how tightly it pulled across his bladder. "You bet. You too." He had to get outside before everything blew. "I'll see you."

"Yeah." Cletis stuffed himself into the chair. "I'll see you."

The cold, like the darkness, had settled more deeply. When Clark was free of the motel's outside light, he circled its edge to room 110. There was no light inside, no car outside, and tentacles of ice scrabbled up the window. He went inside with excitement pounding against his temples. He left the room light off, then remembered he'd forgotten a flashlight. Never do this professionally, he thought, if you can't remember something as elementary as that.

He tried to remember the layout of these rooms, but it had been too

316

long since he'd seen one. Shins had evolved in order to find furniture in the dark, and Clark's performed admirably. With ease he located the bed, a chair, and a desk beneath the curtained window. Painful little lights blinked in his brain like Walter's burglar alarm. Oh, Walter. Clark had no time to think about him now.

His hand brushed over the desk's cheap, plastic veneer. His fingers touched pens, papers, and a book. Good. It was what he had come for, but it would have to come later.

He fumbled blindly past the desk, found a door, and went inside, feeling beneath his boots the carpet turn to tile. He shut the door and turned on the light, then dropped his pants with a frantic effort and aimed for the toilet bowl. His breath rushed out as if he had been holding it for as long as he had his water. God, what genuine plea-sure—if you wait long enough, pissing is as good as sex. He thought of Emma and thought of that first night he had spent with her. He thought of all the nights he had spent with her, and of all the nights he would.

Will you marry me? After Nora, I mean.

We'll see.

Yeah, he thought, we'll see. But I've got to clear my mind. Ted Lewell comes first.

His force was almost dissipated—piss, like life, goes in a rush. With the last of his reserves and the hope that Ted Lewell would return with diarrhea he dropped the seat and wetted it. He wondered briefly if a forensic test existed that could identify a criminal by urinal splash pat-terns. Maybe piss held DNA and they could tag you that way. Wonder turned to apprehension until he remembered that the investigating of-ficer would probably be Jergen Burnett. Even with the VCR burglar under his belt, Jergen was still Jergen, maybe even more so. Clark pon-dered the relation between the rate of anxiety-induced ulcers in the criminal population and police incompetence. You think the damnedest things committing crimes, he thought. Christ. I'm a criminal.

He left the door cracked open just enough to throw a sliver of light across the desk. He recognized Rose Wilson's diary—it was opened somewhere toward the end, and resting on a scattering of papers beside a red loose-leaf notebook. He took the diary, the notebook, and the papers, tossed the key under the bed, then hurried outside. He thought as he pulled shut the door that his boots must have left tracks in the bathroom. He'd left the damned light on, too. Never do this for a living, he thought, anywhere but in Credibull.

He walked by the lake, looked out at the icehouses, and thought about Walter again. The bulky papers beneath his arm pulled him back to his task. He could shove them through a hole in the ice, but then something might show up in the spring. He could just keep them, but hell, he didn't want them, and he especially didn't want to be caught with them. Well, he thought, there's nothing nicer on a cold winter's night than a warm fire. He hurried past the nursing home.

He didn't go inside when he reached the house, though his fingertips were numb, his cheeks so cold they felt as if the bone was exposed. He walked past the garbage can, stopped, then came back and studied its lid. It had been almost a year ago now, almost to the day, and almost this time of night, that Nora had fallen. It was funny how momentous deeds lined up like that. He wondered what would happen next year. Maybe Maynard would go. Maybe he would already be gone. Clark hoped so—like cold water, he imagined it better to leap into death than wade in. He shook his head. What kind of thing is it to hope for a friend's death? And the hell of it was he was being compassionate.

He removed the lid from the can and lifted out the single bag. He dropped the papers inside, then carefully dragged the can back to the garage and left it outside the door. Inside he found nestled beside the lawn mower his red gasoline can. As he picked it up, cold and arthritis worked over his body like a boxer carefully selecting his blows. His vision clouded in pain and the arthritis pulled him down like the weight of a pack or rifle barrel. Cold water sloshed in his boots and sucked at his thighs; a dirty, salty reek stung his nostrils. When he heard the heavy, ripping, blood-spattered booms he wanted to cry like a child. But when he wiped his eyes clear the water was only the winter's cold, the booming only the blood in his ears. The reek was only a memory, the weight was only a can, only a can, God bless it. Things can come back so fast they scare you.

He left the garage door open to light his work. He splashed gasoline more generously than he needed to into the can, but hesitated before reaching into his pocket for the lighter Agnes had given him for Christmas. Hell, he thought, I'm not reaching into that with a flame.

He picked up the diary to act as a starter, but it was heavier than the can had been, as heavy as the war had been, a lead memory that slipped free of his fingers. It fell into shadows where he gratefully could not see it. As he splashed more gas onto the papers he thought of Maynard again. The lighter was warm from the heat of his leg and blazed at the flint's first spark. He reached into the can for a sheet of paper, lit it, and dropped it back inside.

The whoosh of flame was a blinding vision, a Damascus road. He jumped back, slipped, and went down hard on his tailbone. He felt a terrible fear as cold as the ground beneath him, as cold as the air sucking in his chest. One leg was numb and gone.

Fear subsided into a breath-tugging thrill as he felt a welcome, throbbing pain just below his kneecap. He tentatively bent both legs. He felt beside that one pain only the general pain in his ass. He raised his eyes to thank the stars, those blessed and merciful guardians. He stood slowly, bracing his hands on the ground, snow crystals working beneath his mitten cuffs to gnaw sorely on his wrists. By the time he was standing, the fire had died to flames that only occasionally licked beyond the top of the can. He had to rub his singed, fused eyelashes before he could blink.

The loose papers curled in agony. Bits of them floated upward, then fell again like repentant but rejected souls. The notebook was burning well, but the diary had fallen closed and would not light. He went into the garage for a hoe. When he stirred them open, the diary's pages snapped like disapproving tongues.

As he stared at his crime he thought about hell and God. Perhaps God was a constipated God sitting on his throne with a roll of heavenly toilet paper beside him, and judgment has nothing to do with justice but with how much spicy food he had eaten the night before. The crisp remains of the paper rose and fell, rose and fell. Perhaps the afterlife is an ash can. Our sins burn, but we are not purged. They rise to simply fall upon us again.

He stirred the ashes slowly, as if performing an act of meditation. The fire was too bright for his eyes. When he looked up he could no longer see the stars.

Chapter

14

The phone was ringing when he went into the house. He ran into
fatalism like a wall—he had not expected that the time to pay the
piper would come so quickly. Perhaps he had underestimated Jergen.
More likely, someone had seen him go into Lewell's room.

It was not until he picked up the receiver that he began to wonder
why they were trying to arrest him over the phone. Was he so danger-
ous that no one dared confront him? Supergeezer.

"Mr. Holstrom?" a female voice said.

The Credibull police force had no female employees. He relaxed like a released rubber band. "Yes?"

"This is Mrs. Trodahl at the nursing home."

Ah yes, he thought, the bitch nurse's stringy companion. The Weed Woman. "I remember you."

"Your wife has taken a turn for the worse."

He had forgotten about Nora. He searched his conscience for her eyes and had difficulty finding them. Something was very wrong. "What do you mean, a turn for the worse?"

The Weed Woman hesitated. "You might like to visit her tonight. We don't think she'll last until morning."

The receiver grew very heavy in his hand; his fingertips went numb. There should be joy, he thought; I should feel like dancing. He tried to analyze this strange melancholy and failed. All he could think of was her name, over and over again. Nora. Nora. All he could do was focus on what he could find of her eyes.

"Mr. Holstrom?" the Weed Woman asked.

Nora, he thought, Nora. "Yes?"

"Are you all right?"

Am I all right? That was a hell of a question. Like it or not or love her or not, his wife of forty-six years was about to leave him. He felt suddenly very alone and very sorry for Nora. She'd always just lain there; now she would just lie there forever. There'd be no way to measure the spot on the wall she'd be staring at.

"Mr. Holstrom?"

"Yes?"

"Would you like me to call a clergyman?"

He shook his head, as if through the receiver she could see him. "No. I'll be in."

"Are you all right?" she asked again.

"Yeah. I'll be in."

He hung up the phone without waiting to hear more, then stared quietly through the window at the darkness. A heavy numbness pulled over his head like a dank wool blanket. This moment he had been waiting for was now so god-be-damned anticlimactic. He never wanted it to be like this. Nora, he thought. Nora. He felt he was going to cry.

He went to her bedroom and stared at her empty, dust-covered bed. He remembered each detail of how she had looked that first time he had seen her, how incredibly young she had looked, how incredibly vibrant. He shook his head. What are you thinking? She had only been young and vibrant compared to her youth and vibrancy now. And you, old boy, have never been much of either.

He felt a heavy age and sorrow settle upon him. With a shock he found that he could not remember his youth. How could that be—at the Sunset Motel just an hour before he had dropped his pennies and looked up under Hannah's dress. No, he explained to himself, you are remembering remembering. As he saw it now his coins had fallen from withered fingers, and when he'd crouched beside Hannah's stool, sharp pains had flashed in his shoulder and knees. He'd been an old man in his youth and an old man when he'd married an old woman, and from his loins an old child had sprung.

Clark could hardly stand with the weight of only his life on his shoulders; the added weight of his wife's and his son's drove him backward onto the bed and into the mattress. All lives center here, he thought; on this point the universe collapses. He rolled onto his side, his face in the bedspread, smelling in it both dust and her scent. Her eyes flickered, went out, then flickered again. Nora.

By the time the bus drops him off, Clark is angry at Deloris, angry at himself. He wants an outlet for this anger and the courage to release it. He knows that courage can only be found in the amber tint of a bottle. Alcohol frees expression; it makes a man a man.

"Hi, Clark," the Double-Trouble bartender says. He has short hair, black horn-rimmed glasses, and a World War II airborne tattoo on the inside of his forearm. He smells of cigarettes and shaving cream. "Missed you last night."

"I was in the Cities." Clark wants a bottle. He doesn't want conversation.

"Oh, that's right. The third weekend of the month. What brings you home early?"

Clark doesn't answer; instead he buys a bottle and leans against the bar. The whiskey grants him his courage and accentuates his anger. It is a double blessing.

"It's goddamned cold out," he tells no one. He tucks the bottle under his arm, then leaves without saying good-bye.

I can't think about this, he thought; I can't let myself think about this. He forced himself off the mattress, to his feet, and out the front door. He possessed only the strength of a child, the strength of an old man, and the fitful, bitter *whoosh* from the Dodge's vent only added to his weakness. He drove numbly onto St. Anne's Road and down the highway. Ice crystals flashed before his headlights, as if even the darkness had frozen. A dull glow leaked through Ambrose's front doors; a silver shadow flickered in the lounge. *The Late Show* must have been on.

"Hello, Mr. Holstrom." The Weed Woman glowed dully herself, a tall, thin specter, a ghost run through a ringer. He nodded his greeting. "I'll leave you alone with her."

"Thank you."

He shuffled past the lounge. Within it waited an assortment of silvered or bald heads, wheelchair handgrips sticking from each ear like horns on demons. Maynard paced behind the others as if on guard, muttering.

"Maynard," Clark said quietly.

Maynard turned his back on Clark. "Got to get the crop in," he muttered. "Corn and beans."

"Maynard, can you understand me? Nora's dying."

Maynard turned. "Corn and beans," he said more loudly. A few tired faces looked at him, craggy in the shadows. "Got to get home! Got to get the crop in!"

"Sure, Maynard." The words fell from Clark's lips like dying butter-flies. "Sure."

The Weed Woman followed him down the hall. Maynard's mutter-ing blended into the sludge of laugh tracks and clever banter oozing from the television. Clark stopped at Nora's door. He looked at the nurse.

"I just wanted to make sure you were all right," she said.

"I'm fine." Maybe she wasn't a bad sort after all. "Thank you."

"I'll be up front if you need anything."

"Thank you."

Clark went inside. Nora lay as always, but something was missing or departing fast. A dead smell hung mustily in the air. That or a memory.

"Nora," he said as he sat down. He struggled to draw what was left of her out of her eyes.

Well, she said in a whisper, *you win.*

"There are no winners," he answered.

Now you have what you want. Until death do us part. I'd call that a victory.

"You can't believe that I wanted this."

Her eyes grew hard. *I think I can.*

The cold is as gaudy as the bar sign flashing above his head. His breath climbs into his eyes. He is angry at the whole world and drunk enough to believe that he stands colossally above it. King of the beasts again.

He walks to St. Anne's Road with his shoulders hunched, one cheek tucked behind his upturned collar. The bottle presses his side like a lover. The sight of his house and the thought of the woman that awaits him within it rise high enough in his throat to make him wonder if he is about to be sick. Domestic tranquillity, he thinks—shit. But he can hold down his marriage as well as he can his liquor. He takes pride in that.

The wind has driven the loose snow to settle in the shelter between the two drifts on each side of his driveway. There are fresh tire tracks in it, leading south, vanishing quickly with the wind. He stumbles through them and into the house. The sudden warmth fails to comfort him. She damn well better be home. And where the hell was the kid?

"Nora?" he calls.

Her voice drifts around the corner from their bedroom. "Al?" she asks.

She lay there now, staring up, seeing nothing, seeing all. Clark couldn't hide from her. He never could. He wondered if he ever would.

You're free to fuck what's-her-name now. Isn't that the word you use? Fuck? Such an economical word. I can't understand why they relegated it to profanity.

He reached into her lap for her hand. It held a scalding touch, as if the last of her life was flaring in its pores. "Please, Nora. Let's not part like this."

We parted a long time ago.

He stared at that leathery, familiar bag of a face, loved and unloved, light and darkness, as monochrome as Emma's apartment. He didn't say anything.

I know every memory you possess, she said, *every feeling. And I know what you're thinking now.*

He closed his eyes and pressed the heels of his hands into their sockets. He tried to keep his teeth from gritting and failed. What he was trying to keep from thinking about, what he had spent thirty-five years training himself not to think about, skirted the edges of his consciousness, tried to slip through the age cracks within it, and more and more he couldn't keep it away. If she kept this up, if she kept this up . . .

His hands trembled; the pressure against his eyes raised soft flashes of silver light. "I am not responsible for this, Nora. I am not!"

But Clark, she said, *you are.*

• •

"Al?" she asks again.

Who the hell is Al? He slams his bottle down upon the television. The liquor laps against its side.

"I'm glad you came back, Al. Come to bed."

Who the hell is Al? He is filled with the anger unique to the adulterous cuckold—some fucker named Al has been fucking his wife. He stomps to the bedroom, his fists in clenches as he pounds open the door, Deloris's derisive laughter driving him to great and drunken deeds. Nora is lying on the bed, one uncovered breast lying limply. The heavy smell of sweat and sex enrages him.

"Clark," she says as she covers herself.

His anger overwhelms him, seizing his sanity and taking his mind. He runs to the bed, his arm raised, and slaps her with the back of his hand, using all the power the liquor has given him. "Who the hell is Al, you bitch?"

His hands were still pressed against his eyes. His throat ached—he must have been panting or screaming. "If you know what I'm thinking, Nora, then tell me what it is."

Her eyes watched him, but they would not answer. They had become God's eyes, as big and mute and silent as always.

"Say it, Nora," he pleaded. "I need to hear it from you." The pleading left little rips in his chest, little stabs of pain. "Say it." He wiped his face and looked at her. He closed his eyes to study her gaze. "Say it, because I can't."

Her eyes remained silent. Their oppressive, accusatory gaze set his mind spinning loose from his body. To hell, to hell, God in heaven, to hell with those dull, accusing eyes. He clawed inside to hang on to who he knew himself not to be. He thought he would scream and he might have been screaming when suddenly the gaze faded, the eyes closed. They did not open again.

He was splayed across the chair. His throat was raw; sweat pooled against his eyelids. When he opened them he saw only the ceiling; his heart thumped dully in his ears. Nora lay heavily on the bed. He knew that all she had said was true.

"Nora?" He threw her name into that gray world between happiness and sorrow. He still needed to hear an answer. She offered and could offer none. "Nora."

He took her hand. She did not drive him away because what had really been Nora had left, as the warmth he felt against his fingers soon would be. He looked into her eyes, placed his hand beneath her nostrils, felt for her breath, and felt nothing. He closed her eyes with his palm—it was funny how lifeless they felt. Relief mixed with sorrow and exaltation and a fear to know that she was gone. Well, he thought, it had been a hell of a way for that to end. But Nora, he thought, oh, Nora. Tears were running down his cheeks.

He sat in the chair for an hour, only staring. The darkness deepened as the warmth left both her and him. He was contemplating his coldness when Mrs. Trodahl looked in through the door.

"Excuse me, Mr. Holstrom. I don't mean to intrude. I thought Maynard Tewle might have wandered by."

"I haven't seen him." His voice stuck to his tongue.

"Oh, goodness." The cords in her neck pulled tight like guitar strings as she glanced down the hall. "Oh, goodness."

Clark looked up. "What's the matter?"

"It's nothing." She paused. "I can't find him."

That's nothing? Clark stood. "He's not in the building?"

"I didn't mean that. I just can't find him."

"How long has it been?"

"I don't know. Perhaps an hour."

He looked at Nora again. He felt no need to apologize for leaving, because no one was there to apologize to. "My wife is gone," he said.

"I'm sorry." She rested her hand on his arm. "It's for the best."

"I suppose."

"I'm sorry that I can't be of more help, but I really must find Maynard Tewle."

"Yes. I'll help you." Clark stepped from the room, turning his back on Nora. "I'll look outside."

"I'll look in here."

"If you don't find him, call the police."

Clark hurried away. Mrs. Trodahl followed more slowly, sticking her head into each door. Halfway down the hall Clark stopped for only a second. Well, Nora, he thought. Good-bye.

The wind had blown snow across the walk in little drifts that crunched like beetles beneath his feet. Prints ran from the door into the darkness with a stride Clark feared Maynard could not maintain. The highway in both directions revealed only shadows. Cold is an unconquerable predator. Christ. Clark winced. To be out in this in slippers.

The Dodge started fitfully. Clark remembered the night at the mall when it had not started at all. He thought of Emma, then pushed the thought away. He wished all memories were so submissive.

His wedding ring has left a line on her cheek like a red scar. She retreats with a whimper beneath the sheet, then comes out with teeth bared, eyes hot, flailing fingernails searching for his eyes. He steps back, keeps stepping back, fear trembling in his breath as she charges him. He remembers Deloris. This, he knows, is not Deloris. His drunken courage returns. He is in a battle he cannot but win.

Clark's headlights caught the footprints as they followed the highway east. "Corn and beans," he heard himself say. "Got to get the crop in." Christ.

He hits Nora hard in the stomach. As she bends, he brings his knee up beneath her chin hard enough to clatter her teeth like dinner plates.

329

She careens back onto the bed, blood and vomit on her lips. He leaps upon her with one knee in her stomach, his hands around her throat. Her face is crimson. The stink of bile mixes with the sweat and sex.

"Who the hell is Al, you bitch?" he demands. The rage in his fingers does not allow her words.

With her face turning blue he finally releases her. "Why should you care?" she asks when she can. "You have your lover and I have mine."

He slaps her hard enough to wonder if he has broken a knuckle. He can hardly believe what he sees. "Who the hell is Al?"

"One day you'll burn for this," she says. "Do you know that?" Her swollen lips smile a hateful triumph.

He was turning the corner onto St. Anne's Road too quickly. His back tires slipped in a wide arc that made the world spin, as if his head were twirling shrapnel or chips off a cheekbone. The spinning ceased abruptly; he banged his head on the window. When his eyes cleared the car was angled into a drift and he was staring at the feed store, at the bench where he and Maynard had spent so many mornings. Dull aches pulsed all over him, his knees, his shoulder, his head, his ribs. He closed his eyes. When he opened them, he saw the streetlight above the alley. It gave him a sudden idea—perhaps he would be lucky.

He shifted into reverse and stepped on the accelerator. Wheels spun on the wind-driven snow, caught on asphalt, and jerked the car onto the road. He shifted again; the light at the alley drew him. He turned onto the alley ruts, stomped on the accelerator, and did not let off it until he saw Maynard's house.

Clark shakes her by the throat, bouncing her head off the mattress. The look on her face, the whimper on her lips—but the hatred does not leave her eyes.

"Every third weekend of every month," she chokes out. "I figured it out long before you did, you dumb bastard."

The windows were dark; he had expected them to be. The unshoveled walk rolled out from the door like a tongue tasting the night. It held no footprints. He checked the backyard anyway.

"Maynard? Maynard!"

The only answer came from a mocking wind. He struggled through the drift beside the stairs as he had done with Barb a lifetime before. The snow in the backyard looked swept clean; cardboard covered the window Maynard had run his hand through. All Clark could think about was all the time he was wasting.

He started the Dodge and raced back toward the alley. When he reached St. Anne's Road he turned hard to the right. Tires spun, but somehow he maintained control. He raced out of town, the wind blowing hard across the yielding fields, the snow reaching across the asphalt in front of him with skeleton fingers. He drove near the shoulder where his headlights would illuminate both the asphalt and the drifts. He searched for footprints in the whiteness. The awful familiarity of the night stripped away at a frightening rate the layers protecting him from his memory.

I know what you're thinking, Nora had said.

Clark releases her throat to hit her again. She rolls on her side, convulses, and spews vomit onto the sheet. It flecks the sweat on her chest, the blood on her lips; it covers in a sheen the swelling beside her eye. She smiles. Her teeth are outlined in red. Christ. She smiles.

"The only cock I'd ever seen was yours," she says. "It's nice to finally have a man in me."

Clark roars as he leaps upon her, pins her arms into the vomit with

331

his knees, then slams his fists first into one eye, then the other. He hits her until the sweat drips from his nose, until the fight is beaten out of her. My God, Clark thinks. He revels in power.

"Please," she says. "Please." Her voice is the voice of a frightened child. A light dies in her eyes.

He stops only from exhaustion. His labored breath affords him time to think. Al, Al. He remembers the tire tracks leading out along St. Anne's Road toward the Tewle farm. Toward the Wilson farm.

"It's that fucker, Albert Wilson, isn't it?" he demands.

She does not speak or look at him. The smell of her pollutes the air. Though there is blood in her mouth and vomit on her cheeks, there are no tears in her eyes.

A snowbank leered before him. He jerked the steering wheel to the left, felt the back tires slip out, then felt the front right tire catch on the edge of the asphalt and snap him across the road. He went into the far ditch with a thud, angled so deeply that the drift washed over the windshield. He banged his forehead on the steering wheel; the tears blinded him. He heard only an incredible, awful silence.

He clutched at the pain in his forehead as if he could yank it out. When it cleared, he breathed a quick, cold sigh, and looked up at what the angle of the roof let him see of the sky. He prayed, for perhaps God was a compassionate God who knew the pain of frigid cold, who lived not in heaven but in space's eternal night. He tried backing out, then cursed as the car settled deeper.

"Well, God," he muttered, "then this is how it will be."

"It's that fucker, Albert Wilson, isn't it?" Clark repeats.

She nods, a barely perceptible but blatantly defeated movement. He strides into the living room, shrugs on his coat, and jams his feet into his shoes. He goes back into the bedroom. Nora is lying on her back in the stink and the filth with her hands clasped over her crotch. Her eyes are dry, her face bland, her body not moving. Clark grasps her throat and leers into her face.

"If you ever say a word of this to anyone," he says, "I'll kill you. I'll kill you in the most horrible way that I can." He pauses as he thinks of the clincher, then smiles. "And then I'll kill the kid."

He had fallen forward somehow. His arms were sunk in snow to his elbows; tiny crystals snapped at his nose like dogs. He pulled his hands free and stared at the scars he had made in the drift's innocent surface. Oh, Walter, he thought, my son. Oh Walter, my son, the things I have said, the things I have done have cursed you. How could you have been anything other than what you have become? His fingers outlined the scars he had made in the drift. Oh, Walter. My son.

Clark watches Nora until he knows that she understands exactly what he has said, until the light in her eyes dies into a complete and final submission. He leaves the bedroom and the house. He comes back only for the bottle.

He is too angry to think of anything but following Wilson's tire tracks, dying now in the wind. As he runs, weather and time anneal the rage into a calculating, first-degree hardness. He uncaps the bottle and warms his throat with the liquor. In the distance he sees the church steeple and Maynard Tewle's silo. He sees the Wilson farm. He throws the bottle to the side and begins to run. Within a few strides he hears a hammer pounding.

• •

In the distance, Clark saw the Wilson farm and the church steeple beyond it. The howling wind spit snow in his face and forced him to cover his eyes. The wind, his memories, the cold, and his sorrow were things to fear, and suddenly the snow became something to fear intensely. In it and in this road were more awful memories than all the bloody beaches, than all the French countryside, than all the Ardennes could muster. In this snow and on this road, in memories trained to hide beneath thirty-five long years, lived an act that defined a life that had never paid its due.

Clark flings the shed door open. Wilson turns, then drops his hammer when Clark punches him in the face. Wilson falls, one arm sweeping cans from the workbench. Clark picks the hammer up from the floor; he brings it down again. Wilson's groans meld by the third blow into crunches and wet, sopping sounds. Wilson is lying there. Pieces of Wilson are lying there. He is a broken mess soaking into the hard-packed earthen floor.

Clark is kneeling beside the body, gasping, his face dappled with gore—Christ, he thinks, this is just like France. Blood lies like spilled paint, hardware is scattered. Shattered teeth are hidden treasures. He smells blood and shit and urine and something metallic he can't name. God in heaven, he thinks as he looks at Wilson, God in heaven. Fear washes away the rage and leaves him naked before all-powerful eyes. He flees with little sensibility.

He drops the hammer into a drift beside the culvert running under the driveway. Blowing snow buries the sin.

He was stumbling through a drift two hundred yards south of the car. It was right here, he thought, right here where I threw the bottle. It was right here on the way back where I found it again, where I used it to wash the blood from my face. The whiskey had been hellishly cold—liquor takes so long to freeze. Like guilt.

It was as cold tonight as that whiskey had been, colder now in old blood washing over old bones, in old and rancid guilt. He'd murdered Nora that day as surely as he had Albert Wilson; he'd beaten her life from her like the stiffness from a side of beef. He had murdered Dwayne and Rose that day, too, murdered Maynard in a way, murdered his reputation, shifted suspicion onto him until Father Callahan had taken upon himself the sins of the world. But salvation so freely offered he should have known could just as easily be lost; it had been stolen by a writer from Chicago. He'd had to shift suspicions again. Maynard, he thought, my friend. My friend?

He kicked free of the drift, stepped unto the road, and broke into an old man's run. The stars were no longer merciful guardians. The stars were eyes. They were the eyes of the dead staring, eyes in which he sought forgiveness they didn't offer. Helen was up there, enmeshed in pawned-off stories of infidelity. Wilson was up there, who might know a cuckold's fury, with Rose who had died too old and Dwayne who had died too young to have had the chance. And Nora now, who had been broken beyond the point of forgiveness, was up there, too. But he had tried, God, how he had tried. To change.

The Wilson farm was closer now—in a drift on the right side of the road he saw a footprint's faint outline. He tried to keep his mind on it, on the ones that followed, but the eternal and uncaring stars were looking down too darkly. Nora was too distant. She was gone, Albert and Rose and Dwayne were gone, Callahan was gone, Helen was gone, too—their forgiveness was light-years beyond him. Maynard Tewle was the only person remaining who could offer it. Maybe he remained. My God, Clark thought. Maybe.

The *maybe* quickened his pace, made his heart pound, and pulled the cold air sorely into his lungs. The Wilson farm bore upon him like a warning. Over the field across the road blew a snowy sheen that Clark was certain hid something. He stumbled toward it. His shadow suddenly stretched in front of him as if even it wished to flee his presence.

Headlights, the harsh groan of a cold engine. The shadow focused. He turned to be blinded.

A gray sedan stopped alongside him, its tires popping on the snow. A window rolled down, then a voice came out into the night in choppy white breathlike messages from a signal fire. "You bastard. You son of a bitch. You took them."

What the hell was this? Clark wondered. Who the hell was this?

Ted Lewell emerged as the words dissipated, his face white and almost glowing. It took Clark a moment to remember that he had broken into his motel room only a few hours before. Too much had been happening, too much present, too much past. Selective memory.

"You took the diary and all of my goddamned notes, you bastard!"

Clark had no time for this. "You have to help me find Maynard Tewle."

"I don't give a damn about Maynard Tewle. Fat-assed Cletis Meadows told me you had been at the motel tonight. Where the hell are they?"

To hell with your notes, Clark thought, and to hell with the diary. What do you need them for? I'll give you a damned confession. "Help me. Maynard Tewle is out in this somewhere."

"I know. I called Burnett after you stole my stuff. I want my stuff."

Urgency left Clark incapable of anger. "Please."

Lewell sighed. "Fuck." A heavy cloud obscured his face. "Get in."

Clark hurried around the front of the car and climbed in onto the passenger's seat. The warmth from the vent he felt he didn't deserve. "I think he went out to where his farm had been." Before his eyes returned to the fields he glanced at the face beside him, shining a dull green in the light of the dashboard. "How did you know where I'd be?"

"Where the hell else would you be?" Lewell wiped the corners of his mouth and shivered. They crawled toward the church. "What is he doing out on a night like this?"

"He doesn't know it's a night like this."

The moon peeked above the horizon, smiling and wise. The wind paused to inhale; the snow for a moment settled. In the field across the road from the Wilson farm a shadow rose. Its arms were out, its head back, shadows flapping loosely beneath its arms.

"There he is," Lewell said.

Clark twisted his ankle as he stepped from the car—he hadn't waited for it to stop. He broke into as fast of a limp as he was capable, its pain a foreign thing. Maynard's voice carried across the field like a memory.

"Helen? Helen!"

The limp jarred Clark's knees. His breath came much more quickly than the last time he had run down this road. Maynard was wandering where the farm buildings had stood, his arms spread as if in puzzlement, his robe fluttering in the wind.

"Maynard!"

"Helen!"

Maynard danced in the snow across the field, some ancient, insane fairy living in a fantastical time. He stopped suddenly; his arms dropped. Like the wind he moaned sharply, then fell forward onto his knees. He fell forward again with his face in the snow.

The ice the wind bore drove into Clark's cheeks like needles. He dropped into the ditch, tripped, then fell forward, the cold and his fatigue complete. He could not see Maynard from where he lay—when he thought of Dante's hell and the unforgiven who inhabited it, a panic gripped him. He scrambled on his hands and knees up, over, and through a drift, out onto the windswept field, hard beneath his knees like spikes and diamonds. He stood. Maynard lay still in the moonlight, his robe flapping against the furrows. Clark ran toward him, fell again, then crawled the rest of the way. He rolled Maynard onto his back with the last of his strength and searched his face, blue in the night, frosty white in the cold.

"Maynard?"

Maynard said nothing. Clark shook him, looked to the sky, bled out a prayer, and received no answer. He looked down again. Maynard's eyelids fluttered. "Maynard?"

"Helen?" His only movement was the sudden wildness in his eyes.

"It's Clark, Maynard."

"Helen?"

"It's Clark. I have to tell you something."

"Helen, I didn't mean to do it. You know I didn't mean to do it."

"Maynard, please, I have to tell you something." Clark looked up. Lewell was just coming around the front of his car, turning up his collar, his footsteps silent beneath the rising wind. "Maynard," Clark said softly, "I killed Albert Wilson."

"Helen, I didn't mean to do it."

"You have to forgive me. You're the only person left who can."

Maynard's hand gripped Clark's shoulder, strong now in its dying, a farmer's strength, a farmer's hands. "Helen, I didn't mean to do it!"

"Please, Maynard." Clark's chest was an open sore, the pain of thirty-five years swelling and breaking. Tears in his eyes dripped to splatter on the blue and white and dying skin. "Please forgive me."

"I didn't!" Maynard's eyes reflected an unmitigated desperation. "Good night, Helen." He only managed to whisper.

"Maynard—"

"Good night, Helen!"

"Please, Maynard." Words dripped from Clark's chin with the tears.

"Helen! Good night!"

Clark wept beneath two huge and terrible weights: the death of a five-decade friendship and the realization that salvation was and would always remain an alien thing. There was no redemption here, not in this madness. There was no friend, either; he was already gone. "Good night, Maynard," was all he could say.

Maynard's eyes cleared. He seemed for a second to be the old Maynard sitting on the feed store bench, talking about Bogey and Bergman. The old Maynard with the seed cap pulled low over his eyes, the old, innocent, maligned Maynard. He'd have been a randy monster if not for his ticker, his god-be-damned killer of a ticker. He smiled faintly before his face twisted; his grip on Clark's shoulder fell to clutch weakly his own chest. The smile faded, the blue lips parted, and his head went back to stare at the stars, to seek with blind eyes the new star that was all his own.

Clark touched Maynard's cheeks; he touched his lips, his eyes. He cried. He cried because he had killed this life as he had killed so many others, as he had killed his own. His head went back as if he, too, were dying. He stared up at the stars, seeking their redemption, seeking a kindly face of God.

A life of searching ended here; he finally knew who God was. God was not a merciful God; he was not a vengeful God, either. God was only a laughing God, and he was not laughing a laugh of mirth or derision, but a maniacal one. Perhaps at one time he had created this world, perhaps he had given it order, but he stared at it now in total incomprehension. He was an old God with an old God's afflictions. He was a demented God who sat on his throne peering blindly, knees tucked tightly beneath his chin, hands clutching ankles, rocking, ever rocking, insane lips working wildly, bellows echoing through heaven's empty halls. When you pray to a laughing God, expect only laughter. He cannot hear your prayers.

"Is he all right?"

Ted Lewell's voice was so close it was frightening. Clark glanced over his shoulder, through the bitter wind consuming his tears. "No, he's not all right."

"I want my notes."

"You and your notes can go to hell. Maynard is dead."

"Then they can't hurt him."

"I burned them, you bastard."

Lewell didn't say anything for a moment. "The hell you did."

"I burned everything. The garbage can behind my house is probably still warm."

They waited in the darkness, Lewell standing behind Clark, Clark holding Maynard's face in his lap. Waiting for what, Clark didn't want to admit. Waiting for the truth. Waiting for him to finally exhume his buried life. He could see in his mind what he needed to tell Lewell, how he needed to say it. He could not make himself say the words.

"It doesn't make any difference, you know," Lewell said. "The story isn't in the notes. It isn't even in the diary."

"Then where is it?"

"The story is here, in his words. You can't protect him from what he's said. Nice try, Clark, but I win." Lewell paused; his gloating carried on the wind. God bellowed his laughter across a cold and silent sky. "This will make one hell of an ending."

Clark twisted inside. What do you say? In an insane and laughing universe, all words whirl nonsensically. "You win. Go find Jergen. Get him out here."

Lewell chuckled; his feet crunched in snow. "I thought for a while it was you. I thought that in the diary Rose was talking about your wife. But your wife didn't fuck around, did she? Only you did. You and Helen and Albert Wilson."

"You found that out?"

"I found that out. It will make a hell of a story, don't you think?"

"Please. Go find Jergen."

Lewell chuckled again. His footsteps trudged into the winter's moaning. Clark looked at the stars, into the eternal night; he stared at that maniacal and unforgiving sky. He looked down and saw in his lap a great and ancient god's twisted visage. He cradled Maynard's heavy face to his chest because he could not stand to look at it anymore.

Lewell's car started. Headlights flashed shadows, then the sound of the engine faded. The wind-driven snow burned Clark's face like sandpaper.

"I'm sorry, my friend. I'm sorry." Clark searched through the stars and cried.

Chapter

15

Tuesday was dark and heavy with clouds, a blanket on the world. At just after two in the afternoon, Clark was sitting alone in the front pew of St. Luke's Lutheran Church—Walter had not come. Nora lay ten feet in front of him in a casket lined with silk. She'd left behind the linen, but not the sterilized smell, not the sterile efficiency. It was colder here.

The minister droned with the stoicism that a lack of acquaintance with the deceased breeds. Nora lay as she had always lain, leather face spread across a pillow, liver-spotted hands folded, except that her eyes were closed—Clark wondered what she was seeing. Maynard's funeral was going on out at St. Anne's. It was poorly attended, Clark guessed; probably just Barb and Brian, the kids, and Father Charlie. Since the weekend, rumors about Lewell's book had made anathema for Maynard Tewle again in vogue.

Clark stared blindly at the casket. It isn't true that you reap what you sow. You reap what others think you've sown. What others have sown for you.

Richard Sanders, the protestant funeral director, came forward to shut the casket. Nora was finally gone, her eyes gone on Saturday night and the rest of her gone now. A blue of sympathetic faces solemnly greeted him at the door, weathered, bald men and women with silver wigs reeking of Wal-Mart perfume. Cold, perfunctory sorrow—it was nothing they all hadn't been through before.

The solemn gathering snaked in a procession of vehicles out to the community cemetery on Crystal Lake's north shore, where Nora would wait on a mausoleum shelf with the rest of the winter's dead until the weather warmed to at least the level of the funeralgoers' sympathy. Such are our ways.

After the service, Clark walked from the grave to stand on a hill overlooking the lake. He stared across tombstones and ice to the lake's southern shore, across the blowing snow, across a gray, silent world that had, like Nora, been beaten into submission. Men and women again moved quietly past him, shaking his hand and patting his shoulder. It was funny how they all thought Nora had left this world so gently. If only they knew. Dylan Thomas would have been proud of her eyes.

He turned from the lake to watch the mourners straggle back to their cars. We're all broken in the end, he supposed. Hands in his pockets, feeling the cold, he thought nothing more, though he heard, in the part of his mind where memories had been hidden, a laughter. He looked at the sky. He tried to penetrate its murkiness and failed. Somewhere out there was a creator who only fools believed held the soul of understanding. The laughter proved there was no understanding.

He walked slowly down the hill, favoring his sore ankle. Richard

Sanders waited beside his limousine with his mouth set in a practiced, sorrowful line. Clark stopped at the road to let Elmer Tornquist drive by. He waved. He waved as Bert Finchley drove by, too—Bert's long face the car window could hardly frame. Bert lifted a hand from the steering wheel and nodded, as if he knew the hiding of secrets was something they shared.

Clark and Sanders sat together in the limousine's backseat. Sanders's daughter acted as chauffeur, her long auburn hair spread over her shoulders like the sphinx. It was a family business.

"Are you all right?" Sanders asked as they passed the nursing home.

Clark searched the building. There was nothing inside he recognized. "Yeah. Take me home."

"The reception—"

"Take me home."

Sanders nodded. "If there's anything I can do."

"Sure."

The sun shouldered through the clouds; the world turned bright again. The light off the elevator blinded him as the limousine paused at St. Anne's Road. He thought of Arnold Andresen beating his lambs into the ground, of Maynard sitting on the feed store bench, of Albert Wilson, of Helen, of Nora. He saw them staring up from a sanctuary floor, staring down from a dark, frostbitten sky. Why could he never leave eyes behind?

His spirit rolled queasily when he saw Emma's car in front of his house. He almost got out of the car and ran, so tempted he was to flee, to flee as he had from the war, from Indiana, from life. He didn't only because running required a youthful energy he no longer possessed. She was standing in the doorway.

"I read about Nora in the paper. I'm sorry." She was wearing a thick sweater and slacks, her hair pulled back severely. She looked old, but she looked her age, and she looked lovely. In the fifties he had seen Deloris's age as something to be disdained. Well, in the fifties he had been a different man. Or he hoped he had been.

He walked into the house and shut the door behind him. Emma

took his hand after he had removed his glove. She had a cold touch, as cold as the snow in that field, as cold as Maynard's face had been. His own cold reflected.

"Are you all right?" she asked.

"Sure."

His slow, sad ache intensified toward exhaustion. Life is too big, too crazy; he collapsed wearily onto the sofa. "Thanks for coming by."

She sat beside him. "Really? Or have I made a mistake?"

"I'm just so tired."

"Of course you are."

They sat silently. Emma leaned into him, then backed away when he stiffened. What do I do about her? he wondered. What do I do? He turned to study her face and found he could hardly see it. She was hidden by those funeral clouds, by a snowy sheen. His life of lies was too much around him.

He thought about the feel in his hand of Deloris's hair, of Nora's throat, of Albert's hammer. He thought about lifting that wrench in the historical society, the surety he had felt that, yes, he could almost with delight bring it down. He shook his head. The hell if you're a different man. The hell.

"I'll go," she said.

"No. I'm just tired." He stood, wanting to be near her and run from her at the same time. "I just need a few minutes."

He felt her watching him as he walked to the basement door. He climbed slowly down the steps, feeling in every inch of descent his age grow, and turned on the light to protect himself from the darkness. The Credibull model leered at him; a life as broken as it was leered at him, too. He could not shake the sense that even in laughter the world knew justice.

He looked at the phone sitting on the workbench. I ought to call him, he thought. I ought to call him and end this right. He picked up the receiver, then listened for Emma above him. He heard nothing but the dial tone's undercurrent. He punched out the number as if he were poking out the last years of his life.

Cletis answered. Cletis always answered. "Sunset Motel. Hello?"

"Hi, Cletis. It's Clark."

"Clark, how are you doing?" Cletis paused awkwardly. "Sorry. Dumb question." He paused awkwardly again. "It was a nice funeral."

"Cletis, could you put me through to room one-ten?"

"Are you after that writer? He checked out yesterday morning."

Clark rubbed his forehead. Hell. Oh, hell. "Did he say where he was going?"

"Home, I guess. His research is done and he has to write up that book. It'll put Credibull on the map. Kind of nice to think about."

"Sure. We can add it in with the ice cream sundae."

"The what?"

"The ice cream sundae might have been invented here."

"Is that a fact?"

"Talk to Agnes Miller about it."

"Is that really a fact?"

"I can't talk now, Cletis. I have to make some phone calls."

"Oh, sure. Sorry about Nora, Clark."

"Yeah."

He hung up the phone and took out his wallet. In the back he found, limp and warm with body heat, the business card Ted Lewell had given him when he had first come to Credibull, back when Nora and Maynard had been alive, when Helen had been cooking roast beef dinners, when Clark had still believed life, like wives, could be cheated. The card listed two Chicago numbers: Ted Lewell, business and home. Clark wondered where he would be today. Justice was now reduced to a fifty-fifty and correctable shot. If you're wrong, you can try again and make it right. A credo to live by.

The phone rang. He picked up the receiver expecting sympathy, but heard only long-distance static. Someone from Indiana maybe. Someone from Chicago.

"Hello?" he asked. Only static answered him. "Hello?"

"Dad?"

Christ, oh Christ. Walter. Something leaped in Clark's chest, caught on a lump in his throat, and left him for a moment unable to speak.

"Dad?"

"Walter?"

"Hi, Dad."

"Walter, where the hell are you?"

"It's hard to say, Dad."

"What do you mean, it's hard to say? You don't know where you are?"

"No, I mean that it's hard to say. It's some Mexican word, and I don't speak Mexican. It sounds like *chili pepper*."

"You're in Chili Pepper, Mexico? What are you doing in Chili Pepper, Mexico?"

"I had to go somewhere. If you'd looked at our books, you'd know that."

"I looked at the books." A lot of angry creditors would be looking at them, too, a lot of angry state and federal agencies. Walter had shifted location to match his shift of responsibility. A mover and a shaker. "Why Mexico?"

"I met this guy in San Diego, and he suggested I come in on this deal with him. We're going to buy up cheap Mexican land and sell it for a fortune to Los Angeles yuppies as vacation lots. He's got most of the groundwork laid, but he needs someone in on it who has a little business expertise. It's really hopping, Dad. It's not like that computer thing."

Yeah, Clark thought, I've heard that word *hopping* before. "Your mother died on Saturday."

"Jesus." Walter fell silent. God be damned, Clark thought, why'd you have to tell him like that? God *was* damned—he was sitting on his throne and rocking, probably soiling himself. Drool dripping from his chin. "I'm sorry, Dad."

"I am, too."

"Are you really?" An edge came to Walter's voice. "It clears the way for you and this Emma, doesn't it?"

"Don't start, Walter." Too many thoughts clamored in Clark's head.

He wasn't sure what he wanted to say. "I don't think I'll be seeing Emma anymore." He hadn't expected that to come out.

"You sound like me and Amber. I had to dump her when I came down here."

"Sure. How are you really doing, Walter?"

"You know me. And the women, Dad, the women. They're everywhere."

Especially in the magazines, Clark thought, or on calendars. Legs spread in close-up shots for the discriminating cunt connoisseur. Please, Walter, not this.

"Dad, I can't stay on long. It costs a fortune."

Clark heard traffic in the background and wondered if Chili Pepper, Mexico, was really where he was calling from. "Sure, Walter. Can I get your number?"

"This number is temporary. I'll see you, all right?"

"Are you coming home?"

"I'll call when I can. Bye, Dad."

Clark choked on the words he knew he was supposed to say. "Sure." It came out like a cough.

"Dad?"

"Yeah?"

"All I ever wanted for any of us was to be happy. Do you believe that?"

"Yes," Clark said. "I believe that." Isn't that all anyone wants?

"I'll call soon. Bye."

"Bye."

The receiver clicked; the line went dead. *And I'll kill the kid*, Clark remembered. *And I'll kill the kid*. It all comes back, he thought, like ashes rising and falling; like vultures swooping, it all comes back. Walter. He wanted to cry. My son.

He sat quietly for a long time, staring dully, words echoing in his mind. He found he was staring at the card on the table. He picked it up and concentrated on its delicate texture. Well, he thought, bring it full circle. Let both hell and the vultures have their fill.

347

He listened for Emma and heard nothing. He picked up the receiver and shut his eyes to keep the world from dropping into the dial tone's buzzing confusion. Behind it all he heard that laugh, that lunatic laugh that was this world's foundation. His free hand came up to grip his temples. It shook with the force of the universe and the past.

Some say that time is an illusion, that all things are happening continually. If that were so, then he was now killing Albert Wilson, was now threatening to kill Walter, was beating Nora to within an inch of her life. He was holding Emma on the last midnight of every year, he was listening to a church bell continuously toll. He was the man he was then, the man he was now, and they were the same and they were different and we are all wrong, we are all wrong: light and darkness exist in the same place, in the same instant, black-and-white like a monochrome apartment. How can it be that such polarities exist together? It was chaos. It was maniacal laughter.

With all the force of his will, Clark could not tear his fingers away. God laughed. He gripped his ankles and chuckled through his knees.

The touch of two warm hands jolted Clark, like the touch of cold snow. Emma's scent surrounded him, filled his mind, filled his soul. His hand dropped as hers ran over his chest, as he felt her cheek against his. The buzzing of the receiver drifted far away—her touch was the only solid thing in this world. Thank you, he thought, with pure and profound obeisance. Thank you, Emma.

"I hope I'm not intruding." Her voice was music.

"No. God, no."

"I'm so sorry, Clark. I'm so sorry that I don't know what to say."

He left the receiver on the bench as his hands rose gratefully to hold her wrists. He felt only their warmth, a slow-burning fire. "You being here says enough."

She held him tightly before placing the receiver in its cradle. The buzzing died; the chaos receded. He climbed her out of it rung after rung. Thank you, Emma.

"Who were you calling?"

He shuddered out a sigh. What should he say? The truth? But that was the truth then, and Emma was the truth now. Then and now happen at once, truth and falsity exist together. This was not Nora, not Walter, not Helen, not Maynard, not even Albert Wilson. This was Emma. But it also was them all.

Life was a sensible insanity, was light and darkness in the same place. You cannot choose one without choosing the other.

He looked at the card and felt suddenly sure of himself. He crumpled it in his hand. "No one."

She held him tightly. He reveled in her aroma, in her touch, in her rock solidity. "Have you eaten?" she asked.

"No."

"Would you like some lunch? I'll make something."

He raised her hand to his lips and kissed it. "Yes."

She straightened, then held his shoulder in a grip more sure than the world. "I'll see what's in the kitchen. Are you coming up?"

"In a moment."

She released him. He listened to her climb the steps.

He was still surrounded by chaos, the divine laughter still rolled, but with the touch of a hand and a cheek, the grip on a shoulder, everything had changed. He wanted to join the laughter; he could not help from doing so. Squeaks erupted from the corners of his lips; he had to cover his mouth with both hands to keep from bellowing into this cold and white and brilliant world. He picked up the phone and dropped it gleefully to the concrete floor. The receiver fell free, bounced once, and lay as broken as the model beside it. As broken as that old life.

Clark finally knew the truth, or finally knew how to deal with it. The past and the future, the good and the bad, lay shattered and irrelevant. God is a laughing, demented God, an old God who wallows in madness. His home is a padded room.

All people seek salvation. So few understand that its shattered road lay in convincing God that your laughter is as maniacal as his is. We must revel in chaos.

Clark stood. The pains in his ankle, shoulder, and knees were miraculously gone, hidden beneath lunatic mirth, the way of the world, truth—God was damned and Clark felt young again. He shut off the light, let that old life fall into its deserved darkness, and scampered up the stairs like a boy. He marveled at the sound of Emma banging pots in the kitchen. It was a strange, new symphony.